The Ruffian on the Stair

THE RUFFIAN
ON THE STAIR

Gary Newman

Constable • London

Constable & Robinson Ltd
3 The Lanchesters
162 Fulham Palace Road
London W6 9ER
www.constablerobinson.com

First published in the UK by Constable,
an imprint of Constable & Robinson, 2008

First US edition published by SohoConstable,
an imprint of Soho Press, 2008

Soho Press, Inc.
853 Broadway
New York, NY 10003
www.sohopress.com

A copy of the British Library Cataloguing in Publication
Data is available from the British Library

UK ISBN: 978-1-84529-637-7

US ISBN: 978-1-56947-543-0
US Library of Congress number: 2008019054

Printed and bound in the EU

1 3 5 7 9 10 8 6 4 2

Chapter One

Going over this in my little corner of the early 2000s, I still haven't come to terms with what's happened. Never shall, completely, I suppose, but let's start with the notebook. God! I was actually pleased when, all innocently, it arrived with the rest of my legendary grandfather's effects in the banal Jiffy bag from the lawyer in Jersey. On an April Saturday it was, by the normal postman's van, on his daily visit to my lighthouse at the foot of the headland in the Essex mudflat where I live – more or less – as a freelance writer. Gardening articles and occasional film biographies are my subjects, by the way – one or two of you might even have read some of my stuff – but back to the notebook. As to how it turned up at all with the other things, the lawyer explained in his covering letter:

Dear Mr Rolvenden,

I'm enclosing some possessions of your late grandfather and namesake, Sebastian Rolvenden DD. As you no doubt know, he was vicar of St Marc's here from October 1919 till June 1940, when he and his lady were rounded up by the Germans with other former mainland residents and sent into internment in Germany. The objects enclosed were left on the doorstep of my office in a supermarket carrier bag, and I don't envisage that the donor will be traced, nor do I have any knowledge of the contents of the written matter. I understand

5

*you still own a property on the island, and will be happy to
see you on your next visit to Jersey.*
                              Yours sincerely,
                              H. E. Le Touzel

As soon as the Jiffy bag had arrived and I'd opened it,
Leah – my significant other – and I had started to run
through the contents, and I'd lit immediately on the notebook. It was scuffed, crumbling and ancient, the Victorian
forerunner of the marble-backed jobs you could buy in
post offices for fifty pence or so up till about ten years ago.
Many of the pages had clearly been torn out. I'd turned
back the cover and there, on the first, untitled page, was
my grandfather's hasty, angular handwriting in faded
black ink. But the contents were something different, as we
soon learnt when I began to read them out to my companion who sat with one neat, firm leg under her in the
window seat and rummaged through the Jiffy bag.

'*Julian Rawbeck is a great artist,*' I read out my grandfather's words, '*but he paints in blood. What fate drew me to
the Arches on that cursed evening? The sign – yes, the sign on
Gatti's music hall – "Miss Carrie Bugle – Colour in the
Shadows – Artiste of the Adagio". Then the fume and roar inside
the hall, the reek of tobacco, stale beer and staler clothes. And
Rawbeck lounging against the gilded column, with his handsome
coffin-plate of a face that I was to come to know so well gazing
dreamily at the lithe, red figure on the stage. She was redeemed
from the dark backdrop by the white dazzle of the lime. Rawbeck
must have noticed my gaping stare, for the cold, good-humoured
eyes were turned to mine.*

'*"Like a snake, hey, sir?" he'd said in his lah-de-dah drawl.
"Your two hands might span the hips . . ." I was young enough
to blush, then, and I glared back, stung by his invasion of my
very thoughts, and he laughed, evidently pleased at having read
them. Then, after Carrie's troubling form had left the stage, to
thunderous applause, Rawbeck had given me an ironical bow,
waving his hand towards the long bar. There was something*

6

strangely inviting, and at the same time take-it-or-leave-it, in his gesture, which countered my first instinct to turn my back on him and leave – if only I had obeyed my instinct! – and I joined him rather uneasily at the bar.

'"A sherry cobbler, sir!" he said, with a tinkling, youthful laugh. "Cools the blood, don't yer know . . ."

'Rawbeck talked well, with a sort of raffish erudition mixed with coarseness of the lowest sort, beginning with Carrie in particular and proceeding to Beauty in general – the only thing that redeemed life from the slime, he avowed. He then touched on his inspiration, France, for which he had a passion. When I mentioned tentatively that I had briefly studied art in Paris, our affinity, Rawbeck declared, was sealed, and I earned my first invitation to his high studio in the dim cavern of a street on Camden Hill. I recall the high night sky in jewel-case velvet, all roaring with stars, and – a typical trick from the box of the Master Illusionist – her there, all lithe and dressed again in red. She was Rawbeck's model, and owed much of her reputation on the halls in no small part to his brilliant posters of her. She eyed me with a frankness that made me blush again to the roots of my hair, and the artist's teasing laughter rang out again.

'"I'll wager you'd like those legs round your neck, hey, sir?"

'Carrie hooted with vulgar laughter, but as drink was plied – there were kindred spirits at the gathering – and my host became more outrageous, I found, little by little, that I could listen without blushing. And so, at twenty-four, my slavery began – he cheering me on – and my consequent descent into hell.'

Here there was a gap in the narrative, a wad of pages having been torn out of the notebook at some time. When my grandfather's handwriting took up again after the gap, it was more broken in style, produced, as it seemed, in fits and starts, the downward strokes fairly cutting into the brittle paper. The fresh text began with a title.

'The Horror . . .' I read out again from the notebook, and Leah put down the Bible she'd been examining and gave me her full attention, her dark, almond eyes sombre. 'The Anniversary, and Convocation in Great College Street – with the drinking of the Lapland Mushroom potion – Lord! How can I have been so weak! And all for her! The regale laid on this time in honour of that vile, lisping queen, Toland, for the sake of Rawbeck's credit with him. With P. F.'s dirge on the flute solemnly mocking me in the background, then the Invocation – blasphemous farce! – and Toland's blubber lips at my ear – more a kiss than a whisper. He lisps that I am to be Seer tonight.

'I drink the potion – it is gall unspeakable! I retch and retch, amid the circle of dark heads round the glowing brazier, with Toland's silly voice bleating all the while. The purgatory of pain, then, after an aeon of time, a great ease and concord of the senses. I breathe colours and taste sounds, smell lightness or heaviness, smoothness or roughness, as if I were caressing them with the linings of my nostrils. I expand into vastness, then into a dot of infinite smallness, and the whole universe is filled with my laughter. And the colours! Glowing and coalescing, beyond the range of the prism – colours to which I cannot put names – then confluence into the "white radiance of eternity," and I am White itself. Boundless joy, beyond thought, beyond the shabby husk of the ego – I have slipped the chains of the tedious jailer behind the eyes. Then a moment of terror: what if I should expand to fill the entire universe? Endless diffusion? But then I laugh again: I am the universe!

'Now I sense myself leaving Convocation, at first in a disembodied swirl until I become conscious of the silver head of my stick in my palm, which is as sensitive as a second palate. Indeed, I taste the silver – nutmeg and lemon – through that very palm. Now the shock of the sooty London night air – I am reminded that I have lungs, after all, raw bellows sifting the onion of the oxygen from the soot. Then the hardness of the pavement under my unsteady legs, and the cab-bell jingling like some temple cymbal. I glide somehow into the cab and sink, intoxicated, into the leather upholstery. The cab lurches off down the hill, and I know no more.

'The Awakening. It is calm and cold, and – Lord! – I am naked! Pitch darkness all around me, then, as my eyes become accustomed to the obscurity, some crack lets in a grey, dimity light. I am no longer a lordly stalker of eternity, drunk on the Mushroom, but a shivering, naked worm. I slip my legs over the side of the bed and stand upright, and, in my doing so, a bombshell of pain explodes inside my head, and I groan out loud. But I am now shivering uncontrollably, and I stoop and grope on the floor for the reassurance of my clothes and boots, find them and somehow pull them on. My mouth is dry as a furnace, and the scimitar that is cleaving my head gives way to a steady throb, like the engine of a steamer. A wave of nausea sweeps over me, and, providentially, the toe of my boot rings against the rim of a chamber pot under the valance. I draw it out quickly, and, stooping again, relieve my stomach.

'Almost myself once more, I cast my gaze round the shadows of the stale-smelling room, with its few looming blocks of furniture. There is a chink of drawn curtain, and a tenuous ray of yellow gaslight coming in, no doubt from a street lamp outside. I pick up my stick and hat from the bed and make for the curtain, only to stumble against a heavy object on the floor. I lose my balance, and fall down beside the object. I raise myself to my knees and grope along the thing – soft, clothed – a body! My questing hands reach a watch-chain, then, higher up, I gasp as I pull my hands away from a wet obscenity. I climb to my feet, then rush over to the curtains, which I tear apart. The light from the lamp outside streams into the mean room, and I swing round towards the object on the floor, to be mocked – but not for the last time – by Rawbeck's extinct, ironic smile. The eyes are glazed, and under his chin a red ruin.

'I dash for the unlocked door, then, fumbling in my pockets for my handkerchief, try to wipe off the blood from my hands as I negotiate the landing and flight of rickety stairs. Then an afterthought stops me in my tracks – my stick! Back, shuddering with loathing, to the room, where I retrieve it, then down the stairs again into the lobby of what is evidently some low public house. There is a double door with frosted windows, and the image of a galleon in full sail, and the stale smells of beer and tobacco. I pause in the grey, dawn light, unable to resist a shuddering glance back up the stairs: it is as if the slaughtered

9

Rawbeck were beckoning me: "A sherry cobbler, sir – nothing like it for cooling the blood . . ."

'Am I going mad? As I glance up the stairs, I notice a stairhead window with an outside gas lamp illuminating the alternating ruby-and-blue stain along the edges of the glass. The design beguiles me, somehow, then I look down at my hands – in spite of my frantic efforts with my handkerchief, the fingernails are still clotted red, like the talons of a ravening beast. Cain's mark . . . Lord! Can I have done this thing? I cannot remember – farewell, peace of mind.

'At last, I turn on my heels and face the street doorway. I grasp for the door bolts, and find – thank God! – the handle of a spring lock. A turn and a click, and I am outside. I pull the brim of my wideawake over my face as I shut the door gently behind me before hurrying off into the cold, greasy streets. I am in some mean quarter of London, one entirely unfamiliar to me. All is silent and deserted, and, my brain beating, I shuffle along for what seems ages. I have a vague sense of water nearby – the Thames? A canal? I rush ahead, thinking only of escape, then a shabby thoroughfare comes into view, with closed shops, and, yes, a stationary hansom ahead.

'I approach the cab, and tap the dozing driver's seat with my stick. I give him the name of the nearest railway station to my diggings, and climb in. The cabbie yawns, and without a word, drives off at an easy canter. Once ensconced in the protective darkness, and lulled by the gentle rhythm of the cab-bell, I feel my overstretched nerves slacken, and I slip into slumber before I am woken up by the cabbie's voice. I climb out, pay him and dismiss him, then make for my rooms, letting myself in with the latch-key. I tiptoe up the carpeted stairs to my quarters and immediately begin to stuff some clothes into a carpet-bag. I go to the dressing table, and clear my things from it, but my razor is not there . . .

'I freeze, as, with my mind's eye, I find myself standing again at the foot of the stairs in the house of horror, and, inconsequentially, the window on the stairhead that adjoins the fatal room flashes before me. The throbbing ruby of the window's *stained glass edging seems to reflect the crimson of the throat of what lies inside the room. I shudder again, and return to my senses – the missing razor . . . And then there is relief when I reflect that, though the razor is an heirloom, the initials on the handle are not mine, and so it cannot be traced back to me. Already I am thinking like a fugitive scoundrel! Should I then go to the police? But my people – no, it is unthinkable. And what of my dearest Cecily? She knows nothing of what my life has been of late: am I to repay her steadfastness with this? And if she should find out about Carrie? No, it is not to be thought of. I must go abroad, efface myself and spare the innocent, but how can I ever forgive myself?'*

There the writing in the notebook trailed off into a flurry of biblical chapter and verse titles, then a spate of disjointed entries.

'Rivers,' I went on reading from the notebook. *'Home in the East – Soundings A – Reuben's Court – Smoking Altars . . .'*

'More visions?' Leah's deep voice, with its ghost of Leeds, chipped in. 'Looks like young Sebastian's been at the magic mushrooms again!'

'Ah!' I said. 'Some more joined-up text. Let's see . . .'

I carried on reading out my grandfather's confessions.

'The studio in Montmartre – I know the madness of jealousy again: she is a very devil! I return from the Salon and find the Vickybird with her – lying on our bed. Lounging, slack-jawed, Cockney impudence – he is after money again, and I don't doubt, the other thing . . . And Cecily's gift almost gone – it was to have been my redemption – my escape! I am not fit to kiss the hem of her gown!

'The Vickybird lounges off, laughing at my futile railing, then Carrie takes up her billingsgate again, and the mockery of her dance when I first saw her in Gatti's. Her abuse turns to tipsy wheedling – her breath stinks of drink, and her blouse is stale, but I cannot, cannot, resist . . .'

Here another page of the notebook was torn out, so we'd never know how my grandfather coped with Carrie's raunchy allure on that occasion. I went straight on to the next page, with all of Leah's attention now from the window seat.

'She is in drink again – I blot out the horrid words – and for the first time I see how ugly she can be – a blowsy slut. Now I could smash down the absurd, bobbing, ginger mop, and the white face, with its squirming, loose lips. Our eyes meet, and, suddenly, hers become calm and sly: she has seen my resolve. It is done between us – over. I know I desire her no longer, and I am free. Her voice is even and indifferent now, and I freeze with horror as she talks of Rawbeck, confirming my worst fears. The Vickybird and the drawings, especially LXXXIII, must be found at all costs, unless – God forbid! – Carbonero already has them, and they are on sale in his atelier. Then, her parting shot – her "condition", as she puts it, and am I man enough to assume my responsibilities? But I had anticipated that: the arrangements are already in place.'

At this point the narrative made one of its abrupt shifts of topic, resuming on the next page under a new heading.

'Gare du Nord,' I read out from the scruffy little book. *'My Angel, my Goddess is there. We embrace, and I am embedded in the very scent of home. I am unmanned for a moment, and she comforts me, stopping my blurted confessions with her dearest finger. Then the boat-train hisses and clanks its arrival, and Cecily draws her veil down firmly as we enter the compartment, with the prospect of England and salvation in front of us.'*

There were only blank pages after that, and I put down the book on the cane sofa.

'Well,' Leah said with a low whistle, 'is that a story, or is it a story! This is your next book, Seb – you know that, don't you?'

'It's been dropped in my lap like a gift,' I said with a sort of wonder. 'There's always been a virtual rule of silence in the family about my grandfather's early life, before he became a clergyman, and now this! I'd no idea he'd studied art in Paris, for one thing, or that my grandmother had pulled him out of such a scrape . . .'

'She'd have been his Cecily, his Angel and so on, who

"took him away from all that" at the Paris station to a new life in England?'

'Right. There was a belief in the family that she'd supported him through his ordination course at Cambridge – paid his college fees and so on – till he'd been ordained as a clergyman and they'd got married. Highly irregular in those days.'

'Quite a girl, by the sound of her – clearly the balls of the partnership.'

'She had money of her own, I gather, but Grandfather was quite skint – his father'd been some sort of impoverished parson, living more or less on genteel charity towards the end of his life. As I say, we weren't told much about that side of the family. I've always been fascinated by my grandfather Rolvenden's legend – it was always an unspoken assumption that he'd been remarkable in some way in his life, but when you asked how, a sort of barrier would come up, and the subject would be changed. He was rather a hero of mine, and the fact that I was given his first name did nothing to detract from that. As a boy, I was forever weaving tales in my mind of what Grandfather's secret life had been. I usually came to the conclusion that he'd done something heroic – usually in the North-West Frontier line – but for reasons of national honour had sworn himself and his family to secrecy. And now this . . .'

'Did you actually know your grandparents?'

'Grandfather Rolvenden died in 1950 – two years before I was born – but I remember Nanny Rolvenden. I recall our last meeting in particular – in the garden of their house in Malmesbury. One of the gardens that sweeps down to the river. It was a sunlit, late June day, all motes and dragon-flies. Magical. She was quite tall, and pretty formidable in a nice way, with a handsome, high-boned face and her hair in – what did they call the sort of plaits in a ring round their ears?'

'Earphones,' Leah helped out.

'Right, and a sort of tweed costume with a long skirt and sensible shoes. I don't remember the exact conversation we had – what do you talk about to a six-year-old kid? But there was one remark she made that I'll never forget. She'd stooped, then stroked my hair and cheeks with her thin, cool hands. Then a funny expression came into her eyes – sort of solemn and avid – and she grasped my shoulders quite hard, then said as if to herself or to someone over my shoulder: "The issue is good." Just that, then she'd sprung upright again, and with an "Inside for strawberries!" the spell had been broken. Since I've got older I've had the feeling that there was something else to my grandmother's words about the "issue being good" – something beyond mere grown-up approval of a six-year-old. She died not long after that: it'd have been 1958.'

'This is really creepy, Seb . . .' Leah cut across my bows. 'Look . . .'

I went over to the window seat and sat beside her. She'd taken a bundle of letters from a linen flap on the inside cover of the family Bible she'd taken out of the Jiffy bag, and was reading one of them. I stooped over the letter, to read the signature at the end: *Cecily*.

'It's Nanny Rolvenden's signature!' I exclaimed. 'Let me see the letters . . .'

Just then the doorbell rang.

'Sugar!' I said. 'Saturday – that'll be the window cleaner for his money. Be back in a sec.'

The window cleaner also doubled as a jobbing builder, and he'd been trying to persuade me to let him repoint my walls for some weeks now, so the 'sec' stretched to five minutes before I was able to foil his hard-sell technique, pay him and see him off at last.

'Has he been hustling again?' Leah said with a throaty chuckle as I returned to her and the letters.

'Mostly Grandfather's handwriting,' I went on as I examined the faded ink on the stiff sheets, 'but some with Nanny Rolvenden's. What a find! Listen . . .'

I read out the letter Leah had been handling when she'd called my attention to the bundle. It was written from Nanny's father's vicarage near Malvern in the Christmas of 1893. Miss Cecily Woodruff, as she'd been then, was writing to her 'Dearest Jack', my grandfather's middle name having been John. It was unremarkable banter – Parson Woodruff not at all favourable to the attentions paid to his daughter by a penniless Cambridge under-graduate, as Grandfather had then been, so no invitation down for Christmas.

In the next envelope, addressed *Poste Restante, Malvern*, no doubt to avoid its being intercepted by Nanny's par-ents, was my grandfather's impassioned reply, with the usual eternal vows, responded to with maidenly badinage from Nanny in the next letter in the New Year. All con-ventional enough, but poignantly moving to me: 'Dearest Jack' and 'Dearest Cecily' were one with the sunlight now.

'You certainly don't take after your grandad in looks,' Leah remarked from the fireplace, where she was study-ing his fine-featured, bearded face in the silver-framed photograph on the mantelpiece. How often I'd stared into the large, unquiet eyes in that faded photograph, thinking what Leah had just said. My high-cheekboned, hatchet fea-tures had got me the nickname of 'Ming the Mong' at the tenth-rate public school on the south coast where Dad had dumped me.

'I know,' I finally replied to my companion's observation. 'Did he have the eyes?'

'Mmm . . . no, or I'd surely have heard of it. I think I'm the only one in the family who has them; at least, I've never met any relations with one brown eye and the other bright green . . . Oh, listen to this: it's from six years later . . .'

The letter from my grandfather to my grandmother in Malvern which had now caught my attention bore no address at its head, and was dated Good Friday, 1900.

'*My Dearest Cecily, Your finger stopped the confession that*

15

was on my lips in the train from Paris, but I feel duty-bound to let you know the worst about me, to lay before you the record of my past profligacy. In doing so, I am all too conscious of the risk I am running of my forfeiting forever what undeserved favour I may have found in your eyes. I feel, however, that I cannot in fairness withhold from you the full picture of "a man in all the truth of nature". I have striven always to show you my poor best, and now you must judge me at my worst, weighing my qualities in the balance. But be assured that, whatever consider-ations may sway you, upon your verdict will hang all my hopes for happiness, now and for the future. In Chancery, Jack.'

'That must be a sort of covering letter for the little note-book,' Leah said, 'with all its confessions. Written months after Julian Rawbeck's disappearance.'

'And Grandfather must've kept quiet all that time about what he knew.'

Just then, as I was handling the Bible, another envelope slipped out of it. I laid the Bible, open at the page, on the little Egyptian side table, and picked up the envelope from the floor. The address – *Poste Restante, Marylebone* – was in Nanny's handwriting, and as I drew out the letter, a hank of shining auburn hair, bound in white silk ribbon, lay in the fold.

'It was grey when I knew Nanny,' I murmured, as, lost in a timeless moment, I brushed the lock of hair against my lips.

I felt Leah's arms slip round me as I read on. The letter was from the same Malvern vicarage, dated Easter Monday, presumably in the same year, 1900.

'Dearest Jack, I thought Chancery was for orphans, and you're rather old for that, nor I must confess am I much flattered to be compared by implication to the Lord Chancellor! Thank you for the little notebook, which I'm sure is very interesting – we may read it together one day – but for now you have indeed "shown me your best", and that best is more than good enough for me, so I return the book to you unread. As for the hopes you say repose in my "verdict", I trust you will find in me the most

lenient of judges when I affirm that I ask for nothing better than to be allowed to try to bring those hopes to pass. Ever, Your Cecily'

'They're wonderful letters, Seb,' Leah murmured, giving me a squeeze.

'I couldn't have wished for . . . Hello . . .'

'What is it?'

I'd happened to glance at the pages of the open Bible on the table, and was caught by the verse at the head of one of the leaves that had enclosed Nanny's roundabout acceptance letter of Grandfather's confession-cum-proposal. I picked the Bible up and read: *'He that over-cometh the same shall be clothed in white raiment; and I will not blot out his name out of the book of Life.'*

'Revelations,' Leah remarked.

'It sounds a bit sinister.'

'A definite case of religious mania,' Leah now pronounced, reverting to the psychology lecturer she was. 'Clearly obsessional: your grandfather felt himself "unworthy" of salvation at the hands of Cecily, especially in the light of the stuff in the notebook about his unregenerate art-student phase: his lust for the music hall girl, the goings-on with magic mushrooms in the artist's house on Camden Hill, and finally, the extraordinary passages in the notebook about the murder of the artist, Rawbeck. It's symbolic that your grandfather should mark the page with the stuff about atonement – "overcoming" – with your grandmother's acceptance letter. He's overcome his worst side, and so reached a sort of salvation. Interesting.'

I reverently replaced the letters, with the hank of hair, in their respective envelopes, and slid them back into the linen flap at the back of the Bible before laying it on the table with the Jiffy bag and picking up the tatty notebook again. Leah and I then went over to the antique cane sofa that my ex-wife Reet had chosen for our last home together, but that had been a divorce and a share-out ago. My new love and I made ourselves comfortable in front of the chattering, scarlet wood fire in its arched fireplace, then Leah turned to me and seemed to take me in, as if for the first time.

'What is it?' I asked with a little laugh. 'What have I done now?'

'I'm wondering if I've been sleeping with the grandson of a Victorian murderer . . .'

Chapter Two

Leah's words gave me an odd frisson – fear? Or even a shade of vicarious guilt? No – absurd! I leapt to the defence of my grandfather and hero.

'No,' I protested. 'You're jumping the gun. There are a number of possibilities: this guy Toland in the notebook, for instance, who's at the magic mushroom bash in Rawbeck's place on Camden Hill in 1899.'

'The "lisping queen", you mean, who's bankrolling Rawbeck?'

'Right. From the description in the notebook, Toland obviously fancies my grandfather. What if the idea is for Rawbeck to dope my grandfather, then have him taken to the seedy pub, so that Toland can have his way with him? Toland and Rawbeck fall out over the payment, there's a fight, Rawbeck gets the worst of it, and young Sebastian's left drugged there as the patsy. Or again, Rawbeck – an obvious toff, if a streetwise one – could've been rolled for his money by opportunistic local heroes from the pub downstairs. He puts up a fight – maybe he's armed – a razor comes out, and he gets unzipped, with Grandfather left starkers upstairs for the coppers to find later on . . .'

'But your grandad says in his notebook that he felt Rawbeck's watch-chain on his dead body: surely lowlife thieves wouldn't have left a watch behind?'

'Mmm . . . you've got a point there, but maybe they panicked, and then again, it could all have been a mushroom-induced hallucination on my grandfather's part.'

'But Rawbeck disappeared right enough – that wasn't an hallucination.'

'God!' I exclaimed. 'If what we've just read had come out at the time, it would've been the scandal of the century, given Rawbeck's notoriety.'

'I wouldn't mind knowing more about him,' Leah said thoughtfully.

'He was Anglo-Swedish, a French-trained Impressionist, reputed to have been a Diabolist. Bit of a raver, too, involved in a number of society scandals. When he disappeared in 1899, it was rumoured a masterpiece he'd been working on had disappeared, too. That's all I know about him at the moment, but I'm certainly going to work on it!'

'And those mysterious names in the notebook – one was an address, wasn't it? Reuben's Court . . .'

She got up and walked over to the bookshelves, where she took down a directory and flicked through its pages.

'Here, Seb – in the London street plan – there *is* a Reuben's Court near Gunnersbury station.'

'That area wouldn't have been built up in the 1890s,' I said. 'Don't tell me there's a Smoking Altars Avenue, too!'

Leah laughed and returned to the sofa while I fished out the rest of the contents of the Jiffy bag.

'What have we here?' I mused as I took out an ancient *Crockford's Clerical Directory* and a linen-backed, 1871 street map of London.

'And that music hall artiste, Carrie,' Leah went on, 'the artist Rawbeck's model. She must've followed your grandad to Paris after Rawbeck had disappeared, then her fancy man, the Vickybird – sounds charming! – comes and joins them. What a nice little earner your grandad must've been for them – a regular meal-ticket . . .'

'Until he finds out about the Vickybird's pinching his drawings – I'd give a lot to know what was so incriminating about them!'

'Why he was so scared at the prospect of the Vickybird selling them to that Paris art dealer – whatsisname?'

I put the old street map and the *Crockford* back in the Jiffy bag and consulted the relevant page in the notebook.

'Carbonero,' I said, jumping up from the sofa and pacing the room. 'This is sensational! When I think of what my grandfather's life was later on – when he'd married Nanny and become a vicar, the Reverend Sebastian Rolvenden DD – it's unbelievable!'

'I'm not so sure,' Leah said in an even voice, the psychologist taking over again. 'In a way, his behaviour's all of a piece – in his rackety magic mushroom days, he's as earnest, intense and questioning in his vices as I'm sure he was later in life in his duties as a blameless clergyman. The same integrity, the same innocence, if you like, and we do change as we get older. As I read him from this notebook, though, he's got one serious flaw – a potentially damaging one . . .'

'Oh, what's that?'

'No sense of humour: it's the essential stabilizer in most of us, a sort of thermostat of the sense of proportion.'

'But there's surely not much scope for a sense of humour in the events he's describing – he's a virtual slave, his mind mushed up by dope . . .'

'Mmm . . . possibly, and that stuff about Carrie's "condition" – she's pregnant. It looks as if you may have a set of unknown cousins, Seb! Maybe French ones, at that! And those Rawbeck drawings the Vickybird pinched from your grandfather in Paris – they must be worth quite a bit now.'

'There's so much I've got to find out . . .'

My companion looked up at me in a quizzical sort of way.

'Well, when you do find out, I hope the truth's to your liking.'

My query about this remark was drowned out by the bleeping of Leah's mobile.

'Yes, all right, Mum,' she replied to the caller in a soothing tone, 'I should be there about three o'clock – see you.'

One of Leah's home visits north, more frequent now in

21

Easter Vacation time than in her ever-more-pressurized term weekends. She switched off the mobile and faced me, then glanced down at the Jiffy bag cornucopia on the table.

'Well, I'll leave you with Grandad for now, then – you'll be all right over the weekend? If you get really down, there's the tablets, but try to lay off them as much as you can.'

I got up, drew Leah gently to me, and kissed her on the mouth, and she nodded again at the bag.

'Give me a ring if you find out anything else – it's interesting.'

After she'd gone I went over to the window to see her car disappear northwards along the headland, to be swallowed up in the grey Essex flatland. Leah had been wonderful after the smash – after I'd finally split from Reet and the sky had fallen in round me. I still hadn't really come to terms with it – there'd been our son, Paul, to consider, for one thing – and now I just frankly wanted to blot it all out of my mind. He was all right, anyway, a capable young man virtually running the smallholding at the Holt, and, if anything, he was even more committed to it than Reet. If Reet would let me blot it out, that is, but no – it was all over.

I glanced out over the mudflats, and could hear the high creaking of gulls. When Paul was five or six he'd started coming out with me gathering seaweed off Dunstanburgh – our ecological period – for the cottage potato patch. The seaweed heap was one of Reet's wheezes. My little son had found a big whelk shell and an ancient tarred-canvas shoulder bag, which he'd donned proudly, and I'd fled in mock terror with him when we'd found an alien-looking purple jellyfish in a rock crevice. Why couldn't it have stayed like that forever? It had been in that same holiday cottage that he'd confronted me fifteen years later during our last ghastly 'family' gathering together, an angry, husky young bloke with red hair spitting out his contempt at me. I didn't know him, and he didn't know me.

22

I went on gazing across the flats: it was peaceful out there, and you couldn't see where the land ended and the sea began. What if you just set off across the flats and kept on walking – No! I must be firm. I was past the head-banging stage, I had Leah, and hadn't I just got a parcel from my long-dead grandfather? Sort of. A message to tell me that before he'd become a clergyman of otherworldly goodness at the turn of the last century he'd been a bohemian lecher in lowlife London, a crony of the most enigmatic of English Impressionist masters, an art student in Paris and a partaker of scheduled substances. What's more, he'd dallied with and probably fathered a child on one of the toasts of the Victorian music hall, narrowly escaped a fate worse than death at the hands of a blubber-lipped sybarite called Toland, only to wake up above a slum pub to find the corpse of his Svengali, Julian Rawbeck RA, between him and a discreet exit. To cap it all, he'd been saved by the bell in the form of my late grandmother Cecily's majority money. You don't get many letters like that from your grandad.

Then there was the actual covering letter from Lawyer Le Touzel in Jersey, on whose doorstep the contents of the Jiffy bag had been dumped. He 'didn't envisage that the donor would be traced', and I could guess why. No doubt some shamefaced heir, who'd discovered the stuff in his old dad's or grandfather's attic, booty of my English-born grandparents' vicarage looted by neighbours after the big German round-up in the summer of 1940. My aunt in Malmesbury, Nanny Rolvenden's niece, had once told me how my grandmother had described to her how she and my grandfather had been sent by the Germans to a camp near Freiburg, but that, both of them being over sixty, they'd been repatriated to England via the Swiss Red Cross.

My grandparents had gone back to Jersey straight after Liberation, only to find their vicarage ransacked and gutted – doors, floors and window frames gone for firewood – with none of their former neighbours and parishioners knowing anything about it ... They'd never gone back, though over the years Reet and I had spent several holidays in the beachside cottage, which had been left in one piece after the war, owing to its having been a billet for a couple of German officers. Even today, they tend not to talk too much about the war on the island – live and let live, and all that. I suspected that that had been the subtext, too, of Lawyer Le Touzel's doubts expressed in his letter as to the 'donor' of the Jiffy bag contents ever being traced. But I'll bet that, back in the 1940s, my grand-father had a few sleepless nights over who might be reading his stolen notebook!

Funny, but recently I'd been fishing around in vain for a subject for my next book, then this lot drops out of the sky on me. If ever I'd wanted to write a book on some-thing, this was it. Leah was going to be an invaluable help to me here, too, with her cutting intelligence and insight, just as she'd been invaluable to me since the smash. I'd met her at a party I'd been invited to by my old crony Frank Hague at his boathouse in Wivenhoe, when he'd thought I needed to be taken out of myself, reintroduced to life sort-of-thing. When I'd told Leah I'd read Botany and Spanish at university, we'd launched into a confab about heredity, an issue she was into as a major part of her study of human behaviour and its causes. We'd liked the same music, loathed the same politicians, and the rela-tionship had really taken off – one up to Frank.

I'd known Frank ever since school, and our paths had kept crossing over the years until he'd opened his antique shop in Wivenhoe, though he still spent quite a lot of his time up in London, an aspect of his life he didn't talk about much. Frank's wife, Pat, taught English at the nearby university, where Leah taught psychology. Frank was known to be seriously well off, though they used the flat over the shop as a sort of perch, and lived fairly mod-estly there. Of course they had the boathouse in the nearby marina, and there was talk of a place near Grasse on the French Riviera. I suspected that Frank's relations with the taxman weren't all that effusive, and that Pat kept on with her job because she liked it and was damned good at it, judging by the heavyweight literary biographies she'd written, and the Readership she'd recently been appointed to. Frank, if rumour was to be believed, had several odd gaps in his CV dating from his London period, which the envious attributed to brushes with the law, but, as I've said, I owed my meeting with Leah to him, not to mention the way he'd negotiated the purchase of my present home for me after the smash.

After so many years of marriage to an inveterate clinger, I loved Leah's self-containment, too – if ever there was a case of anyone being her own woman, Leah Rooney was it. But she had her work at the university, too, and I, what was I working on? *Tod Slaughter, His Life and Crimes* ... Tweaking up the first draft, to be precise. It's funny how I got on to writing film biographies: after years of patient hacking as a staffer on gardening mags, I'd had the idea of celebrating all the holiday Saturday matinées of my boy-hood, and had my first go with *The Lugosi No One Knew*, and, hey presto! – a late-flowering little niche as a film biographer. I even consult on it. I largely owe my starting to write again to Leah, too.

But damn it! That reminded me I'd promised to have lunch with Frank and Pat Hague in Wivenhoe: in my excitement over the arrival of the package from Jersey I'd clean forgotten about the date. Make it short and sweet, though – there's sure to be a twist in the tail – trust Frank! – and I feel uneasy with Pat now since what happened during our last foursome in the cottage in Jersey. I really think Pat gets a buzz now out of putting me alongside Frank, then giving me nods and winks. I feel really guilty with regard to Frank, too, though I've long been aware that he and Pat go their own ways in these matters. All the same, keep it short.

I glanced at the clock on the mantelpiece – time to get a move on. I took up the Jiffy bag with its contents – there'd be time after lunch to do it all justice – and was about to put away the little marble-backed notebook, too, but something prompted me to keep it by me. Call it superstition, what you will, but I wanted to have the feeling of carrying my grandfather's truth with me. I went over to the bureau and locked the bag in the deep bottom compartment, then returned to the sofa where I'd left my jacket and slipped the notebook into the inside pocket before pulling it on and going out to the car.

I bowled along meditatively over the causeway under the huge, lowering grey skies: the Easter hols might be just a week away, but the weather certainly wasn't performing to script. At one point, a wind-tossed willow branch from a ditch-side hedge lashed its skeletal fingers against the windscreen, and I recalled the encounter between Pip and Magwitch in the graveyard in the 'lone, shivering marshes' in the 1946 film version of *Great Expectations*. It was all a bit sad. I slipped in a cassette of the *Enigma Variations* – why not be low-spirited in style . . .

Reet didn't like Elgar – thought it was 'sick Romanticism'. She couldn't abide Pat, either, after the Jersey cottage incident – no, I wasn't really looking forward to lunch. And Frank – we were after all such unlikely friends. We hadn't been what you'd have called close chums at school, but there'd been a sort of attraction of opposites, and with me being as sturdy and uncertain of temper as he was small and unsure of himself, I was always an insurance against the bullies. I suppose it was their attentions that had left him with the slight stammer that still dogged him, but they must also have honed his knack of weighing people up, spotting their weaknesses, and how he might make them serve his turn. Frank took the insider's satisfaction in showing you the ropes: when Reet and I had left university, he in fact had found our first London flat for us, and later, when we'd got into organic smallholding – Reet actually doing it, and I writing it up – he'd used his local contacts to find the Holt for us, which Reet and my son Paul were still farming. Frank'll fix it . . .

And now I was helping him out with his film memorabilia website – that was in all likelihood what the lunch would be leading to. Funny, though, but – Christ! – how do you tell someone: Look, Frank, I've known you for forty years, and you've been of great help to me in more than one crisis in my life – don't think I don't sincerely appreciate it – but, well . . . the thing is, I don't really like you . . . And Pat: I still felt bad about how we'd behaved together in Jersey, though she'd made the running. Just do the lunch, ignore her tricks, help him with the website, over and out.

Just then it started to rain, and the strings in the Elgar music really got to me – the tears of things. I'm sorry, Frank, you're an eager, manipulative little man, but I'm sure you've been my friend in your own way, and I'll do what I can for you.

The windscreen-wiper was dispersing rivulets now – grey rivulets, like floods of tears – enough Elgar. God, I wish I were going home to Leah afterwards. Leah would only have the best of me – I'd see to that. What was that Grandfather Rolvenden had quoted in his proposal to Nanny? *A man in all the truth of nature.* Yes. The masts of the marina were coming into view: straight round it and up to the shop.

It was a fair lunch, cooked by Frank – salmon and a nice sauce, with Chardonnay – and Pat started in with her indignation at the new marking policy now being enforced at the university, just the latest, according to her, in a long series of target-driven lunacies being foisted on the weary toilers of Academe.

'TLAC!' she hooted in her brittle, throaty voice. 'I ask you, what sort of a name's that for a policy!'

'TLC with something extra added!' Frank cracked, his

nondescript, bearded face creasing and his snuffling little laugh escaping. 'Shows how much they think of you.'

'There was a Mexican rain god called Tlaloc,' I said, contributing my twopennyworth, to a curl of the nostrils of Pat's handsome prow of a nose.

'At least he did something bloody useful!'

'What's the new rule all about, then?' I asked, more seriously.

'Just the fifty-word appreciation at the foot of *each* exam paper, but next year we're to be given a new treat – RAE, Research Assessment Exercise – a minimum of four papers in accredited publications. I suppose if we can find time, we'll be able to sneak behind the bike sheds and do a little clandestine teaching or writing in our subjects.'

'And the Dylan Thomas book?' I put in brightly, wondering how such a hard-favoured woman could be so sexy.

'Next sabbatical,' Pat snorted. 'I'm going to stay in Swansea to really absorb Dylan's background.'

'You could apply for a travel grant,' Frank stammered in his uncertain way, the foxy grey eyes taking us in through the oblong specs, then, when he saw that we were laughing, he laughed his own apologetic snuffle, too.

'Ha, bloody ha,' Pat retorted, as Frank got up deftly and started to clear away the lunch things. As soon as he was out of the room, Pat locked her leg round mine under the table. I recalled the strength of those strapping brown legs on that warm, curtained afternoon in Jersey two summers before.

'It's no good, Pat, I . . .'

'It was good then, Seb.'

'Think of Frank – you're . . .'

'You were married then, too, Seb, and what does Frank care? He has his little hobbies in London. I like a man who's not a rabbit, and I make you laugh, too, don't I? It's nice to be with a woman who's not a hysteric, isn't it?'

'It's different now, Pat.'

28

'Still smitten by the little trick-cyclist, are we?'

This reference to Leah really hit home: if Pat should try to spoil things between her and me . . .

'You want me, don't you, Seb?'

I surveyed the firm bust under the tight jumper, then the taut neck and the jutting chin and the nut-brown, freckled face with the big nose and insolent, provocative dark eyes, the half-open, thickish lips and the tusky gap-teeth. I said nothing, but was all too well aware that the confusion and longing in my eyes and in every line of my face must be screaming 'Yes!' to her last question. Sensing her triumph, Pat's eyes softened, and she smiled, the crows' feet coming into play at the edges of her eyes doing nothing to lessen her allure. She slipped her leg out from mine and got up lazily.

'I'll leave you little boys to your train sets,' she said simply, and left the room.

Shortly afterwards, I heard a powerful car engine rev up and then drive away. I resolved to keep away from her in future: it only worked when I was with her. Pat had been right: I still lusted after her, I did relish her totally disabused sense of humour, admired her sheer dash, but I was afraid of her coldness, which was like staring down a deep, dark well.

'Seb . . .' Frank said as he came back into the room, breaking my reverie. 'Grab a drink and come into the workroom: I'd like you to take a look at the blurb I've blocked out for the new website. I'm not sure the register's quite right for the States . . .'

It was as if we were back at school again, and I was helping Frank with his prep, but this time it was with his antique dealer's website rather than with a Latin prose. As he explained what he was aiming at, part of my mind went back to Pat; or rather to the car she'd driven off in not long before: it had been a vintage black Bristol 400. There must be all sorts of ways a bored, clever woman can get back at the man she despises but who pays for her lifestyle. You don't come by a car like that on the proceeds of teaching Eng. Lit. and almost finishing a book on Dylan Thomas.

And why did Frank put up with it? There was clearly no longer any sympathy between them. Habit? Or maybe Pat revelled in her power over him? I thought again of his unspecified London activities: maybe the answer lay there, and in what Pat knew about them.

But back to Frank's workroom and his new website: we quickly agreed on something for the text, then, after he'd asked rather pointedly if I was all right – why not just ask whether I was still taking the tablets? – I thanked him for the lunch and left. I was a bit puzzled as to why he'd asked me along at all, since my 'help' with the website had merely consisted in confirming all his suggestions. My doubts, though, were quickly forgotten in my relief at getting clear of the fraught, *ménage-à-trois* atmosphere that had reigned in the Hagues' flat.

Once outside, I breathed in the fresh air with gusto. My mind soon went back to the Jiffy bag that had arrived that morning, with its intriguing contents, and the vow I'd made to learn more about Julian Rawbeck, the disappeared Impressionist painter. It occurred to me that the local library would still be open, so I nipped along there and managed to find a copy of Rothenstein's authoritative biography of Julian Rawbeck – good weekend reading.

I regained my car, got in with the book, and soon I was driving back over the flats in the raw, April greyness towards my empty watchtower. It was now far too late for tea, and too early for dinner, and I was still dogged by my bad feelings over how I stood with Frank and Pat. Like my attraction to Pat, my friendly feelings towards Frank only operated while I was actually there with him. I felt false – a man of straw. Perhaps I should move away – strike out for a completely new start – you could write articles for gardening magazines or biographies of defunct film actors wherever they had modems and telephone jacks. But then the lighthouse hove into view. A squatter version of the usual workaday nineteenth- and twentieth-century models you see today, square at the base, with three storeys and a pyramidal, leaded roof with a finial on top. I could see the discreet, green front door now, then the two, single-room storeys and attic – where the light had been in the old days – one room above the other like building blocks, each with its squarish, many-paned window. They did lighthouses very tastefully in 1720. I loved the vast view from the second-floor bedroom, too, with marsh, sea and sky joining in a sort of silver truce. No: I didn't think I'd move after all.

Once inside, I made coffee, and, moving to the sitting room and my cane-backed armchair, plunked the coffee mug on the side table and reached automatically for the phone. But then I recalled that Leah usually went out with her mother on the first evenings of her Leeds visits, and, besides, I didn't want to be forever bleating after her like a lost sheep. I desperately wanted her to respect me. I remembered Grandfather Rolvenden's letter to his love, Cecily: *I have striven always to show you my poor best* . . . I put the receiver back down on its rest.

To the Jiffy bag, then, and the earthly effects of Sebastian John Rolvenden. The street map first, I thought – I hadn't really looked at that. A handsome linen-backed affair from 1871, with Highgate a scattered village and open country east of Hackney Marshes. I smiled on reading on the yellow inside folder that no more than a shilling should be paid for cab journeys within the 'four-mile circle', and was duly impressed to learn that the India Office might be visited by the public on Mondays, Wednesdays and Fridays. I scanned the actual street plan, and, hello – what was this? Markings. Faint, pencilled crosses – half a dozen of them scattered at points within a two-mile radius roughly east of King's Cross station. I examined the map back and front, but there were no other markings or

31

additions to the printed text. So the X's marked what spots? That would need further investigation.

I carefully refolded the map and put it aside, turning my attention to the *Crockford*. It was for 1940, the year my Rolvenden grandparents had been collared by the Germans in Jersey. On first riffle, no inscriptions or markings to be seen aside from the printed text. Then the Bible, and in its cloth flap the bundle of letters between my grandfather and grandmother way back in their courting days in the 1890s. I went carefully through the letters again, and was struck more than ever by the contrast between my grandfather's expressed personality and Nanny's – or Miss Cecily Woodruff as she appeared in most of them. His tense earnestness, without a glimmer of humour – I was fully behind Leah's diagnosis on that one now – and Nanny's rather mocking, affectionate common sense. It was certainly how I remembered her. They'd been each other's complements, I supposed. But what Sebastian Rolvenden had been through . . .

I was getting ready to replace the letters in their bundle when – what was this? – there was another sheet jammed into the envelope which contained one of my grandfather's letters to Nanny. A single sheet, folded once, but too big to slide easily out of the envelope. I tugged it out, to find that it was cheap, rather slippery notepaper, written in a completely different hand from his, and in French! There was no accompanying envelope. The address at the head of the sheet was *L'Oustalet Grau, Balmes le Vidame, Niort, Deux Sèvres*. It was written in fairly basic French, so I was able to get the gist of the text:

Dear Monsieur Rolvenden,

I'm writing to you on behalf of my husband Laurent, who has been very ill these last three months, owing to the wounds he suffered during the War – affected lungs. [I think this answered to poumons atteints.*] Because of his illness, he is unable to work, and now we find ourselves in a desperate situ-*

32

ation. Laurent has often spoken to me about you, always describing you as a real gentleman ['gentleman' written in English], *and we would be eternally in your debt if you could help us in our difficulties.*

May God bless you.

Respectfully,
Odette Pidgeon

The English-surname spelling of 'Pidgeon', too – and this Laurent's damaged lungs suggested poison gas, hence the First World War rather than the Second. I wondered how he'd ended up afterwards in Niort, and whence his impressions of my grandfather as a 'gentleman'? I refolded the sheet of notepaper, and was about to slip it back into its envelope, when the faintest of faded-ink inscriptions on the back of the sheet caught my eye. My heart began to pound as I recognized my grandfather's handwriting: *Secured. P. died 11th March, before my help could reach him. Pax cineribus.* So why 'peace to (Pidgeon's) ashes'? Just conventional piety or an element of reconciliation or even forgiveness on Sebastian's part? And what had been 'secured'? And 11th March of what year? I replaced the sheet in the envelope.

Curiouser and curiouser. Throughout my life, my grandfather's elusive memory had echoed like a grace note. He'd died before I'd been born, and neither Nanny nor my own father had ever really talked to me about him. All through the dreary endurance of my boarding-school boyhood I'd woven romantic fantasies round his memory, and now it was as if he'd jumped out of his photo and was standing beside me!

I went back to the Jiffy bag for the Bible, with Nanny's acceptance letter of my grandfather's proposal of marriage tucked between the pages of Revelations. I opened the Bible at the first page of the two marked by the letter, and read the line that had struck me the first time I'd read the letter: *He that overcometh the same shall be clothed in white*

raiment; and I will not blot out his name out of the book of Life.
White ... Hadn't white figured in the unreformed young
Sebastian's drug-trip impressions in the tatty notebook?
'The white radiance of eternity, and I am White!' or some-
thing along those lines. I'd take another look at that.

I slipped the envelope back in the Bible, then, snapping
it shut, got up in a sort of exaltation and began to pace the
room, for all the world like some hellfire preacher, with the
Good Book under my arm. I fingered the top edge rest-
lessly, and became aware of a bump. I raised the volume
to my eyes – the cloth marker – of course, all old Bibles
had cloth markers like shoelaces. Since the inspiration
seemed to be on me that evening, I opened the Bible at the
marked page and read the top line: *The woman thou gavest
me, Lord, tempted me.* I looked upwards and felt a tingle run
up my spine as I found myself looking into my grandfather's large, unquiet eyes, as they seemed to reach out to
me from the framed photograph on the mantelpiece. The
eyes seemed to be more anxious than ever over the fine
features and discreetly bearded, pointed chin. It was as if
he was trying to warn me about something.

Chapter Three

Sunday was a day of rest – I suppose. Up at ten past eight after an informative late night read of the Rawbeck biography, and there'd been progress on the sleeping pill front – none needed to go over. A long, hot bath, ditto breakfast, then a quick drive along the headland and sharp right down the willow lane to the village for a paper and a pinta, and so back again. The paper didn't detain me long – nothing of interest in the reviews – and so straight out into the high-skied, April glory to sow my onions.

I favoured the traditional varieties, and I glanced with satisfaction at the sterling names on the three packets I'd be sowing that morning: Bedfordshire Champion for firm keeping, Ailsa Craig for size and sweetness, and, if you liked the violet-tinged, French type, the chosen variety of the Breton onion men, Rouge Pâle de Niort. Niort again – Madame Odette Pidgeon had written the begging letter to my grandfather from there, the letter I'd found the evening before, spatchcocked in a too-small envelope. I wondered if, on a fine April morning just like this, way back in the pre-war, poor Laurent Pidgeon had sown the same variety in his *potager* before his 'affected lungs' had done for him? Just as my reverend namesake had pronounced his solemn Latin peace on him in his enigmatic note on the back of the letter, I paid my own tribute.

'This row's in your memory, Laurent,' I said superstitiously as I stooped and sprinkled the hard little black carapaces along the drill in the stiff loam.

I worked on in silence till the packets were empty, then I covered the drills gently with the rake before standing up straight awhile to stretch my back as the sun soaked through my closed eyelids. I thought of my next port of call: salty-tanged Mersea Island and the super fish restaurant in the village there. A couple of bumpers of chilled, bone-dry Chablis with my fish would soon dispel any stray fantods.

The roads were empty for a Sunday – the gathering cloud and the northwester explained that – and I'd a clear run past the bird sanctuary and on to the B1025, then straight down among the creeks and willows of the flatland, and so over the bridge to the island and West Mersea. I pulled up and parked outside the rough-and-ready little building with the whitewashed walls – half a dozen cars outside already – and got out and stretched my legs. The northwester was gathering strength – I instinctively zipped my old bomber jacket further up my chest – but the sky was clearing into the buoyant vastness of a Constable flatscape. There was a Thames barge out on the Nass – 'Red sails in the sunset, way out on the sea . . .' Brrr . . . parky, though, out in the wind.

I hurried inside the restaurant, which was chock-a-block, and amid the hubbub – oh, no! – Pat Hague. In a rollnecked sweater and waving to me from a window table – the only one I could see with a free seat. She'd obviously not come in her big old vintage car, or I'd have been forewarned outside: here we go . . .

'Let's order!' she said brightly, as if we'd been on a date, and I slid helplessly into the facing chair and smouldered, half at her importunity, and half at my own gutlessness in not just walking out again.

'I thought a couple of nice chunks of cod with their white sauce,' Pat was going on brightly, rubbing her rather large, shapely hands, 'and a bottle of Alsace –'

'Chablis,' I countered firmly, 'and how did you know I'd be here?'

A hoarse laugh, and the freckled skin stretched taut on either side of the characterful prow of a nose.

'You're a creature of habit, Seb, and, besides, it's a pretty good place – first-rate, fresh fish, done simply to perfection – and so real, don't you think? You can catch the Essex drawl above the *EastEnders* voices.'

I did tend to gravitate here of a Sunday – it was a ritual I didn't like to interrupt – but latterly with Leah sitting where this clever, loose cannon of a woman was sitting now. What the *hell* was she up to? Just then a bustling little body in a green overall with a navy-blue cardigan over it and with frizzy coal-black hair came over and took our order, and was soon back with our wine. She poured out our first glasses.

'Fish'll be ready in a jiff: d'you want chips with it?'

We both nodded eagerly, and the *patronne* bustled away. Pat fixed her bold eyes on mine, and took a sip from her glass.

'Frank and I popped over to see Reet after the auction last week in Walberswick,' she said evenly, by way, I suppose, of mental torture.

'I wish you wouldn't . . .'

'She's our friend, too, Seb,' Pat replied, without batting an eyelid. 'She still talks about you – a lot . . .'

I'd have said something hot and strong, but just then our food arrived.

'Here's some parsley,' the coal-haired missus said, plonking a china dishful of the stuff on to the table.

'Smallholding's flourishing,' Pat went on about her visit to my ex-wife and son, as she tucked into her fish. 'That's Paul's side – he's developed into such a hunk, hasn't he? He's got your shoulders . . . The Long Barn's fitted up now, and they're expecting students in –'

'Why did Frank ask me up yesterday?' I interrupted. 'There wasn't really any more to be done to the website.'

'He's fascinated by you – you're so different from him.'

I must have looked puzzled, for Pat laughed.

'Seb, what hand does Frank write with?'

'I, er . . .'

Pat laughed again, spontaneously and loudly.

'God! You've known him for forty years and never noticed he was left-handed, have you? You're priceless – the last of the great egotists! He often tells me about your fight at school with Neill, the bully, you know . . .'

'Oh, that . . .'

Neill had been a chubby, determined chap – good at games – and had given Frank, as well as others, a pretty bad time in our first year in Big School. Not that I'd come to the rescue, or anything like that – I'm a firm believer in keeping your head down in unfavourable situations, such as school – but when Neill had taken it into his head to smash the lid off my pencil case in a Latin class, I'd seen red and jabbed the jagged end of the lid into his fat mush. He'd clutched his bleeding face and run screaming to Matron, while 'Pablo' the Latin master had just blinked and quietly escorted me to the Head's study. We didn't have any more bother from Neill, and Frank had just sort of tagged along behind me after that.

'Neill had it coming to him,' I replied to Pat, 'but I didn't do it for Frank. All ancient history now.'

'And is that what you and I are to be in future? Ancient history?'

'We've been over that, Pat. I want you while you're there, and I like your talk, but we're bad for each other – do I have to draw a picture?'

Brutal enough, but Pat's smile was as bright and tiger-ish as ever, though I fancied I glimpsed something hard in her eyes, and in my mind's nostril I thought I caught a tang of burning boats. She held my gaze for quite five seconds.

'What are you staring at, Pat? Are you all right?'

'Oh, just looking deep into your eyes, Seb. It's always rather intriguing, you know, what with one being brown and the other green.'

'You've had time to get used to that.'

It was my turn to be disconcerted when my rather compulsory lunch date burst into a rorty hoot of mocking laughter.

'Perhaps I see the truth in them.'

From then on, the conversation turned on Pat's book on Dylan Thomas, then she left the table, and I went on alone, eating the excellent meal without tasting it. My Sunday had been bitched, my lunch had been bitched, and I felt as if I'd been violated by this clever, restless woman, whom I now definitely hated. Would she take my words of dismissal to heart?

'By-ee!' she cried from the counter, jacket on again. 'I've already settled.'

She gave me a silly, parting twinkle with her talons and threaded her way through the surrounding tables, and so out of the restaurant. I wriggled my bomber jacket off the back of the chair, dragged it on, got up, and with a nod to the missus, left the place, too.

I kicked around the edges of the car park and looked over the flats for a couple of minutes, just to clear my mind. Pat – damn her! – in mentioning my son, Paul, had reopened the reverie I'd had not long before, about my final row with him two years previously. I suppose that had marked the beginning of my breakdown; at any rate, I couldn't remember a thing between the row with Paul in the cottage in Northumberland that morning and finding myself at the wheel of my car late in the evening of the same day, staring out to sea from the edge of some cliffs. Or had it been some other cliffs somewhere else? The thing seemed important, somehow. Just then the wind got to me again, and, with the reflection that at least there weren't any bloody cliffs to speak of in Essex, I made for my car and the road back home to some work, followed by a nice, foody, blotto evening with the rest of the Rothenstein biography of Julian Rawbeck that I'd borrowed from the library in Wivenhoe the previous afternoon.

Next morning, Monday, I'd an appointment with my agent, Eve Solander, in London, and I decided that, after we'd done our business, I'd check out the crosses I'd found on my grandfather's London street map. In her little perch in Lisle Street, Eve brought me up to date with my writing projects: the prospective English publishers of my book *Tod Slaughter, His Life and Crimes* were holding out for the US rights, and the sales of my last book were dwindling fairly rapidly – the usual tidings of imminent insolvency.

After I'd left Eve's office I pressed on with the second agenda of my London visit: the mysterious pencilled crosses on what I assumed to have been my grandfather's street plan. I chose King's Cross station as the starting point of my recce, since the crosses on the map were clustered round there. The first two crosses led me south-east to Clerkenwell, and seemed to mark a couple of old pubs in corners of the district as yet untarted up for residence for the upwardly mobile. The sort of hostelries where tourists tend not to tarry for long at the opinionated bars or on the gashed vinyl seats.

I ordered a half-lager in the nearest one, to be joined at the bar by a twitching, bare-armed youth with greenish skin and white eyelashes. He seemed high on something, and his glottal jargon was beyond me, so I just drank up and went, glancing up the stairs as I left the pub. I was on the lookout for the staircase described in my grandfather's notebook, the one in the pub, where, according to his account, the artist Rawbeck had been so gorily done in in an upstairs room in 1899. No luck here, though, no stained glass windows, beguiling or otherwise, being visible on the top landing.

The next water-hole on the map – *if* the cross had been to mark the pub – was surrounded by humdrum, low-rise business premises, refaced in the Fifties and Sixties. The pub itself was another rough-and-ready one. It seemed to be one where codgers hung out, judging by the characters with baseball caps and trainers to their BHS suits, who stood at the bar parroting the usual tabloid rant. I ordered another half-lager, and, just to live a little, a bagful of smoky bacon crisps, then casually asked mine host if he knew how old the pub was.

'1910 – George the Fifth's coronation's stamped on some of the bricks.'

Eleven years after Rawbeck's disappearance, then, so no good for my purposes.

'What I say is,' a tipsy oldster next to me spluttered in my ear, 'this country can only take so many –'

'Yeah, I'm bailing out now,' I said, finishing my lager and leaving.

Outside, I made for the third cross on the map, which answered to a narrow little ethnic cafeteria in a backwater behind Farringdon Road station. I didn't even bother to go in there – for one thing, the lager and crisps I'd taken earlier on were bloating my stomach uncomfortably, and for another, I knew there could be no possible connection between this post-war pastiche art deco building and the murder pub of my grandfather's horrified account of 1899. I stood glumly outside for a moment, and faced the opposite buildings, which were equally humdrum and out of period. The banality of the building immediately opposite was relieved a bit by its garish white-and-blue fascia, and a stationary van in matching colours outside it. The Greek colours, I reflected idly, as I made my way back to the station.

I hadn't found the fatal pub, then, on this first sortie, and my thoughts turned naturally to the corpse, Julian Rawbeck RA, Impressionist master, Diabolist, cadger and conman. I'd glanced at his stuff in the galleries, of course, but maybe a look-in at the National Gallery would expose an aspect I might have missed. At last I reached the station: next stop Charing Cross.

At the Gallery off Trafalgar Square, I didn't need to borrow a soundtrack headset in the central hall: thanks to my reading of the excellent Rothenstein biography of

41

Rawbeck, I'd now a fair idea of the basics of his life. Born in Halifax in 1852, of Swedish parents – the name had originally been spelt Råbäck – Julian had been educated at the Moravian Brothers School in the Black Forest and the University of Paris. On summer excursions to Dieppe he'd hung round the Impressionists, living on an allowance from his wool-broker father, then on air after his father's death in 1875, while trying to be an artist. Then there's a gap – the biographers had given free rein to their imaginations concerning this – till Rawbeck resurfaced in London in 1883, and this time he *was* an artist.

He brought bags of talent, and plunged into dope, Diabolism, a brief marriage for money, affairs, and a grudged RA status in 1891. And lots of controversy, appearing as a witness in the Bowness Trial in 1893: did young Lord Bowness fall over the cliffs under Stairs Castle while under the influence of something illegal, or was he pushed? Horsewhipped by Major Giffard-Chant on the steps of the Reform Club in 1895 for writing in praise of Oscar Wilde in the *Mercure de France*, and so on, and so on. There was no knowing now whether Julian Rawbeck had been mad or bad, but he'd certainly been dangerous to know.

I found his exhibits in the East Wing. A modest four canvases – two of early derivative stuff from his Paris period, but the third, his self-portrait *Harlequin*, glowed. I stared into the level, self-confident gaze of the cold grey eyes, set close into the thin nose, in the square, pink face. The eyes gave nothing away, but the artist's supreme mastery of colour worked its usual magic. I recalled my grandfather's notebook rhapsodies about actually *tasting* colours.

Then I came to Rawbeck's acknowledged masterpiece: *Colour in the Shadows*, with the dazzling white of the can-can girl's frou-frou as she held her shapely leg under the knee muting the tone of the receding scarlet of her dress and of the curtains behind her into the near-black of the background.

'Some see a parallel with Sickert,' a fruity hoarse whisper in an Irish accent came from somewhere behind my shoulder, 'but the treatment of colour is quite different – none of those dull reds and browns.'

I turned to meet the humorous blue stare of a shortish, bullet-headed man of about forty. He'd a camera case slung over the shoulder of his buff macintosh, and his already-silvering hair was cut militarily short.

'Both artists were interested in the music hall, weren't they?' I replied.

'Because it was trendy in France then – they were all trying to be French.'

'She certainly wasn't French,' I said, nodding at the ginger-headed cancan girl in the painting, whom I knew from the account in my grandfather's notebook to have been his youthful femme fatale of the music hall, Carrie Bugle.

'Is that so?' the man said, the smile that creased the pleasant, blunt features widening. 'What was she, then?'

'Oh,' I hedged, fearing I'd already said too much, 'she looks English to me.'

'Enjoy!' the puckish man said, still smiling, and with a nod walked briskly off.

I looked at my watch: one-twenty already, and the gaseous lager and crisps had killed my appetite for lunch. I didn't feel like traipsing round London in search of the other crosses on my grandfather's street map, either – another day – so I made for the tube for Liverpool Street, en route home.

That evening, Leah rang and invited me over to a pasta supper in her flat in the university grounds. I filled her in about the pre-war begging letter from Madame Pidgeon in Niort I'd found among Grandfather's things on the Saturday evening, and without a word she got up and left the room. She came back and handed me a glossy brochure, which I held open at the folded-back page.

'I took Mum to Leeds Art Gallery yesterday afternoon,'

Leah said, then, with a nod at the brochure I was holding: 'They've a Rawbeck of their very own.'

I took in the illustration in the brochure. It was a charcoal sketch of the back and legs of a beautiful young male body, contorted round a sort of blasted tree trunk. The face was invisible except for part of the jaw, the head being more or less absorbed into the tree trunk. The caption read: *Sketch for* Ariel Bound, and at the end of the short blurb: *Model believed to have been the 'L.V.P.' associated with a number of other Rawbeck studies.*

'L.P.,' I said, the penny dropping. 'Laurent – Laurence – Pidgeon.'

'Middle V. might be Victor, and pigeons are birds . . .'

I recalled the later Paris entry in my grandfather's notebook, about the 'lounging, insolent Cockney' who'd carried on with his Carrie, who'd pinched and possibly sold on his compromising Rawbeck sketches, and who'd figured in some horrifying revelation of Carrie's at the time of their final break.

'God!' I whispered, the hairs standing up on the back of my neck. 'The Vickybird's back!'

Chapter Four

An article on new varieties of garden bamboo for the *Dumfries Herald* kept me away from the Jiffy bag mystery till Wednesday, when I found on rummaging through my files that I hadn't the pics I needed to meet the delivery deadline. Groaning at the prospect of having to trundle up to London again to use the picture library, I took some comfort from the fact that at least I could press on there with sussing out the data in my grandfather's old notebook and street plan.

As I settled into my seat in the scruffy London pacer-train in Colchester station – thank God the morning rush-hour was long over – I reflected on how Leah's turning-up of the Rawbeck sketch in the Leeds Art Gallery brochure had opened a whole new window on the affair. Now we were pretty sure we had the Vickybird in the frame. Odd how alive these characters still seemed, even after they'd been in the grave for so many decades. The ripples of my grandfather's London nightmare in 1899, too, were proving wider than I might have thought, with possible continuing link-ups with Jersey and France.

As the train rumbled free of Colchester I fished the old marbled notebook out of my inside pocket: what was the street where the magic mushroom session had taken place, before my grandfather had woken up beside the artist Rawbeck's body in the room above the sleazy pub? Ah, that was it: Great College Street – 'Convocation in Great College Street' – it sounded positively ecclesiastical.

I unfurled the 1871 street map, and noted that there was no pencilled cross marked anywhere along Great College Street, which I knew was behind the Houses of Parliament. Like the marked places I'd already visited on the Monday, the remaining three were clustered at points east of King's Cross station, the farthest out in the Hackney Marsh district. Some sort of pattern to the cluster?

By the time I'd finished my musings, the train was trundling into the refurbished gloom of Liverpool Street station, and, as soon as I'd got out, I made a beeline for the picture library where I needed to borrow the pics for my article. The business took half an hour, then I took a tube to Westminster.

Armed with the squared-up, antique map, along with a modern street guide for reference, I made for Great Smith Street, and so down to the junction with Little Smith Street, then sharp left up the end of Tufton Street, to face the flint front of the Westminster School gate-surround at the head of Great College Street.

I strolled slowly down the narrow street, the side opposite the school being taken up by, first, a red-brick, churchy-looking shop, whose windows revealed piled-up building materials inside. Next was the school Art Department – both buildings having a post-1914 look to them – before the discreet recess of Barton Street and its handsome Georgian houses. I paused and took in the side street – now, that was just the sort of place you'd have had a discreet little magic mushroom session in – then with a sigh reflected that, no, Grandfather had written Great College Street, and he must've known . . .

I walked on in the direction of the river, across the opening to Barton Street, and came, more promisingly, to a block of eighteenth-century buildings, under refurbishment and still in Great College Street. Not a soul or a blue plaque in sight. Finally, I came to the opening to Little College Street, with, across the road, the lofty bulk of a Victorian building, the last in Great College Street not part of Westminster School. I crossed the street, to find that the building was a stately hotel, with, before it, the vast loom of the Big Ben clocktower, with the Thames at its foot. And that seemed to be it. Apart from the little assembly of Georgian houses under refurbishment before you hit the hotel at the end of the street, it was pretty clear that Westminster School now effectively occupied both sides. And again, even in 1899, it would have been a pretty high-profile area to have held Diabolist sessions in; unless some of the Diabolists had been MPs or clergymen.

I turned my back on the Mother of Parliaments, and, crossing to the other side of Great College Street, thoughtfully retraced my steps. They'd have detailed OS maps of Victorian London in the new public library in Westminster Town Hall, I mused, and made my way to Victoria Street. There, I found that at the time of Julian Rawbeck's disappearance in 1899 there'd in fact been *two* Great College Streets, the one I'd just visited, and one – named after the Royal Veterinary College – in the Camden Town area. Looking in my modern street guide, I saw that the Camden Town alternative now went under the name of *Royal* College Street. The district had a certain resonance, too, for hadn't my grandfather mentioned in his notebook that Julian Rawbeck had had a studio on Camden Hill?

Spurred on now by the thrill of the chase, I made for the tube again, and Camden Town station. Not knowing that part of London very well, I got out at the Camden High Street exit instead of the one at the back which gave on to Kentish Town Road, and so blundered about for a while in the sleazy Gothland round Inverness Street market. Using my modern street guide, I jostled my way through the throng of young tourists, trendseekers and oddbods like myself until I'd found my bearings amid the grubby tat of the gorblimey fascias under the crumbling, Regency-looking upper storeys.

Having reorientated myself, I crossed the canal at Starbuck's, curved up Castlehaven and Hawley Roads, and faced the roaring confluence with Kentish Town Road and Camden Street, which ran parallel with Royal College Street.

Yes, I could cross the street here and use the side street on the other side as a short cut to Royal College Street. I took my life in my hands and nipped across, then took the pavement of the genteel side street – Jeffreys Street – that led down to the head of Royal College Street.

Jeffreys Street had nice, Regency-looking terrace houses on both sides, two-storeyed, cream-painted on the ground-floor walls, with ironwork grilles under the upper windows and the original iron railings round the areas. Barriers at either end shut the street off from school- and rat-runners, as well as from the roaring traffic on the two parallel thoroughfares.

By then I'd almost reached the opening to Royal College Street – so far, so ... but hang on ... there was a commemorative plaque on the wall of one of the cream-painted houses at the end of Jeffreys Street: *Sir Tarquin Rivers, traveller and writer, lived here, 1893–1899*. 1899 again, and Rivers rang a bell. I tried to remember as I walked on, but couldn't quite make the connection: it'd come to me later on, no doubt.

There's quite a lot of Royal College Street, and whatever dingy romance my grandfather might have found there in its gaslit and cab-belled days has long since dissipated amid the roaring utilitarianism of the modern streetscape. A weary succession of rundown Victorian terraces till you crossed the canal at Lyme Street, then, on the hospital side, the Brutalist rash of the Parcelforce depot, then more Victorian blight, with nary a mark or plaque on either side to give me a scent of my youthful grandfather's world. Then, on the last crumbling house-but-one on the hospital side ...

I crossed the road at the zebra crossing and viewed the front of the house: unaltered from Victorian times, for all I could see, except for the concrete sills of the windows of the upper storeys. Sash window frames with catches on the central bars, a battered door with a grotty area down on its right, and there, on the blistered, buff wall between two windows, a square wooden plaque with the words: *The French poets Paul Verlaine and Arthur Rimbaud lived here May–July 1873*. The adjoining house, just before the gateway to the car park of the Beaumont Animal Hospital, marked the end of the road for my purposes, and I made my way to the bus stop in Crowndale Road.

While I waited for the bus that would take me to King's Cross, en route to Liverpool Street, and so home with the pics that would enable me to meet the deadline for my article that day, I went over my impressions. Verlaine and Rimbaud had been the Punk Poets of their time, into all sorts of now-illegal substances, and hadn't Rimbaud dealt with synaesthesia in his poetry? The name given to interchange of sense impressions: smelling sounds, tasting colours etc. '*Correspondances*', I think he'd called them. My grandfather had recorded just such impressions in his description in his notebook of the effects of his having imbibed the magic mushroom potion. I felt I was on the right track.

An hour later, I was seated in the train home, and I pulled out Grandfather's notebook and went over the entries again, mulling over the fantastic story he told.

Briefly, in the autumn or winter – he describes the London air then as 'raw', and it was established that Rawbeck had disappeared in the November – of 1899, he becomes involved with a bohemian group based in Great College Street – as it was then called – in Camden. Whose house it is isn't stated, but Rawbeck is clearly calling the shots. Also present is a 'queen' called Toland, whose 'credit' Rawbeck enjoys, and who slobbers over my youthful grandfather. There's also a 'P. F.', who obliges with a dirge on the flute. There's a sense that there are others present, too, but with no details as to their identity, which suggests that my forebear was writing up the notes for his own reference.

At the session, young Sebastian is chosen as 'Seer', who through the medium of a magic mushroom potion will presumably provide mystic revelations for the rest of the 'Convocation'. My grandfather is undergoing this, and other ordeals, for the sake of access to Carrie Bugle, a girl from the music halls, access that can only be attained through the artist, Julian Rawbeck, whose model Carrie is.

After the 'Convocation', my grandfather makes his way – or is escorted – semi-conscious and hallucinating, into a hansom cab, from which he's decanted, unconscious, into the upper room of a pub in some rough area of London, somewhere with 'water on his left'. The young man comes to, naked, on a dingy bed, and, while dressing, stumbles over the body of Julian Rawbeck, the latter's throat cut. My grandfather flees the room, apparently unobserved, in the early hours of the morning and, on leaving the pub, clocks a charismatic red-and-blue stained-glass edging to the window of the landing. He reaches his digs, and on packing hurriedly for the Continent, notices that his razor's missing.

Young Sebastian Rolvenden then heads for Paris, where he's joined by music hall girl and artist's model Carrie, now free of her Svengali, Rawbeck. But Carrie has a fancy man in attendance, the racily nicknamed 'Vickybird', possibly the Laurent or Laurence Pidgeon whose French wife Odette a generation later will send a begging letter from Niort in France to my grandfather in his Jersey vicarage.

In Paris, Carrie and the Vickybird batten on my grandfather, until, sometime in the following year, 1900, the Vickybird steals some drawings that are somehow of great significance to Grandfather, and possibly sells them on to a Paris art dealer, Carbonero. There's some link-up with the Roman numeral LXXXIII.

Meanwhile, Grandfather and Carrie, who's now increasingly drunken and 'blowsy', as well as pregnant, come to the parting of the ways, but not before she's horrified him with some unspecified revelation about the fate of Rawbeck. My grandfather makes arrangements for the coming child, while Cecily, his long-suffering fiancée in England, comes into her majority-money and comes over to Paris to take him away from all that. So ended the notebook entries.

I laid the notebook in my lap and looked out of the compartment window: the train was skirting the A12, and would soon be coming into Hatfield Peverel. But how much of my grandfather's account had been true, how much hallucination or, as Leah suggested, psychological bogeymen induced by guilt feelings? As for what had happened in the real world after the notebook entries, Cecily paid for Grandfather's ordination course at Cambridge, he set up as a parson, and they married and produced my father, Athelstan Hugh Rolvenden – 'A. H.' to all and sundry. For my grandfather there'd followed a blameless life as a clergyman, first in Cambridge, then in Jersey, and finally at Malmesbury, where he'd died in 1950, in a house owned by Nanny's family, the Woodruffs.

But happy ever afterwards? I hardly think so: the impression I'd got was that my grandfather had passed the rest of his life in a sort of haunted unease, which seemed to have been visited on my own father, 'A.H.', who'd appeared to go constantly apologizing through life. Dad had been sandy-haired and shy, and had passed his days quietly as an aircraft designer at Calshot. He'd only married at forty-three, and my mother, who'd been a bookshop assistant in Harrogate when he was conducting an army course in a nearby country house during the war, did a bunk in 1958, when I was six. She'd been dark and vivacious – as sociable as Dad had been shy – with brown eyes and a snub nose, and had worn her wavy hair like the Rank Charm School film starlets of the day.

Dad hadn't been able to cope with me – too busy, for one thing: he was a technical director at Calshot by then – and had simply bunged me into a series of boarding schools.

He'd never remarried, and had remained quietly shrugging his shoulders – 'Search me, old lad . . .' – and smoking his pipe till he'd died in 1971. If I'd had to invent an epitaph for him, I think it would have been: 'He kept his head down.'

The train pulled out of Hatfield Peverel, and I returned to the battered notebook in my lap. I opened it again, this time at the page with the enigmatic, disjointed entries: *Rivers – Home in the East – Soundings A*. But which rivers? The Seine? The Thames? Whose Home in the East? And Soundings A had more of the ring of a recording studio than something from way back in 1900. And where was Reuben's Court, if not in prosaic, too-modern Gunnersbury Park? And Smoking Altars? These would have to be tackled methodically, one at a time.

Then at least one penny dropped: Rivers. The name on the plaque on the house in Jeffreys Street, the one that led into Great College Street. Not a river, but a man. Could the Rivers in the notebook have been Tarquin Rivers, who'd been a traveller and writer, and who'd left the house in Camden in 1899, the year of Julian Rawbeck's disappearance?

I was too impatient to wait till I got home to look it up on the Internet, so as soon as the train pulled into Colchester, I reclaimed my car from the station car park and made for the reference library and their past numbers of *Who's Who*. The 1913 edition had the most complete summing-up of Rivers' life, for it had been in that year that he'd died of typhoid at Homs in Syria. Born in 1865 into an army family near Croscomb in Somerset, Tarquin Soane Rivers had been educated at Wellington, then had gone up to Balliol to take a First in Arabic and Persian before joining the Sudan Civil Service – 'Blues ruling Blacks' – in 1887. In 1891 he'd resigned 'somewhat abruptly' from the Service in order to indulge his lifelong passion for travel in the 'desert places of the world', basing himself loosely in London during the brief intervals between journeys. A lifelong bachelor, he'd published four collections of sonnets and numerous travel books before his death.

It wasn't a long entry in *Who's Who*, so I made for the non-fiction department, to find that they'd a collection of poems by Rivers in the reserve stack. It was called *Baalbek*, and I got the girl to dig it out for me. When she had, I went over to a seat and skimmed through the slim volume, the Introduction giving me the gist of where the writer was coming from: *A minor poet, whose marked individuality and subjectivity of theme did not recommend him to the coteries of his day, Rivers gives the fullest expression to his enigmatic genius in his haunting, almost hallucinatory evocations of the landscapes and cultures of the Levant. In more than one of these sonnets, Rivers' explorations of the theme of unattainable, 'distant' love clearly evoke the* Amor de lonh *of the medieval troubadour Rudel, as does his skilful use of the Arabic convention of the* ghazal, *in which the true identity of the adored object – often of the same sex as the writer – is hidden among virtuoso conceits. Among the poems gathered here, there is a peculiarly elusive quality to the sonnet 'Baalbek', first fruit of Rivers' last oriental period after he left England forever in 1899 . . .*

That year again! When the Camden Convocation – along with Julian Rawbeck – had so abruptly vanished. I glanced at my watch, remembering that I still had pics to process and an article to email, so just read the flagship sonnet 'Baalbek' as a taster. It was all about deserts, heart's desires and the Oasis that must always dissolve as in a mirage. I remembered the old Piaf number, 'Mon Légionnaire': 'He was thin, he was handsome, he smelt good – of the hot sand.' Who'd Rivers' legionnaire been? Whose male identity had he covered up in the Arabic conceits of the sonnet? With a final glance at my watch – I was cutting it thin, now – I flicked back the pages to the Dedication at the front. It was only four letters, and there flashed through my mind the image of a lonely, sand-blown cairn of stones in the middle of an endless desert as I took the words in. They read simply: *To S. R.*

Chapter Five

I got home just after three-thirty, and dashed up to my study and tore immediately into the gardening article, finally emailing it to Dumfries at twenty past four. After that, it was straight downstairs to get myself a mug of coffee and a crunch of biscuits before tackling Grandfather's notebook and letters again. I'd now be able to read them in the light of my new discoveries, in particular that of Rivers, the Camden-based desert wanderer of the turn of the last century.

I found that there was only one mention of Rivers in all of the Jiffy bag texts, and that was confined to the notebook entries in the 'disjointed' section. Of course, Rivers' Camden address and the fact that he'd left England for good in the year of Rawbeck's disappearance might have been pure coincidence, but if the 'S. R.' of the dedication of his *Baalbek* book of sonnets had stood for Sebastian Rolvenden, we were into exciting new territory . . .

But then there were Reuben's Court, Smoking Altars and Home in the East to crack, not to mention Soundings A. And if only I knew who else – apart from P. F., the lugubrious flautist – had been at the Camden Hill Convocation on the night of my grandfather's horrible awakening in the unidentified house with the beguiling stairhead window . . .

The tentative quack of a car horn outside broke my reverie. I plonked my mug down on the side table and went over to the window. Leah? She'd told me she was up

54

to her neck in compiling exam papers. I twitched the curtain aside, half-ready to groan with dismay at the sight of Pat Hague's boxy, black vintage car, but my heart sank into my shoes when I saw the familiar – in both senses – Land Rover parked on the headland, and my ex-wife Reet getting out of it. She was dressed any old how in an anorak, woollies and denims, with the scuffed oil-rigger's half-boots she usually wore on the smallholding. Her hair was now its natural grey, but she was as spare and graceful as she'd ever been.

At first I felt totally confused and abashed, as you do towards someone who knows everything about you, but with whom you're not right. I hadn't given much thought up to then about how I might feel if I ever ran into her again – the relief had been so total when I'd walked out of the divorce court the year before – but I found that what I actually felt was shame – and, yes, a sort of subdued excitement. She looked calm enough as she walked up to the front door, which I ran forward to open.

'Coffee?' was all I could say as, shaking her head, she wiped her boots on the front doormat. 'Please . . .' I heard myself saying.

'All right, then,' Reet said indifferently, and I scurried off to the kitchen.

I drew her a mugful from the brew I'd made not long before, and returned to the sitting room, where she was sitting on the cane sofa she'd bought herself for our first home an age before. I took a seat at the other end.

'I've been to London,' my ex-wife said as I plied her with coffee – milk, but no sugar. 'Just turned off the A12.'

It must be important, I thought, then: if this was Pat Hague's work . . .

'You didn't arrange these . . .' Reet said with a little smile as with her long fingers, reddened by country living, she stroked the brightly coloured cushions on the sofa.

'Er, no,' I said: had Pat been talking to her about Leah?

'You've not been well?'

I could cheerfully have wrung Pat's neck.

'Been a bit under the weather, but I'm fine now.'

She glanced at me reproachfully, and I noticed how firmly her high-coloured skin still held over the high-bridged nose and high cheekbones.

'I've been under the weather, too – Seb, have you been sending a private detective to watch me?'

'No!' I yelped angrily, spluttering over my coffee. 'Of all the . . . Who's been telling you . . .'

'Sorry, then . . . It's just that lately there's been a car parked on the side road behind the stables and once actually inside the trees at the Holt. Paul waited behind the hedge the other day for the driver to come back. When he did, he said he was looking for Mr Sebastian Rolvenden, and Paul told him you didn't live there any more. Paul said he'd looked on the top of the dashboard of the car – a light-grey Nissan Micra – and there'd been a copy of our book there, and a map of Jersey.'

Reet and I had co-authored a book on our organic experiment at the smallholding years back – the snooper at the Holt must have got our address out of it – and now there was another possible Jersey connection. I remembered the odd little encounter I'd had at the end of my visit to the Rawbeck collection at the National Gallery on Monday.

'Was he a bullet-headed little man, by any chance?' I ventured. 'Stubbly grey hair, round blue eyes and a cooing voice with an Irish accent?'

'Yes, that's pretty well how Paul described him – d'you know him, then?'

'No, but I'm beginning to think he might know me: he spoke to me, or rather behind me, at the National Gallery on Monday. Did he tell Paul his name?'

'No, he asked him where you were now, and, er . . . Paul said he'd no idea . . .'

I smiled a grim little smile: I could well imagine how forcefully my son would have responded to such a query.

'Then the man just said there'd been a misunderstand-

ing,' Reet went on, 'and drove off. I wouldn't have bothered you, but . . .'

'Did Paul suggest I'd been sending a private detective to
the Holt?'

Reet put her mug down and, getting up, went over to
the back window. 'The kitchen garden's looking lovely,
Seb – you're more suited to working on a small scale.'

She then swung round to face me, real disquiet in her
eyes this time.

'Why were you at the National Gallery, Seb?'

'Mmm . . . to look at some, er . . . Impressionists – something I'm working on at the moment. Why do you ask?'

She seemed on the point of saying something, but hesi-
tated before replying.

'I just thought it might've been something to do with the
man who came to the Holt.'

'Reet, if our friend shows up again, will you send him
down here to me?'

'All right – if that's what you want – but I hope it's
all right.'

I got up and walked over to her, gently touching her
sleeve. I wanted to say something to her, but didn't know
what it was.

Reet softly disengaged my hand from her arm and
started to make for the door.

'Well,' she said, 'must be going. Evening chores waiting
and all that.'

She paused in the doorway, and the anxious expression
came back into her eyes.

'Seb, you're a clever guy, but you can't always see.'

'What d'you mean?'

'Just that the truth doesn't always set you free – Bye,
take care . . .'

I stood at the door, till the Land Rover had disappeared
up the headland. What had all that been in aid of? I could
understand Reet's desire to head off a potential dust-up
between me and Paul over his private detective notion

– there'd been enough spats between us in recent years –
but what could it possibly have been to her if I'd visited
the National Gallery recently? And that stuff about my not
'seeing'? I also wanted to know what the puckish Irish
bloke who'd buttonholed me in the Gallery was up to.
I still had a strong suspicion, however, that Pat Hague's
fine Italian hand might be in this, so on finally shutting
the door and going back inside, I rang the Hagues' number in Wivenhoe, Frank answering my request to speak to
his wife.

'Pat?' he replied. 'Not in – destination unknown. Mine
not to reason why – not at the boathouse at the last count
– maybe on the trail of the Bard of Swansea.'

'Could you ask her to ring me up when you see her
next?'

'Righto – that all?'

'That's all, Frank – thanks and cheers.'

I put down the receiver and returned to my new discovery: Sir Tarquin Rivers' possible connection with the
Camden Hill Convocation, and the dedication of his book
of poems to someone with at least my grandfather's
initials. I'd started another browse in Grandfather's notebook, when, around five, Leah rang from the university to
ask how I was. I excitedly explained about my new find in
London that afternoon.

'Rivers,' Leah repeated, 'Tarquin. Right, I'll try the
English section in the University Library – see you round
seven-thirty – and have my dinner ready!'

I laughed, rang off, and returned to my grandfather's
notebook. I riffled the meagre pages – such a wad torn out
– but wasn't there something I'd forgotten in my concentration on the surviving text? What they did in the best old
crime films? I went over to the bureau and rustled up a
soft-leaded pencil, then began to shade the first blank
sheet after the torn-out section. But there was no imprint
outlined in the pencil-shading. Leave it for now – there
was dinner to get ready.

A couple of hours later, Leah was sitting in my kitchen opposite me, looking enigmatically over the leek dumplings.

'You've found something out, haven't you?' I quizzed her.

'Watch this space,' she said, even more enigmatically. 'These are nice dumplings . . .'

After the meal, we took our wineglasses over to the sitting-room sofa, and Leah looked dreamily into the fire as I enlarged on what I'd told her earlier about my findings in Camden Town.

'How long is it since you took any medication?' my companion asked, as if she hadn't been listening, and cutting off my stream of excited speculation.

'Damned if I can remember . . .'

The soft olive features turned smilingly in my direction.

'Good – soon you'll be completely back into life.'

'And who've I got to thank for that?' I murmured, caressing Leah's firm, plump thigh as I sought her mouth.

'Aren't you interested in what I found out in the University Library?' she asked, pushing me away good-humouredly.

'Yes – Rivers . . .'

Leah pulled a folded A4 sheet from the pocket of her denim top, unfolded the paper and started to explain.

'This is Tarquin Rivers' foreword from a 1907 collection of his poems: *Salix Babylonica* . . .'

'The Willow of Babylon,' I translated aloud. 'In the Bible, that's what the exiles hung their harps on, wasn't it?'

'. . . and wept,' Leah capped my paraphrase, 'when they remembered Zion.'

'Exile,' I said. 'Longing – Rivers' theme song.'

'Well,' my companion went on, 'I think he explains here why he left England.'

Now I sat bolt upright on the sofa, all attention.

'*As to my reason for leaving my native land,*' Leah read out Rivers' words, '*suffice it to say that, roaming on a sleepless*

*night in London, and idly following the hot-chestnut man home,
I chanced upon a jewelled casement in a mean house. I entered
the room whose door the casement guarded, and found inside a
truth whose burden I knew I could not bear under English skies.
That truth, with its burden, is still with me, and will remain
with me forever.'*

'The "jewelled casement"!' I exclaimed. 'The red-and-
blue stained glass that Grandfather said in his notebook
"beguiled" him on the landing window as he was doing
his runner from the pub where he woke up with
Rawbeck's body!'

'Rivers' "burden",' Leah suggested. 'What was in the
room . . .'

'But what was his part in it?' I said, clapping down my
wineglass on the side table, getting up and pacing the
room in my agitation. 'Was Rivers there while Rawbeck
was still alive? Did Rivers in fact do him in? In that case,
he wouldn't have *dared* come back to his "native land" . . .'

'And where was your grandad when Rivers barged – if
he did – into the murder room? Remember, if the S. R. in
Rivers' dedication of the other book stood for Sebastian
Rolvenden, Rivers was probably mad about the boy. Deep
waters . . .'

'And we know now that Rivers' night-wander through
London was after pub-closing time – very late at night in
Victorian days . . .'

'Oh?' Leah challenged. 'How do we know that from
what I've just read?'

'You haven't had my experience in researching, my dear
– over the years a hack becomes a repository of useless
knowledge. In those days, hot-chestnut and hot-potato
sellers used to gather in front of the pubs at closing time
to catch the home-going revellers.'

'Like burger stalls today.'

'Right, and the fact that Rivers was following the hot-
chestnut men *home* after a night's trade indicates that the
pubs would have been well and truly empty by that time.

There'd have been no witnesses to whatever his part was in what went on in the murder room over the pub Grandfather describes in his notebook. We're narrowing it down.'

'What's the next move, then?' Leah asked as she forked into her third dumpling.

'Examine the surrounding events of the time; after, say, the beginning of November – Rawbeck was last seen by his associates in the London art world around that time – 1899. Any reported events in London – crimes, arrests, anything – that might have a resonance with my grandfather's account in the notebook.'

'A trawl through the newspaper archives . . .'

'My pigeon in Colchester tomorrow.'

And so, next morning, after Leah had driven off to the university and her exam papers after breakfast, I cleared my Inbox – a little Spanish translation job for an art gallery in Gateshead, with a fairly elastic deadline – then got into my car and drove again to the Colchester Reference Library. For the next hour or so, I pored over microfiche spools of their back copies of *The Times* for November and December 1899.

There was no reference to Julian Rawbeck in any of them, which was to be expected in the case of such an elusive character. He'd been capable of goofing off on the spur of the moment to Malaga or Algiers – anywhere – and prowling around there alone and incognito for months on end in search of inspiration. In this light, it wasn't surprising that his absence only began to be noticed months after the time-window I was exploring.

I went on trawling carefully through each edition of the paper, from house property adverts to foreign news, through the Court Circular to the obits, without spotting anything with seeming relevance to the Rawbeck Affair. Then something caught my eye – a full name I could put significant initials to – in one of the small inside news columns in the issue of Friday, 11th November:

Suicide of Musician

The body of Mr Philip Forbuoys, aged about thirty, was taken from the Thames last night under Tower Bridge. Mr Forbuoys, who was unmarried and had rooms in Camden Town, was an executant of the classical flute, and according to his landlady, had seemed to be in low spirits for some time. Some indication of his intention to take his own life was provided by the fact that he appeared to have bought a second-hand razor in the course of the day of his death, his own being still upon the washstand of his lodgings, where he had left it upon leaving the house yesterday morning. The fact that he had seemed to have changed his mind during the course of the day, and chosen water as the means of his death, was indicated by the stones found in his pockets, along with the second-hand razor, after the discovery of his body. Mr Forbuoys had studied music in Germany, and was well known in artistic circles in London. The matter is now in the hands of the Coroner.

I sat back on the seat of the library carrel, and stared, unseeing, into the screen of the spool projector. Even through the dry language of the old *Times* report something of the blackness in the hapless flautist Forbuoys' mind before he'd taken the final plunge into the deadly eddies under the piers of Tower Bridge came through to me. I pictured in my mind the 'Convocation' scene in my grandfather's account, with his description of his writhings, to the accompaniment of a mournful tune on the flute, under the effects of the magic mushroom potion. I wondered whether the unfortunate Philip Forbuoys – the flautist 'P. F.' in my grandfather's account – had been aware at the time that he'd been playing his own funeral dirge.

Chapter Six

I joined Leah for lunch in the university cafeteria, near-deserted in this vacation-time, and we did a post-mortem on my morning's find among the back numbers of *The Times* in the nearby City Library.

'Mmm . . .' Leah murmured thoughtfully over her undistinguished chicken curry. 'On the face of it, given the way all the other circumstances fall into place, it's unlikely to have been coincidence.'

'None at all – P. F. in my grandfather's notebook – Philip Forbuoys in the *Times* article on his suicide – both flautists – Forbuoys' death on virtually the same day as Rawbeck's disappearance.'

'Which from the article's dateline – 11th November 1899 – we can pin down to the 10th of that month. And I think we know now from the article who took your grandad's family-heirloom razor from his digs . . .'

'Right!' I agreed. 'Forbuoys . . . But did he take it along beforehand to the pub to murder Rawbeck and leave it there to frame my grandfather –'

'Or did he turn up at the pub after Rawbeck's murder, and take it *away* from the murder room to *save* your grandad? The flute player and your grandad may even have been in cahoots to get rid of Rawbeck, and as time goes by young Sebastian simply blots the thing out of his mind: not like me at all, so I couldn't have done it –'

'No, Leah! Grandfather didn't kill Rawbeck – I'm absolutely convinced of that: in his notebook he's

63

genuinely puzzled as to what could've happened in the sleazy room above the pub that night. His account's just, well . . . right.'

'So now we've lined up Rawbeck himself, your grandad, the rich "queen", Toland, Forbuoys the flute player, and possibly the poet and explorer, Rivers, too, at the Camden Convocation on the night of 10th November 1899. But were there others present? Not much likelihood of finding out now, of course, after all this time . . .'

'Don't say that, Leah! Look at how much we've discovered already – and all of it unknown to the biographers and theorizers about Rawbeck and his fate.'

'I must say it's proving excellent therapy for you,' Leah remarked with her smoky chuckle. 'You're all bright-eyed and bushy-tailed!'

I sat back in my chair and gently pushed away the plate with the ruins of my meal. Who better to establish the truth about the first Sebastian Rolvenden than his grandson? I then returned to the matter in hand.

'I think we can rule out Toland – provisionally, at any rate – from the list of main suspects in Rawbeck's murder.'

'He of the wet-kiss whisper,' my companion said with a chuckle. 'Pathic type – *he'd* have been the one lying on the bed awaiting the lad of his dreams. The initiative would've had to come from young Sebastian, and there's no indication he was that way given, either active or passive.'

'His revulsion toward Toland's pretty clear in his notebook entry, anyway.'

'Toland could've had other motivations,' Leah suggested. 'According to your grandad in his account, Toland was Rawbeck's creditor. There are a number of reasons why Toland might've been paying him off: for procuring young men for his queenly tastes, for instance, or for arranging drugs for him and so on.'

'As well as the obvious one,' I said. 'Blackmail. Remember that at the time Oscar Wilde had hardly finished his two years' hard labour for merely paddling in the shallows of "the love that dare not speak its name". If it was blackmail, then Toland had an excellent motive for doing Rawbeck in.'

'Or maybe a jealous spat over a young man got out of hand, and Toland went for Rawbeck with a razor.'

'I'd like to know in what order they all left the Convocation that night,' I said.

'In any event, I'd say Rawbeck left last, as he was the host.'

'We don't know for sure that the Convocation was in Rawbeck's house – he had more than one hideaway scattered round London. For that matter, it's very possible that Tarquin Rivers was host, since his house is in the right area.'

'Well,' Leah said, 'my money's on Rawbeck as master of ceremonies that night. Rivers strikes me as the ironical observer type: he was a travel writer, for heaven's sake.'

'He certainly seemed committed where my grandfather was concerned.'

'Ah, yes – dedicating his poems of exile to "S. R." But, then again, as far as clinching evidence goes, it might just as well have been to "Sally Robinson".'

'Nevertheless, it all ties in.'

'And what about the crosses marked on the old London street plan?' Leah changed tack. 'You said they were mostly pubs.'

'Mmm ... but not all date back as far as 1899. Clearly, Grandfather was trying to track down the one with the room above where he found – or hallucinated – Rawbeck's body. Some at least of the modern buildings I sussed out could've been built on the sites of pubs standing in my grandfather's time. '

'No sign of the magic window at the head of the stairs?'

I shook my head. 'Not after a hundred years and two world wars,' then, changing the subject: 'Leah, what physical effects would taking a magic mushroom potion have had on my grandfather? It may be important in assessing

65

his state of mind on the night of the murder, as well as his movements.'

'In the case of *Psilocybe chionophila* – the Lapland Mushroom – severe gut-ache on taking the stuff – that's described in his notebook account – then, after half an hour or so, the Wacky World effects he also describes: euphoria, sense of detachment and consequent loss of any sense of time, all combined with an extraordinary sense of *focus* on things – hence his stuff about being a "seer" – and possible synaesthetic effects – tasting colours, smelling sounds, and so on – including extreme sensitivity to stimuli on the skin. That's the intense stage, during which, well, to all intents and purposes he wouldn't really have been in this world.'

'How long would the intense stage have lasted?'

'About three hours, depending on the dose and make-up of the subject, but there could be effects of varying strength and frequency over nine hours.'

'Including the periods when my grandfather was actually zonked out in cabs to and from the murder room – again, if that wasn't a hallucinatory effect, too?'

'Total unconsciousness isn't typical of the state, but what he took in recollection to have been sleep or unconsciousness could simply have been memory blanks caused by the mushroom.'

'So we're talking about twelve hours or so during which my grandfather was effectively no longer in control of his thoughts or actions?'

'That's about the size of it: anything could've happened within that period without his really knowing about it. How old did you say your grandad was when he died?'

'Seventy-five.'

'He must've had a constitution like a locomotive! Often the case with these frail, ethereal-looking little guys. And wasn't there a missing masterpiece that Rawbeck was supposed to have been working on when he disappeared?

66

Maybe that was what the Vickybird pinched from your grandad in Paris?'

'No, they're different things: it was some *drawings* the Vickybird stole from Grandfather. Rawbeck's missing masterpiece was believed to have been entitled *The Ruffian on the Stair*.'

'Who's the Ruffian?' Leah asked.

'And where's the bloody stair!' I protested, as we both got up laughing from the table, and, slinging on our coats, took our trays back to the counter.

'What next, then?' Leah asked as we moved towards the exit.

'I want to find out more about Toland. He was clearly well off, but didn't walk the Victorian businessman's walk. I suspect he belonged to some aesthetic in-clique of the time.'

'All that camp *Mapp and Lucia* stuff, you mean? Mauve music at the Café Royal, and so on?'

'That sort of thing, and he sounds pretty flamboyant, too: a character like that could hardly have escaped the memoir writers of the time. I think a good, long session in the London Library tomorrow . . .'

'Which is Good Friday.' Leah brought me back to earth.

I cursed my absentmindedness, and I couldn't borrow my companion's university library ticket for today, either, since they had photos on them.

'Leah, could you be an absolute star, and –'

'*No*, Seb – I've work to do – you know I'm setting exams. There must be dozens of books on Eng. Lit. in the nineteenth century in the stacks, and I simply can't spare the time . . .'

'Leah,' I wheedled, trying to conceal the urgency of growing obsession with a tone of mock tragedy, 'my psychological health – my very identity – may be at stake, and you've said yourself what a deal of good this new interest's doing me.'

Leah's nose wrinkled as we crossed the bleak concrete

helipad of the central university concourse, and then she relented.

'I may pop down for ten minutes when I'm finished at the department, but I can't promise.'

'Drinks on me at the Crown afterwards – seven-thirtyish?'

Another olive scowl, and I grabbed her round the waist and nuzzled the scent of her black hair.

'Talk about a star,' I said. 'You're a positive Oscar!'

I drove back home and got on with the Spanish translation job that had come in that morning's email, and at four o'clock, Pat Hague rang me.

'Frank said you asked for me yesterday?'

'Yes, Pat, he said he didn't know where you were.'

'In the university library, as a matter of fact, where I've been most of the last few weeks: your psychologist friend will confirm that.'

'Leah? Ah, yes – she's been looking up a few things for me. In the English section, that would've been?'

'Where else? That's where Dylan's to be found. What is it you want? Me?'

I ignored the tease.

'Pat, you said on Sunday that you'd been talking to Reet at the Holt the other week – you and Frank had been up to Walberswick for some auction.'

'Yes?'

'Has any stranger asked you where she lives recently?'

'No, what sort of stranger had you in mind?'

'Shortish, stumpy man, with short grey hair, big, baby-blue eyes and a crooning voice with an Irish accent. Drives a light-coloured Nissan Micra, and may have some connection with Jersey.'

There was a pause, then Pat laughed.

'Dear me, Seb – the pangs of jealousy, is it? A bit of competition up at the Holt? I shouldn't worry, though – however your ex copes with the needs of nature, you're still the one she's carrying the torch for. So this stranger at the

Holt was "driving a light-coloured Nissan Micra, and may have some connection with Jersey . . ." You sound like a *Crimestoppers* voice-over! A propos, remember the connection we had in Jersey . . .'

I was being well and truly wound up, but something occurred to me: maybe this conversation would turn out to be of some use after all.

'Pat, you're an English don –'

'Don't remind me! So?'

'For research purposes, where did well-off British artistic gays hang out round about 1900?'

'Capri: Compton Mackenzie sends that scene up in *Vestal Fire*. It's a quite funny novel, in a faded way. Any particular figure in mind?'

'A man called Toland – I don't know if he was a writer – I don't think so.'

'Mmm . . . name doesn't ring any bells with me.'

'Thanks, anyway. Oh, and Pat . . . please lay off Reet.'

The laugh again. 'Conscience pricking, Seb? That's rich coming from you – if you can't do the time, don't do the crime.'

'All the same . . .'

She just chuckled again, and my hand began to tremble, and I crashed the telephone receiver down in its cradle. It was true what she'd said about my adultery, and I hated myself anew for it, but I hated her a thousand times more for rubbing my nose in it. Reet had never slept around when we'd been together, and I . . . But here we go, round and round, again – no, I had this funny guy Toland to look into, one of the jokers who'd been with my grandfather at the Diabolist do in Camden in 1899.

I was really looking forward to what Leah might turn up in the university library again, and what was that Pat had just said about seeing her there the day before in the English section? Funny Leah hadn't mentioned seeing Pat there, but it was a biggish place, and no doubt Leah would have been buried in some study carrel or other. I recalled something, and smiled. The only other academic psycho-logist I'd ever known had been a friend at university, and she'd ended up living in a cave in Almeria with twenty-odd dogs. Leah, though, was one psychologist who wasn't barmy, and I wasn't going to let Pat spoil things between us.

Leah joined me that evening in the Crown Inn in Wivenhoe, and, after I'd brought our drinks back from the bar to our window table, she pulled a tattered old book with a red plastic flash on the spine from her bag and handed it over without a word. I put our glasses on the table, sat down, and read out the title further up the spine of the book:

'*Black Wine: Memoirs of a Victorian Decadent* by Leon Asche.'

'I found mentions of Toland in a few books on the period,' Leah said, after she'd taken a draught from her pint. 'But no more than mentions: Jimmy Toland was also there, sort of thing. This author, Asche, actually knew him later on in life – the book's really a summing-up of the period.'

'Twenty years after the period,' I remarked, on glancing inside at the publication date of the first impression – 1921.

'The author only gives Toland a short passage,' Leah went on, 'and he obviously assumes the reader'll know all about the basics of Toland's life – pity he never seems to have published anything himself. I've marked the page with a slip of paper.'

I eagerly turned to the marked page, which was in the chapter entitled 'Naval Occasions'.

'Last para,' Leah prompted.

I turned to the spot and read on:

Also still occasionally to be found greeting the Jack Tars on the Chatham 'up' platform at Waterloo was the brave, forlorn form of Jimmy Toland, his familiar chubby delineaments now shielded with rouge against the ravages of time.

70

Returning from business in Rochester one autumn evening in 1913, my eye caught his on the crowded platform. We exchanged a few conventional words – can anything be more mutually embarrassing than to bump into a friend from better times? – and he moved up the platform again, and so out of my ken.

I stood dismayed for a moment amid the steam and smut as I recalled the 'days of redder roses and madder wine' in his lovely villa above the bay in Posilippo before financial reverses around the time of the Diamond Jubilee confined him to his little flat in Mornington Crescent. I do not know how – or indeed, if – he weathered the inflation after the war, for I have never seen him since . . .

Then the writer went on to someone else he'd known. Posilippo was near Naples, wasn't it? Pat Hague hadn't been far wrong with Capri, which was just across the Bay. I took a gulp of my Guinness.

'The Diamond Jubilee was in 1897,' I remarked to Leah.

'And Rawbeck disappeared "around" that time – 1899, to be precise – so could blackmail have been at the root of Toland's "financial reverses"?'

'Hang on,' I said. 'There's a touch of the "dog that didn't bark in the night" about this.'

'How d'you mean?'

'After Rawbeck vanishes, the rest of the known members of the so-called Convocation all do runners, in one way or another – my grandfather to Paris, followed by Rawbeck's ex-models, Carrie Bugle and the Vickybird, Tarquin Rivers to the Near East and poor flautist Philip Forbuoys to the bottom of the Thames. All except Toland. He does the opposite – he apparently never sets foot *outside* England again . . .'

'You think that speaks for his innocence? Then why does his money drain away over the years?'

'If he was paying blackmail, it goes on for a long time – but we're building bricks without straw.'

I thanked Leah profusely for her efforts in the university library and left the matter there for the moment. I asked her how her day had gone, after which I drove her back to her flat on campus, where we had a bite of supper before I drove home to the lighthouse. Somehow I couldn't settle down to anything there – too many 'thoughts that could not be thought' – so I just decided to turn in earlyish.

I was fastening the bolt on the back door when a sharp clink, as of something being rapped sharply against glass, reached me from outside. The shed . . . I listened for the wind – maybe a rake handle being blown against the window of the shed – but all was still. I had all sorts of things in the shed other than garden tools – better check it out. I walked round to the cupboard where my fuse-boxes were housed and took out the torch I kept there, then returned to the back door, quietly slid the bolt free and slipped out into the garden.

In the cold moonlight all seemed OK on the side of the shed that faced the house door, so I made my way down the path and behind the shed, where a beech hedge shielded the garden from the little byroad that turned off the headland. In the leafy gully so formed I almost walked into the broad, anoraked back of someone who was plying the ray of a torch through the window of the shed.

I was about to pull back for safety, when the figure swung round, and I took in the face – monk-like in the hood of the anorak – of the short, bullet-headed man who'd spoken to me in the National Gallery on the Monday of that week. The candid blue eyes were round and intent now, like those of a startled baby who's just been caught in the act of doing something naughty. The man's free hand shot into the pocket of his waterproof, and with a click pulled out something which flashed in the torchlight. I flinched instinctively as I made out the blade – dog-legged for action – of an old-fashioned cut-throat razor.

Chapter Seven

Suddenly, the intruder relaxed, and, smiling, flicked the razor shut and flung it to me. I fielded it with my free hand.

'Handsome thing!' he cooed. 'What d'you make of the initials?'

'Who the hell . . .' I spluttered.

'Oh, excuse me . . .'

The man in the anorak fished in his pocket again and produced a business card, which I took with the forefinger and thumb of the hand that was still palming the razor. I took a step back, and, still blinking up distrustfully from moment to moment, shone the beam of my torch on to the card and read: *Liam Brogan, Antiques*, with a good St Helier address off Halkett Place, and the usual contact information underneath.

'It's pretty chilly for late April, isn't it?' Brogan hinted pleasantly.

I eyed him suspiciously again, and he threw up his arms.

'Frisk away!'

I reflected that, if he'd been bent on real mischief, he'd have used the thing with the warm, smooth handle I was still clutching.

'Straight ahead and round the shed,' I directed, 'and keep well in front of me.'

He went ahead of me indoors, and into the sitting room, where he installed himself in a cane armchair in front of the fire, which I revived with a split log. I put down my torch on the side table and glanced at the razor again. Yellowing ivory, with gold trimmings, and a cartouche in the same metal in the middle, with the cursive initials *D. B. R.* I opened the razor gingerly and examined the broad, concave blade with its copperplate inscription: *Chas. Beffreys, Piccadilly.* I gave the edge of the blade the merest brush with the side of my thumb, and shuddered involuntarily.

'They had good hearts in their bellies in those days,' my unexpected guest said with a chortle: 'facing that thing every morning!'

I was definitely intrigued by the final R. of the initials on the handle of the razor, which I reclosed carefully and laid on the table again, along with my visitor's business card.

'Yes,' Brogan went on, looking meaningfully over at the drinks cupboard on the back wall, 'a very chilly night for April . . .'

There might be an advantage in loosening his tongue, I thought, and went over to the cupboard.

'I've some Irish stuff, here,' I said. 'Bushmill's . . .'

'Just what the doctor ordered, Mr Rolvenden – neat, thank you kindly.'

I came back with the whiskey, and handed it to the compact figure with the merry eyes. He stared at me for a second or two, between his first sips of whiskey.

'I should've thought you'd have been able to follow me home from the National Gallery on Monday,' I said from the other armchair.

'Escalator conked out in Baker Street underground station, and by the time I'd got to the entrance, you were gone. Make anything of the initials on the razor?'

I shook my head – Brogan would have to do the talking.

'Daines Bartlett Rolvenden, midshipman, Royal Navy – made for him in 1816. Beffreys have a complete record of all their customers since they started in 1797. They've no record of any more being made for your family since then.'

'There was a long run of poor rural parsons for the rest of the nineteenth century – they wouldn't have run to customized West End accessories.'

'Ah . . .' Brogan went on. 'D. B. Rolvenden died in 1877, and I assume the razor would have passed to his son, Francis Skeat Rolvenden, then when he died in 1894, to his son – your grandfather and namesake, Sebastian John Rolvenden.'

'You're quite a living compendium, Mr Brogan.'

An eager light came into the little man's eyes.

'It's not just the money – oh, no! – the chase is everything to me! When I've a full provenance for an object, it's, it's . . . like possession itself!'

'And the full provenance of the razor?'

Brogan took another sip from his glass and a sly look came back into his eyes.

'A lot of fresh stuff coming on to the market over in Jersey, Mr Rolvenden. An old feller from one of the rural parishes – no need to go into details, but all above board – used to bring all sorts of things in to me. He died very recently, more's the pity . . .'

Would the rural parish have been St Marc's, I wondered, where my grandfather had been vicar and where I still owned a beachside farmhouse? And would the 'old feller' who'd sold the razor to Brogan have been the parishioner who'd looted Grandfather's vicarage when he'd been interned by the Germans in 1940? If so, it probably meant that the contents of the Jiffy bag that Lawyer Le Touzel had forwarded to me after the 'old feller's' death had been just one step behind Brogan . . . In that case, I'd stepped on his toes big-time, and would have to box cleverly with him.

'You rather alarmed my wife and son in Suffolk, the other day, Mr Brogan.'

'Yes, and I'm terribly sorry if I've caused you embarrassment. You see, I got your details from the blurb of the book you wrote with your lady, and I'd no idea you and she were no longer . . .'

I recalled a detail of his visit to the Holt, as recounted to me by Reet when she'd called on me on the Wednesday afternoon.

'You haven't been an antique dealer in Jersey for long, Mr Brogan.'

The eyes became positively saucer-like.

'Oh, and how do you make that out?'

'You still need a road map to get round the island.'

'Ah, nice one! The map in my car – your son – a very observant young man! As for my visit here tonight, thing is, it took me longer to find this place than I thought it would – it's a sort of a backwater of a backwater . . .'

'That's one of the reasons why I like it. As a matter of interest, how did you find me here?'

'Your regular gardening article in the *Dumfries Herald* – just out today. I read it online. About garden bamboos. In the article you mention your "new venture, your light-house in Essex . . ."'

You had to hand it to him: Brogan was thorough.

'Right,' my puckish visitor went on, 'but when I did eventually find this place, it was so late I wasn't sure whether to bother you with a call. I thought it might be better just to note the spot and come back in the morn-ing, but when I saw the gap in the hedge that adjoins the shed . . .'

'Professional curiosity did the rest.'

'In one, Mr Rolvenden!'

'Well, I don't keep any family mementoes in the shed, and I certainly haven't anything in the antiques line to sell, so it's very late, and if you don't mind . . .'

Brogan smiled on, seemingly undeterred, then reached in his pocket for something, and handed it across to me.

'All sorts of things coming on the market on the island . . .' he remarked brightly.

The object was a platinum tiepin. In tiny diamonds was

the stylized monogram *J. R.*, which I recognized as Julian Rawbeck's from his paintings. I was lost in speculation as I gazed at the rich little trifle, and by the time I'd looked up again, Brogan was on his feet and examining the photographs on the mantelpiece. I got up and joined him, noticing in passing that the razor and the business card he'd given me were no longer on the side table where I'd put them. I handed him back the tiepin without a word.

'Let me guess,' he said, pocketing the jewelled Rawbeck relic, while nodding in the direction of the sharp-featured, bearded face in the framed photograph. 'That's your grandfather.'

'Yes,' I said.

'I'll bet he could tell quite a story, Mr Rolvenden: quite a story.'

With the thought that my dead grandfather was already telling me a remarkable story, I showed the opportunistic dealer to the front door.

'I suppose your Micra's hidden away somewhere in the undergrowth,' I said, as I switched on the porch light.

'A discreet little model, Mr Rolvenden,' Brogan said, busy with a pencil on the back of the business card he'd handed me not long before. There was complete confidence in his voice as, on handing me back the card, he made his parting remark.

'Well, we know where to find each other, now. I'll be on the mainland for at least a month, and I look forward to seeing you again. Goodnight; or rather, morning!'

In the light of the porch lamp, I looked at the writing on the back of the card. The address of a London hotel and a mobile number. If what I'd just examined had been the razor my grandfather had missed when he'd returned to his digs after fleeing the murder room in 1899, and if the victim Rawbeck's tiepin had been part of the stuff looted from my grandfather's vicarage in Jersey in 1940, then, yes, I thought I would be seeing Liam Brogan again.

I switched off the porch light and shut and bolted the

front door, then went and did as much for the back door before returning to the sitting room. I looked up at the clock: a quarter to one. I remembered the anxiety Brogan's visit had caused Reet – would she still be up? I sat down on the sofa and rang the Holt.

'Mum's gone to bed,' my son Paul answered shortly. 'What d'you want?'

'The little guy in the Micra who's been nosing around up at your end's just been here to see me. He's an antique dealer.'

'He didn't look like a knocker to me.'

'No, he's a real dealer – an offbeat character, but I don't think he'll bother you again – he's only after me. If you'll just tell your mother first thing – set her mind at rest.'

There was a tense silence at the other end, and I sensed I'd said the wrong thing.

'She seemed worried when she called here on Wednesday,' I went on, 'and I only thought I'd –'

'You're a fine one to talk about setting her mind at rest – just leave her alone: you've made her unhappy enough already.'

'I'll ring her myself in the morning,' I said wearily.

There was a short silence, then the voice came back more calmly.

'Don't bother – I'll tell her – but don't think –'

'Goodnight, Paul.'

I put the receiver down, then held my head in my hands for a little while, just to compose myself again. Yes – Brogan – just how much did he know about my search for the truth about my grandfather and his part in the disappearance of Julian Rawbeck? He'd seemed very confident I'd rise to the bait, in the form of the monogrammed tiepin – just left the next move to me. At any rate, I seemed to have picked up another shadow. And yet another connection with Jersey . . .

I remembered my last stay in the farmhouse there with Reet, Frank and Pat, a thousand years and two summers before. How it had all started with Pat. That afternoon, I'd seen everyone – or so I'd thought – off at the gate, Frank and Reet having decided to trek down to the reed ponds at La Mielle du Moro on the bay. In my mind's eye, I saw the sweep of the bay: the low-lying, rich fields and the few whitewashed farmhouses, their walls incandescent in the July glare, then, higher up, the gorse scrub that led up to the abrupt, granite escarpment.

Reet had always been a bit of a twitcher, and I knew the RSPB hide at La Mielle would claim her for the rest of the afternoon. Frank, too, would have been busy with his camera, for nowhere seemed real to him unless he'd captured every detail of it on film. If he hadn't snapped it, he hadn't really been there. I'd stayed behind to make some phone calls to the mainland, and Pat had taken the Land Rover to drive into St Helier for shopping – or so she'd said.

Yes, and there'd been the funny incident at the gate with the solemn little boy as my company had got ready to set off. He'd been walking with his father along the footpath to the beach when he'd stopped and confronted us, then, after he'd stared intently at me for a moment, he'd turned to his dad and, pointing at me, asked him if I was 'the man in the shed'. We'd all laughed, and the father of the little boy had grinned sheepishly and led his charge – his head turned, still staring at me – away along the path.

Frank had then made one of his impromptu cracks about my having been up to my old tricks somewhere – to a sharp look from Reet – and the party had broken up, to go our separate ways; in my case, to stay behind in the farmhouse.

Funny how often Frank hits the mark with his tactless blurtings: when Pat had come back to the farmhouse on some pretext ten minutes or so later, I'd got up to some of my 'tricks' with her. She'd made it fairly obvious what she'd expected of me, and what with the heat, the still, charged air, and her, all brown and spare in her shorts and blue top, I'd played the part more than willingly.

Hence the misunderstanding between us. I'd thought then from her approach that she'd meant it – as I had – to be a mere episode, leaving no traces – a sort of fit of absentmindedness on a hot afternoon, as these things happen. But Pat had something more in mind. Even then – if I'd resisted her the second time – I might have been able to nip it in the bud. That had been when, two months after the Jersey farmhouse incident, Reet and Paul had been over in Belgium for the Florilegium thing. Frank had been on one of his trips to the States, and Pat had turned up in her provocative way that Sunday afternoon at the Holt. I hadn't resisted, and so it had gone on, hence the present merry dance she was leading me.

'Pish!' The collapsing log on the fire brought me out of my reverie, and back to the chill, early hours of Good Friday in my lighthouse in Essex. I looked up at the photo of my grandfather on the mantelpiece, wondering inconsequentially if he was disapproving of such unholy reflections on this most solemn of religious festivals. I turned to the clock – one-thirty, and time for bed – but I lay awake upstairs for quite some time, chewing over the visit I'd just had from the Irish antique dealer.

Hadn't I overlooked something rather obvious about the heirloom razor he'd shown me, the one with my naval forebear's initials on it? If it had been the one found in Philip Forbuoys' pocket after his body had been fished out of the Thames in 1899, how could it have been found among my grandfather's effects years later?

The razor the River Police had found on Forbuoys' body had been used in evidence at the Coroner's post-mortem, so how could it have found its way back to my grandfather in Paris? What did the authorities do with bits of evidence after court hearings? File them away somewhere? Return them to the owners or the next-of-kin? Flog them off at a Crown auction? There was still no solid evidence to connect the razor my grandfather had missed from his wash-stand in his digs in Victorian London, and which Brogan had produced so melodramatically an hour previously, with the one that had been found on Philip Forbuoys' body.

And Brogan's motives: he'd clearly invested a lot in this show, gone to prodigious pains to track down the rest of my grandfather's stolen Jersey hoard, but surely he was after bigger game than the trinkets he'd flashed in front of me like a party magician? What was the Big Prize? I thought back to the legend of Rawbeck's lost masterpiece, *The Ruffian on the Stair*. Its price – if it existed, and were to be unearthed today – would surely run into six or even seven figures. Now there was a prize worthy of the Irish dealer's efforts . . .

I knew Rawbeck had taken many of the titles of his paintings and drawings from literature, a typical Victorian trait. *The Ruffian on the Stair* rang a bell with me: I seemed to connect it with something about your being 'Captain of your fate, Master of your soul,' or was it the other way round? Ah! Henley – W. E. Henley – that was the writer! I remembered now, but 'The Ruffian' had been another poem of his: how had that gone? Yes:

> *Madam Life's a piece in bloom*
> *Death goes dogging everywhere:*
> *She's the tenant of the room,*
> *He's the ruffian on the stair.*

The Ruffian on the Stair, then, was Death.

Chapter Eight

I woke very late to full day on that Good Friday morning, and all, I congratulated myself, without my having popped a single pill. The sun was streaming in through the square-paned window, and out in the garden a blackbird was shrieking its heart out like a working men's club turn. I remembered the previous night's encounter, and in my musing, morning mind wondered how Liam Brogan would be marking the Crucifixion on this most solemn of days. No doubt he'd have a full programme of skulduggeries lined up – who cared nowadays?

I got up, showered and dressed and went downstairs to make some coffee and toast. I looked into the sitting room, and glancing at the white ash in the hearth, realized that for the first time that year it was mild enough to leave the fire unlit.

After breakfast I drifted unwillingly upstairs again to my workroom to check my Inbox: nothing, not even from Leah. She'd said she'd be working on at the university, and I decided not to bother her till she actually got in touch again. I sat vacantly in front of the blue screen for a moment or two – a little bit of rewrite still to do on the Tod Slaughter biography, but nothing terribly urgent. My gaze strayed to the window, where the sun was egging me on like a feckless companion. I'd walk out into the springtime morning – along the headland to the marshes. I closed down the computer and went downstairs again, donned my old leather bomber jacket and left by the front door.

I drew in deep draughts of salt air as I strode down the tarmac of the headland, the sea-reek having been displaced for a moment on the breeze by the faint, hay fever aroma of sun-warmed broom blossom. As I drew nearer the muddy vastness of creeks and marshes the sea-influence began to reassert itself over the pervasive scent of broom, and I stood still for a moment, closed my eyes, and thought of nothing. Why couldn't this be enough?

I started walking again, the tarmac swerving back inland, and brushed the village – well, just a couple of straggling bunches of farm buildings, really. The place was known simply as Headland, with the squat, twelfth-century church as focal point. There were three churches in the parish, served by the one vicar, and Holy Trinity, Headland, was used only on certain high holy days in the year, of which this was the most solemn.

Standing back a bit, I could hear over the cluster of cars parked on the rough grass of the glebe, and through the low, Norman-arched open doorway, the organ strains to 'I was glad when they said unto me, Let us enter the house of the Lord'. I took this as a sign, and went in rather awkwardly and perched on the edge of the pew nearest the door. As the solemnities unfolded up front, I closed my eyes in the Norman coolness and meditated. I'd had the usual youthful intimations and inklings of Glory, but as our time becomes more limited these fade, and I'm no exception to this process. It was soothing, though – definitely.

Then they sang 'There is a green hill far away', and all my half-forgotten religious education came back to me on a wave of unworthiness. Wasn't I the grandson of an ordained priest, and what had I made of the life that God had given me? What clean thing had I to offer up to Him? A knockabout career of lucky hobbies, and a wife and son I'd betrayed and failed. Unworthy ...

I got up and went out, and began to retrace my steps back down the headland, but, as I went, I felt an odd vulnerability in the small of my back. I looked over my shoulder, and saw a tall, slim man standing all alone in the churchyard. The sun was behind him, so I couldn't make out any features, but he was looking in my direction. The fancy came into my head that he was like an unravelled question mark. I looked ahead again and walked on. Suddenly, the sun went in, and the breeze that had earlier brought the scent of broom now brought drops of rain. I hurried homewards.

I'd had notions of having lunch on Mersea Island, but the prospect of hordes of Bank Holiday trippers put me off that idea, so on arriving back at the lighthouse I simply washed down a pie with a mugful of coffee, then went straight upstairs to my computer. I got stuck into the 'little' rewrite job, which as nearly always happens involved much complicated tying-up of loose ends opened up in the surrounding text. The upshot of it was that it wasn't till nearly seven-thirty in the evening that I could slump back in my cane chair downstairs and shut my stinging eyes for a spell.

After a few minutes, I dragged myself up and went into the kitchen, where I uncorked a bottle of Merlot and poured myself a glass before supping off a slab of cheese between two hunks of wholemeal bread. As I munched and grew mellower with the soft wine, I mulled over the Rawbeck business, and in particular the new aspect of it introduced so theatrically by Liam Brogan the previous night.

My grandfather, then, had done his runner from the murder room over the lowlife pub on that November night in 1899, then, on packing his things in his digs before decamping to Paris, had noticed that his initialled, family-heirloom razor was gone from the washstand. On the same night, Philip Forbuoys, who played the flute at the magic mushroom session at which my grandfather was also present in the house on Camden Hill only hours before, apparently fills his pockets with stones, jumps into

84

the Thames and drowns. According to the contemporary *Times* report, Forbuoys 'apparently' bought a second-hand razor earlier that day, since his own was found afterwards in his lodgings.

Now, on the eve of Good Friday more than a century later, Liam Brogan produces my grandfather's long-missing heirloom razor, looted, as far as I knew, from his effects by a Jersey neighbour in the troubled invasion summer of 1940. Working on the assumption that Grandfather didn't use his own razor to cut Julian Rawbeck's throat and absentmindedly leave it behind, the crucial question was: where had the razor been between the time it went missing from Grandfather's London digs on 10th November 1899, and the time, sometime this year, when Liam Brogan presumably bought it from the old rogue who'd been my grandfather's thieving parishioner? Did Grandfather get it back from someone in the meantime, and in which case, from whom? And, most crucially of all, was it the razor that had cut Julian Rawbeck's throat?

I recharged my glass with Merlot and went back into the sitting room, where I got the fire going again with old fish-and-chip paper and wood shavings. I rested a half-log on the blaze, retired to the cane armchair, and pursued my train of thought in comfort. My ear felt cold leather, and I reached up to my bomber jacket, which I'd draped over the back of the chair. Instinctively, my hand went for my grandfather's notebook in the inside pocket. It would all be in there, I thought: the answer to the riddle would be in there somewhere . . .

I riffled through the tired pages of the cheap little book, my attention lighting on the section with the disjointed phrases: *Rivers* we now knew, *Reuben's Court* we thought we'd dealt with for the time being, and *Smoking Altars* looked literary, but *Home in the East* and *Soundings A*? Figuring as they did in this record of what must have been the most shattering events in my grandfather's life, they must have been of crucial importance to an understanding of the Rawbeck affair, but what did they mean? I glanced up at the mantelpiece and searched my grandfather's eyes in the photograph, but he was saying nothing . . .

I sighed, and was about to lay the notebook aside: might as well throw dice for an answer . . . But yes, there was a modern equivalent of dice: the Internet. I got up and found Grandfather's 1871 street plan, and took it upstairs with his battered notebook, and started up the computer. I got into the search engine, and typed *Home in the East* into the box, then clicked on Search.

A long list of Indian restaurants and takeaways appeared: in Luton, Leicester, Coventry and Peterborough, with one in London. I clicked on the London one: it was in Iceland Road, in Hackney. In my grandfather's young days, Hackney was for the most part a humdrum, lower middle-class residential district, but with shady patches and rough edges to it. I reached over my desk for the modern London street plan, and found the grid with Iceland Road in it. Comparing this with the equivalent on the 1871 map, my suspicions were confirmed: virtually the whole district had been ripped out to make way for the northern approach road to the Blackwall Tunnel.

The pub with the horror room above it must long since have been swept away, and the stairhead window with the beguiling colours shattered into a million ruby and blue fragments by the blind snout of the bulldozer. But, hang on, Iceland Road went down at right angles to the Lee Navigation Canal. I recalled the detail in Grandfather's account of his flight from the murder room in that raw, pre-dawn in the November of 1899: *water on my left*. And *Soundings A* came immediately after *Rivers* in the notebook. Was there any street or other townscape feature with Soundings in its name?

I looked up the index of the modern London street plan: there was a Sounds Lodge, but that was in Swanley. Turning to the 1871 map, I trawled my magnifying glass from the desk drawer and ran it carefully over the upper left-hand corner of the dirty, linen-backed paper. Iceland Road was there, branching off towards the canal at right angles towards the bulge of the easterly sweep of the Old Ford Road, as it must have been before the modern approach road had been built. And, yes! – there, bisecting the semicircle drawn by the sweep of the Old Ford Road, was Soundings Alley – hence the A.

But what made me spring back in my seat with excitement was the little black box on the old map, just a little up the curve of the Old Ford Road, with the words *Home in the East*. This was more like it! I returned to the computer keyboard, typed in *Hackney Home in the East*, clicked on Search, and directly the earnest face of a Victorian philanthropist flashed on to the screen. I took in the introductory text at the bottom of the photo:

Nonconformist Julius Benn, late of Manchester, in 1851 moved with his wife Ann to London, to take up work in the London City Mission in Stepney, the couple eventually moving farther north to Hackney, where they opened the Home in the East, a refuge for homeless boys in the East End.

I scrolled down and read the rest, but there was nothing there that I could tie in with my grandfather's astonishing adventure. I supposed it would all be gone, now. So: Rivers, a boys' home in Hackney, an alley through the Old Ford Road, and a canal that bordered the marshes. Link them all up, and Bob's your uncle!

I turned to the old street map again, and gave the spot that featured the boys' home and Soundings Alley a good once-over with the magnifying glass, but no sign of any pencilled markings. But, although I still couldn't link them all up logically yet, I'd at least cracked the rest of the enigmatic references in the notebook – with the nagging exception of Smoking Altars, of course. I immediately rang Leah at the university to tell her about my findings.

'Interesting,' was her initial response. 'Now all you've got to do is get some actual *meaning* out of the stuff.'

Something occurred to me.

'Yes,' I replied, 'it's possible, too, that Grandfather only marked the places on the map that he'd already checked out. The complete *list* of places still to be checked out by him in his search for the murder room could've been on one of the pages of the notebook that have been torn out. And that raises the question of who tore out the pages – but I'm jumping the gun.'

'Yes,' Leah said. 'I think you've done well – made real progress – and as for the torn-out pages, didn't this old guy in Jersey who's supposed to have pinched your grandad's things have kids?'

'Yes, a son, and now a grandson – the little lad who pointed me out to Reet and Frank and Pat Hague a couple of years ago when we were all on holiday on the island.'

'The kid who asked his dad if you were the man in the shed?'

'Right, but what are you getting at?'

'Well, kids like nothing better than scribbling in books and tearing the pages out of them, so I don't think there's any need your going on flights of fantasy about who might have had dark motives for tearing out evidence.'

'Typical common sense,' I remarked. 'Leah, what would I do without you?'

'I shudder to think.'

I laughed, but then something else came to mind.

'The little boy in Jersey might've been playing with my grandfather's things in his grandad's shed,' I mused aloud, 'but why should he have asked if *I* had been in it? To my knowledge, I've never been inside a shed in Jersey in my life.'

'Search me, I'm no child psychologist, but this is a real lead, Seb: will you be going up to Hackney?'

'I'll ring the Local Studies people there after the holidays, and if there's anything left of the district as it was in

1899, I'll go and suss it out. I'm afraid on first blush, though, it looks as if the approach road to the Blackwall Tunnel is all there is to be seen there now. What are you doing this evening?'

'I've some people from the department coming round for a meal – how about my popping over lateish tomorrow morning?'

'Fine – we can talk it all over.'

I rang off, then went back upstairs, shut down the computer and started to pace the workroom, my brain racing with fresh speculation, until weariness took over. Before heading downstairs again, I glanced out of the window at the marshscape. It was dusk now, with a riding moon visible in the gaps between the clouds: a tame contrast to the 'sky roaring with stars' as described by my grandfather in his notebook account of the mushroom session on Camden Hill way back in 1899.

I was turning away, when something caught my eye far off on the headland. It was a straight, motionless human figure, but in the dimity light I couldn't make out which way it was looking: straight at me, or out into the distance where marsh and sea joined. I peered at the figure for some time, but it remained steadfastly motionless, then I finally pulled myself away. Some citizen exercising his dog, I reasoned as I went down the stairs, or a late-night fisherman probing for lugworms in the mud. All the same, it gave you the creeps seeing him standing there like a statue. Just then I shuddered, as if someone had walked over my grave . . .

Chapter Nine

Next morning, Saturday, Leah arrived around eleven-thirty, having cleared her desk at the university, and we talked over my Internet finds of the previous day. The upshot was, we decided to drive up to Hackney to do a bit of field research; and in particular, round the subject of the Home in the East.

The weather being a bit on the lowering side, we had a fairly clear run to London, accessing the particular district of Hackney we were interested in by the A11. Iceland Road – what there was of it – ran down from a cluster of industrial buildings just east of the A102 to the Lee River. The whole area was cut through by the A11 and the A102 motorway, which converged on the Blackwall Tunnel, and amid the trading-estate bleakness, there was no trace to be seen of the Hackney of 1899. I parked the car on a space near the Northern Outfall Sewer, and we surveyed the twenty-first-century desolation.

'It's all been swept away,' Leah remarked. 'Nothing of the original streets – not even the directions.'

'Mmm . . . Iceland Road's about the only street in Grandfather's 1871 map that's still in the same place.'

We retreated, somewhat deflated, to the nearest seriously populated area round the bus garage in nearby Bow, and sought out a safe-looking parking space near a decent pub, where we ordered lagers and tikka baked spuds, and made our numbers with the older regulars.

'All gone in the bombing, mate,' or variants thereof was

all we got in response to our enquiries about Soundings Alley, Victorian pubs with colourful windows, Homes in the East or legendary murders. As for the rest, the usual inner city bleakscape of isolated stumps of scruffy pre-war brick terrace, unplanned scatters of council housing, plonked, willy-nilly, over the former street-grid, Brutalist concrete municipal utilities, roaring motorways and unexplained wastes, and all done over by the graffiti –maxims of the gawky – of the local redundant youth. It seemed you had to look farther north and west for the better-preserved pre-war streets, now being furiously gentrified – the ones 'worth burgling', as one pub wiseacre had put it. Of course, it being the Easter weekend, the usual information sources were closed, so I'd have to contact them on Tuesday. We tried in another couple of pubs, but with the same result: my grandfather's East Hackney was gone.

At last I drove my uncomplaining companion – she said she'd enjoyed the crack in the East End pubs – home to Essex and the university, where she'd be entertaining some colleagues later on, then started through the little township towards my lighthouse. But first, if he was at home in the flat above his shop, I'd some questions to put to Frank Hague about potential fellow antique dealers in the vicinity, particularly puckish Irish ones who shone torches through shed windows after midnight . . . This would be an especially convenient time to call on him, since Pat was always at the boathouse at weekends.

Driving slowly past Frank's shop, I caught the eye of the man himself in the window. He grinned at me, and made an elbow-bending gesture – one for the road? – so I pulled up in a space farther up and went back to the shop. He unlocked the door, with its Closed sign sported, and invited me cheerfully into the wax-smelling front shop, with its mellow-coloured oak, walnut and mahogany wares. I went in, and Frank closed the door again, and clicked the little brass inside-hasp shut behind us.

'Midnight oil . . .' I remarked chirpily, as Frank led me

into his backroom-cum-workshop with its couple of done-in, 1830 leather armchairs in front of the original fire grate with the electric fire in it. I sank into a flaking armchair, while my host rustled up drinks from the bric-a-brac that filled the room.

'You know how it is, Seb,' he remarked, handing me a glass of malt whisky before flinging himself, glass in hand, into the opposite chair. 'We poor tradesmen have to work all the hours God sends.'

'I should be so poor,' I murmured, after I'd taken my first smoothly smoky sip, 'drinking malt like this . . .'

A snuffle of laughter.

'My one vice, boss!' Frank exclaimed.

'And the rest . . .'

'How's the scribbling lark going, then?' my old school chum asked.

'My last book's now in the Amazon six-figure rating – thank God for gardening magazines . . . Something I'd been meaning to ask you, Frank – trade matter . . .'

The hazel eyes behind the narrow-framed specs turned foxy again.

'I'm always ready to talk business, Seb – fire away.'

I fished in my pockets, and found Liam Brogan's business card, which I passed to Frank.

'Has he come into your ken, Frank?'

'Yes, he was here on Thursday afternoon, actually. Do you know him?'

My host handed me back the card.

'I know him now,' I said. 'He came round to the lighthouse on the, er . . . knock, late on Thursday night.'

'Right – busy character – he told me someone had recommended me to him at the salerooms in Walberswick the other week.'

'As the doyen of the local dealers?'

The snuffling laugh again. 'Naturally – last court of appeal, and all that.'

'I hope I'm not breaking any professional taboo or anything, but what's he after round here?'

'He thinks someone local may be sitting on a lost Impressionist masterpiece – a major *minor* Impressionist one, if you see what I mean.'

I nodded and took another sip of the fine whisky.

'Did he specify which masterpiece?'

'Not really,' Frank replied. 'I got the impression he was following up some lead from Jersey. He struck me as a slippery type – just picking my brains, but I charge for that.'

'Quite right, too! For your information, though, I'm pretty sure the painting's *The Ruffian on the Stair*, by Julian Rawbeck, circa 1899.'

Frank's eyes glittered, and he drew his head back sharply.

'When I saw the Jersey address on the guy's card,' he went on, 'I thought straightaway of you – the farmhouse over there, and all. You haven't got the painting, have you, Seb?'

The last remark was in fun, of course, but I kept a straight face.

'If I had, how much would it be worth to me?'

'Well, it's a legendary – almost mythical – painting, what with Rawbeck's disappearance at the turn of the last century, and so on – no one's actually *seen* it, as far as is known. And with a provenance like that – and Rawbeck *was* a good painter, quite apart from anything else – shall we start the bidding at, say, half a million?'

I reflected that, for that kind of money, quite a lot of people would be prepared to do a lot more than shine a torch through the back window of your shed at dead of night.

'That was all Brogan wanted?' I went on. 'Information on the painting?'

'Mmm ... yes, and to say that he'd be offering a few

93

articles himself at the sale at Walberswick on Friday, and hoped he'd see me there.'

'I wonder if Brogan'll be offering articles on a Rawbeck theme?' I probed. 'Smoke out potential local Rawbeck collectors by using a sprat to catch a mackerel . . .'

'Just what I was thinking, Seb – he's flying a kite down here in the sticks.'

'Will you be going to the auction, Frank?'

'Oh, I don't know – I've a lot on at the moment.'

'I can take a hint!' I said, getting rather creakily to my feet – it had been a long day – and putting my empty glass down on Frank's desk. 'As smooth a drop of malt as ever I tasted.'

'Any time, Seb.'

'Well, thanks again for the drink – I'll leave you poor tradesmen to your toil.'

Frank escorted me to the shop door, and saw me out, then, just as I was stepping on to the pavement:

'Lock up carefully before you turn in tonight, Seb, and watch out . . .'

'Oh?' I said, half turning my head. 'What for?'

'The Ruffian on the Stair!'

I laughed back and said my final goodnight before the key rattled in the lock of the shop door, to be followed soon after by the whirring of the descending security shutters. You never quite knew where you were with Frank. And, yes, I'd definitely be looking in at Friday's auction sale in Walberswick.

Sunday was a lot more restful than Saturday had been; in fact, things were almost back to post-convalescent normal. I'd had my looked-forward-to fish lunch with Leah in West Mersea, then we'd come back to the lighthouse and had a lovely, lazy day together, watching telly, listening to music, not saying anything when we hadn't anything to say – just being contentedly around each other. I began to think I was completely out of the woods . . .

On the chilly, overcast Easter Monday morning, Leah

drove back to her flat to do some work, and not long after a delivery van drove up with a package of shallots I'd ordered for spring planting. A silly mishap occurred around this episode, for, forgetting that my front gate was off the latch, I leant on it with one hand while taking the package from the delivery man with the other. Of course, the unlatched gate gave way under my grasp, and I fell forward with it. Luckily, the delivery man had the presence of mind to grab both of my arms and steady me, saving me from falling on my face.

After I'd gone indoors again, I felt an odd sensation of déjà vu, as if all of this had somehow happened before. It was as if I'd had some sort of familiar prompt, but I was damned if I knew to what action. I quickly shook this mood off and went upstairs to my computer to get on with my next gardening article for the *Dumfries Herald*, knocking off for coffee at around eleven.

The next thing I can remember clearly was standing in the vegetable garden, looking down at a plump, purple shallot which I was holding in the palm of my outstretched hand. I looked in a very detached way at the ground, to see a row and a half of planted shallots, with the mostly emptied packaging the delivery man had brought them in that morning lying at my grimy-booted feet. I remembered my almost falling through the unlatched gate, and his grabbing me by the arms to stop me falling, then I'd gone upstairs to work, had stopped for coffee at eleven, and . . .

I looked at my wristwatch: five forty-six. Where had the day gone? The computer would tell me, I thought, then, stooping briefly to firm the shallot clove in its row, I dashed indoors and upstairs to my workroom. The computer screen was dead, and the display and printer lights out. I sat down and switched the computer on, then opened the document I'd been working on that morning – 'dumf126' – and there it was, my week's gardening article for the *Dumfries Herald*. I read it through, and it seemed crisp, cogent and readable, and unmistakably in my style. The work must have been duly saved, then, and, yes, the word count was 600 up on the last effort. I must have just done it all on automatic pilot! So no harm done there – ah! The kitchen . . .

Hurrying back downstairs, I found the morning's breakfast things still in the sink. I'd evidently not cooked lunch, and, no, when I pedalled open the little waste bin, there wasn't a pizza delivery box or any other takeaway packaging in it. Had I eaten out? I ducked through the back door and got into the car outside, then checked the fuel gauge: I'd filled the tank at a station in West Mersea on the previous day, the last time I remembered using the car, and now the gauge registered near-empty . . . Where had I been?

I rang Leah, and explained things.

'You certainly haven't been near me today,' she replied. 'I put it down to the after-effects of all the medication you've been taking lately; that and the obsessive way you tend to work at times. You haven't been hitting the vino, have you?'

'No, just my usual couple of glasses with dinner.'

'Mmm . . . when's your next appointment with your doctor?'

'Friday, as a matter of fact: at two o'clock.'

'He seems pretty good – see what he says – but, in the meantime, as you say, no harm seems to have been done, so I should just carry on as usual, but gently . . .'

So I did. Next day, Tuesday, I rang the Hackney Local History people about my quest for the pub with the magic window, then, on driving out to the shops, just made it to the nearest filling station on the few drops of petrol left in my tank after my unlogged, forgotten drive the day before. It'd come back, I reassured myself – something'll trigger it off, and it'll all come back to me – then I just got on with my life.

The Hackney findings arrived in Thursday morning's

post. The Home in the East was long gone, and the only late Victorian crime of any notoriety that could be connected to a local public house had taken place near the Christmas of 1893, six years before Rawbeck's disappearance. This had been the murder of Mrs Bella Nye, landlady of the Ring of Bells in Lefevre Road, just down from the Old Ford Road station. Mrs Nye had been bludgeoned to death, apparently in the course of a disturbed burglary. The assistant at the local history centre in Hackney had kindly enclosed a photocopy of the relevant column of the *East London Advertiser* of the day, and had added in her letter that no one had ever been brought to book for the crime. I rang up Leah, and told her the news.

'1893?' she'd responded. 'Six years before Rawbeck's disappearance, and of course the pub will have gone with the wind by now.'

'Yes,' I said, referring to the Hackney letter, 'apparently there's a Lefevre Walk, now, but it's modern, and it isn't aligned on the same plan as the former Lefevre Road.'

'Mrs Bella Nye . . .' Leah said. 'Does the name suggest anything to you?'

'No, but let's file it for future reference.'

'Will you be going to this auction sale in Walberswick tomorrow?' Leah changed tack.

'Oh, yes – Brogan the antiques man from Jersey's clearly going to offer Rawbeck objects there because he believes *The Ruffian on the Stair*'s being held somewhere in the district.'

'Julian Rawbeck's so-called lost masterpiece?'

'Right: Brogan wants to use the sale to smoke out the owner. I can't think of any other reason why a flash dealer like him should be footling about in the sticks like that. I want to be there to see who it might draw out of the woodwork.'

'Don't they have viewings before sales?' Leah suggested. 'That may draw even more bods out of the woodwork.'

'Dammit, yes! Thanks for telling me – I'll keep you posted!'

I reached for the Yellow Pages for the number of the auction room, to confirm that the viewing would be on that day, then, having done so, got into my car and hit the A12, arriving in the little Suffolk seaport an hour and a half later.

The salerooms were in a converted Methodist chapel, and Brogan's ticketed lot was a framed print of a head-and-naked-torso sketch of two young men, in the style of Leonardo. The youths in the drawing were sitting back-to-back – there was no perspective background detail at all – and their eyes were half closed, their faces relaxed in a dreamy, satiated sort of a trance. The words on the label said: *Morte Moriantur, attributed to Julian Rawbeck RA, 1852 –*, the artist's death-date being left significantly blank.

But I scarcely had eyes for all that, my gaze being riveted on the features of one of the young men in the print. Shade his hair more lightly, add some wrinkles to the small, fine features and a neat imperial to the chin, and the face was that of my grandfather in the framed photograph on my sitting-room mantelpiece!

'Remarkable resemblance, isn't there, Mr Rolvenden?' cooed a now familiar voice behind me.

I turned to face Liam Brogan, resplendent in an orange Irish tweed three-piece and huge yellow butterfly bow tie.

'With this expression,' he went on, waving a blunt-fingered, pink hand at the figure on the print, 'you miss the haunted look in the eyes in the photograph of your grandfather in your lighthouse, but it's a fascinating study. Looking at it, they seem half asleep, but what if they suddenly woke up to full life! Or if someone broke in on them? What would their expressions change to then? Didn't you tell me you were a linguist, Mr Rolvenden?'

I hadn't, but decided to play his game for now.

'More or less – why?'

'What does the title mean?'

'Roughly: Let them die the death . . .'

'Does it, now, but that's Rawbeck all over: always a bizarre twist somewhere along the line.'

'It must be valuable, then.'

'Mmm . . . depends. Normally, a print of a sketch of a fairly dodgy attribution to a minor master wouldn't fetch all that much, but since the prints are so rare and the original lost – this is the only print that's ever come my way – and considering Rawbeck's notoriety . . .'

'Things might get quite interesting on the day . . .'

'As you say. May we look forward to seeing you here tomorrow, Mr Rolvenden?'

I glanced again at the printed sketch of my youthful grandfather and his nameless companion, and nodded at the little bullet-headed man in the big yellow bow tie. He nodded too, with a rather smug smile, then moved off to talk to someone else in the crowd. There was a little knot of about half a dozen people round the Rawbeck study, but I scanned their features in vain for any family resemblance. I strolled through the rest of the exhibits for ten minutes or so, then went outside to ring Leah on my mobile and put her in the picture.

'The other young man in the print didn't ring any bells with me,' I said, 'but his companion was definitely my grandfather. They were both nude, too – don't you see the tie-in?'

'Frankly, no.'

'In his notebook, Grandfather describes how he wakes up in the sleazy room above the pub naked – Rawbeck could've given him the magic mushroom potion in order to use him for unwitting nude poses and more decadent subjects.'

'Far-fetched, Seb: there's another humdrum conclusion you could draw from the study, as you've just described it. After all, your grandfather's not alone in the sketch, and there's the title: "Let them die the death . . ."'

'Mmm . . . forbidden love, you mean?'

'A clear implication of it.'

Something occurred to me, and I fairly whooped into the mobile.

'Leah! Could this be the sketch – or rather a print of it – my grandfather got so worked up about in his notebook?'

'The one the Vickybird was supposed to have pinched from him in Paris in 1899, you mean, and to have sold on to the Paris art dealer – whatsisname?'

'Carbonero! Grandfather writes about how disastrous it'd be for him if the sketch and its subject got abroad . . .'

I heard Leah's deep chuckle from the other end.

'Mmm . . .' she murmured. 'What if your grandmother's folk had got wind of it in England? Can you imagine them up from Malvern on a staid Sunday outing to the National Gallery, squinting at it through their lorgnettes, then recognizing who the second male nude was! Bang would have gone young Sebastian's marriage prospects with his Cecily, whether she'd been of age or not. And there's another aspect to it . . .'

'Go on.'

'Well, the obvious one! Didn't you say Brogan's just told you that no one's ever seen the original sketch?'

'That's right.'

'Well, then, maybe Rawbeck just sat on it to keep his power over your grandfather – play along with me, or I'll put it on display, sort of thing – what a great motive that would've given your grandad for doing him in!'

I don't mind admitting that for a moment Leah's logic shook my conviction of my grandfather's innocence.

'If he'd murdered Rawbeck just to get the sketch back,' I conceded glumly, 'it's no wonder he was frantic when he realized the Vickybird had done a runner with it. But wait a bit: it's a *print* of the sketch on display here in the sale-room, so the original must've gone public at some time or other, or presumably there wouldn't have been any prints in existence. And in 1899 Grandfather would have had no way of knowing whether Rawbeck had had lithos engraved of the sketch, so there'd have been no point in his doing Rawbeck in to get it away from him.'

'Or prints could've been made from the original after it had been stolen from your grandfather's vicarage in Jersey in 1940.'

'It's the timing of the thing, Leah, we don't know enough yet about the timing ... And as for Rawbeck's disappearance – probable murder – my grandfather's scribbled account runs absolutely true. He's clearly horrified when he finds Rawbeck's body, and is determined to find out the truth about the incident – the pencilled crosses on the London street plan tell us that.'

'But he was drugged to the eyeballs: in that state he might've done anything –'

'No, he couldn't have murdered Rawbeck in a fit of absent . . .'

The words died from my lips when I remembered *my* long fit of forgetfulness on the Monday before.

'What was that you were saying?' Leah asked. 'Are you all right?'

'Yes, I was saying I didn't believe Grandfather could've murdered Rawbeck in a fit of absentmindedness. Anyway, I'm sure I'm on the track of something here, and I'll certainly be at the auction tomorrow.'

And so next morning, I found myself again among the crowd in the bleak, iron-raftered auction hall. I was ready for anything, and had equipped myself at the office with a numbered bidder's label on a stick. I worked my way near the front of the hall, and scanned the crowd. Brogan was there, smiling and bow-tied, and so was Pat Hague – I instinctively tried to make myself small – and, to my great disconcertment, my ex-wife, Reet. Now what had brought her here, of all people I knew the least interested in art or antiques?

Brogan smiled and nodded at me across the hall, and I nodded slightly back. It was eleven o'clock, and, the Rawbeck print being Lot No. 51, I hadn't seen the point of coming in earlier. The rap of the auctioneer's gavel focused my attention on the proceedings up front – Lot No. 37 was going to someone in the doorway. As the auctioneer droned the introduction to Lot No. 38, I stood on tiptoe and continued my scanning of the crowd, praying all the while that neither Pat nor Reet had seen me come in. Turning my head back towards the entrance, I spotted a rather striking figure leaning against the side of the doorway: a tall, slim, youngish man, in a foreign suit and wearing dark glasses. An international bidder? There seemed something oddly familiar about him . . .

'Now Lot 39,' the auctioneer was droning on. 'This fine Belleek butterdish – lot of interest in this, and I'm starting the bidding at eighty pounds . . .'

My attention wandered, and – oh, no! – Pat Hague was making a beeline for me through the crowd, like the periscope of a hunter-killer submarine. She was in a buff trouser suit, with black blouse and shoes, and was wearing her most tigerish grin. She slipped her arm through mine – she must've known Reet was in the room – and cocked her head against mine in a conspiratorial sort of way.

'Belleek's always a good seller,' she began, 'especially when the lacework isn't damaged.'

'You talk like an old hand.'

'Of course – didn't you know? Frank's got me into the inner circle.'

'I half expected to see him here, too.'

'Not disappointed, I hope – you've always got me . . .'

Pat snuggled her coarse dark hair into my shoulder, and I wriggled in my embarrassment and annoyance.

'Don't you care about Frank?' I hissed. 'This place'll be full of people who know him and do business with him.'

'Love laughs at auctioneers! Ooh, look! There's Reet . . .'

My uninvited companion's grin became even more ferocious as she twinkled her fingers over the heads of the other spectators in the direction of my ex-wife's greying head. I gritted my teeth as Reet glanced sadly over in our direction: she looked tense and tired, and I thought I read a question in her eyes before I flinched mine away from hers. I felt a disconcerting jag of protectiveness towards her, which changed almost in the same moment to guilty rage as I tore my elbow from Pat's grip.

'Don't worry, Seb,' she said, all unconcerned. 'She'll always forgive you – she'll always be there.'

'I hate you, Pat!' I growled, loudly enough to bring a disapproving glance from over the auctioneer's half-track spectacles. 'I loathe you with all my being!'

'Ooh! There's passion for you! It means I'm still in with a chance – must be going – someone over there I want to talk to . . .'

A last finger-twinkle, and she was off again, no doubt delighted at having created the effect she'd been aiming at. Embarrassed, I moved away from the clearly disapproving couple in front, who'd obviously heard every word of my nasty little exchange with Pat. Were they members of Frank Hague's circle? I peered over the heads of the crowd again, but Reet must've shifted her position too, for I couldn't see her. The tall, foreign-looking man in dark glasses was now standing up unsupported by the wall of the entrance, and was looking at his watch. Could he be a Rawbeck collector? I scanned another twenty degrees to the left, and caught Liam Brogan's round, blue gaze: it was as if he'd never taken his eyes off me since I'd come into the place. What had he made then of my little performance with Pat Hague?

'Lot No. 51 . . .'

This was it! I swung my attention back to the auctioneer.

'A rare print of a late sketch by Julian Rawbeck RA, of the English Impressionist School, circa 1895, and entitled *Morte Moriantur*. Wonderful draughtsmanship . . . We've had a great deal of interest expressed in this, and I have to start the bidding at eight hundred pounds.'

A tension ran through the room, and I could hear people

here and there muttering into mobile phones, a man with one to his ear kicking off the bidding with a nod towards the podium. The thousand-pound barrier was soon broken, and I glanced round briefly to see how the dark-spectacled Joe Cool in the doorway was taking it all, but he was leaning against the wall again, his arms refolded, just calmly watching the hall.

The bidding mounted, and at eighteen hundred pounds most of the mobiles were switched off.

'Going, then, at eighteen hundred pounds, I'm selling at eighteen hundred . . .'

A thin, familiar hand shot up from the crowd, and I stood on tiptoe again – Reet, for Pete's sake! Reet was bidding against eighteen hundred pounds . . .

'Eighteen-fifty, madam – do I hear nineteen hundred anywhere? I'll take nineteen hundred . . .'

A grim-faced nod from a stocky, sharp-suited man just in front of me.

'Nineteen hundred, sir – do I hear nineteen-fifty? – one-nine-five-oh?'

The gavel was poised in mid-air, and you could have heard a pin drop, then a shapely brown hand, with a glittering gold chain at the wrist – Pat Hague's hand – shot up with a wiggle from the crowd.

'Against you, then, sir, at nineteen-fifty – at nineteen hundred and fifty pounds . . .'

The stocky man in front of me nodded again, and muttered something into his mobile, then, wooden-faced, put it back in his pocket and folded his arms. There was a flurry from Pat's patch, and her hand shot up again, waving this time for good measure.

'With you, darling,' the auctioneer barked, to laughter. 'Don't worry . . . Two thousand now, sir – it's against you – do I hear two thousand and fifty?'

The stocky man kept his arms folded, and just shook his head at the auctioneer.

'I shall sell, then, at two thousand – selling at two thousand – another fifty anywhere?'

A tense couple of moments, then the gavel crashed down on the pulpit top.

'Sold to the lady in the buff costume . . .'

Pat waved her paddle – No. 33 – frantically in the air.

'No. 33. Now Lot No. 52 – a piece of delightful celadon-glaze . . .'

Pat suddenly appeared beside me, waving the numbered paddle under my nose.

'You must be barmy!' I gasped.

'Oh, I don't think so. I see no reason why I shouldn't make a tidy profit on the print – unless, of course, I decide to make you a present of it. But in that case, you'd have to come and get it, wouldn't you . . .'

Chapter Ten

I walked back into the saleroom to take a final look round, and Brogan buttonholed me.

'An interesting response to the Rawbeck print,' he said. 'You know the lady?'

'Yes,' I replied, with a weariness I couldn't conceal, 'I do know the lady . . .'

Pat could take a running jump, I thought, if she imagined I was going to run after her for the print. I could remember the details of it without playing games with her, the main thing being that one of the nude young men in the sketch was my grandfather and namesake, Sebastian Rolvenden.

'Why didn't you put it up for sale in London?' I asked Brogan. 'I'm sure it'd have fetched far more there than a couple of thousand.'

'Every object has its fate, Mr Rolvenden.'

With a civil nod, the dealer left me and rejoined the crowd of onlookers and bidders. I stood in the entrance portal for a while – by then the tall Joe Cool in dark glasses had left the wall to prop itself up – and took in the crowd for a final time. No longer any sign of Pat or Reet, and, apart from Brogan, no one else I knew. I turned and went out into the street again, glancing at my wristwatch: ten past twelve – just time for a quick pub lunch before I set off to keep my medical appointment in Wivenhoe at two.

I was on the road again by twelve-thirty, and as I made for the A12, I noticed that the red flag was up over the cluster of black fishermen's huts down round the Blyth estuary: that meant the fleet was back, and there'd be fresh fish on sale. Pity I hadn't time to stop . . .

As I drove, I pondered over the events that had just passed in the saleroom: Pat's action in buying the Rawbeck print I could understand – winding me up, as well as acquiring a no-doubt saleable article – but Reet, why on earth would she have wanted the print? For one thing, they weren't exactly rolling in money at the Holt, and eighteen hundred quid would have made an appreciable increase in their overdraft. No, moneywise, it was crazy . . . And it wasn't for the intrinsic beauty of the object, as neither Reet nor Paul was artistic in that way. It must be something to do with my grandfather, then. Reet had been to the viewing, and, at any rate, must've recognized my grandfather in one of the young chaps in the sketch.

There was another aspect, I supposed: as well as being my grandfather, Sebastian the Elder was Paul's great-grandfather, too, so maybe Reet had tried to buy the sketch for my son. But surely not – Paul had always pooh-poohed my interest in someone who for him had been no more than – in his words – an 'old Victorian vicar' . . . And what – or who – had prompted Reet to go to the auction-viewing in the first place? These speculations occupied me till I'd crossed into Essex and reached my doctor's surgery in the old detached Victorian house outside Wivenhoe just in time for my appointment.

'And how long have you been off your medication?' was Dr Cousins' first question after he'd taken my blood pressure, which was tolerable.

'Oh, the best part of a fortnight, doctor.'

'And you're sleeping well without your tablets?'

'Pretty well.'

'That's good – very good!'

The thin, bald man's blue eyes glittered at me over the oblong lenses.

'So many depressions are situational,' he went on, 'and

good sleep patterns are largely a matter of habit – it's always good to be able to get along without drugs. Are you writing again?'

'Mmm . . . as busy as ever.'

'Excellent! That's a sure sign of recovery. Have you been under any severe emotional stress lately?'

I thought of Pat's winding me up, but now I had Leah – my rock.

'That side of my life's going well at the moment, doctor – touch wood . . .'

'Amen to that! It counts for so much . . . Anything else since I last saw you?'

I described the odd memory blank I'd had on the Monday, when I couldn't recall anything between eleven in the morning and nearly six in the evening. Dr Cousins' brow wrinkled into a frown.

'That's quite a long time, and you're sure that you went through all your normal daily schedule, in spite of the loss of memory?'

'Yes, just as I've described: it's as if I'd gone through the day as planned, only I wasn't there at the time.'

'Quite. It can't be an after-effect of ECT, either, since you haven't had the treatment. What's your normal alcohol consumption?'

'Oh, a couple of glasses of wine with dinner, usually, and a pint of beer now and again. I'm not normally a spirits-drinker.'

'Did you feel faint at any time before your memory lapse? Any headache? Dizziness or difficulties with breathing?'

'No, I felt busy and purposeful – just getting on with things.'

'And did your tongue feel at all sore afterwards – after you'd come to yourself while you were planting the shallots in the garden?'

'My tongue?'

'Folk tend to bite their tongues in epileptic fits, but I see that doesn't apply in your case.'

The doctor excused himself, and tapped rapidly on the keyboard of his computer for a minute or so.

'Mmm ... no clues in your file ... Tell me, Mr Rolvenden, is there any record of fits or seizures in your family?'

'No – nothing of that kind. Nothing at all.'

'And have you had any blows on the head, any sudden shocks that might have triggered this incident on Monday?'

'No, only ...'

'Yes, go on ...'

I told him how on going to the front gate on the Monday morning to take the package with the shallots from the delivery man, I'd leant on the unlatched gate, and the man had had to grab my arms to save me from falling forward.

'And you didn't actually fall, or hurt yourself in any way?'

'Not in any way, doctor. Is there anything wrong with me?'

Dr Cousins settled back in his swivel chair for a moment, contemplating me.

'Mmm ...' he murmured. 'Amnesia rather than actual disturbance of consciousness, and no apparent loss of physical function at all. And you've never experienced anything like this before? For as long as six or seven hours at a stretch, that is?'

'No, nothing like that.'

The doctor looked serious, and leant forward towards me.

'Mr Rolvenden,' he began solemnly, 'd'you know what I think?'

I gulped, anticipating the worst.

'No, doctor – what?'

'I think you're doing fine! As for this memory lapse, it's in all probability a one-off. We all sink into reveries,

109

experience absentmindedness from time to time, but I'm willing to put money on your being in full control. Now you're a brain-worker, and that lays you particularly open to mental effects such as the one you've described – have you anything in your work at the moment, for instance, that you're finding particularly challenging?'

'As a matter of fact, I'm researching the most unusual and engrossing subject that's ever come my way . . .'

Dr Cousins spread out his hands.

'There you are. Perhaps you're overdoing things – just working too hard. Why not plant more shallots!'

And that was that. Good, then – my session with the doctor had gone very breezily. I made for my car, and decided to drive straight up to the university in search of Leah, in order to give her all my news. As I drove, I had a bit of an afterthought to Dr Cousins' questioning: strictly speaking, I *had* had a serious memory lapse before. At the time of my final family row with Reet and Paul in the cottage at Dunstanburgh, in Northumberland, more than a year before. It was something I didn't care to remember in any circumstances . . .

I'd had the row at the time, stormed out of the cottage, and the next thing I'd remembered was sitting in my parked car on the edge of some cliffs. I recalled the turf landscape, the wheeling gulls overhead, the fresh wind in my hot eyes through the open window, and the sweep of the bay, with, in the sunshine, the dazzling chalk of the cliffside.

The next thing I'd remembered after that had been sitting in my then-rented cottage in Essex – Frank Hague had later found the lighthouse for me after my final split with Reet – and wondering how I'd got there from Northumberland. Just a gap. The cliffs had seemed significant at the time, though – I've never felt easy around cliffs . . .

Well, no use going over that again – leave it alone and get on with my life. At the university, I discovered that

Leah was in confab with some of her departmental colleagues, so I left a message and jumped into a lift to the Level Five general common room, where I lolled for a while over coffee and magazines until, at around four, Leah came up and joined me.

'I've got something to tell you . . .' we both said in unison, then burst out laughing as Leah flopped down in the next seat and put down her document folder on the little table in front.

'You go first,' I said from the drinks dispenser, as I got a coffee for her.

'I had some business in London this morning,' Leah began, taking a sheet from her folder. 'At the City University. In fact, my car's still there, worse luck – I had to call in the AA. Broken lead in the steering. I thought that, with the Family Records Centre in Myddelton Street being so handy, I might as well pop in, and *voilà!*'

My companion's rounded arm shot out, and I took the proffered printout, handing her her coffee with my free hand. I sat down and read the contents of the sheet, which was a photocopy of a page of the 1891 Census, with the Ring of Bells pub, landlady Mrs Bella Jean Nye, underlined by Leah.

'The lady who was murdered in that pub in 1893,' I recapped, 'according to the info the Hackney Local Studies people sent me. Lefevre Road and the Ring of Bells weren't far from the Home in the East and Soundings Alley, mentioned in Grandfather's notebook.'

'But look who she had working for her . . .'

I scanned down the list of the hapless landlady's resident staff in 1891, then gave a low whistle at the last name entered.

'*Laurence Victor Pidgeon,*' I quoted aloud. '*Age: 16. Boots and cellar boy . . .*'

'The Vickybird certainly seems to have seen life,' Leah remarked, then, echoing my thoughts: 'I wonder if he was still pub boots-cum-cellar boy when Mrs Nye was murdered two years after the census was taken?'

'If he'd had a hand in the murder,' I speculated, 'and Rawbeck had somehow found out about it, what a blackmail handle he'd have had over the Vickybird!'

'And what a motive the Vickybird would've then had for doing Rawbeck in!'

I put down my coffee beaker and stared across the tired Eighties decor.

'Leah, I wonder if the Ring of Bells was . . .'

'The pub below the room your grandad woke up in beside Rawbeck's body? Very unlikely, I'd have thought: if the Vickybird had already been involved in one murder committed there, he'd hardly have come back six years later to dirty his own doorstep, so to speak. It would've been an insane risk to have taken.'

'I'm not saying the Vickybird was necessarily there when Rawbeck was murdered in 1899, any more than that his was the actual hand that struck poor Mrs Nye down six years before, but he may have been on the inside in both capers. The fact that both crimes were committed in such a strictly defined area – triangulated in my grandfather's notebook – draws us farther and farther away from coincidence as an explanation.'

'I'm with you there – something was definitely rotten in the state of Hackney Marshes.'

I thought about the legend of Rawbeck's lost masterpiece, *The Ruffian on the Stair*, and had an idea.

'Leah, remember the missing Rawbeck painting – the one he was supposed to be working on when he disappeared?'

'Mmm . . . *The Ruffian on the Stair*. Go on . . .'

'Let's just suppose – kick the idea around – that the Vickybird had modelled for the Ruffian – Death – and there was an actual staircase in the painting . . .'

Leah's eyes took on a sombre expression.

'A staircase,' she went on, 'with a distinctive, ruby-and-blue window on the top landing . . .'

'And let's further suppose it had been the staircase of the pub where the Vickybird or his mates had done in the landlady in 1893 . . .'

'Seeing the painting,' Leah carried on my line of thought, 'any local copper might've recognized the staircase window, and recognized the Vickybird in it from the earlier investigations into the murder of Mrs Nye . . .'

'Not evidence against him, but it might have amused Rawbeck to watch the Vickybird squirm a bit – remind him of where he stood . . .'

'Brr . . .' Leah said, then brought me back to earth: 'But how did you get on at the auction in Walberswick, and how did your appointment with Dr Cousins go?'

I brought her up to date with my doings, and in particular Pat's extraordinary bid for the Rawbeck print of my grandfather and the other, unidentified young man.

'Hmph,' Leah grunted, an ironical smile dimpling her olive cheek.

'You don't seem surprised,' I remarked.

'Oh, no – I'm sure a chance to wind you up big-time would have come cheap to Pat for a couple of grand – the bidder's paddle you had in your hand would've been like a red rag to a bull.'

'I only had that as cover – I was there to have a look at the company, not to buy anything, but I suppose she wasn't to know that.'

'No doubt Frank'll sell the print on at a whacking profit, knowing him, but be warned, Seb, Pat means to get you – she's not the sort of woman you taste like a hard chocolate, then put back in the box.'

'And I still can't fathom what on earth prompted Reet to bid eighteen hundred quid for the print,' I went on. 'I wonder if someone's been getting at her?'

'Maybe part of Pat's winding-up operation – didn't

you say Pat told you she'd been up to see Reet at her smallholding?'

'Mmm . . . if that woman . . .'

Leah reached across and gave my hand a squeeze.

'Never mind, love,' she said. 'The main thing is that the doctor's given you the all-clear.'

The conversation then changed tack to medical matters, till, near five, I invited the carless Leah home for dinner, and she spent the night with me at the lighthouse. Next morning, as I was driving her back to the university, I needed to stop at a filling station, and we both got a taste of Pat Hague's persistence.

'Oh-oh . . .' Leah had muttered through the car window.

I craned round, to see Pat's little everyday car pulling up at the pump next to the one I was using. She got out of the car – she was dressed in a windcheater over a track-suit, and with trainers on her feet, suggesting a visit to some sort of keep-fit function. Pat came up and shone a bright, false smile at both of us as she began to ply her respective pump nozzle.

'Talk about the long arm of . . .' she remarked cheerfully.

Some coincidence, I thought.

Pat then craned over towards my car window, where inside Leah was clearly trying to shrink into the upholstery.

'Read your letter in last Thursday's *Guardian*, Leah,' the *belle laide* screeched through the open window at my companion. 'Congratulations – you gave that dork Druridge's article a good pasting . . .'

I recalled that Leah and the said journalist had been engaged in some correspondence-column duel over nuclear power, but it was the first time I'd been aware that Pat Hague had had any interest in the issue.

'I thought he needed answering,' Leah replied lamely, in a voice that registered less than her usual self-confidence.

'You certainly did that, love!' Pat roared cheerfully. 'Hot and strong!'

114

My anger rose at Leah's obvious discomfiture: why didn't the bloody woman fill up and go . . .

Pat finished filling up her tank, hooked up the nozzle, and turned to make for the counter, but before doing so she stooped and peered through the window of my car. Leah just sat there rigidly, staring at the indifferent tin-stream on the road beyond the pull-in. I saw a world of malice in Pat's eyes as she addressed my companion again.

'Yes, Leah,' she said. 'You really gave it to that journo in your letter in last week's paper – your name was all over it.'

Chapter Eleven

'I wonder what all that was in aid of?' I said to Leah, when we were back on the road to Wivenhoe again.

My companion shrugged. 'Life's too short . . . The more seriously we take Pat's tricks, the more fool us.'

'I'm with you there!'

'Seb, the business of your memory lapses . . .'

'Yes?'

'You mentioned that, after your last family row with Reet and Paul in Dunstanburgh, you found yourself sitting at the wheel of your parked car, looking over some cliffs.'

'That's right: over a year ago. I'd no recall at all of driving there from our cottage in Dunstanburgh.'

'The cliffs would've been at Embleton Bay.'

'You know the area?'

'Mum and Dad had some friends in Jesmond in Newcastle,' Leah explained. 'We spent a couple of summers in their chalet near Alnmouth when I was a kid – it made a change from Scarborough, where we usually went. And you've no recollection at all of how you got there?'

'No, and I've always had an odd dread of cliffs. The incident I described would've been a vague memory of flight, I suppose – ending in white cliffs. It's disquieting not being able to remember significant parts of one's life.'

'We've all got things we'd rather not remember – a sort of moral amnesia.'

'Some sort of guilt complex, you mean?'

'If you like,' Leah said. 'I certainly agree with your doctor about ruling out epilepsy.'

'Aren't shrinks – saving your reverence – supposed to be all for bringing it all out into the open?'

'For one thing, I don't happen to be a shrink, as you're pleased to put it – I've no actual medical qualifications – and for another, some things are best left buried.'

'So the truth doesn't necessarily set you free?'

Leah's pleasant heart of a face was turned to me, and her dark eyes were grave.

'The truth isn't for the weak.'

'Well, thanks a bundle, Leah!'

She patted my knee.

'I didn't mean it like that, but it's something you should think about: that applies to all this stuff about your grandfather, too.'

'Ah, but now that I've decided to write a book about it, it'll count as therapy.'

We fell silent for a while, then I drove on to a straight, narrow road through heavy arable land, the tractors busy on it, with their usual train of white gulls. In the distance, the faint popping of practice fire could just be heard from the direction of Colchester army base.

'What have you got planned for the rest of the day?' I asked.

'Marking bloody scripts – freshers' terminal tests.'

'Do I detect a hint of disillusionment?'

'It's the same every year, now – same subjects, same questions, same students: they seem to come out of a six-pack . . . I've had twelve years of it now.'

'Any sabbaticals in the pipeline?'

'I've a term free in a couple of years' time, but ideally, I want out.'

'Really? Any other line in mind?'

'I'd like to live the way you do – you're a lucky sod in many ways, Seb – but what else does a thirty-seven-year-old psychology lecturer do?'

117

I laughed.

'Marry a poor sap with money, like Frank Hague – like Pat did.'

'Pat's a Reader,' Leah replied. 'She's good at her subject, and she's written quite a lot, too. Pity she happens to be barmy . . .'

'What do you want most of all, Leah?'

'What everyone wants – to be fully myself.'

'And what would that take?'

'Money!' she pronounced, making her already deep voice positively boom. 'Lots of it!'

We both laughed.

'Fine chance,' Leah finally remarked, with an ironic sigh.

By now I was driving under the vast entrance portal of the main university building, then I turned off in the direction of the high-rise where Leah's flat was housed. I reflected that, if I worked here and came into money, the first thing I'd do would be to get the hell out and buy some accommodation on a more human scale. I pulled up, and Leah got out.

'What'll you be up to?' she asked me, as she slung her shoulder bag on.

'Unavoidable shopping in Colchester,' I said. 'I've been dodging it for as long as I could.'

'Ciao,' Leah said, pecking me on the cheek.

'Catch up with you, darling.'

She turned and strode towards the entrance to the block, and I drove back in the direction of Colchester. After our little talk in the car, I felt I'd glimpsed a new side to Leah, not having guessed before at the evident depths of her discontent. To me, she was a clever, sexy young woman, on top of her profession and her world, to the extent, even, of giving time to a wreck like me. To herself, though – allowing for the ever-tightening screw of academic bureaucracy that was demoralizing the whole profession – it seemed she was a bored academic, approaching middle age, and with nowhere else to go. And that stuff – half-serious

118

though it might have been – about money: well, at least I could be sure she wasn't interested in me for mine . . .

Having got my shopping in a bit earlier than normal, I popped into my favourite second-hand bookshop. I eventually arrived at the English poetry section, and felt a tingle of excitement when on its shelves I made out *The Magus*, by Tarquin Rivers, on the spine of a slim, cloth-bound volume. Rivers, again – that erstwhile member of Julian Rawbeck's Camden Hill Convocation, and pensive night-wanderer and discoverer of devastating truths in 1899 East Hackney. Who was it who'd said that if you looked long enough for something, it ended up by looking for you? I opened the book, and found from the date of the edition – 1952 – that it had come out two years after my grandfather's death and nearly forty years after that of its author, Rivers, in the Near East.

I skimmed through the stiff, deckled pages of this book of Rivers' 'hitherto unpublished poems', to find that it was only a hundred and thirty pages long, and that there were only about twenty lines of text in the middle of each page. It was priced very reasonably – I'd have it.

That afternoon, after a scratch lunch, I sat down in my cane armchair at home and read through Rivers' book in one sitting. It was highly varied in subject matter – from the poet's public school and college reminiscences, through the meaning of Beauty and so on to his travels in the Near East. Like most 'previously unpublished' collections by dead, once eminent folk, it soon became clear why the poems hadn't found publishers during Rivers' lifetime: they were obviously not his best work. The lack of a central theme and of the dark emotional intensity of his later Near Eastern poems made for facile and not very interesting reading, except for the last – 'The Burial of the Magus'.

The poem was set in Syria during the Roman Empire, and its narrator is Creon, a worldly-wise soldier-philosopher. Creon relates how Esdras, a naive young provincial scholar, comes up to Antioch in search of a

119

teacher. While listening to the various philosophers in the market-place, Esdras spots Cleoma, a 'lascivious hand-maid' of Simeon, a celebrated Magus. Enslaved by Cleoma, Esdras through her finds his way to Simeon, who becomes his guru.

Esdras soon becomes disillusioned with the Magus, who he sees is a manipulative sensualist, using his powers to dupe rich fools into parting with their money. Part of Simeon the Magus's racket is procuring young men, through drugs and blackmail, to cater for the 'unholy loves' of his wealthy followers. To Esdras's dismay, he learns that the Magus is using his love for Cleoma to groom him for the attentions of Lollius, a rich and foolish Roman sensualist, who's a member of the Magus's circle. Faced with the Magus's machinations, Esdras feels power-less – his attraction to his guru's creature, Cleoma, is too strong – to avoid the loathsome role being prepared for him.

Rivers goes on in his poem to explain how, meanwhile, the slave Silas, an 'unclean minion' of the Magus, and Cleoma's lover, conspires with other disgruntled depend-ants of the Magus to kill him, planning to incriminate the hapless Esdras, whom Silas hates on account of his rivalry for Cleoma's favours.

With all of this going on, the narrator, Creon, who's an occasional sitter-in at the Magus's more legitimate lectures, gets to know Esdras, in whom he finds the Ideal Friend he's been seeking all his life – 'In our One, there is neither Thee nor Me.' Creon soon sees through the way the Magus, Silas and Cleoma are using Esdras for their re-spective ends, and pities his young friend as 'the Seer, who cannot see . . .'

The poem goes on to describe how Creon uncovers Silas's plot to destroy his master and put the blame on Esdras, and late one night, follows two members of the band of plotters to a 'low tavern' in the Bactrian Quarter, where they've already lured the Magus. Muffling himself in his cloak, Creon awaits developments outside the tavern, but to his alarm, two other plotters arrive, shouting and singing like revellers, while propping between them a drugged Esdras. The 'revellers' shout for girls, and drag the seemingly drunk Esdras upstairs.

Creon waits in the street, his fears mounting, till, half an hour later, the clients of the tavern stream out and the innkeeper douses the lamps. Fearing he's left things too late, Creon crosses the road and hides in the shadows of an alleyway next to the tavern door, where he waits for the way to be clear for him to sneak in. He's about to do so, when all four plotters slink out of the tavern – minus Esdras.

The poem moves to its climax as a now thoroughly alarmed Creon waits for the plotters to go their ways, then slips unseen into the tavern entrance and makes his way upstairs, where he finds the Magus, dead and with his throat cut, in a squalid room with a window 'that signified an Emperor's blood'. Creon looks all over for Esdras, but he's not there – he must have come to in time to sneak out of the tavern somehow. To that extent, the plotters' scheme to incriminate Esdras has come unstuck, but there's still the problem of the Magus's body . . .

Here Creon does some quick thinking: the best thing he can do is to get the body out of the tavern, and, 'hard by Reuben's ground', to 'ash it in unhallowed fire'. There can be no religious ceremony for the Magus, 'only nearby, the undying smoke.' Creon then buries the ashes so that no one will know of the Magus's fate, and, whatever the evil Silas and his fellow plotters may say later, Esdras can never be accused of the Magus's murder.

The endpiece to the poem describes how, after Creon has got rid of the Magus's remains and put Esdras in the clear, his young friend is more besotted with Cleoma than ever, and has no time for Creon . . . Finally disillusioned with earthly attachments, Creon wanders off into the desert to seek truth as a hermit. So ended 'The Burial of the Magus'.

And so, I thought, sitting in my cane chair back in the early 2000s, ended the mystery of how Julian Rawbeck had met his death! For Antioch, read Camden Hill, and for the era of Imperial Rome, read 1899 . . . Rawbeck, of course, appears as the Magus. All the circumstances of the Camden Hill Convocation set-up were mirrored in the poem, which was a barely disguised confession by Rivers – 'Creon' in the poem – that he'd been the one who'd got rid of Rawbeck's body after my grandfather – clearly 'Esdras' – had woken from his drugged trance beside it! 'Cleoma' had been a dead ringer, too, for Carrie Bugle, and who could the malign slave 'Silas' have been in real life but Laurence Victor Pidgeon – the Vickybird? And 'Silas' had led the plot to murder the Magus/Rawbeck.

My hands trembling with excitement, I read through the poem again, just to see if I hadn't missed anything. No: it was all there, down to poor Jimmie Toland as the rich Roman fool, Lollius, who'd fancied the candid lad, Esdras . . . Then there was the description in the poem of where the Magus's body had been cremated: 'hard by Reuben's ground . . .' Where had I seen that before? I put the book down on the side table, and, jumping up, made for the kitchen, where I'd left my jacket, and took Grandfather's notebook out of the pocket. Turning to the page with the enigmatic disjointed entries, I found what I was looking for: *Reuben's Court* and *Smoking Altars*. The latter expression could well tie in with the 'undying smoke' that was the only funerary mark of the Magus's cremation in the description in Rivers' poem. But why should smoke from a funeral pyre be 'undying'? If that was only a poetic effect, it was a pretty lame one. I dashed back into the sitting room, hopping up and down in triumph – 'Got it! Cracked it!' – then rang Leah and blurted out the details of my new discovery.

'The poem's clearly cathartic on Rivers' part,' was my companion's initial reaction. 'Getting the fact that he'd burned Rawbeck's body off his chest. And I think the fact that the poem wasn't published until forty years after his death strongly suggests that he never meant it to be published in his lifetime. And after all Rivers' efforts, your grandad still only had eyes for Carrie . . .'

'But this Reuben's Court reference is still stumping us,' I complained.

'Though the Smoking Altars mention in your grandad's notebook could tie in with the "eternal smoke" Rivers says in his poem marks the grave of the Magus – Rawbeck. Remember, I looked up Reuben's Court in the modern London street guide . . .'

'Mmm . . . you found one near Gunnersbury station, but that area presumably wasn't built up in 1899, and there's none in the East End on my grandfather's 1871 map.'

'Seb, have you thought about the fact that your grandfather was using an 1871 map in 1899, a gap of twenty-eight years?'

'You're right! There'd have been slum clearance and so on in the meantime. I may have been looking for places – streets and houses – that Grandfather knew, but mightn't have figured on his 1871 map . . .'

'Yes,' Leah went on, 'the map would just have served for general reference, as we might use a 1980s map today, if we found one lying around.'

'Right. But back to how Rivers might have got rid of Rawbeck's ashes: what about actual burial grounds around Hackney? They'd be the obvious places to scatter someone's ashes without arousing suspicion, and there can't have been that much chopping and changing round of graveyards. There may be something suggestive, too, in the surrounding streets and features.'

'It's worth trying – process of elimination, and all that. Keep me posted, Seb.'

I rang off, then got the 1871 street map and spread it out on the floor. I then got my magnifying glass out of the bureau and knelt over the map. I'd make the radial point of my circle the Home in the East in Hackney.

Moving westwards from there – there was only open country to the east – the first cemetery of note was the Victoria Park one, and there were no Reuben references in the surrounding streets. Moving on from there, the same applied to the Jews' Burial Ground, just south of the park, in front of the Mile End Workhouse. A bit farther west, alongside the Whitechapel Workhouse, was another Jews' Burial Ground, off North Street, which, reasonably enough, branched north, off the Whitechapel Road. Still no features with a Reuben label, though . . .

I sat back for a think: right, call in the professionals. I glanced at my watch: three-fifteen – the Central Library in Colchester should still be open. I got up off the floor and went over to the side table with the Yellow Pages, and rang the library. I was referred to a helpful voice, to whom I explained the situation.

'You say your map's the 1871 one?' asked the young girl on the desk.

'That's right,' I said. 'But the events I'm researching took place in 1899.'

There was a short interval, filled with the click of fingers on a keyboard.

'We've the 1894 Ordnance Survey map of East London: it's pretty exhaustive. And it's cemeteries and street or place names with Reuben or Smoke you're after?'

'That's it.'

'Could I ring you back?'

She could, and I spent the next twenty minutes rummaging in vain through my reference books for anything on East London topography pre-1899. Then the phone rang, and I dashed over to answer it.

'There's a Jews' Burial Ground north of the Whitechapel Road,' said the pleasant female voice. 'It's marked "disused" on the XVII. II Middlesex Sheet of the 1894 OS map. Bordered on the east by Brady Street.'

'Ah! That's marked North Street in the 1871 map – the

street must've been renamed between 1871 and the time of your map.'

'And there's a Reuben Street,' the voice went on, 'branching off eastwards again from Brady Street – just opposite the Burial Ground, in fact.'

'Excellent! And the Smoke or Smoking connection?'

'Mmm . . . not as such, but . . .'

'Yes – please go on.'

The girl at the other end laughed.

'Not unless you count the smoke that would've come from the Animal Charcoal Works in those days – the Works abutted directly on to the Burial Ground.'

'That's really splendid – better than I could have hoped for. Many, many thanks – you've been a great help!'

I put the receiver down, and, in a fever of excitement, started to pace the room. It all fitted! After Rivers nips up the stairs into the murder room above the pub in East Hackney, to find my grandfather gone and Rawbeck's corpse lying there, he manages – with help, surely? – to get the body of the artist into a coach or cart. He then takes it somewhere where he can safely burn it, and scatters the ashes in the Whitechapel Road Burial Ground, which is 'hard by' if not Reuben's Ground in Rivers' poem, then at least Reuben Street, near the eastern, Brady Street boundary of the Burial Ground. And, as it says in the poem of the Magus's cremated remains, Rawbeck's ashes will receive a tribute of 'eternal' – or as long as the nearby Animal Charcoal Works' chimney lasts – smoke.

My brain was racing, and as I always do on such occasions, I went out into the garden to try to restore my equilibrium. Time to mulch the clematis on the east wall – it would give them a boost, and they liked a cool, moist root-run. It was good to be in the open air, and I whistled a tune as I wheeled a half-barrowload of rotted-down seaweed from the compost bin behind the shed to the clematis clump under the window. I'd trained the plant up a trellis, on two main stems, which forked, one stem on each side of the window, from the stump below.

I couldn't help wrinkling my nose as I forked the compost out of the barrow and laid it in a three-inch layer round the roots of the climber: no matter how long you left seaweed to rot, it always kept some of its sewage-like pong. Having worked my way round the whole border, I gave a last pat to the surface of the mulch with my fork, slung the tool in the barrow, and wheeled both back to the shed.

Once indoors again, I cleaned up, then settled down in my cane armchair with a mug of coffee and a barrel of ginger-snaps. I considered the question of motives in the Rawbeck Affair. Rawbeck had set up his show for power and money – easy one. My grandfather's drawn in because he's crazy for Carrie Bugle, and he can only get to her through her Svengali, Rawbeck. Tarquin Rivers joins initially for esoteric knowledge, then things become increasingly complicated by a platonic pash he conceives for my youthful grandfather. Jimmie Toland joins Convocation through exuberant silliness and because he knows Rawbeck can procure young men for him. Laurence Victor Pidgeon, the Vickybird, is a chancer, and there's probably been some sort of blackmail-nexus that binds him to Rawbeck. The Vickybird above all wants out, and the indications were that he'd killed Rawbeck to achieve this.

But Philip Forbuoys the flute player, what motivates – if that's the word – him to jump into the Thames? What ill has he that's not for mending? And Carrie herself, how does she see all this? Is it all just rip-roaring fun for the girl from Gatti's music hall, as she plays the Vickybird against Rawbeck, and both against my wet young grandfather? Ta-ra-ra-boom-de-ay . . . It struck me that with her experienced, cynical eye, she'd have seen through them all. Maybe poor Forbuoys longed for her, too?

Then there'd been Carrie's surname, Bugle. Just right for

her and her profession, as if it had been designed by a publicity man. Had it been her real name, though?

I put my mug down on the side table, and, getting up, made my way over to the bureau, and the London Residential phone book. I stood and flicked down the 'B' columns: half a dozen variations on the theme of 'bugler,' two almost-spellings of Carrie's surname, six Trumps and seven Trumpers, but nary a Bugle as spelt. Maybe the name had originally been something more prosaic, like Budgell, but her manager had thought Bugle would add a touch of charisma?

I flicked the wad of pages idly back – there were Pidgeons, too, and a dozen or so Nyes, but none in Hackney. In any case, how could you just work down the list, cheerily enquiring: 'Good afternoon, could you by any chance be descended from a Victorian music hall dancer who'd something to do with cutting the throat of the artist she occasionally modelled for?' Or, in the Vickybird's case: 'Hello! Would your great-grandfather have been a psychopathic pub cellar boy who bashed his landlady's skull in in 1893?'

I decided to leave it all there for the time being, and the evening jogged along through supper to an early bed, but not for long, because for some reason I woke up suddenly in the pre-dawn of that Sunday morning. I turned over – and over again – but couldn't get back to sleep – don't say it was going to have to be the sleeping pills again – until, when it was more or less daylight, I got up grumpily, dragged on my robe and went downstairs.

On my way to the kitchen, I paused at the open door of the sitting room – something wrong. I went in and took a look round: everything seemed as I'd left it when I'd turned in on the previous evening, but yes, I could smell the sea . . . I glanced down at the carpet, and it was as if some sea-creature had flopped and hobbled across the floor: there were brownish stains in a huddle under the mantelpiece and round the bureau at the other side, then a trail of them leading to the window. I walked over to it, and flung aside the curtains, to let in the grey morning light. The windowsill was muddied with some of the seaweed compost I'd been applying under the window the previous evening, and there were little heaps of sawdust where someone had drilled up the window-hasp, which was cocked up at ninety degrees.

I pushed open the windows, and, stooping out, saw footprints deep in the newly applied mulch below. Cursing myself for not having installed window-locks immediately on buying the house, I hurried back in, my hands trembling with anger, and went and checked the front and back doors, which were locked and bolted from the inside, as I'd left them on turning in the night before.

Next I turned my attention to the sitting room, where everything appeared to be in place, including my grandfather, the anxiety in his large eyes frozen forever in his silver-framed photograph. A new fear surged through me, and, foolishly, I reached into the pocket of my robe for the key to the bureau compartment, where the Jiffy bag from Jersey was lodged.

Cursing myself again, I dashed upstairs for my jacket, in the pockets of which – along with my grandfather's precious notebook – I found the bureau keys. Back downstairs, I unlocked the bureau-compartment, and, praying as I worked, checked all the items – 1871 OS street map of London, Bible, *Crockford*, and all the letters – in the Jiffy bag. I checked the contents of every envelope, including those in the folder in the back of the Bible, and the one sandwiched between its pages. All there – thank God! – but, hang on – the overlarge letter that had been squeezed into an envelope that was too small for it – the letter written to my grandfather in French from Madame Pidgeon in Niort before the war – was gone.

Chapter Twelve

I went outside to examine the footprints in the mulch: a big foot – size ten or even eleven – and quite a shallow impression, in spite of the softness of the seaweed compost. I weigh just under thirteen stone, and the imprint of my shod feet on soft earth is noticeably deeper. Barring a little man with outsize feet – very rare, in my experience – we were looking for a tall, thin man, with big feet; one, moreover, who was agile enough to break into a house and nip through a window so as not to awaken the upstairs occupant. A fairly young man, then.

The above criteria ruled out Liam Brogan, even if he'd been stupid enough to have taken a second pop at my property within days of my having caught him at his midnight tampering with my shed. My son Paul was fairly tall – five-ten-and-a-bit – and wiry with it, but he took a size eight shoe, and the idea of his doing anything quietly just made me smile. The shoe-test also ruled out Reet, as well as Frank and Pat Hague – I knew Pat's narrow, brown feet pretty well, with or without shoes. As for Leah – just for the sake of elimination – she was tiny. Plainly ridiculous.

Who did that leave, then? I recalled the tall, lanky figure I'd seen standing with his back to the sun in Headland churchyard on Good Friday morning, and the tall man I'd seen out on the headland itself the other evening in the dimity light, when I hadn't been sure whether he'd been looking out to sea or at my lighthouse. In addition, there'd been the Joe Cool in the foreign-looking clothes and dark glasses who'd propped up the wall of the Walberswick auction room two days before. They all – or perhaps it had been the same man? – fitted my Identikit description of the previous night's burglar.

Just then the shrill song of a blackbird broke my train of thought, and I shivered as it was borne in on me that there was nothing between my skin and the chill April air but an old bathrobe. I flopped back indoors on slippered feet, bolted the door behind me, and ducked into the bathroom and ran a bath. As I kicked off the slippers, I wondered where my night visitor might have chucked his incriminating, seaweed-ponging shoes. Which roadside ditch or unwitting council-tax-paying citizen's wheelie bin might be holding them at that moment?

I slipped off the robe and climbed into the steaming bath, where I sank luxuriously into the hot water. My night intruder would no doubt be over the hills and far away by now, and with part of my grandfather's life history in his pocket. I minded that very much. But, hang on: the fact that he'd only taken the pre-war letter from Madame Pidgeon in Niort, and had left all the other letters, suggested that he already had a fair idea of what was in them: the details of the early life of Sebastian Rolvenden the First. In any case, the stolen letter had been from a Pidgeon, suggesting a tie-in with the Vickybird's role in Grandfather's distant ordeal.

What then was the big-footed burglar's game? Nothing altruistic, judging by his entry to the lighthouse. I sank back deeper into the joint-caressing hot water, and narrowed my eyes like some sybaritic pasha. If Big Foot needed to know about me as much as I now felt I needed to know about him, it was a racing certainty our paths would cross again, and then ... I sloshed upright in the bath again, as I realized that I wasn't the only Rolvenden within an hour's drive – I remembered how put out Reet and Paul had been when Brogan had been mooching around the Holt. I must warn them. I got out of the bath

130

and dried myself, pulled on my robe, then went to the sitting-room phone and rang the Holt, Reet answering. No need to apologize for the early call – they were always up with the larks.

'Watch out for a tall, youngish bloke,' I warned her. 'He's broken in here last night.'

'You're all right?'

'Mmm . . . slept through the whole thing, more's the pity.'

'What did he take?'

'An old letter to my grandfather.'

'You're still going on with that stuff? Really, Seb – it's your life – but you should lay off all that . . .'

Disappointment registered in Reet's tone: she'd never had much patience with this preoccupation of mine with my grandfather, regarding it as an unhealthy King Charles's Head that kept me tied to aspects of my childhood immaturity.

'You've no idea who this man is?' Reet went on. 'Nothing to do with the little guy who came round in the Micra, is it? The antiques man? Paul said if he comes around again, he'll –'

'I don't know if there's any connection between them, but I think I've seen the man who broke in – if it was him – before. Tall, lanky, foreign-looking chap in dark glasses at the saleroom in Walberswick the other day . . .'

There was a pregnant silence at the other end for a couple of moments.

'All right, Seb – thanks for telling me. I'll be on the alert – I'll tell Paul as soon as he comes in.'

'Right – bye,' I signed off, feeling a pang at no longer being able to add the 'darling' I'd have used two years and more before.

And that was it: when I'd mentioned the Walberswick auction sale, not a word from Reet as to why she'd been there herself. Let alone why, more annoyingly, she'd made an extravagant bid for an object connected to my

131

grandfather, whom she'd just been dismissing again as an unhealthy obsession of mine! I sat back in the chair and recalled the breakfasts we'd had in our first little flat in Earl's Court, when we'd just been married. She wearing the ancient, checked woollen dressing gown Dad had chucked out, her long red hair combed over to one side as she'd sat with both hands round the coffee mug, talking in the quirky, dogmatic way I'd then been in love with: right and wrong, black and white, cut and dried . . . Youth! And how warm the white skin of her cheek and neck had been to the lips – so white, yet so warm. The days that were gone – I had so many of them now. But *why* hadn't she mentioned being at the auction . . .?

It was no use: I just couldn't sit around at home. Having broken into one Rolvenden house and got away scot-free with his haul, Big Foot wasn't going to wait long before having a crack at the Holt. I looked at the mantelpiece clock: still only six forty-five. I could easily make it up to the Holt, do a recce there, and be down in West Mersea in time for my beloved ritual Sunday lunch with Leah. A good breakfast, then, and a quick dash up the A12 for an unscheduled visit to the Suffolk coast.

I got to the Holt at eight-forty, and parked discreetly in the piney hollow on a sand ridge that gave the farmstead its name. The little wood rose abruptly amid the gorse waste that formed a belt between the eroded seashore and the farmland of the hinterland. The hollow was at the end of a rough track that led off the A12, so I was in a position to watch any traffic going in the direction of the farm. It would have been here that Brogan had parked, I supposed, before Paul had shooed him away that day. I guessed that, after the first wave of farm chores, Reet and Paul would be sitting down to a late breakfast. I got out of the car with my little set of field-glasses, had a look round – no company in the quiet pine thicket – and clambered up to the top of the ridge.

Dead weed stalks cracked like gunshots under my feet

as I made my way up, and there was an ominous croaking of crows above me, as the disturbed birds wheeled blackly round the tree canopies. At the summit of the ridge, I plied my glasses over the grey sea, as it lapped and foamed on to the rotted black fingers of the breakwaters. Under the overcast skies, there was nobody on the beach, and in the distance I could vaguely hear the lin-lan of a church bell – someone getting some practice in, no doubt, before actually summoning the worshippers in a couple of hours' time.

I swept the glasses landward – apart from the ridge I was on, there was only a vast, green flatness, with, immediately below me, the buildings of the Rolvenden farmstead. The family Land Rover was parked at the front door of the red-brick, Dutch-tiled farmhouse, and there were three cars parked in the yard formed by the three sides of the single-storeyed farm-adjuncts. Hadn't Pat Hague told me they now had students in residence?

Ah! Reet had just come out by the kitchen door of the farmhouse, with a bucket: she was making for the garden compost bin, near the tunnel cloches. She looked purposeful and unconcerned. And there was Paul's head popping out of the door – he'd be making some remark after his mother. My son was smiling. A peaceful, normal scene, then: no suggestion in it that they'd been troubled by any uninvited callers. I sighed inwardly with relief, and made back down to the car.

Once inside the vehicle again, I wondered if, unseen by me, the Tall Man might be making the selfsame reconnaissance as I was? Maybe he was watching me now from some concealed hide or vantage point ... If so, where would he be staying? Not in the nearby village of Thruxton-under-Holt – he'd stick out like a sore thumb in one of the farmhouse B&Bs there. Unless he was yo-yoing it from London – hard going – or from some bigger town like Bury or Ipswich, Southwold was the likeliest place.

Not too far away, but big enough to be anonymous. Better give it a look-see . . .

I pulled out slowly, and crept along the path to the main road again, then set off for the couth seaside residential town. Good morning, Southwold . . . As I drove on, I reflected that, at that moment, Leah would be just stirring in her concrete tower, Frank Hague would be twitching his whiskers nervously over his breakfast Sunday paper in anticipation of the day's wheeling and dealing, and Pat would be amusing herself – probably not alone – in their weekend boathouse in the Wivenhoe Marina. Liam Brogan would no doubt be glittering punters over breakfast in some small, but discreetly expensive London hotel, and Big Foot, the tick who'd stunk out my sitting room with seaweed compost and pinched Madame Pidgeon's letter to my grandfather, where would he be, and what would he be doing?

Just then I entered Reydon, where the service population of Southwold – Hampstead-on-Sea to the irreverent – was housed. Then I'd hit Southwold itself, with its Toytown fishermen's cottages, jolly white lighthouse and self-consciously idiosyncratic beach huts of many colours. I knew Reet found the town's charms resistible – the first time we'd gone there, she'd dismissed it with the remark that the brewery was the only 'real' thing about the place.

I slowed down to a cruise, looking to see what I might see, especially in the forecourts of hotels and pub-inns. A goodly scatter of foreign number plates –mainly German – in the car parks of the respective hostelries; then, a hundred yards or so beyond the lighthouse, a Renault with a French number plate.

Distinctly interesting, I thought, in connection with the foreign clothes of the tall Joe Cool in the auction rooms and the French ramifications of the Rawbeck Affair.

I pulled up in the first available space, about a hundred yards ahead. I then sat back and had a think: how to approach this one? I couldn't very well barge into the place where the French car was parked – the Low Light Inn – because if the car belonged to the lanky individual who'd been shadowing me, I wanted to keep tabs on him. A discreet enquiry by phone, I thought – the Low Light Inn displayed its phone number prominently on its fascia. I took out my mobile, and rang the number.

'Good morning,' came the bright, professional voice. 'Low Light Inn – I'm Dot Steel. Can I help you?'

'Good morning, Mrs Steel.' I returned her greeting. 'I believe you've a French gentleman staying with you at the moment . . .'

'Ah, you're Mr Rolvenden, aren't you?' she said cheerfully. 'Monsieur Ramier's left a message . . .'

Chapter Thirteen

That fairly knocked me off my perch, and then I realized what had happened, my suspicion being confirmed immediately in Mrs Steel's next sentence.

'I recognized your voice, Mr Rolvenden; in fact, I was going to ring your mother . . .'

She'd obviously taken me for my son, Paul, our voices being very similar.

'Mum's busy at the moment,' I improvised, trying my best to sound relaxed and youthful. 'I can pass on Monsieur Ramier's message to her if you like.'

'He just wanted to tell your mother that if he isn't here on time tomorrow morning, could she possibly hang on a bit till he arrives? She won't have to wait long, as he's checking out at eleven-thirty.'

'Oh, righto,' I said. 'I'll let her know.'

'Thanks for calling, Mr Rolvenden.'

I put the phone away, relief struggling with elation within me. I could easily have blown the whole thing. Now just what had Reet to say to this mysterious Frenchman next morning around eleven? Curiouser and curiouser: I had to check this man out, and I'd certainly be coming back to Southwold in the morning. *This* 'Mr Rolvenden' would be keeping the appointment, too, but I'd see that no one knew anything about it . . . Now for West Mersea and my lunch date with Leah: I'd have a lot to talk to her about.

A couple of hours later in the little fish restaurant, I was bringing Leah up to date with the burglary at the light-house the previous night, along with the Southwold developments, as we downed our oysters-with-Tabasco.

'It's Joe Cool, all right,' Leah said. 'The guy in the dark glasses at the auction – your ex-wife was there, too, didn't you say? There's something going on between them . . .'

'You're surely not suggesting Reet had anything to do with the burglary at my place?'

'No, but it looks as if the same man did your lighthouse over – his description fits that of the skinny bloke you say's been stalking you lately.'

'Mmm . . .' I murmured. 'And of everything portable in the house, he only took the Odette Pidgeon letter: he left the rest of my grandfather's things. I wonder if it's connected to whatever it is he's after – the real prize, I mean?'

'The lost Rawbeck painting?' Leah suggested. *'The Ruffian on the Stair?'*

'I don't see why not; after all, that's what Brogan's after. He told Frank Hague as much the other week. Why not a French antique dealer, too?'

'Like a pack of vultures . . .'

'And if a legitimate dealer like Brogan's willing to try to break into my shed at dead of night . . .'

'Then,' Leah began, 'this Joe Cool, or Monsieur – whats-isname?'

'Ramier,' I prompted.

'Well,' she went on, 'no reason why this Monsieur Ramier should stick at a little burglary to get what he wants. This is red hot, Seb, and I don't mean the Tabasco! Will you be sussing out this date your wife's got with Ramier tomorrow?'

'You bet I am!'

'Watch your step, then,' Leah said darkly.

Ten-thirty next morning, Monday, found me in Southwold, strolling Byronically along the pebble beach in front of the Low Light Inn. I was dressed in a naff raincoat and tweed cap I'd bought in an Oxfam shop, and the addition of a pair of dark glasses, I hoped, would enhance my disguise. I pretended, with a sparse handful of other passing gawpers and dog-walkers, to take an interest in the occasional sea traffic, while keeping a weather eye on the front of the inn where I knew my ex-wife had business to do with the tall man who seemed to have been following me around lately.

One good sign: Monsieur Ramier's – if that was his name – Renault was still parked in front of the inn, so my failure to pass on the landlady's message to Reet that he might be late for their date looked irrelevant now. Unless, of course, the lady had rung her since, to check on whether 'her son' had passed on the message . . . But no reason why she should have, and, in any case, eleven o'clock should see the thing resolved, one way or another.

I spotted a container ship on the horizon, and levelled my field-glasses at it: it was like a great blue shoebox, floating on its side. I then paused awhile to consider the ranks of rainbow-hued beach huts with their wacky names: Hickey Doola, Kate 'n' Sidney, Fernando's Hideaway . . . I recalled that in summer they had a sort of Tea Cult here on the beach, everyone plying everyone else with pots of tea, like some tribal bonding ceremony.

You'd need something stronger than tea, though, I thought, to counter the effects of this whipping wind, as, with watering eyes behind the dark glasses, I turned my head slightly and took a sly dekko through the glasses at the front of the Low Light Inn. Yes – Reet's Land Rover! She was getting out, striding purposefully – her face looked set and angry – up to the front door of the inn. Dared I walk right up to the esplanade, and sit on one of the benches with my back to the hostelry? I'd brought a shaving mirror along to act as periscope . . .

I crunched up the pebble strand to the low brick wall that edged the road, took a last look out to sea, then clambered up, and so on to a bench to read my paper. I sat like that for about ten minutes, when, through my little square of shaving mirror, I caught the reverse image of Reet as she appeared at the door of the inn again. She was leaving the place in a tearing hurry, her face red with fury – it went with her once-red hair! – and positively flung herself into the Land Rover and roared off in the direction of the Holt. The rendezvous with Monsieur Ramier had evidently not gone well . . .

Phew! I hadn't seen her in such a state since we'd been together, but Reet's temper was the feature that really let her down, and Paul had inherited it from her, along with the carrot-coloured hair. I went over a hundred-and-one speculations as to why she'd been so angry with her vis-à-vis, then the man himself emerged from the inn.

It was Joe Cool, all right – the tall, thin man I'd noticed at the auction – even down to the dark glasses. He'd a car jacket flung over his dark suit, and his lean, pale face was set in a sort of determined scowl. If I was going to keep tabs on him, though, I'd better look slippy, because he was even at that moment bundling his holdall into the boot of his Renault.

I got up from the bench, and, with my back still to the forecourt of the inn, slowly folded my paper round the shaving mirror and slid both into the side pocket of my nondescript raincoat. Then, nonchalantly slipping one hand into the other pocket, where the little pair of field-glasses lay, I crossed the road well ahead of the inn, and began to saunter the hundred paces or so to my car. I smiled as, halfway along my route, my attention was drawn to a creaking and jingling of horse harness from the road. It was one of Southwold's carefully preserved bits of character: Prince and Sovereign patiently plodding in front of their dray, on the way back to the brewery after delivering the morning's brew. The wind suddenly veered offshore, and I caught the aroma of malt from the brewery, mingled with the smoky tang of the fish-drying sheds. As the dray jingled slowly by, I reflected with satisfaction that

Joe Cool in his Renault would have to hang on a bit to let the dray-horses get clear.

He didn't wait long, though, for moments later, the Renault zipped by me in the road. I pulled the silly glasses off and stuffed them into my pocket as I dashed for my car. I soon got in and set off on the road: if this Ramier was going anywhere, he'd be making for the A12. I threaded my way carefully through the narrow streets of the Lilliputian resort, and my luck was in: at the end of the feeder road, I spotted the Renault with its French number plate as it pulled out of a thin queue of vehicles that had been waiting in front of me to join the arterial road.

By the time I'd got into the stream on the main road, Ramier's car was almost lost to sight ahead of me. I accelerated, discreetly overtaking the competition, till he was visible ahead of me, and from then on it was a clear run down behind him in the direction of Wivenhoe: could he be making for the little haven? Perhaps he was on his way to visit my lighthouse on the headland?

But no: he shot past the opening to the minor road that led to my place, and drove straight on in the direction of the marina, with its tinny-rattling masts and chi-chi water-side conversions. I immediately thought of Pat Hague and the Hagues' boathouse here, where Pat seemed to spend most of her spare time these days. My suspicions hardened as the Renault slowed abruptly and drove into the marina car park.

I didn't want to seem as if I was driving up his back, so did a lap of the marina, after which, just as I was returning to drive into the car park, I saw the tall man in the car jacket and dark glasses scanning the buildings along the water's edge. By now I was sure he was making for the Hagues' weekend retreat, and such was my confidence in this hunch that I decided to give him five minutes before going off in pursuit. I found a parking space, parked my car, and strolled up to the machine to get a sticker, before walking casually down to the Hagues' boathouse.

There, on the decking at the back of the low, blue-and-white painted building – the side facing the water of the creek – I found the tall man trying the door handle. I walked softly up, then, leaving a fair distance between him and me – you never knew – glanced briefly from behind him down at his formally shod feet. Size tens, at least. His hair was stiff and fairish, done in a sort of overgrown crewcut which veered to one side, like that of Tintin in the cartoons.

'I don't think anyone's in,' I remarked quietly from behind the man.

He swung round and took me in through the glasses for a moment.

'Evidently,' was his calm reply in slightly accented English. 'Perhaps you know where I may find Mrs Hague?'

I had the feeling that this was one of the turning points of my life.

'I can't help you there,' I said. 'By the way, I'm Sebastian Rolvenden.'

The man drew himself up straight from the door handle, and, taking off the dark glasses – his eyes were a warm, reddish-brown – smiled rather deliberately and held out a long, thin hand to be shaken.

'My name is Paul Ramier – it would be nice if we could talk somewhere.'

Which we did, over a smart-sandwich lunch in the cafeteria of a nearby swish yachting-gear emporium.

'I have a small hotel in Berneval, on the coast of Normandy – perhaps you know it?'

I shook my head, and Pat's caller went on between sips from his Stella.

'This is my spring holiday, but I am also looking for my roots.'

'And they spread as far as Suffolk?' I asked, biting a wodge off my salami baguette.

'Let me start from the beginning.'

'Be my guest . . .'

'My great-grandmother killed my great-grandfather, Mr Rolvenden . . .'

I paused in mid-chomp and stared into the narrow brown eyes, set above the high cheekbones of my interlocutor.

'In 1909,' he went on undramatically. 'A *crime passionnel*, you understand . . .'

I nodded in what I hoped was an understanding fashion.

'When there is no *entente* between a couple, and there is poverty . . .'

'What happened to your great-grandmother?' I asked.

'Two years in prison, and there was a little boy of two years – my grandfather. My great-grandfather's parents took care of him while his mother was in prison.'

'And the Rolvenden connection?'

'By 1921 my great-grandmother had become alienated from all the rest of the family, and was desperate. She took my grandfather – he was then thirteen years – to Jersey, because she knew an English priest there from her earlier days in Paris. The priest was very kind, and he found a place for them to live, and helped my grandfather find his first job in a tomato house. That good priest was your grandfather, Mr Rolvenden, and he has a very honoured place in the hearts of my family. But if you will permit me, Mr Rolvenden, your grandfather lived so long ago, yet you are of an *âge mûr* only – not yet old . . .'

'My father –' I explained, 'your "good Jersey priest's" son – was born in 1900, and didn't get married till he was forty-three, and I wasn't born till nine years later, in 1952, two years after my grandfather died.'

'Ah, I see – it explains itself.'

142

'And did your great-grandmother and her son settle down in Jersey?' I asked.

'My grandfather was called back to France in 1925 for his military service, and he called my great-grandmother back there two years later, after he had finished his service. By then he worked on *les chantiers* . . .'

'Building sites?'

'Correct – building sites, assembling fairs and circuses in summer, then on farms during the harvest. He was a strong man, not afraid of work. He married my grandmother in 1930, and my father was born soon after. My great-grandmother died in 1933. The war came, and in 1940 my grandfather's year was called. After the *débâcle*, his regiment was embarked from Dunkirk to England, then, after the regiment had been regrouped under de Gaulle, it was Madagascar, the Near East – *tous azimuts* – all the quarters of the compass . . .'

'Did your grandfather look up my grandfather after the war?' I asked.

Ramier spread his arms. 'That is what I would very much like to know. After the war, my grandfather returned to France, but my grandmother had grown independent, and no longer wanted him. My father by then was fifteen years old, and hardly knew his father. There was disagreement, my grandfather started to drink, and finally, in 1947, he left the house and joined the Merchant Marine in Cherbourg under a false name, so the company could not take from his salary to send to his wife.'

'How did she find out about this?'

'Because from time to time my grandfather sent cards to Bernard Marti, an old army comrade in Cherbourg, who was still friendly with the family. When she discovered where my grandfather was, my grandmother could have taken him to court for her support and my father's, but she was a hardworking woman, and did not choose to do this, especially after my father began to work, too.'

143

'What happened to this, er . . . old army comrade of your grandfather's who blew the whistle on him?'

'Bernard Marti? He is alive today at over ninety years. He lives in Dieppe with his daughter.'

'And your grandmother and father would have been in Berneval at this time?'

'Yes, my grandmother had gone there during the war to work as a housekeeper, and later with my father opened the family hotel. They were the most industrious people.'

'And you're now carrying on the business there.'

'That is correct.'

'So your grandfather – the one who knew my grandfather in Jersey and joined the Merchant Navy – simply disappeared after the war?'

'As I have said, he used false papers to avoid paying my mother her *cotisation* from his salary, and since then we hear nothing of him.'

'And you've nothing left of him – photographs, letters – anything?'

A smile creased the long, pale face, as Ramier reached into his inside pocket and drew out a picture postcard, encased in a polythene wallet.

'Monsieur Marti, my grandfather's ex-comrade in Dieppe, was kind enough to give me this.'

I took the proffered card, in its protective wallet, and looked at the picture. A blurred colour representation of Piccadilly Circus, with 1950s cars in evidence. On the message side was Monsieur Marti's name and French address under a threepenny stamp with the head of a youthful Queen on it, and the cancellation date 8th August 1955. The message read only: *Cher Bernard – Tu te souviens? Philippe.* What was Philippe asking Bernard to remember, though?

'The date over the stamp's the tenth anniversary of the end of the war in Europe,' I commented. 'VE Day. Maybe your grandfather and his ex-comrade took part in the

Victory Parade and celebrations in London in 1945, and that's what he's asking Marti if he remembers?'

'*C'est ça!*' my companion agreed.

I had a mental picture of a couple of sharp-featured French likely lads, surrounded by raving peroxide-blonde girls with Betty Grable hairdos and wearing pillar-box red lipstick. Quite a few jars sunk, no doubt, and quite a bit of grass flattened . . .

'Since then,' Ramier was going on, 'nothing . . .'

One thing was sure, I reflected: Philippe couldn't have looked up my grandfather on his nostalgic trip to England in 1955, since he'd died five years before.

'Wars unsettle people,' I remarked, handing the postcard back to Ramier. 'Maybe your grandfather emigrated – Canada? Australia?'

'In spite of all, I am sure the point of departure is here in England. I typed in your grandfather's name on the Internet, and there is a village called Rolvenden in the county of Kent. Also your name came up – you are an author – two authors together, in the county of Suffolk with your wife!'

'Not two any more . . .'

Ramier made a sympathetic grimace.

'Evidently,' he went on. 'I searched in the telephone book for the Holt, which you describe in your book, and found your name in the list. I called the number, and Mrs Rolvenden answered, and she offered to come and talk to me in my hotel. Perhaps you are wondering why I came to Mrs Hague's house?'

I was, rather, but just let this smooth character go on.

'On Friday I attended the saleroom at Walberswick because I saw previously on a website that a print I was interested in was to be offered there. Mrs Hague bought it, and I understand her husband is an *antiquaire* here.'

I nodded.

'Is the print connected with your search for your, er . . . roots, Monsieur Ramier?'

'Yes, it is connected indirectly with my great-grandmother.'

'Ah, yes – the lady who, er, committed the *crime passionnel* in 1909 . . .'

'Yes, she was English.'

'Oh? Might I ask her name?'

'But of course, it is a charming and musical name: Bugle. Carrie Bugle.'

Chapter Fourteen

I sat back in a sort of awe, which, judging by the narrow, complacent smile on Ramier's face, had not been unexpected by him. The last thing recorded of Carrie in Grandfather's notebook had been her declaration that she was pregnant by him, and his consequent 'arrangements' for that eventuality.

'Was there any knowledge in your family,' I asked the Frenchman, 'of your great-grandmother's having a child before she met your great-grandfather in 1907?'

Ramier spread his hands.

'If so, it has not come down to my generation.'

My mind went back to Leah's speculation that I might have a whole brood of French cousins. And now I'd just learned that, not only had Carrie Bugle had a child by my grandfather, but she'd later married a Frenchman, had a son by him, then killed her husband in the course of a domestic . . .

'Do you know what part of England your great-grandmother came from?'

'My father told me once that my grandfather, Philippe, had told him she came from Broome, but did not say much more about her, except that she drank a lot – when life is hard, one must have something – and was not polite.'

'And,' I pressed, 'I suppose your father would've been too young really to have known your great-grandmother, Carrie?'

'He was only aged three years when she died in 1933. The alcoholism . . .'

I sighed as the realization of what Carrie Bugle's later life had been passed through my mind: it was all too clear. But, as for her origins: Broome?

'Lord knows how many place names there are in Britain with variants of "broom" in them.' I voiced my doubts as to this aspect.

The French visitor spread his hands again.

'Don't I know it . . . You cannot help me, then, Mr Rolvenden?'

'Not at the moment, but if anything comes my way, how can I contact you?'

'My plans are very, er . . . changeable at the moment, perhaps you could . . .'

I fumbled in my jacket for a business card with my contact details – better a phone call than waking up to more seaweed stinks in the sitting room . . . The long Frenchman took the card, then we got up. There was another round of handshakes, and we put on our outside things.

'May I say again, Mr Rolvenden, what a pleasure to meet the grandson of a benefactor of my family! We must keep in touch.'

I nodded without too much enthusiasm.

'Now,' Ramier said, 'I think I shall call on Mr Frank Hague the *antiquaire*.'

We moved to the door, then parted on the pavement.

'*Au revoir*, Mr Rolvenden.'

I gave an absorbed parting nod before making for my car, but my mind was engrossed by what this Ramier had just told me. 'Broome . . .' I muttered out loud, as the Frenchman's car roared away in the distance. Then the penny dropped, and I stopped in my tracks and roared with laughter. To a French ear, 'Broome' was what Carrie's 'Brum' would've sounded like: Miss Bugle had been from Birmingham . . .

The first thing I thought of was the Family Records

Centre in Islington: did I have time for a quick trip up to London? I was up to schedule with the film bio and I could catch up with whatever might be in my Inbox after tea, burning the midnight oil, if necessary. In view of this godsend that had just fallen into my lap, I could hardly see how I could resist making the trip.

Settled, then, but first – before I forgot – I'd have to pop into the stationer's in Colchester to lay in a fresh stock of printer paper. I always forgot printer paper if I left it to the journey back. This little detour didn't take long, but as I drove away from the stationer's in the nearby provincial centre, something caught my eye among the shops: a white fascia with *The Triada Health Club* in blue lettering. It seemed to signify something, somehow – not the name, but the colour scheme, perhaps. And hadn't Pat Hague, I mused, been in tracksuit and trainers – health-club gear – when she'd buttonholed Leah at the filling station on Saturday morning with her mysterious provocation about Leah's *Guardian* letter?

Such fleeting impressions, however, were soon driven from my mind by the impact made on it by what Ramier had just told me. First of all, I didn't believe for a moment that the Frenchman had simply swanned over the Channel for a holiday themed round a search for his English roots. For one thing, he'd claimed to be a hotelier – presumably in a modest way of business – in Berneval, but, in view of the fact that the holiday season was just getting under way, it was a funny time to take a break. Then, by Ramier's own admission, the Rawbeck print at the auction we'd both attended in Walberswick had had some connection with his family tree. I didn't buy his just having happened to spot the lot advertised on some website or other.

And what lay behind Reet's confab with him that morning? Above all, why had she been in such a rage, both on entering the guest house Ramier had been staying in in Southwold, and on leaving it after the interview? Scarcely the response you'd have expected to a friendly chat about genealogy ... And she'd been after the bloody Rawbeck print of what looked my grandfather and the other model, too! It occurred to me: what if the other young man in the sketch had been modelled by the Vickybird? I felt as if I were fighting some sort of duel in a darkened cellar ...

These speculations accompanied me all the way to the Family Records Centre in London, where I traced Carrie Bugle through the 1881 Census to Birmingham: Castle Bromwich Workhouse, to be precise, in the orphanage of which she'd been dumped in 1877. No doubt the Master of the workhouse – in the tradition of *Oliver Twist* – had assigned a surname to her associated with her immediate discovery. Perhaps the catsmeat man had been around with his bugle when she'd been discovered. Despite the way she'd conned and cozened my grandfather in Paris, I began to feel for Carrie: 'to know everything is to forgive everything ...' Well, maybe I'd leave a question mark at the end of that adage for the moment.

Further along, there was no record of her in the 1891 Census, either for Birmingham or London, nor did she appear in the one for 1901, so I assumed she'd been on her travels from the age of fourteen or so, and had fetched up in London after the 1891 Census had been taken. Then a meteoric career on the music halls and as an artist's model, with Julian Rawbeck as her Svengali. She'd fled after my grandfather to Paris after Rawbeck's disappearance in 1899, followed shortly afterward by the Vickybird, so that would explain her absence from the 1901 Census.

It looked as if, like the Vickybird, Carrie had stayed permanently out of England, unless you counted her stay, with her son, Philippe, under my grandfather's protection in Jersey from 1921 to 1925, as residence in England. Knowing Nanny Rolvenden, she'd have taken even the overwhelming Carrie in her stride. And did Carrie's arrival on the island prompt Nanny to carry out her suggestion in her acceptance letter to Grandfather's proposal of marriage that, one day, they'd both read through the confessions in his little notebook?

I pictured the young Sebastian Rolvenden the First in 1900, living the *vie de Bohème* in Paris, swooning over Carrie's stale blouse, with the Vickybird stealing a slice off the loaf whenever his back's turned . . . But it was the bare bones of Carrie's life that stirred me: dumped on the steps of a workhouse as soon as she's born, out on to the streets at fourteen, then a brief glow of glory on the halls – Gatti's, with 'Tom Tinsley in the Chair!' – followed by a sort of immortality on Rawbeck's canvas, then murder and horror, with flight to Paris, and a child by my grandfather.

Afterwards, after he's left her for comfort and respectability in England, her long, booze-fuelled decline: a mismatch with a Frenchman, another child, then she kills her husband, followed by jail, then temporary refuge with my grandfather again in Jersey, then back after her son to France, and more booze amid the poverty that, like an untreated toothache, never leaves her, until death wraps its white cocoon round her at the age of fifty-six. But Carrie was by no means finished with me yet . . .

'You look lost – need any help with the computer?'

This from a thin young staffer in shirtsleeves, with a shaven skull and ginger bristles at the sides, and keen, helpful eyes behind thickish specs. I shall remember him . . .

'Er, no . . .' I said, startled out of my reverie. 'Just that I've discovered something a bit disconcerting.'

'Tracing your family line?'

'You could say that – indirectly.'

The young man's next statement had a hint in it of the confidential, as well as the professional – he clearly liked his job.

'It sounds obvious,' he went on, 'but you'd be surprised how many people jump a generation or two when they're researching their family histories. They think they know all there is to be known about, say, their grandparents, so

151

they tend to skip that generation, and often even that of their parents, which is a mistake.'

Of course it had been Carrie Bugle I'd been after on this occasion, but the assistant's remarks fitted my case, too – during my occasional researches into my grandfather in the past, I'd always started automatically with him. Nearer home, I don't think I'd ever even seen my own rather colourless father's birth certificate. I didn't know, for instance, whether you had to produce someone's birth certificate to register their death, and in Dad's case his old pal Bill Wallace in Lympne had had to do the necessary when he'd died suddenly in 1971 while staying with Bill. At the time, I'd been backpacking in Crete.

Come to think of it, I was rather hazy as to exactly where Dad had been born: I'd always assumed it had been in Cambridge, where my grandparents had settled after Sebastian the First's arrival back from Paris in 1900 to read for ordination as a parson. Grandfather had had his first curacy in Cambridge, too. Just for the record, it might be interesting to know where Dad had been born . . .

'I'd like to start with my father,' I said to the helpful assistant. 'He was born in 1900 – in Cambridge, I think.'

The young man showed me the ropes, and I started off, drawing blanks at Cambridge and the ecclesiastical rookery of Ely, seventeen miles away. Nor had the London Registries of the day known the infant A.H. Rolvenden. I caught the eye of the helpful assistant again, and he came back over to me. I explained the impasse I was in.

'Any record of foreign service in your family at the time?' he suggested. 'Armed services? British Empire?'

'His father – my grandfather – was a clergyman, actually.'

'Mmm . . . missions abroad – some postings were quite short. Does your family have any strong connection with a foreign country?'

'Not unless you count the Channel Islands as "foreign" . . . My grandfather's mother was a Jersey girl, but to my

152

knowledge, neither of my grandparents had any contact with the island until my grandfather went out there as a clergyman in 1919. He'd served as an army padre in France during the 1914 war, but apart from that, there was no foreign connection, unless, of course . . .'

'Yes? Go on.'

'My grandfather was an art student in Paris in the 1890s, and didn't come back to England till the spring of 1900.'

'Ah, right . . . If your grandparents were in France at the time, your father's birth may have been registered at the British Embassy in Paris.'

'Have you records of that here?'

'We do – let's see . . .'

When the assistant had come up with the information, he didn't seem a bit surprised by the gasp I couldn't help giving out – he must have seen so many such reactions before on the part of searchers like myself.

'Didn't I tell you?' the young man said quietly, as the bluish light of the computer screen was reflected by the lenses of his glasses, making him look like a hatless alchemist. 'It's always interesting to start at the beginning.'

'Interesting,' was hardly the word to describe my reaction, as I sat there, trying to adjust to the information on the cyberspace image of the copy of the handwritten entry, and trying to take in its full implications. But there it all was, inescapable: Sebastian John Rolvenden, aged twenty-five and described as a 'theological student', had indeed registered the birth of his son, Athelstan Hugh Rolvenden, at the British Embassy in Paris on 11th August 1900, the mother's name being given as Caroline Ann Bugle, aged twenty-three and described as 'of no occupation'.

Chapter Fifteen

Once outside the Family Records Office again, I made my way thoughtfully down Myddelton Street in search of my car. The preoccupied London faces on the street wore much the same expressions, but I felt I'd come out of the Centre a different Seb Rolvenden from the one who'd gone in. So the 'arrangements' my grandfather had made for Carrie's child had included his going with her – what did one wear to register offices in 1900? – to the British Embassy in Paris, and having it put on record that he was the father.

And this child – my father-to-be, 'A.H.' – hadn't been spirited away afterwards, hole-in-corner fashion, to some orphanage, but taken to England to be brought up by Grandfather and Nanny Rolvenden as their son. At that moment, as I walked the indifferent London pavement, Nanny's high-nosed face, with its confident smile, appeared in my mind's eye. To have taken on Dad as her own like that – what a woman! My already-high esteem for her had now shot sky-high. All right, I now knew she hadn't been my grandmother in the biological way, but love had its rights and title deeds, too, and by that token, I felt Nanny had been more my grandmother than ever!

Then there'd been Nanny's cryptic remark about me in the garden in Malmesbury when I was six, to the effect that 'the issue had been good' – I saw that remark in a new light, now. God bless her!

But back to Dad – how had this background affected him? He must've been told about his origins, because for one thing, he'd have needed his birth certificate for his first passport, but not a word to me about it ... God! I still couldn't take it in – I was Carrie Bugle's grandson! And when Carrie had come back into my grandfather's ken when she'd sought refuge, with her son by her French marriage, under his protection in Jersey in 1921, how had my staid young design-draughtsman father taken it? Though he'd already started his career in England, he must've come over occasionally in the holidays to visit Grandfather and Nanny in Jersey. Or had he? I mustn't think in twenty-first-century terms: such a meeting would've been socially impossible for Nanny, and if the situation had become known, it would have meant the end of Grandfather's career in the Church. No: some sort of pretext must have been cooked up, and Carrie and her son sworn to secrecy. I wonder, though, whether Carrie, Dad's real mother, had ever yearned to see her firstborn again? They were all silent now ...

But what tension there must have been in the vicarage, and what relief for Grandfather and Nanny when Philippe had got his French call-up papers, and Carrie had eventually followed him back to France. And then, a couple of years later, in 1927, my grandfather gets the hard-luck letter from the wife of the old thorn in his flesh – the Vickybird. All Sebastian would have needed to complete his unease would have been the appearance of the ghost of Rawbeck, Jacob Marley-like, with a gap where his throat should have been!

I sat in the car for a good five minutes, mulling things over in my mind, before deciding on my next move. It was just four o'clock, and now I was in London I thought I might as well check up, from the coded verses in Tarquin Rivers' poem 'The Burial of the Magus', the details of how he'd disposed of Julian Rawbeck's body. Bethnal Green station would be as good a starting-off point as any for the nearby Jews' Burial Ground. I drove off, weaving east-wards through the growing traffic, and found a parking space fairly easily near the station, but I sensed that it wasn't the sort of place to park in for too long . . .

I got out, and the walk in the fresh air did me good at first, but the gritty shabbiness of the East End soon got to me, and I felt my spirits sink as I emerged into the green space that was all that was left of the old cemetery. The most outstanding inscriptions there were the graffiti, gibberish of blown-out minds, and the only votive offerings on view plastic carrier bags, discarded pizza boxes, plastic bottles, stray trainers and worse.

I looked around me: besides Brady Street, the only thor-oughfare of any size was parallel Collingwood Street. Of the 1899 Reuben Street – disguised as Reuben's Court in Rivers' poem – there was now no trace, nor was there any-thing on the ground to mark where the Animal Charcoal Works – source of the Undying Smoke in the poem about the Magus – had stood. What had I expected after more than a century?

I turned round and went back up Brady Street again, recapitulating the narrative hidden in Rivers' poem as I walked. It's the night, then, of 11th November 1899, and Rivers is watching, unobserved, on the side of the road that faces the East Hackney pub where Rawbeck's body is found. Rivers witnesses the comings and goings that con-firm his suspicions that my grandfather's being set up for what's happened upstairs. He sees the four conspirators in the caper leave the pub – the way I read it, on the actual night Rivers would have seen my grandfather stagger out afterwards, too, but for obvious reasons omits this from the poem.

Well, then: Rivers, unable to wait any longer, rushes up to the murder room to find the artist's dead body, but no Sebastian Rolvenden. He decides to put his beloved 'S.R.' in the clear by disposing of Rawbeck's corpse, which, from the mention of 'ash' in the poem, he does by some form of cremation. First of all, though, he's got to get the artist's body out of the room, on to the landing with the stained-glass window, and down the staircase to the street. Ways and means . . .

I knew that Rivers was an ex-army man and an explorer in high-risk regions of the world, so I assumed he was pretty able-bodied; even so, Rawbeck was fairly hefty himself, and without an accomplice, how could Rivers possibly have carried his – literally – dead weight out of the pub and away unobserved?

Ah! But there'd have been at least one potential accomplice at the head of every street in London at the time – late-night cabbies . . . Rivers would have been used to blood and gore from his army days, so it's no great ordeal for him to tidy up the corpse, muffle a scarf round the lacerated neck, and ram the hat over the head. Gloves, too, would hide the coldness of the dead man's hands.

Rivers then checks that the way's clear, nips out and whistles up a cab: 'Gentleman upstairs has had one-over-the-eight, cabbie – I'll dash you an extra florin if you'll come up and help me down with him and get him into the cab . . .' Routine for the cabbie, and in the dark and murk of a late-autumn night he'd have had neither the visibility nor the incentive to examine the tipsy, unconscious gent too closely. It would have needed nerve on Rivers' part, of course, but his life had been one long risk . . .

That left me with the little matter of exactly how Rivers would have cremated Rawbeck's corpse without arousing too much attention – a fire would have had to be arranged . . . Where better to find out what fires had been laid on that night in the East End than in the columns of the archive issues of the *East London Advertiser*? As soon as I'd got into my car again – and not without a little sigh of relief that it was still there and in one piece – I drove to Tower Hamlets Local History Library and got them to rustle up the microfiched numbers of the *Advertiser* for November 1899. I found what I wanted in the 12th

November issue – just a single paragraph, under the title: *Fatal Fire in Pereira Street*:

The remains of an unidentified man were found in the early hours of this morning amid the ashes of an outhouse of the Collingwood Arms public house in Pereira Street, Bethnal Green. The wooden structure had been used as a coalhouse and oil-store, and a rum bottle and the fragments of a clay pipe were found at the fatal scene. It would seem that some unfortunate vagrant had used the outhouse as a shelter for the night, and, while in an intoxicated state, had lit his pipe near a paraffin-can, thus unwittingly causing the conflagration. An inquest is to be held on Friday.

I scrolled up the following Friday's number of the paper, to find an even shorter report on the inquest: death by misadventure, victim unknown. Just another faceless vagrant going under the wheels of London. Rivers must have known the Collingwood Arms, and that it had an oil-store in the back yard: maybe he'd accidentally strayed into the shed one night, on his way to the pub jakes. Nor would the cabbie have been fazed by a couple of toffs' – or at least the conscious one – asking to be put down among the bins behind a lowlife pub in Bethnal Green. Toffs had their amusements lined up in all sorts of funny places, and maybe Rivers had increased the cabbie's tip to five bob . . .

And, of course, when much later Rawbeck's absence from his known haunts had begun to be noticed, there'd have been absolutely nothing to connect his seeming disappearance with the death of an unknown tramp in an oil-store blaze in Bethnal Green. Certainly, in the standard books on Rawbeck I'd read to date, there'd been no hint of such a connection, though many allusions had been made to the artist's penchant for hanging out in low places.

But there was another figure who'd gone missing on that autumn early morning in 1899 – Forbuoys the flautist.

He reminded me of the songbird in the French *chanson*, desperately singing to attract a mate. Had Carrie been at the bottom of the mental turmoil that had led him to his quietus in the dark waters of the Thames, his pockets filled with stones – and a razor that wasn't his own?

If my guess was right, I could picture the fatal scene at Convocation, with Forbuoys playing his dirge on the flute for the benefit of the gathered illuminati, then the company breaks up, Rawbeck leaving first, then my grandfather – whether under his own steam or helped – then Rivers, who has his own plans for the night . . . If my surmise was right, for Forbuoys everything would have taken on the shape of Carrie: perhaps he'd thought Rawbeck and my grandfather were sneaking off after *her* that night . . . Maybe the pub with the magic window *had* been a former meeting place for the showgirl and whoever in the Camden Hill circle might be enjoying her favours at the time, all except lonely Philip Forbuoys, that is. Maybe he'd followed Carrie to the pub on previous occasions, longing but not daring . . .

Anyway, it all comes to a head. Forbuoys, an obsessive type, finally cracks – if he can't have Carrie, he'll eliminate the principal opposition – Rawbeck and my grandfather – with one master-stroke. Rawbeck will die on the spot, and the young Sebastian will hang later for his murder. At the end of the magic mushroom session, having laid his plans, Philip Forbuoys leaves the house, equipped with either my grandfather's or a second-hand razor, and makes for the pub in East Hackney.

Imagine his horror when, on arriving in the assignation room, he finds neither Rawbeck nor my grandfather, the artist having already been done in by the Vickybird, young Sebastian having already come out of his trance on the bed and done a runner, and Tarquin Rivers having got rid of the artist's body. The drama has already been played out . . . Forbuoys looks round the room, only to see a phantasmagoria of blood. Unhinged, he flees the scene, and an agonized wander through the City of Dreadful Night follows, till the poor flautist finds some sort of peace in the black eddies under Tower Bridge. As my grandfather might have put it: *pax cineribus.*

The only initiate not in on the murder of his guru and pandar, Rawbeck, is effete Jimmie Toland, whose innocence is borne out by the fact that he's the only one of the principal players who doesn't run away after Rawbeck's disappearance. No doubt things are explained to Jimmie later by the Vickybird or his London representative. They'd have pointed out to him, too, how urgently desirable it was that the Vice Squad shouldn't come into possession of proof of what his private life had been, and of the part they might play in keeping it all among friends. At a price, of course ... The Vickybird would have remembered how Rawbeck had blackmailed *him* into being nice to Jimmie and his more exotic clients, and, with the boot on the other foot, wouldn't have been kind to Toland.

It all held together, I mused, as I drove back to Essex on that late afternoon. I decided to stop off at Frank Hague's shop in Wivenhoe to find out if the Frenchman, Ramier, whom I'd caught that forenoon trying the door of their boathouse, had been to see Frank, as he'd said he would.

Frank must have been on his travels since I'd last seen him, nine days before, for there was a car-park ticket marked Folkestone on the windscreen of his shabby Ford, which I found parked in the entrance to the cobbled yard at the side of his shop. He was busy with a customer when I went into the front shop, so I walked over to the wall where his pictures hung, pride of place going to an actual Stanley Spencer sketch, though a very minor one. It was a little pencil job of a Thirties shopgirl – *Woolworth's Girl* – her bobbed hair pulled in with a grip, and a peculiarly moving look on her face made up of equal parts of weariness and wistful unintelligence. The old-fashioned doorbell tinged behind me as the customer left.

160

'How Spencer loved his subjects . . .' came Frank's voice over my shoulder.

'Mmm . . . he thought people were all holy.'

'I could never take that leap,' Frank said. 'I just see them as human.'

'Bit of a tall order, isn't it? But I suppose that's the difference between the likes of us and a genius. Take a fiver for it?'

'Plus a few noughts! How's tricks?'

'Trickier than ever – how's France?'

For a moment, I could read consternation on the ruddy, bearded face.

'The car-park ticket on your banger outside – Folkestone . . .'

'Oh, that – no, not France. I was down in Folkestone yesterday – at a fair.'

'Anything interesting?'

'Just browsing – pictures and prints – I'm trying to build up a competence in it. Funny you should mention France . . .'

'Oh?' I said, pricking up my mental ears.

'There was a Frenchman in here round lunchtime, looking at the pictures, just as you've been doing.'

'Was he after anything in particular?'

'Not really – he said he was studying the English "sensibility", as he put it. Nice chap – you get more and more Continentals coming over now – I'm all for that.'

Monsieur Ramier must have been casing the shop, I reflected, just as he'd been casing the Hagues' boathouse earlier on in the day.

'I'm all for them coming over, too,' I took up Frank's thread, 'but it depends on what they've come over for.'

'I'm sure you're going to tell me what this is all about, Seb.'

'Was this Frenchman tall and thin – formal suit – with his hair in a Tintin quiff?'

'Yes. Go on.'

161

'I was going to say that he says his name's Ramier, and I caught him trying the handle of the boathouse door this morning. I referred him to this shop, in fact.'

'Ah, you just happened to call at the boathouse, then?'

I thought I detected the suggestion of a taunt in Frank's voice – the Pat thing – but maybe it was just my conscience.

'I followed him to the boathouse, in fact. He's been sniffing round the lighthouse and other places I've been to recently. He said he was looking for Pat, and I know she spends a lot of time there.'

No doubt there'd be a number of callers at their joint weekend retreat – now Pat's province – that Frank wouldn't know about, nor, I guessed, want to know about.

'Just thought I'd tell you,' I concluded. 'Bods trying doors when they think no one's looking's a bit out of order.'

'I appreciate it, Seb – thanks for telling me. I'll warn Pat, and we'll be double-checking locks and alarms in future.'

I refused Frank's offer of a drink, left and went back to my car, wondering whether I should have said more to Frank, but no – Pat was his wife, and I'd given him fair warning about Ramier. She'd insisted on buying the damned Rawbeck print at the auction in the first place, so let her take the consequences, whatever they were going to be. Clearly, one of them was that she was going to be given the stalking treatment by the inquisitive Frenchman.

I stopped in my tracks for a moment: I'd referred to Ramier as a 'bod' and 'the Frenchman', but if there was anything in the story he'd told me over brunch in the yacht-emporium cafeteria – if he really was descended from Carrie Bugle – then we were related! *Mon cousin*, or whatever! Really, what I'd learned just a few hours before at the Family Records Centre in London was going to take some getting used to . . .

But now I simply had to tell Leah about my latest – and up to now most momentous – findings. I got into the car

162

and drove straight to her flat on the university campus. I found her in, and we sat on the sofa in her little sitting room and talked over what I'd discovered up in London.

'Your father's origins explain his behaviour,' she remarked. 'His diffidence – his obvious desire to sink into the background.'

'Like an uninvited guest,' I remarked.

'Yes, when he found out he wasn't really your grandmother's son, he'd have felt like an imposter – there on sufferance.'

'I'm sure Nanny would have given him all the affection, and Grandfather the security, he'd needed for a happy life.'

'I don't doubt that one bit, but your dad would've *known* ... He'd have internalized the thing, probably thought that if he was discreet about it, saw to it that it never went beyond the family circle – and the half-dozen or so anonymous figures who'd have been privy to his birth certificate – then it wouldn't make any odds. Just build his life *around* it, but be discreet – above all, be discreet ...'

'I'd never really seen it in that light, Leah, but it makes sense, especially in the light of social attitudes in Dad's day. He had to protect his identity – that's so important to us, after all.'

'Oh, but it's *all* we've got, Seb ... It goes without saying that your father would have been totally screwed up about sex, too. Probably no girlfriends in his youth, not getting married till he was in his forties. I wonder what gave him the confidence then?'

'Dad went straight from school into an engineering apprenticeship – he ended up as a technical director in a big aircraft plant near Southampton. He was very much on the technical side, and came into his own during the war as a sort of army boffin. What few real friendships he made during his life all dated from the war.'

'That boost to his self-image – along with the uniform

– would have given him just enough self-confidence to make a play for your mother.'

'She was an assistant – no doubt bored stiff with the job – in a bookshop in Harrogate when Dad was running an army course near there. He told me that on about six separate occasions he'd gone into the shop and bought completely unreadable books, just for an excuse to get into conversation with her! He was tall and slim, then, with sandy hair – quite good-looking in the English fashion. I can just imagine his initial chat-up line: "Girl like you must get pretty cheesed off in a hole-in-corner place like this . . ."'

We both chuckled.

'And you must've been gobsmacked,' Leah went on, 'to find out that Carrie Bugle had been *your* real grand-mother.'

'I'll say, but it hasn't really sunk in yet.'

'You say that your grandfather fixed up Carrie and her other son, Philippe, with jobs and accommodation on Jersey?'

'Mmm . . . from 1921 till 1925, when Philippe got called up for the French army. They'd been on their uppers in France, and Grandfather had done the decent thing by them.'

'And I'll bet that Carrie's booze habit would have given him plenty of opportunities to develop his Christian forbearance!'

We both laughed.

'And you really think your grandfather and Nanny Rolvenden actually succeeded in keeping your father away from Carrie and his half-brother in Jersey? Your father'd have had school holidays, Christmasses and so on . . .'

'Dad would've been twenty-one when his real mother and her son landed on the island, and by then he'd have had his nose well and truly to the grindstone at his job in Southampton. As for Carrie and Philippe, I'm sure there'd have been some sort of understanding between Dad and Grandfather.'

'*So* many compartments to your grandfather's life!' Leah exclaimed. 'And how uneasy your father must've been: never off guard, always the Keeper of the Secret . . .'

'I feel a lot closer to Dad now, after what I've just learned in London.'

'I daresay, Seb, but think of Carrie, too – your newly discovered grandmother – when all's said and done, she was a music hall artiste and celebrated model – her image is still to be seen in art galleries and prints. Rejoice and be proud, dammit – she was a star!'

I laughed, but then a sudden sadness overwhelmed me.

'Right, right, Leah, but, God – they're all gone: Grandfather with his compartments and confessions, Carrie with her flaming red hair and hips like a snake's, Dad with his pipe and his reticences, Nanny with her character and kindness and her hair in earphones. All gone as if they'd never been: just temporary smears of sensation . . .'

Something avid and challenging came into Leah's dark eyes.

'Then it's all the more important, Seb, that we make them enjoyable sensations.'

I moved across the sofa to meet her.

Chapter Sixteen

Two days later, on the Wednesday evening, I received an unprecedented visit from my son Paul. Unprecedented, because, as far as I knew, it was the first time he'd ever set foot on the headland. Added to my usual feelings towards my estranged son – guilt, sorrow, irrational anger at him for not loving me – was the conviction that what he'd now come to see me for was not for the ears of his mother. He could always have phoned or emailed me: no, it must be important to him.

I came downstairs from my computer, answered his ring at the door, and ushered him into the sitting room, where he flung himself on to the cane sofa, which creaked in elderly protest. Paul sat and glowered up at me while I struggled for something to say.

'How's your –' I began to dance round the subject of his mother.

'This French guy,' Paul interrupted me. 'Ramier. He was in the village post office at Thruxton this morning – I thought he'd left the area? He checked out of the Low Light in Southwold on Monday morning. Mum said we wouldn't be seeing any more of him: what's going on? Is he working with the little Irish guy? I think it's time you –'

'I don't know about Brogan, but the Frenchman's a hotel-keeper from Normandy – or that's what he says he is – and has a notion we're related through an old flame of Grandfather's. I'm looking into that.'

'Ah, the Adventures of St Sebastian again . . . Christ, Dad – get a life!'

Thanks, at least, for the 'Dad' . . .

'Is that all his game is, then?' Paul went on. 'Genealogy?'

I shook my head. 'Some sort of painting's involved – by a Victorian artist who disappeared in unexplained circumstances way back. Brogan's after it, too, and I daresay there are others. I'm looking into that, too.'

I was waiting for Paul to demand whether I'd put Ramier on to his mother and him, but he didn't, which suggested to me that Reet had already prepared him for the visit to the area by the Frenchman. And not a mention so far of Reet's visit to the auction rooms . . .

'Did Ramier talk to you in the post office this morning?' I went on.

'Just a little nod – he gives me the creeps, with that Men in Black suit and the dark glasses.'

'Well, there's nothing you can do about his being up there: I daresay he'll still be sniffing around for this painting I mentioned, and has it occurred to you . . .'

'What?'

'That he might think that *you're* stalking him . . .'

My son's eyes widened with puzzlement – they were brown like Reet's, and I couldn't help noticing how his features were becoming more and more like mine as they strengthened with age.

'But that's ridiculous, Dad!'

'Have you had any real contact with Ramier? Talked to him, I mean?'

'Not directly: early on last week the landlady from the Low Light Inn rang the Holt when Mum wasn't in, and I took the call.'

So that was how the missus of the Low Light had mistaken my voice for my son's when I'd rung the inn!

'She said a French gentleman had just checked in,' Paul went on, 'and that he wanted to let Mum know he'd be ready for their appointment. When I told Mum later, she said all right, and closed the subject. You know how she can be ... But she's been all sort of preoccupied ever since.'

'Look, Paul: just go about your normal business, take the usual precautions, and don't worry ...'

But my son was distinctly rattled, if the clenched fists and fugitive eyes were anything to go by.

'Ramier's in the open, now,' I went on, 'and he'd be mad to try anything illegal – I just think he's a chancer – maybe a dodgy antique dealer.'

'And that's all he's told you: he thinks he may be related to us, and he's looking for his roots?'

'Straight up and down, my son. I'm on his trail, though.'

'D'you think the little Irish guy and Ramier are working together?'

'A good question – I shall have to look into that.'

'Have you seen the Irish guy since I caught him sniffing around at the Holt?'

'Mmm ... he reckons he's picked up some of Grandfather's stuff in Jersey, and he's trying to suss out how much I know about it.'

'Including this lost painting you mentioned?'

'That's my suspicion – something's opened up in Jersey, something big, that's starting to pull in the dealers. There may be other bods turning up here and in Suffolk, so we'll just have to roll with it.'

'I could go and meet this guy, Brogan, and see what –'

'No, Paul – you've got your plate full enough at the moment, with the development of the smallholding project, and, besides, you're not exactly one of Nature's ambassadors, you know.'

My son smiled – the first time I'd seen him smile since the Troubles – and it was like a blessed truce, but he then snorted with his usual impatience.

'As for Brogan,' I went on, 'rest assured that if I can winkle anything out of him that has any possible bearing on your and Mum's life at the Holt, you'll be the first to know, and the same goes for Ramier.'

Paul was already on his feet, and didn't shake off my hand when I put it lightly on his shoulder. I disengaged the hand as he turned towards the door, then, on the threshold, he turned and faced me, a sort of speculative puzzlement in his eyes.

'D'you really believe this French guy's related to us?'

'I thought you weren't interested in the Saga of St Sebastian . . .' I couldn't resist saying.

My son stepped through the open door on to the pathway.

'Just find out what's going on, Dad – that's all. I don't want Mum upset any more.'

Soon all I could see of my son was the rear of the Land Rover disappearing up the headland. I went indoors to ring Leah up, and bring her up to date about Paul's visit.

'Jealousy!' was her immediate response to my description of my son's call at the lighthouse. 'Plain as eggs.'

'Eh? Really, I don't see what –'

'Oh, come on, Seb! More than a year after your separation from your wife, you and your quest for your grandfather are still a hot topic of conversation at the Holt, and now that this mysterious foreign visitor comes dogging your son's footsteps, it turns out he's only interested in you!'

'I've tried to make amends to Paul – really I have.'

'Tell me, then, Seb: on this visit – the first he's made to your new place, right? – did you ask him how things were going at the Holt? How the new students' annexe was shaping up? If he was short of money? How his love life was going?'

'I just wish I was on those sort of terms with him again – he'd only have told me to get stuffed.'

'But did you think of asking?'

I paused awhile – food for thought – before answering.

'Leah, you said you were getting fed up with teaching,

didn't you? How about working for me as secretary, analyst and sex plaything? Say, ten quid a week?'

'In your dreams! But seriously, I should ring Brogan up and find out if he knows anything about this Frenchman, Ramier.'

'Just about to.'

We exchanged goodbyes, and I rang off. I then rustled up Liam Brogan's business card and rang the number of the Victoria hotel he'd scribbled on it. It seemed he was just on the point of going out, but he'd be happy to give me any information he could. I explained about Ramier, the man in dark glasses, and heard the puckish chuckle from the other end.

'Yes, I spotted him at the auction in Walberswick, too. Bit of a wild card, that 'un, but very plausible with it. He's been round to my place in St Helier, but just to browse. I don't think he's a professional dealer, though: he doesn't really talk the talk.'

'Well, you should know . . . He told me he was a hotel-keeper in Normandy.'

'Is that so? Well, for a hotelier, he seems to have a lot of spare time. By the way, I was on the point of ringing you: I've got something to show you.'

'Yes?'

'Ah, taxi's here. I really have to go now – date with an important client. How about lunch here tomorrow? Hotel restaurant's pretty good – say, twelve-thirty?'

I fell in with this, and went up to London next morning to keep my lunch date with Brogan. The hotel turned out to be a new place, in one of those garden squares behind the Green Line bus concourse at the back of Victoria station. The restaurant was Indonesian, and a beaming Brogan was standing behind one of the tables, his rough, pink hand pointed in my direction like the hand of an old-fashioned country road sign. I went up and squeezed it briefly, then sat in the chair opposite my host's. There was an intriguing-looking buff envelope lying near

170

Brogan's place at the table. He rubbed his hands like an over-eager chef.

'I recomment the *rijstafel*, with some nice, cold lager.'

And very good it was, too. My companion paid the sizzling curry the respect one would have expected from a connoisseur, and the round, pink face under the little mat of silver bristles positively glowed with well-being as he did justice to the meal.

'This Ramier feller you mentioned on the phone yesterday evening,' he said between appreciative little chomps at his food. 'Interesting: sense of things hotting up . . .'

'Talking of hotting up, this is excellent curry.'

Brogan's baby-blue eyes twinkled, and he grinned good-humouredly.

'Not at all bad . . . But Ramier's on the same lines as us.'

So now we were in it together, I thought?

'D'you mean he's after the lost Rawbeck painting, *The Ruffian on the Stair*?'

My vis-à-vis nodded.

'*The Ruffian* . . .' he repeated in confirmation.

The hot towels arrived, and we ordered another round of lagers. Sleepy gamelan music was wafting from the Muzak as Brogan wiped his scarlet face with his towel, then gazed at me in a rather dreamy fashion for a moment.

'Death,' he said abruptly, 'is of course the Ruffian on the Stair. You know the Victorian verse Rawbeck got his title from for the painting?'

I recalled again the opening lines:

> *Madam Life's a piece in bloom*
> *Death goes dogging everywhere:*
> *She's the tenant of the room,*
> *He's the ruffian on the stair.*

Brogan picked up the envelope at his side – one of those jobs with a stiff back to it – and carefully drew out something encased in what looked like tissue paper. He carefully unwrapped the object and held it up to me.

'May I introduce Madam Life,' Brogan announced importantly, 'the tenant of the room.'

It was a sketch – just a few essential charcoal strokes – of a staircase, with, halfway up it, the squat figure of an old woman in Victorian dress, a little bonnet on her drawn-up hair. She was looking out from the sketch, and on her crudely but powerfully drawn features could be read alarm and incipient panic. This was horribly but very well evoked. On the landing of the stairs, waiting in the shadows for Madam Life as she made her way upstairs, was a shaded outline of a male form, malignant intent in his wary crouch. But what caught my attention above all were the rough lines which suggested a landing window, the window being edged by alternate lightly and heavily shaded oblong side panes. Like the window outside the room where my grandfather found Julian Rawbeck's body . . .

'It's not signed,' was my first response.

'It's the lad, though – it's a Rawbeck!' Brogan spluttered, carefully wrapping the acid-free tissue round the square of cartridge paper again, and replacing it in the stiff-backed envelope. 'The power and terseness of the drawing, and the sheer, lively *malice* of it . . .'

'When was it done?'

'The experts put it before 1895, when he started branching out from macabre subjects.'

I kept quiet at this point, but I dated the sketch more precisely to 1893, when Mrs Bella Nye had been murdered in her pub. I suspected she'd been Madam Life as represented in Rawbeck's sketch, with Death, the Ruffian on the landing, played in real life by Laurence Victor Pidgeon, the Vickybird, then Mrs Nye's cellar boy and general kickabout. So this had been one of the blackmail-levers Rawbeck had had against the Vickybird . . .

'Rawbeck doesn't seem to have worked up an actual

painting from the sketch,' Brogan was going on. 'More's the pity.'

And if he had made one, I reflected, the Vickybird would have burnt it on finding it in his master's possessions after he'd murdered him.

'The sketch you've just shown me's about the same size as the print you offered at the Walberswick auction,' I remarked, changing tack slightly. 'Did it come from the same batch in Jersey?'

Brogan's eyes twinkled more frostily than ever. He tapped the side of his nose with a blunt, pink finger.

'Client confidentiality, Mr Rolvenden – client confidentiality . . . I recall at the auction your wife gave that other lady a fair run for her money for the other little Rawbeck work of mine, but then the lady who made the successful bid is married to a dealer. You must know her quite well, Mr Rolvenden: I couldn't help noticing you were in pretty lively conversation with her at the auction.'

So Brogan had witnessed my spat with Pat Hague in the auction room, too.

'I was at school with the lady's husband,' I said. 'We're old friends.'

'And you didn't actually bid for *Morte Moriantur* . . .'

'I'd already had a good look at it at the viewing the day before.'

'You know, Mr Rolvenden, I like Suffolk – the most private of your English counties – and there's an odd melancholy about the coast, a sort of look-thy-last quality as it slides into the sea. I feel I must get to know the region better . . .'

Brogan was drawing me into greater and greater detail, and I knew it would just be a matter of time before he'd put his oar in irretrievably, and compromise my search for the truth about my grandfather. Better wind this up before I'd blurted out too much . . .

'Well, that's certainly a fascinating sketch,' I said,

173

dabbing my lip with the napkin. 'Thank you for showing it to me, and for an excellent lunch!'

We both got up, and exchanged final handshakes across the table.

'You know where to find me, Mr Rolvenden.'

I walked out into the bustle of Belgrave Road again, my mind full of thoughts. I decided to go up across Warwick Way and take a turn round the railed garden of Eccleston Square. It was a spring ritual of mine while in London to do the circuit of the splendid camellias in the square. I crossed to the corner of the leafy pleasance, and the traffic roar seemed to be soothed away by the startling, glossy-dark greenness of the evergreen foliage. The beauty parade began with the lush pink gorgeousness of the riotous blooms of a latish display of Donation, and I made my way deliberately down along the high iron railings, like a meditating monk in a cloister. As I paced, I considered what had passed during my lunch with Liam Brogan.

The Rawbeck artworks, then, and how to fit them into my grandfather's story. The one Reet and Pat had been interested in at the Walberswick auction – *Morte Moriantur* – had been the print of the sketch of my grandfather and another young man in what would have been a highly suggestive and in fact compromising pose in the 1890s of the Oscar Wilde case. This – or rather, the original – I was sure, would have been the Rawbeck work Grandfather mentioned in his notebook as having been stolen by the Vickybird and sold to the Paris art dealer, Carbonero. The one the first Sebastian Rolvenden had been eager to get back at all costs. Why on earth had Reet wanted it, though?

The unattributed charcoal sketch Brogan had just shown me – let's call it *The Tenant of the Room* – I strongly suspected to have been meant by Julian Rawbeck to represent Mrs Nye, the pub landlady who'd been murdered while the Vickybird had been in her employ. Most interestingly, the landing window of the stairs on which Mrs Nye was standing in the sketch confirmed my suspicion that her and Rawbeck's murders, though six years apart, had been committed in the same pub, the Ring of Bells in Lefevre Road, which wasn't far from the Home in the East and Soundings Alley mentioned in my grandfather's notebook.

This charcoal sketch, no doubt, would have been used by the artist as a sort of Sword of Damocles to be held over the head of the Vickybird – a reminder of his crime – to keep him in line. Rawbeck would've had other, more material proofs in his blackmail arsenal against him, I was sure. Whether there'd been a completed version of the sketch in oils, disposed of by the Vickybird after he'd silenced Rawbeck for good, was merely academic now.

As to where Brogan stood in all this, my original theory concerning all the things he'd shown me up to now – the Rolvenden heirloom razor, Julian Rawbeck's platinum tiepin, the *Morte Moriantur* print and now the macabre charcoal sketch – had been strengthened. I was more convinced than ever that the Irish dealer had acquired them from the same person in Jersey that had originally looted my grandfather's effects there in 1940. The original thief had recently died on the island, and his shamefaced heirs had handed what had been left of my grandfather's hoard in their possession – the notebook and the rest of the contents of the Jiffy bag – to Lawyer Le Touzel to send on to me. The one thing Brogan clearly hadn't yet got his eager red hands on, though, was the lost Rawbeck masterpiece, *The Ruffian on the Stair*. The race was still on for that.

'Fahkin' dimbo!'

The curse came from a stretched-out form I'd almost stumbled headlong over, and I found myself muttering an apology to what looked like the leather face, under a stocking-cap, of a Danish bog-burial at my feet. Well and truly wrenched out of my reverie of 1890s East Hackney, I left the vagrant to his sprawlings, and strode back to the main thoroughfare of this corner of modern London in search of my car.

When, a few hours later, I'd got back to my Essex lighthouse, there was something waiting for me in my Inbox: a skittish message from Pat Hague which suggested that she'd managed to squeeze some destabilizing mischief out of the Rawbeck print she'd forked out a couple of grand for at the Walberswick auction.

The message read: *Care to step over to the boathouse for Pidgeon pie?*

Chapter Seventeen

Pat had meant the message as a wind-up, of course, but where had she got the 'Pidgeon'? Some detail of the *Morte Moriantur* sketch I'd missed at the auction viewing, perhaps? Then I groaned inwardly: I was the father of all chumps . . . There could've been something written on the back of the print. I hadn't bothered to ask to be shown it at the time. Brogan would know, of course, but I'd trust him as far as I could throw him. Reet, then – she must've made a thorough examination of the print, to have made a bid of nearly two thousand pounds for it next day. I'd trust her: she'd conceal, but when fairly challenged, would tell the truth. I flopped down in my swivel chair, and, reaching for my mobile, pegged in the number of the Holt. My ex-wife's voice answered.

'Seb here, Reet: that sketch you bid for at the auction the other week . . .'

A pregnant moment followed before Reet answered, with tension in her voice.

'Yes . . . What about it?'

'I'm not going to pry into why you wanted it – that's your business – but could you possibly tell me if there was anything written on the back? I daresay you'd have looked at it closely at the viewing on the Thursday?'

'Why d'you want to know – what's this all about?'

'That's the sixty-four thousand dollar question, dear heart! It's just occurred to me that there might have been something on the back of the print that could provide a clue as to my grandfather's early life. I never thought to look at the back of it at the viewing.'

'Oh, I see . . .'

There was now unmistakable relief in Reet's voice.

'No, Seb, there was nothing written on the back of the print. I looked, and there was nothing at all.'

I thanked her and rang off. So that was that. So where *had* Pat got this 'Pidgeon' angle from? She was playing games, of course, and the very thing she wanted was for me to go down to the boathouse and be baited, and here I was getting ready to do just that . . . But if it was something genuinely new about Laurence Victor Pidgeon, I simply couldn't afford to pass it up. With a sigh of pure defeat, I took up my mobile again and tried the number of the Hagues' boathouse. Flinching in anticipation of Pat's triumphant crowings, I waited for the answering voice, but none came, and eventually the recorded message litany came through.

It was on the tip of my tongue to record the message: 'What about that pie you promised me?' but of course, this must be part of the new game – I had to sit up and beg for my titbit. Angrily, I switched off the mobile – that was it! Sod her – it'd only have been a blag, anyway, and life was too short. I got up off the chair and walked over to the window, staring out across the flats. 'Pidgeon' with a 'd': it was irresistible . . .

I went downstairs to the front door, which I slammed locked behind me, jumped into my car, and drove straight over to the Wivenhoe marina and the Hagues' boathouse, only to find the place locked up and silent. My persistent ringings at the doorbell, then knockings, and finally tappings at the window shutters got no response, and, incandescent, I jumped back in the car and drove home again. Led by the nose again. Leah had been right: I shouldn't be let out on my own . . .

Back at the lighthouse, I flung myself into an article I'd been commissioned to do, and worked single-mindedly on it till nine. The concentration and steady industry needed to complete the task calmed me down, and a hefty omelette afterwards with a couple of glasses of Merlot finished the process. By ten I was in my cane armchair in the sitting room, a mug of coffee at my side. Pat or no Pat, I thought, my researches would go on. Reet was now holding out on me over my quest for my grandfather, and this made me even more determined to get to the bottom of the business. I don't like loose ends – they make me feel tense – and I had to clear the air.

My mind went back to Brogan, and his perpetual pulling of rabbits out of hats to find out what I knew about the Rawbeck affair. Thinking of Brogan made me think of Jersey, the source and beginning of all this, and where, perhaps, the key to the mystery might lie. That discreet island had turned sour on me now, of course, what with my stupid involvement with Pat having begun there. My jag of adulterous lust there a couple of years before had smeared a dirty mark over the happy memories I had of blue bays and sparkling summer seas with Reet and Paul, and, yes, with Frank and Pat in happier circumstances, and other friends we'd had over to stay with us in the farmhouse.

But this was all maundering self-indulgence: to find out, you had to go and look. I remembered the covering letter from Lawyer Le Touzel to the contents of the Jiffy bag, with his invitation to look him up. First, the practicalities: I'd emailed off the article I'd been working on, and wasn't expecting anything else for the next few days, so I had a time window. Where to stay on Jersey? Presumably, the agents would have let the farmhouse – they nearly always managed to fill the place between Good Friday and the end of September, and I hadn't asked for a slot for two years now. In any case, I'd email them. Could I leave it till the weekend? I didn't think lawyers' offices opened on Saturdays, and I was curious to see Le Touzel, so it would have to be tomorrow, Friday.

I'd have loved to take Leah with me, and introduce her to the island, but with term now in full swing I could hardly expect her to reschedule her tutorials at the drop of a hat. Another time, then, for Leah. I'd ring her and let her know my new plan, though – do it now . . .

Next morning, I had an early breakfast, then took a taxi to Stansted and the Jersey flight. My first call on the island was the airport car-hire facility, and on to the tiny, familiar parish of St Marc's. I found Lawyer Le Touzel just after midday in his granite mini-manor of an office in the little township. Le Touzel himself came to greet me amid the computer emplacements of the outer office, and led me into his panelled inner sanctum in a sunlit wing of the building. The furnishings were rich and antique, and dim, older Le Touzels looked down from undistinguished Victorian portraits on the walls.

The suited young lawyer waved me into the stiff, antique chair in front of his wide desk, with its tooled leather top, while he settled into his chair behind it. The whole set-up – like the island these days – stank of money, and I felt distinctly shabby in my Barbour jacket, open checked shirt and jeans. Le Touzel leant forward, arching his long, pink hands on the table, in the process showing off a pair of discreet gold links. He was plumpish in an aquiline way, with longish, dark hair, evidently cut by some chi-chi stylist – Coupes Conseillées in Halkett Place? – and noted me for a moment with his dark eyes. His smile was as impersonal as a treaty, and I was sure that in an earlier era the staff would have referred to him as 'young Mr Le Touzel' . . .

'Had a good crossing, Mr Rolvenden?' came the vaguely Home Counties voice.

'Flew from Stansted, actually.'

180

'Ah – time – tell me about it . . .'

'First of all, I'd like to thank you for sending on my grandfather's things.'

A little fantail with the smooth hands, and the smile grew a little less diplomatic.

'Least we could do, Mr Rolvenden, in view of the fact that your late namesake was such a longstanding client of ours before the – yes, I'm glad you dropped in. You're a writer, Mr Rolvenden?'

'For my sins . . .'

'Ha! Yes – I'm a local history buff myself, when I've the time – and if I could help you, er . . . co-ordinate any enquiries you may wish to make on the island, I'd be more than happy to help. No question of business, you understand . . .'

I wasn't sure I could get my head round the idea of lawyers who did anything for free.

'Our firm,' the lawyer was going on, 'is one of the oldest established on the island, and our network of local contacts is second to none.'

I took that to mean that if I wanted to know anything more about my grandfather, I was to come to him and not nose around upsetting people with possibly embarrassing questions. I decided to jump straight in.

'There seemed to be an interesting subtext to the letter you sent with my grandfather's things – the war . . .'

A conciliatory nod, and the smile became even wryer.

'People die, Mr Rolvenden, and the things they've, er . . . accumulated over a lifetime come out – no need to upset the living – you'll take coffee?'

I thanked him, but shook my head.

'You're planning on staying long?'

'Mmm . . . no. If anything, I just want to get the feel of the island again; there may be something I've missed here about my grandfather's life.'

Le Touzel nodded. 'You own a property on the bay, don't you?'

181

'A farmhouse: I've yet to ring the agents up about it – I'm fairly certain they'll have let it already, but no harm in asking.'

'Good luck, then! As well as being vicar of St Marc's, your grandfather had local connections, too, I believe?'

'His mother was a St Ouen's girl – Alice Le Maistre.'

'Ah, yes – weren't they shipping agents in St Helier?'

'That's right, the farm came to Alice through her mother.'

'Why, you're almost one of us! So, you're just here to soak in the atmosphere – reacquaint yourself with your roots, so to speak?'

'Just about – I don't plan on doing any serious research into family history at the moment, or anything of that sort.'

There was visible relief on the lawyer's face, and his smile began to look positively genuine. He rose from his chair, and I stood up, then he came round and shook my hand.

'If anything else turns up concerning your grandfather, Mr Rolvenden, rest assured I'll be in touch with you – I do enjoy following up island history!'

I thanked him for his time, and insisted I could see myself out. It struck me how tightly the likes of Le Touzel might close ranks if necessary . . . I then rang the letting agency, to find out that new tenants were due to arrive later that afternoon to take up residence in the farmhouse. I'd just go down and take a look at the place, then.

Setting off along the single tarmac thread of country lane, I drove down through the Norman dairy pastures, almost as far as the reservoir which formed the boundary with the neighbouring parish of St Ouen. It was not long before I was confronting the squat, granite barn of St Marc's church, where my grandfather had held the cure of souls from 1919 till the dark year of 1940.

I pulled up on the narrow verge of the lane, got out and viewed the church against the high blue sky of May. It was quiet and deserted, and the double-leafed, studded door was shut. I walked up and grasped one of the pair of iron torques in my hands and gave it a rattle, but it was locked fast, and even after a full minute had passed, there was no response from inside besides the hollow reverberation.

Lingering awhile, I wondered how many times my grandfather, tranquil or angry, had seized that ring, how many times he'd prayed, alone, on his bony knees in front of the slab of an altar I knew was inside, and in expiation of what strange sins? How many confidences had he kept over the years, that man of secrets, things confided to him in the clipped accents of folk more used to the old Jersey patois than to English? And how had he felt when he'd returned after Liberation in 1945, to find that his home had been looted and defiled by some of the very same people whose confessions he must have listened to before he'd been hauled off to internment in Germany? Had he then come into this now-empty church to kneel and pour it all out before the same altar? But they were all gone now . . .

I let go of the ring and walked back to the car amid the ambush of shrill birdsong from the hedges on either side of the lane. I drove the short distance to Grandfather's vicarage, now alienated from the Church and tarted up as a roadhouse hotel-restaurant – no echoes there of any sort . . . Driving briskly past it, I made for St Ouen parish and so to the beach. It was relaxing to see the familiar ward-boundary signs flash by, as lightly and musically as lark-song: Les Hures, L'Amiral, Les Trois Rocques. Only the Norman place-names left now, of course, the last genera-tion of native speakers having had all traces of the patois caned out of them as wartime evacuees in the board schools of urban Lancashire.

Then came the nurseries, the gorse-clumped hillocks and La Mare au Seigneur – St Ouen's Pond – and, finally, the twitchers' paradise of the marshes before the glorious silver-and-blue sweep of the bay, with its gorse-green

183

escarpment, and, on the gentle, seaward slope, the scatter of neat farmhouses. These were positively Scottish-looking, with their whitewashed walls and slate roofs.

I drove down the path and, a hundred yards from the beach, pulled up in front of our farmhouse and got out of the car. The smell of gorse and seaweed hit me in the spring sunshine, with birdsong on all sides, and, in the background, the steady, diastolic swish of the waves on the shore, like a distant groan of discontent. I took in the couth little building, with its white walls, prim-windowed twin storeys and dull grey slates on the roof. Now I was looking at the farmhouse post-childhood, post-marriage, post – damn her! – Pat. I fingered the keys in my pocket: what would it feel like inside?

Actually, it just felt like an empty let, and I went through the minimally furnished rooms, where I found everything in A1 order for the next tenants – one up to the agent – to the main bedroom. I flopped on to the bed and bounced gently on top of the coverlet, then sat up against the headboard, and looked across through the window at the sea. A trudge along the beach, down to the Corbière, would clear my mind of cobwebs. I got up, patted and smoothed the coverlet, then walked out of the farmhouse, locking the door behind me.

Nearer the sea, the breeze got stiffer, and my spirits rose as I strode across the silver sands: this was better than grunts and regrets, better than clapped-out religions and family, with its shames and favouritisms . . . Soon I was skirting the Point, with the Corbière lighthouse atop it. I was squinting out at the glittering immensity of the sea, when, just to remind me that my last meal had been a croissant at six-thirty, my stomach started to rumble. I glanced down at my watch – one-twenty – time to look up some sort of lunch. Unless I wanted a longish drive, the Vicarage Restaurant, just across the boundary in St Marc's, would be the logical place. I trudged back to the car, and, taking my mental farewell of the farmhouse, retraced my route.

On the inside, the Vicarage turned out to be OK as such places go, with a non-themed but decent decor, and an Italian man of about sixty in a suit presiding over things. There weren't that many lunchers, and my lasagne arrived in fairly short order. Eventually, the maître d. strolled across the sparsely occupied room and paused at my table.

'Everything all right, sir? You're enjoying your meal?'

'Mmm . . . salad's nicely dressed – walnut oil . . .'

'Good, sir!'

'Actually,' I said, with the elusive Monsieur Ramier in mind, 'this place was recommended to me by a French friend, who was here a week or two ago.'

'I'm pleased to hear it, sir. We get quite a number of French guests – was he a resident?'

'Mmm . . . he may have been. His name's Ramier.'

The dark man's mouth bowed downwards.

'No, I don't remember such a name – we get so many guests, sir . . .'

'Tall and thin – dark suit – dark glasses outdoors – hair done in a sort of quiff like a cockatoo . . .'

The urbane hotelier's sallow face lit up.

'Ah, yes – the gentleman with all the questions!'

'Questions?'

'Yes, he told me he was related to one of the former vicars here before the place became a hotel, and had there been any of the original furniture and paintings left here? Could he look in the cellar? The loft? And such and so! I showed him one or two nice old things that had been left – a few chairs, a little table – but no paintings. I think he wanted a picture of his ancestor. He was all over the place – the village, the farms, the church . . .'

'St Marc's?'

'Yes, the church just down the road – no one goes there now.'

'Did he stay long?'

'Oh, three-four days.'

It had been Ramier, all right . . .

'That's him!' I remarked with a chuckle. 'He's in England at the moment.'

'Well, sir, I hope they tell him what he wants to know there!'

But not before I find out all about Ramier in Berneval, I thought grimly, washing down a mouthful of garlic bread with the house red. I'd missed the 1.10 hovercraft to St Malo, but let's see what flights there were . . .

I managed to get on a flight to Paris, then there was the usual running around before I started the sticky, three-hour rail journey to Dieppe, arriving at dusk. From there I took a taxi the eight kilometres to Berneval, where Ramier'd said he had a hotel. The only other things I knew about the place were that Oscar Wilde had written *The Ballad of Reading Gaol* there, between 1897 and 1898, and that the town had got seriously in the way of the Normandy landings in 1944.

The reconstructed remnant turned out to be a clean, airy, seaside place – fine for a quiet holiday – but it had the added advantage for me, late that evening, of being quite small – just an enhanced village, really – and therefore easy to suss out. First, I had to find somewhere to lay my head for the night, so where better – if it existed, that was – than Monsieur Ramier's place? I hitched my travelling bag manfully on my shoulder and set off down the main drag.

There was a sufficiency of hotels, as I tramped, bone-weary, along, but none with any suggestion of a name like Ramier on its fascia. I finally slumped down, done in, on a high stool of a bistro at the far end of town, and ordered a cold beer. The proprietor, who was a local lad, had never heard of any Paul Ramier, but if later I didn't have any luck, he'd be able to fix me up with a room at a very reasonable rate.

I thanked him, and said I'd remember his offer, then went out for a last look round: it was dark now, and the lights were on above the hotel and shop fronts. I walked back up the street, and there, over a little bar under the Hôtel Solidor, was a brightly lit sign I hadn't noticed earlier when it hadn't been lit, with a nineteenth-century cancan girl depicted in the middle. She had a mop of orange hair, a dead-white face and pillar-box red lips. Glaring in scarlet letters was the title, in English: *Carrie's Bar*.

Chapter Eighteen

My weariness forgotten for the moment – could it be the same Carrie? – I went into the bar and sat down at the counter next to a trio of loud characters in blue overalls. The barman paused in his animated conversation with them on – what else? – football, and turned his attention to me. He was a chunky, red-faced individual of around forty-five with an adjusted Elvis hairstyle and hairy, gold-laden wrists. I asked for a Stella-hot-dog, and without a word he poured the drink from a dispenser, then turned to a microwave behind him to attend to the snack, which he soon plonked down on the counter in front of me. He told me the price, speaking slowly to allow for my shaky command of his language, and I counted out the money. I summoned up my best French, and, thinking of what Ramier had told me in England about his being a hotelier on a spring break, asked innocently if the *patron* was on holiday.

'*Moi, je suis le patron*,' was the deadpan reply. 'I am the owner . . .'

I then gave a stumbling outline of Ramier's story, the barman's eyes narrowing as I went on. The noisy men in the blue overalls were guffawing and addressing remarks to him, but he clearly only had ears for what I was telling him. At length, he jerked his head over my shoulder, and an attractive, intelligent-looking girl in a blue apron took her place beside me.

'Je vous présente ma fille, Liliane,' he explained. 'She spik good English . . .'

With the proprietor's daughter Liliane to help me with my French and her father with his English, things went more smoothly, but the improvement in communication did nothing to lessen the *patron*'s evident astonishment at what I was telling him.

'Mais, c'est dingue . . .' he said when I'd finished. 'Crezzy . . .'

Crazy because, word for word, Ramier's story about his being Carrie Bugle's great-grandson, including all the family details, applied exactly to the man I was talking to!

'I am Germain Barre!' Liliane translated her father's rapid, indignant French. 'I am the great-grandson of Carrie Bugle! She was a star of the music halls over there in England, and that is why this bar takes its name from her. Do you know that the design of the bar sign outside was taken from a painting of her by a great artist? This man Ramier is an imposter! He has been impersonating me . . .'

'And was your grandfather's name Philippe?' I pressed.

'But of course! As you say, he was Carrie's son, and lived with her in Jersey before the war. He was later embarked at Dunkirk, and was in London before serving with de Gaulle's forces all over the world. Again, as you've just described, he joined the Merchant Navy after the war, but disappeared after visiting England fifty years ago. What does this Ramier look like?'

I described the tall man with the Tintin quiff, and the *patron* rolled his fists out in front of him, snapping both forefingers against his thumbs.

'What did I tell you?' he asked his daughter-cum-interpreter. 'I said I shouldn't have given him Marti's address.'

'Bernard Marti?' I asked. 'Carrie's son Philippe's wartime comrade?'

'That's right: the man you've described came here a

couple of weeks ago, claiming to be a descendant of one of my grandfather's old pre-war friends. He seemed to know more about our family than we did ... He even knew that old Marti had celebrated the end of the war in London in 1945 with my grandfather Philippe. Anyway, the tall man you call Ramier asked if I knew when old Marti had died, and I told him he was in fact still alive, but very frail, and lived with his daughter in Dieppe. The top and bottom of it was, I ended up by giving the man their address.'

'You weren't to know Ramier was a fake,' I said.

So that was how Ramier had got his hands on the postcard from Philippe Barre to Bernard Marti ...

'Who is this Ramier, then?' the *patron* asked via his daughter. 'Some sort of crook?'

I said that my best guess at the moment was that he was some sort of dodgy antique dealer.

'Antique dealer? He's wasting his time here, then ...'

'Barre's the only antique around here!' one of the noisy men in overalls, who'd obviously caught the drift of our conversation, remarked for the benefit of the house, and he and his friends left the bar amid uproarious laughter. They wished the *patron* good evening at the door, and went laughing into the night.

'Did Ramier stay here?' I asked Germain Barre, alluding to the hotel upstairs. 'If so, you must've seen his ID?'

'No, he just came in occasionally and drank at the bar – took a few snacks – and asked a lot of questions – a lot ... If he mentioned his name, I don't remember it – I suppose he might have. That's the way it is in this business – you see so many people, and you're all things to all men. He just sort of carried me along.'

'He's a plausible character,' I confirmed.

'And you, monsieur,' the *patron* began, seeming to take my last remark as a sort of cue. 'Are you in the, er ... antiques business, too?'

Carefully watching the expression in his eyes – how

would he take this? – I took out my business card, and handed it over to Monsieur Barre. He took it in blankly at first, then astonishment mixed with consternation spread all over his face.

'But, it's – this means you're ... The good priest Rolvenden in Jersey ...'

'His grandson!' I said, laughing, and handed over my passport to back up my claim to be a Rolvenden. 'And there's more ...'

As he glanced at my passport photo and details, I fished in my inside pocket, and pulled out the copy of my father's birth certificate, which I handed to Liliane at my side. She gave a low whistle, and looked at me wonderingly with her dark, intelligent eyes.

'*Formidable* ...' she murmured, then, to her father: 'Papa, you'd better take a look at this ...'

He did, with an inaudible whisper, then handed me back the papers and left the bar briefly to flip the Closed sign on the street door, and lock it, an operation followed immediately by the whirr of descending shutters outside.

'You'll be staying here, of course,' the hotelier said as he took my bag with one hand and my elbow with the other and led me, Liliane following, behind the bar into their private quarters. Madame Barre, a stocky lady with bright black eyes and the Midi accent, was summoned from the kitchen, where she'd been watching a blaring television set, and we settled down in the Barres' comfortable sitting room while we talked. And did we have a lot to talk about! By the time, in the unlikely early hours, Germain sat back, his stock of questions exhausted, and gave me a comprehensive look-over, all he could say was: 'So that's why the good pastor Rolvenden helped my great-grandmother Carrie in Jersey – she'd borne his son ...'

'And the lady you call Nanny,' Madame Barre put in, referring to the one I'd always thought of as my grandmother, 'she was a heroine, a really good woman, looking after your father like that, and bringing him up as her own son.'

'To me, she's still my grandmother.'

'*Voilà!*'

'Tell me,' I addressed the hotelier. 'Do you know where Carrie – your great-grandmother and my grandmother – is buried?'

Germain Barre winced slightly and shook his head.

'She died in hospital in Arromanches, but we've never been able to find out where she was buried. A lot of the area was destroyed during the landings in 1944 – the war . . .'

'Germain,' the lady of the house said to her husband, 'Monsieur Rolvenden looks absolutely done in – there's always tomorrow . . .'

Barre jumped to his feet, and, pulling me up, shook both my hands.

'Monsieur Rolvenden – *mon cousin!* – this has been an unforgettable meeting, and of course, we'll be thrilled if you can stay for a while.'

'I'll certainly take up your offer in the future – thank you – but my next stop will be Niort, and in the meantime, I'd like to pay a call in Dieppe.'

'Ah, yes! To see old Marti, my grandfather Philippe's wartime comrade . . .'

It was agreed, then, that next morning, Saturday, Liliane would take me to Dieppe to look up Bernard Marti, who'd spent VE Day in London with Carrie Bugle's son Philippe, my present host's grandfather. As well as helping out my French, Liliane – a friend of the Marti family – could help smooth down any feathers still ruffled by the visit of Barre-impersonator Ramier, who'd pinched the old man's 1955 London postcard from Philippe Barre. After we'd made our visit in Dieppe, I could go on from there farther south to Niort.

Later on, after I'd slept off the edge of my weariness, and taken breakfast *en famille*, Liliane rang up Bernard

Marti's daughter in Dieppe to clear the way for our planned visit to the old man.

'She said not to stay long,' the bright girl told me, 'since his health is not good, and he tires very easily. Otherwise, it should be OK.'

We bought flowers and a bottle of Rivesalte for Marti's daughter before setting off for Dieppe in Liliane's battered little car, and my sympathetic new kinswoman told me something of her own life. She was twenty-four and a graduate of one of the big Parisian *écoles*, who, like tens of thousands in her situation, was kicking around at home, helping in the bar and hotel, till some suitable job turned up. Among her achievements she included her having covered the length and breadth of the United States by Greyhound bus. I told her that, if she ever fancied trying her luck in England, and didn't mind camping out in a disused lighthouse on a marsh, she'd be welcome to stay with me.

Once we'd arrived in Dieppe, Liliane led me to the upper flat of a narrow, shabby building off the rattling fish market on the Ile du Pollet in the port's inner basin. Bernard Marti's daughter was a stout lady, just on the wrong side of seventy, and came out on to the landing in response to Liliane's ring at the doorbell. Before she showed any sign of inviting us in, she said that we had to understand that her father was ninety-six years old, and things had come to a pretty pass when people took advantage of a man of that age ... She was obviously referring to the Tintin-quiffed conman Ramier's visit, and the affair of the purloined VE Day postcard.

But Liliane's reassurances, along with the flowers and the Rivesalte, at last mollified the lady to the extent of her inviting us in. On the strict understanding, she was careful to point out, that the visit was to last no more than five minutes, and that she was to be there in the room throughout.

193

We were ushered into a stuffy little bedroom, full of hideous modernique French furniture of the last-decade-but-five-or-six. Under the tall, single window was an armchair with a shrunken old man in a jacket and zipped-up pullover in it. His bare skull was blotched and yellow, and the middle ground of the waxen face was occupied boldly by a thick white moustache. The knot-veined, bluish right hand was tapping a Zagazig cigarette-paper carton incessantly on the wooden armrest of the chair. The old soldier turned dim, pale eyes on us, and looked blankly as, uninvited, we sat down on the edge of the bed nearest to him.

'Five minutes!' warned the stumpy female Cerberus in the doorway.

I said hello to Monsieur Marti, and he mumbled something that sounded like '*Boujou – boujou . . .*' then, through Liliane, I said I believed he'd been in the army with a kinsman of mine, Philippe Barre.

'Yes, yes, I was in the army – with de Gaulle,' then, with a little smile, a brave stab at English: 'You are from London *Cité*?'

I grinned and nodded encouragingly: did he remember their time in England during the war?

'I've some postcards – Bernadette, where are the postcards from London?'

The lady in the doorway shot us a meaningful look, before telling her father that they'd turn up somewhere later, no doubt . . .

'There were three of us,' the old man was saying, 'like the Three Musketeers . . .'

Three wartime comrades, I thought: I hadn't been prepared for that.

'There was me and Philippe – the two *Dieppois* – and Duzko.'

'Who was Duzko, Monsieur Marti?'

But my question just went over the old man's head.

'We got away in 1940,' he went on. 'We were a team, do

194

you understand? Duzko had been in the Spanish War in '36–7, and knew a network down near the Pyrenees. We got some civvy clothes and made for the border, and Duzko made his number with this guy in Tarbes. He passed us on to a guide – a Spanish Basque in Lannemezan – and we went over the mountains at dead of night. God! The cold . . . There were times when I was sure I was a goner, and the guide wouldn't stop – they never stopped if you held back, you know, because if they were late over the mountains the Fascists would have spotted them in daylight and shot them. Me and Philippe got over, but Duzko . . .'

To our dismay, Marti started to cry – the facile tears of the very old.

'That's it!' his daughter rapped from the door. 'That's enough!'

'Dead in the snow,' the old man snuffled as we made an apologetic exit. 'Dead in the snow . . .'

Liliane and I discussed the visit to the Martis as she drove me and my bag to the car-hire depot which was attached to the train-and-bus station at the far end of town.

'We'd always thought that my great-grandfather Philippe and Bernard Marti had escaped from France through Dunkirk in 1940,' she said. 'And now this story about escaping over the Pyrenees . . .'

'They'd have made for the British Consulate in Barcelona,' I said, 'and been smuggled out via Gibraltar. It was a recognized route for Allied personnel cut off from the northern French ports by the German advance. And who was this Third Musketeer, Duzko?'

'It's a Slav name, I think: there were lots of East European immigrants and refugees in France in those days. No member of my family has ever mentioned such a name to me before, though, and Papa's always talking about Carrie and his grandfather – it's like an, er . . . mania with him . . .'

'Like me and my Grandfather Rolvenden,' I said.

195

The young girl laughed.

'It's so interesting, though,' she remarked. 'Everybody wants to know where they come from.'

But where exactly had this Duzko come from, I asked myself; or rather, where did he fit in? Why had Philippe Barre apparently never mentioned this charismatic ex-comrade to his family? And why had he let them understand that he'd been taken off at Dunkirk in 1940, when, if old Marti was to be believed, they'd got away – minus poor Duzko – across the Pyrenees?

'Here we are at the station,' Liliane said, stopping the car.

She helped me with my bag, then we shook hands warmly amid vows to meet again soon, and she got back into the car. With a last wave, I was about to turn away, when she beckoned from the car, and I went over and leant towards the side window. There was a mischievous smile on the attractive, olive-skinned face, as Liliane delivered her parting shot.

'I think maybe I can help you with the real identity of this Monsieur Ramier you're investigating,' she said almost apologetically.

'Oh, can you – do tell me, then . . .'

'You know, *ramier* in French is a type of pigeon.'

Chapter Nineteen

As I drove south in my hire-car, I mulled over Liliane Barre's conjecture as to Ramier's real name. If she'd been on the right track, it suggested that the man with the Tintin quiff was as arrogant as he was plausible, underestimating the intelligence of people in seeing through his pseudonym. I had to concede, though, that he'd had me fooled: at no time had it occurred to me to look up *ramier* in a French-English dictionary.

So now it was looking as if a modern French descendant of Laurence Victor Pidgeon – the Vickybird of the Rawbeck Legend – had pinched the identity of the latest representative of Carrie Bugle's French family – the Barres – in order to ferret out information about paintings. *The* painting, I was now convinced: *The Ruffian on the Stair* ... It struck me, too, how like his forebear the modern Pidgeon was, with the same conning and stealing from his unwitting marks. But did the modern Vickybird run to murder, too? I'd have to watch my step.

And now there was a new factor in this Duzko, the old comrade of Philippe Barre and Bernard Marti, who'd met his death in the snows of the Pyrenees, and who, for some reason, had been left out of the late Philippe Barre's account of his adventures. 'Duzko' – I wasn't even sure whether it was a first name or a surname, since Frenchmen of Marti's generation habitually referred to their most intimate friends by their surnames. I'd have to await further developments on this one.

I drove on steadily south through the tame countryside, past Rouen, Dreux and Chartres to Blois, where I stopped for a belated lunch and a browse in the local *Grande Poste* among the racks of French District telephone books, to find no Pidgeons listed – with or without the 'd' – in the directory that covered Niort and its environs. Once I'd got there, I'd have to think laterally.

The south-western *autoroute* took me to Poitiers, and so on to Route 68 to the pleasant little town of Niort, on its gentle slope on the left bank of the Sèvre. I found a parking space, then sat down at a pavement table of a bistro on the broad, sunlit main square. By then it was after seven, and, tired though I was, I decided to use the remaining daylight to make a quick recce of the address at the head of Odette Pidgeon's 1927 begging letter to my grandfather.

I drank my coffee quietly for a few minutes, admiring the light-coloured buildings round the square, with their round-tiled roofs, then signalled the waiter, so that I might pay and ask directions to the village of Balmes, where Odette Pidgeon had nursed the ailing Vickybird all those years ago. The waiter knew the village, and told me that it was in a district several kilometres west of the town, in a marshy flatland called Le Palud, on the outskirts of the Marais Poitevin nature reserve. The way, he said with a smile, would be complicated . . .

And so it proved to be, as, half an hour later, I found myself threading my way through a maze of minor roads, paths and ruts in a canalled landscape reminiscent of Holland. The low, whitewashed villages and farms of the *Maraichins* were built on top of ridges, rock-plugs, dykes and other eminences – anything to keep them above sea-flood level – and the squares and rectangles of water-meadows and bean and sunflower fields marked out by the canals and dykes looked fat and prosperous.

I tried to imagine the region in winter, buffeted by the raw westerlies that must roar in unchecked across the flat landscape from the nearby Bay of Biscay. I thought of

198

Laurence Victor Pidgeon with his 'affected lungs', and reflected that it surely couldn't have taken many such winters to see off an undernourished man with war-damaged lungs.

It was all pleasant enough now, though, in the douce Maytime, with the handsome cattle in the willow-hung meadows, the burgeoning crops in the arable fields and the flutter and twitter of birdlife everywhere from the adjoining nature reserve. No signs of the rural distress Odette Pidgeon had hinted at in her pre-war letter, either, in the narrow, single street of low, rendered white cottages that made up the village of Balmes-le-Vidame. Instead, there were neat new cars in front of the trim, crouching dwellings, and blue-rinsed and summer-dressed old ladies at the front doors in place of the pinched figures in shawls and sabots that must have been the order of the day back in the 1920s, when Odette was struggling to keep her 'Laurent' alive. In those days, I reflected, the notion of the EU and its farm subsidies would have seemed like science fiction.

I parked the car just outside the village on a sort of hard shoulder at the side of the blunt dyke along which Balmes's buildings were strung out, and approached a friendly-looking local who was sitting placidly on a bench in front of the second cottage in. I handed him my pre-scribbled note of the address on Odette Pidgeon's letter, and with a brown root of a hand he pushed up the peak of his tartan cloth cap.

'*Oustalet Grau,*' he quoted from my note the name of what must have been the Pidgeons' farmhouse, then, with an apologetic three- or four-toothed grin: '*Connais pas . . .*'

I thanked him for his time, and made my way farther up the street. Of course the house-names of the place must have changed over the years with the tenants, but surely there'd be at least one person left in the village who'd know. I'd an idea, and turned back to the man on the bench, whom I asked where the village postman lived.

With the comment that, if I'd asked him in the first place, he'd have been able to tell me straight away, the man directed me to the house.

The postman turned out to be a thin, sandy-haired man in middle age, and I found him as he was tinkering with a car at the side of his house. He took my interruption in good part, but as to the house-name I was after, he too was reduced to head-scratching. Hang on, though, he'd pop indoors and ask *Maman* –she was over eighty, and a *Balmaise* born and bred: she'd know if anyone did . . .

The postman re-emerged from the house a minute later, with a little stout old lady with prominent brown eyes. She looked me up and down, then smiled and gave me good day, and I repeated my piece to her. She paused awhile, then explained that she'd heard something years ago about an Englishman who'd lived near the village – you didn't see many of them in the *marais* – but of course she'd only been a very little girl at the time, and naturally didn't know his name. The house-name did, however, seem to ring a bell with her. She turned to her son, the postman – wasn't there an *oustalet* owned by the nice retired Dutch couple half a kilometre or so down the road?

I thanked the postman and his mother, and went back to the car, got in and drove straight through the village and out the other end, and kept on driving till I came to a squat, white farmhouse on its own. It had an L-shaped, one-storeyed wing to one side, and a swimming pool in the middle of the lawn where the farmyard must previously have been. On the paved edge of the pool there was a table with a sun umbrella in the middle, and by its side, in twin loungers, a grey couple in happy clothes.

Pulling up at the roadside, I got out and approached the couple, trying my French on them, but mercifully they replied in English, inviting me to take a garden seat under the shade of the umbrella, where the man poured me an orange drink. A nice couple, as the postman's mother had said, Dutch and retired senior schoolteachers. I told them

200

of my quest, but they couldn't help me as far as Pidgeons went, as they'd no idea who'd occupied the farmhouse before they'd bought it. All that had been arranged before they'd finally upped sticks from the Netherlands. Nor had any of the locals mentioned the name to them. They were hoping to run the outbuildings as *gîtes*, but it was early days and they were still learning.

Something occurred to me: I hadn't noticed a church in Balmes: was there one nearby? The man told me that there was a village church of sorts in Trelles, about a kilometre up the road, but it was getting late, and wouldn't I be needing accommodation for the night, or at least a meal? Just then I felt I could have murdered a square meal, and my weariness was like a weight on my back. I fell in readily with both the couple's suggestions: they evidently *were* learning the art of hiring out *gîtes* ...

Next morning, Sunday, I checked out of my *gîte* and drove along to the next village, Trelles, which turned out to be very much like Balmes, in fact, only a tad smaller, but with the added distinction of a small village square, set in from the road in front of the *mairie*. There was an obelisk affair in the middle of the square, which I guessed must be the inevitable war memorial. If the Vickybird had had children, the boys could hardly have missed the war.

I got out of the car, and walked up to the stone obelisk, which turned out to be the 1914–1918 memorial. There were far too many names on it for a place this size, but it was too early for my purposes. Ah, over there on the wall of the *mairie* – a bronze plaque. I walked across the little square to the plaque and examined it: *Morts pour la patrie – 1939–1945*. There was a fair muster of names, though nothing like the number on the First World War obelisk. I looked down the list till I came to the P's: *Paulet, Lionel; Pétiot, Roland; Pézanas, Albert; Piccini, Louis-Philippe*, then, there it was: *Pidgeon, Georges* ...

Galvanized and frustrated at the same time, I looked impatiently up and down the drowsy, late spring street, until logic came to my aid, and I took out a biro and a stray checkout receipt and copied down the thirty-odd names on the plaque. Now for the shop fascias and house fronts . . .

It was, I supposed, testimony to the social mobility of the age that I could only connect three modern features with the names on my improvised list. The first was with the name of a tyre depot, which was closed, the second with a young resident who turned out to be a swimming instructor, and who could only shrug and say '*Connais pas*' in response to my enquiry about Pidgeons, and the third – eureka! – a Madame Paulet, who was a jolly old lady pastrycook. I joined the little queue of locals in her shop for the time-honoured ritual of buying the after-Sunday-lunch cake, chose a scrumptious-looking strawberry tart and asked about Pidgeons in the vicinity.

Yes, she'd known Georges Pidgeon slightly when she'd been a little girl. He'd been a small, thin, dark type – all head. He must have taken after his mother, Odette, then, I thought. No, Madame Paulet couldn't remember his parents – well before her time – but if I wanted to know about the war, I might call in at the corner bistro, where the local codgers hung out. It was just two doors down.

I followed her advice, and ordered a beer in the main bistro, but all the action seemed to be in the back courtyard, where a *boules* game was in progress. I asked the *patron* who among the senior citizens might best fill me in with the history of the village, and he laughed and jerked his head towards the open door that led into the yard.

'Old Alibert – the one in the checked shirt and white cap at the table there. He knows everything about anything!'

I paid the extra on my beer for waiter service, and took my glass into the cool, chestnut-canopied courtyard, where I made for the little wrought-iron table indicated and excused myself into the chair opposite Monsieur Alibert, who was a big-featured old man in dark glasses, and asked him if he'd take a drink with me.

'Willingly!' he boomed, then the Midi accent rolled out in all its glory with: 'English, *hein*? Are you touring the region?'

I nodded and waved through the open door to the *patron*, who came out and took my order for Alibert's beer, the old man shouting his thanks. His loud way of speaking must no doubt have been a pain for the other clients, but it was a boon for my understanding of his French.

'Back in England,' I explained, 'there's a tradition in my family that a friend of my grandfather lived near this very village.'

'Is that so? Another Englishman?'

'Yes, he married a local girl after the 1914 war and had a son, but that was way back – well before your time, monsieur . . .'

It was like a red rag to a bull: rapping his glass back on to the metal table-top, old Alibert leant forward and, after setting his heavy jaw for a moment, accepted my challenge to his local all-knowingness.

'Give me his name!'

'Pidgeon, Laurent Pidgeon.'

The old gaffer settled back in his seat with a triumphant smile on his face, then took a long swig of beer before answering.

'That would've been Georges Pidgeon's old man – died way back in '26 or '27 – I can't really remember him – but I was at school with young Georges . . .'

'You don't say?'

A nod and another swig on the part of my opposite number.

'When all the crap started up again in '39, we were in the same call-up year: I'll be eighty-six in June . . .'

'No!'

'Right enough: when the war broke out I got a posting to Toul, but poor Georges was killed in front of Sedan in 1940. Hardly twenty-one, poor bastard, and with a wife and kid already: God knows what happened to them . . .'

My guess was that Georges Pidgeon's 'kid' had grown up and had a son of his or her own, a son who wore his hair in a Tintin quiff, and whom I'd recently caught in England trying the door of the Hagues' boathouse. A son, moreover, who'd plugged into the background of Carrie Bugle's French family, the Barres, and was even at that moment posing as Philippe Barre as he sniffed around for the scent of Julian Rawbeck's lost masterpiece, *The Ruffian on the Stair*. But I kept quiet amid the metallic clicking of the *boules* on the paved courtyard, and let old Alibert get on with his story.

'Georges was a dreamer,' the old man went on with a faraway smile on his face. 'He had a tale for everything. You've just mentioned his father . . .'

'Yes,' I said, agog to hear something about the Vickybird, 'please go on.'

'Well, Georges used to come in for quite a bit of chaff at school about his dad's being an Englishman – a *rosbif* – you know what kids are – but he used to put a brave face on it – bluster a bit. Did we seriously think his dad would've settled in a dump like Balmes unless he'd had a good reason? That sort of style . . .

'Why, his dad had been a Mr Big in the London underworld, until a toff had blackmailed him for something or other, and he'd had to deal with him. He'd done a runner to France, joined the Foreign Legion, and been sent back up the trenches, where he'd copped a packet, then, later, he'd married his nurse and settled down quietly here. Georges's dad had had to keep a low profile after all that: you had to understand, the *flics* at Scotland Yard had a long arm etc., etc. Talk about shooting a line.'

Alibert wheezed with gravelly laughter for a moment or two, and I sat riveted to my chair: judging by the potted version of the Vickybird's CV my vis-à-vis had just related, young Georges Pidgeon had been no fantasist.

'Did you know Georges's mother, Odette?'

'Poor woman, she was a shadow – a ragged shadow –

she used to fight the shopkeepers for bruised fruit and pork that had gone off. To think the scumbags charged for it! The Spanish War was the time when we could've settled with the bastards – I've always said that, to raise the working class to a proper level of political consciousness, the first requirement is . . .'

We were getting off-subject, so I asked if Alibert had known a family by the name of Barre.

'Barre?' the old man muttered, clearly irritated at my having interrupted him in mid-lecture. 'Once knew a loco driver in Toulouse called Barre – no, it was Barelli . . . Now he was an anarcho-syndicalist . . .'

I seized the hand of the veteran of labour, and told him how much I'd enjoyed our conversation, then got up and made my way to the door, and so back on to the yawning Sunday street. I now knew I was on Pidgeon home territory, but what had passed down the Pidgeon family line about Carrie Bugle and her London adventures? From my conversations with her French descendants, the Barres, in Berneval, it was clear they knew nothing about her relations with Laurence Victor Pidgeon in England, or later in Paris, where he'd upset my grandfather's apple cart with Carrie. But the man I felt sure was the Vickybird's most active modern descendant – Tintin Quiff alias Ramier – certainly knew a lot about the Barres. And the thing I was most sure of: the Vickybird's heir knew all about the legend of the lost Rawbeck masterpiece, as well as my grandfather's connection with the artist – his snooping in Jersey proved that, if nothing else.

I went back over the square and got into my car, carefully laying my strawberry tart on the back seat, then started to pull out of the square, meaning to make for the Charente crossing, then I remembered what the Dutch couple I'd stayed with on the previous night had said about there being a church near Trelles, about a kilometre down the road from churchless Balmes. If Laurence Victor Pidgeon had had a Christian burial, it would presumably have been in the churchyard there. Still short of the kilo-metre, I turned right and drove down the road till I spotted a low, nondescript stone structure to one side of the verge. There was a squared-off forepart of the building, with a cross on top. I pulled up opposite, and got out of the car.

It was one of those low, shapeless French country churches – now clearly disused – with bits dating from most of the periods of the Christian era. You could see the joins, too, in the shape of cracks and slips in the stonework, but it was the graveyard I was interested in. It lay, all overgrown, behind a tumbledown stone wall along the side of the road. I stepped through the gateless open-ing and into the weeds, then started to examine what graves were marked and visible. Here and there I found cleared patches, one or two even with withered flowers on the slabs. Picking up a dead branch to sweep aside the more rampant undergrowth, I started to cover the grave-yard, from top to bottom, until, ten minutes later, I uncov-ered a pathetic, rusted metal plaque, with the words, in raised letters: *Odette Pidgeon – 1885–1952 – Tout s'efface hors le souvenir.* 'Everything wears away, except the memory.' I felt a knot form in my chest as I stood before the grave for a minute or so: a woman of sorrows . . .

Another five minutes brought me to what I'd been look-ing for: a rather smart marble block – paid for by my grandfather, perhaps, after he'd been too late to help the Vickybird in his last illness? – with, in deeply cut, gilded lettering: *Laurence Victor Pidgeon – 1877–1927 – Resurgam.* I murmured the translation to myself: 'I shall rise again.' Suddenly, in spite of the growing warmth of the morning, a shiver ran through me: it was as if somebody was look-ing over my shoulder . . .

Chapter Twenty

With much food for thought, I got back into the car and drove on, eventually crossing the Charente at the big Saintes intersection, then it was the open road again, as far as Bordeaux, where I hoped to catch a flight back to England. I reflected on how tiring it was to be speaking a language you weren't master of, even after only a couple of days. Then I wondered how Duzko had managed with French – Duzko, who hadn't made it across the Pyrenees with Philippe Barre and Bernard Marti in 1940. And if they'd all been inseparable, as old Marti had suggested, why hadn't Philippe Barre told his family about Duzko?

And then a light began to dawn on me: Philippe Barre, by all accounts, had come over to England in the summer of 1955, and then had simply vanished. We could trace the date of his disappearance through the cancellation stamp on the postcard he'd sent old Marti from London in that year.

But it hadn't been the first time Philippe had chosen to disappear: there'd been the time, not long after the end of the war, when he'd split with his wife and joined the French Merchant Navy under a false name, so that they couldn't – as customary – dock his pay and send her maintenance. But then old Marti had blabbed to the Barres and given the game away. Still, Madame Barre hadn't claimed against her husband, so the false name wouldn't have been an issue: Philippe could have gone on sailing the seven seas under it.

Came his second – seemingly final – disappearance in England in 1955, and Philippe Barre would still presumably have been using the same false ID. Whose? Preferably that of someone dead, I'd have assumed, and ideally someone he *knew* was no longer around. Duzko's ID would have done fine ... What if, up on that frozen Pyrenean pass fifteen years before, Philippe had taken on the task of looking up Duzko's people after the war, and possibly returning his few effects – including his ID papers – only to be unable to trace the hapless Third Musketeer's family? It all fitted, and from now on I'd be working on the assumption that Philippe Barre had disappeared in England under Duzko's name and details. But had Philippe chosen to disappear there, or had it happened against his will? And had he just gone to England in the line of his work as a merchant seaman, or for some other reason? Who had been his contacts there?

In 1955 I'd been three years old, Grandfather had been dead for five years, Nanny in Malmesbury still had three years to live, Dad was still alive and in full vigour, and Mother still – more or less – at home. If it had been my grandfather Philippe had come over to see – he may not have known that he was dead – it wouldn't have been the first time, for hadn't he been taken by his mother Carrie to Jersey in the 1920s to seek help from Grandfather? When you're in a jam, who better to go and see than the family benefactor? It was a theory, anyway.

At Bordeaux airport I managed to squeeze on to a flight which got me back to England at some unearthly hour in the morning, and I didn't land up again in my lighthouse in Essex till around eight o'clock, when I just staggered upstairs to bed and crashed out till after two in the afternoon. I then wolfed down a scratch meal before getting up to date with the contents of my Inbox, and then, early in the evening, I rang Leah at the university before driving over to her flat there to give her an eager account of my adventures in Jersey and France.

'This Tintin guy you saw at the auction,' she commented. 'The one you caught trying the Hagues' boathouse door handle and who you now say's the Vickybird's descendant . . .'

'Yes, I'm pretty sure of that, now.'

'I think the place he'd have made for after sussing out you east coast Rolvendens would've been Malmesbury, your grandfather's last address on earth, after all.'

'If he hadn't been snooping around down there before he came up here,' I qualified.

'Let's assume he arrived from France through Stansted, and started from there.'

'Mmm . . . but how would he have known about the Malmesbury connection? When I talked to Carrie Bugle's great-grandson in Berneval, he didn't mention anything about this Pidgeon guy's having asked him about that aspect of our family history, though he'd tried to pump him on just about everything else.'

'If Tintin-Pidgeon had gone round to the nearest library, any halfways competent assistant could've directed him to an old *Crockford*, where he'd have found out what diocese covered your grandfather's last living in Jersey.'

'Winchester – yes, you're right: he could've rung up the Church authorities there and found out my grandfather's last retirement address. Or enquired at Church House in London.'

'Didn't you tell me that an aunt of yours was living in the house in Malmesbury now?'

'Yes – Aunt Hertha – or Dr Hertha Perowne, to give her her full honours. She's the great-granddaughter of Nanny's younger sister, Maud, who married a Malvern music master called Gilchrist. They had a daughter, Faith, who married Frank Perowne, a doctor specializing in tropical medicine. Faith wandered all over the world with him in his various postings. They had a daughter – Aunt Hertha – also a doctor, and a rolling stone for most of her life. Frank Perowne died in what was then

Malaya in 1953, and Faith came back and moved in with her Aunt Cecily – Nanny Rolvenden – herself a widow by then, until Nanny died in 1958, leaving the Malmesbury house to Faith, who in turn left it to Hertha, who lives there now.'

'Well, then,' Leah prescribed in her brisk fashion, 'you know who to contact to find out whether our Pidgeon friend's been down Malmesbury way since you last saw him.'

On that note, I was chased away dinnerless, Leah having a date somewhere else, so I returned to the lighthouse, and, after a meal, spent a reflective evening thinking of Pidgeons, sealing-wax and string. I recalled that I'd written to Hertha in 1996, when I'd first learnt that she'd moved into the old family home in Malmesbury, and asked if she'd known my grandfather personally. I was sure I'd kept the letter she'd written back, and went upstairs and had a rummage in my files for it. I eventually found it, and brought it downstairs to my armchair.

I read through Aunt Hertha's introductory pleasantries: *Having spent a lifetime roaming over the world as a medical busybody, I now propose to keep the Hundred of Malmesbury on its toes . . .* till I got to the bits about my grandfather:

I first met your grandfather in this house not long after the end of the war. It would have been the Christmas of 1946, as I always associate the meeting in my mind with the hard winter of that year and the beginning of the next, which was the coldest I've ever known in England.

I was fourteen at the time, and my parents were in Germany – Daddy was in the Army Medical Corps, and wasn't stood down till later on in the next year – so I was faced with the prospect of having to spend the Christmas hols at school. Nanny Rolvenden, however, came to the rescue, actually turning up at the school for me in her Austin Seven. I'd never met her till then, Daddy's career having taken us all over the place – I still see England as the most interesting of

210

foreign *countries – and what with her and your grandfather having spent so long in Jersey.*

She seemed pretty formidable at first – all nose and tweeds – but a real dear when you got to know her. Anyway, that day she drove me through the snow to their house in Malmesbury, where I'm writing this now, and I was introduced to your grandfather. He was slight – quite little – and must have been striking in his youth, with sharp features and bright, violet eyes. When I met him he had a full head of grey hair and a little, pointed silver beard. He would lean forward and look intently at you when you spoke to him, as if he wanted to understand quite perfectly what you meant. And Nanny would always be hovering in the background, as if she were his keeper, or representative on earth.

I recall your grandfather wasn't wearing a dog-collar, but had on one of those stiff old collars with rounded tips you see in photos of Dr Crippen, and a rich, dark silk tie, with a silver ring under the knot. If you came up on him when he was alone, he always seemed to have an anxious look about him, which would disappear in a jaunty smile when he saw you. He spoke quite quickly, in a high, clear voice, and he'd an occasional habit – quite off-putting – of looking straight through you.

It was a quiet Christmas, with few goodies on account of the rationing, which included fuel. I'd saved a precious box of bonbons which Daddy had somehow rustled up and sent me from Vienna, and gave them to Nanny as my present to them. In turn, your grandfather gave me a copy of – appropriately! – The Box of Delights, which I've still got, and love to read on Christmas Eve. They used to do it on the wireless every year, but I suppose it isn't cool any more.

Some grown-ups I didn't know called round after breakfast on that Christmas morning, but I don't remember going to church, which was odd, but perhaps I've forgotten. We did venture out in the Austin later to pay a few calls, but I've for-gotten the details of that, too.

And that's about it: I suppose your grandparents were the

last of the Victorians, so what does that make us? The last of the Georgians? Do come and stay soon. Sincerely, Hertha Perowne.

I folded up the letter again, and sat back in the armchair. I'd gone down to visit Aunt Hertha after that, and liked the compact, feisty little lady in slacks very much. In Malmesbury she'd joined practically everything in sight, and had soon picked up what she'd described as a 'man friend'.

Aunt Hertha had also shown me the copy of *The Box of Delights* which Grandfather had given her at Christmas 1946. He'd inscribed the flyleaf in his nervous, stabbing handwriting, with the words: *Nothing in this world has ever been loved too much*. I didn't know who the quote had been from, but for me it had added yet another haunting line to the first Sebastian Rolvenden's life story.

After a moment or two's reflection, I reached for the address book at the side of the telephone, found Aunt Hertha's number, and pegged it in.

'Seb Rolvenden here, Aunt Hertha, in Essex. I hope you're keeping well.'

'A1, thanks – lovely to hear from you! What are you writing now?'

'A film biography – Tod Slaughter – d'you remember him?'

'The Sweeney Todd man! You're going back a bit, aren't you? I hope somebody else remembers him . . .'

'The publisher seems to think there'll be one or two. I just wondered if you might have had any French visitors down there, asking about my grandfather?'

'Actually, I was on the point of ringing you about that . . .'

The hunter's tingle ran through me.

'Oh, right?'

'Lanky, ingratiating individual – called round last Tuesday, in fact.'

The day after I'd caught him trying the door of the Hagues' boathouse, I thought: he certainly hadn't let the grass grow under his feet.

'I'd company at the time,' Hertha went on. 'He spoke pretty fair English – said his name was Ramier, and that his family had once been associated with your grandfather. Is that what it's all about?'

'More or less. Could you give me some more detail about the meeting – it might be important. I'll explain fully afterwards.'

'Well, I was pulling some rhubarb in the garden for Steve Hunter – the village copper – at around two that afternoon when this Ramier chap comes up to the gate and asks if a family called Rolvenden had once lived here. I asked who he was, and he reached in his pocket for something, but when Steve came up in his uniform, he seemed to change his mind, and reached into another pocket for what turned out to be a French driving licence . . .'

No doubt as phony as he was, I thought.

'He showed it me,' my aunt went on, 'and Steve, who'd finished picking his rhubarb, left by the gate just before I ushered the Frenchman inside. The man had come a long way, after all, and I didn't think he'd try any funny business after Steve had witnessed his arrival like that. Incidentally, I glimpsed Steve for an instant taking a look at the rear of a car parked in the lane outside – it might have belonged to my visitor.'

'What did he ask you when he'd got inside the house?'

'Well, I took him straight through to the sitting room in front, and he went on a bit about how charming it was, and so on, till I decided to put him out of his misery with a guided tour of the whole house. He seemed especially interested in the pictures on the walls – they're no great cop, as you know: amateur watercolours, and suchlike faded Valentines – and asked if an interest in art ran in the family. I thought: enough pictures, and led him back down into the hall and asked him exactly what connection

213

he had with the Rolvenden family. He said his great-grandfather – or something along those lines – had once worked for your grandfather in France. I knew your grandfather had been donkey's years in Jersey, but France – that was news to me.'

'As a matter of fact, he was a student in Paris at the turn of the last century.'

'Well, now – I didn't know that. Anyway, as I was saying, this French chap kept firing away at me with questions about your grandfather and the Rolvenden clan in general, till I had to explain to him that I'd spent most of my life abroad, and couldn't really tell him much about all that. He then thanked me in his effusive way, and made as if to leave, but stopped in the doorway and said there was just one more thing, and he'd be "infinitely obliged", and so on, but did I know if a "Mr Francis" had any connection with the house or family?'

'Mr Francis?' I said, put out by the appearance of what I then thought was yet another unknown quantity. 'Who he?'

'For a moment I thought he meant Daddy – he'd been called Francis – "Frank" to all and sundry – but when I mentioned this, the Frenchman just shook his head and said that "Mr Francis" was not English. And then he went. What's it all about, then, Seb?'

'This French visitor of yours is called Pidgeon, and I'm pretty sure he's the descendant of a Cockney crook Grandfather got mixed up with way back in the 1890s. Pidgeon's got it into his head that his ancestor knew that Grandfather was in possession of a valuable painting, believed missing, done by Julian Rawbeck, a minor master who vanished in unexplained circumstances in 1899.'

'Well! A real family mystery! I shall have to look into this . . .'

'I'd be really grateful if you'd ask discreetly round the town to see whether Pidgeon's been up to anything else there. Your local bobby friend might play an important part in this . . .'

'Yes, and you'll have to come down so that we can compare notes.'

'Right – thanks – and in the meantime, you have my number.'

I thanked my aunt again, and rang off. The modern Pidgeon, then, was looking for paintings – *a* painting – in my grandfather's old haunts in Malmesbury, but who the hell was 'Mr Francis'? And why should Pidgeon suppose that this new player had ever been in that neck of the woods? It was beginning to look as if, at every turn, just as I thought I was making progress in unravelling this business, another conundrum was tossed playfully in my path.

The next day, Tuesday the 6th, was largely taken up with business connected with the Tod Slaughter book, but just after five that afternoon I was presented with another conundrum – the most unwelcome one to date – in the shape of a visit from two policemen. They were ruddy, clean-looking men, one – Detective Constable Barry Conlon – in his early thirties, and the senior, Detective Sergeant Ian Morris, about fifty. They were dressed in those impossibly formal casuals which form the symbolic uniform of the plain-clothes copper. I ushered them into the sitting room, and on to the cane sofa, while I sat and faced them in my armchair. Conlon, who was faffing around with a document case, glanced discreetly round the room, while Detective Sergeant Morris took a good look at me before his lined, rather baggy face creased into a smile, showing nicotine-yellow teeth.

'I believe you know Mrs Patricia Hague, Mr Rolvenden?'

Christ, what now . . .

'Yes, that's right, Sergeant.'

There was a pause, and more silent scrutiny from the bleary blue eyes.

215

'I hope she's all right ...' I blurted, just to break the silence.

'Oh, I'm sure there's no cause for worry, sir – at the moment – it's just that she seems to have, er ... gone off somewhere without telling anyone, and without leaving any contact details. There's nearly always a simple explanation for these things – maybe a sudden family emergency, a travel hold-up, what have you ...'

'Then what's the problem, Sergeant?'

Conlon's hand went softly into the document case again and he took out a notebook, which, with a pen in the other hand, he held at the ready, while Morris, seemingly ignoring my question, went on in an even voice.

'Can you recall, Mr Rolvenden, when was the last time you saw Mrs Hague?'

'Mmm ... last Thursday round about five-thirty; leastwise, I didn't actually *see* her at the time ...'

'Could you fill that out a bit, sir?'

'Well, I got an email from her round four on Thursday afternoon, and I rang her at the Hagues' boathouse, then, when I got no reply, I drove round there, but there was no one in.'

'It must've been fairly important, Mr Rolvenden, to make you decide to drop everything, so to speak, and drive round there, after you'd already telephoned and got no answer.'

'Er, yes – in the email Mrs Hague had referred to something I'd been researching for a new book – it could've been a breakthrough.'

'So you called round at the boathouse, and no one was in ...'

'No.'

'Why did you ring the boathouse, then call there, instead of first ringing Mrs Hague's flat in Wivenhoe?'

'She seems to spend most of her time at the boathouse, nowadays – it was the most obvious place to try.'

'Right, are you used to going round there to see her?'

216

'Very seldom, in fact: I used to go occasionally at week-ends, when the Hagues both used to entertain friends there, but since then Pat – Mrs Hague – has sort of made it her private domain.'

'And last Thursday afternoon at the boathouse, when you found Mrs Hague wasn't in, what did you do then?'

'Just came back here.'

All the while, Conlon was staring at me, when not busily taking notes.

'Did you try to get in touch with Mrs Hague again later on the Thursday?' Morris went on in his calm, Greater London voice.

'No, I thought that, if her message had been as important as it had first seemed to be, she'd get in touch with me again.'

'And has she since then?'

'No, Sergeant, I haven't heard from her since.'

'And was there anything in this email message she sent you on Thursday to indicate where she might've been going? Any plans or indications that she might be travelling, or seeing someone?'

'Actually, Sergeant, the message was just a one-liner – an invitation to me to come round and eat some pigeon pie.'

The two men exchanged glances, then Morris returned to the attack.

'Pigeon pie, Mr Rolvenden? But you've just told me the message might've represented a vital breakthrough in your research.'

'It might well have been – it was a play on words, you see, Mrs Hague's a bit of a joker – a play on the name "Pidgeon", a man I'm studying in connection with plans for a future book.'

'And do you know where we might contact this Mr Pidgeon?'

'Actually, he died in the 1920s – in France.'

I caught Conlon's cynical gaze, and reflected that my story must be looking all very shaky and silly, and had anyone witnessed my anger when I'd gone to the boat-house that Thursday, when I'd rattled and tugged at the door handle, and banged on the closed shutters?

'Just to fill out the picture, Mr Rolvenden,' Detective Sergeant Morris went on, 'could you help us out with a description of your movements since this, er . . . humorous but important email you got from Mrs Hague last Thursday?'

I did, presenting my French wanderings as a quest for 'Mr Pidgeon', an enigmatic seeker after the lost Rawbeck masterpiece, and taking my time with the French place-names for the benefit of Conlon and his note-taking.

'Sounds like the makings of a good book, Mr Rolvenden,' Morris commented pleasantly when I'd fin-ished my account of my movements. 'I was over there with the wife in '99 – drove through the Burgundy wine region. *Très agréable!*'

I joined rather half-heartedly in the policemen's laughter.

'Tell me, Mr Rolvenden,' Morris said. 'Does the address Cwmdonkin Drive mean anything to you?'

There was a vague resonance in my mind, but I couldn't recall with what.

'Apart from its sounding vaguely Welsh, Sergeant, no.'

'Well, we'll just leave that one for the time being. Now, there's something I'd like you to listen to . . .'

As if on cue, Conlon took something out of his docu-ment case and placed it on the side table. It was a small audio-cassette player. I sat tensely upright as he switched it on, Morris eyeing me like a hawk. What now . . . There was only background drone and some faint clickings for a while, then a disturbing squeal, like the sound a rabbit makes when it's taken by a fox. Then more squeals, until my pulse began to race, and I started to breathe heavily.

'Mummy! Mummy!'

I actually felt faint – I didn't want this.

'It's all right, sir,' Morris murmured reassuringly from the sofa. 'There isn't much more . . .'

'Let go my arms!' the shrill little voice on the cassette went on intolerably. 'Don't want down there! Mummy! Mummy!'

Terror engulfed me. The pitch of the voice was high – a little boy's – but it wasn't a little boy's voice.

'Mummy! Mummy! Mummy!'

By now I was bent double with my head in my hands, and then I felt the Detective Sergeant gripping me, gently raising my shoulders.

'Right!' he said crisply to his subordinate. 'That's enough!'

Detective Constable Conlon switched off the tape of my voice.

Chapter Twenty-One

And then they were gone, with the blank parting statement from Detective Sergeant Morris that if I didn't know how my voice had got on to the tape, which had been found in Pat's office at the university, then they certainly didn't . . . Somehow I had to bridge the gap between fifty-ish, worldly-wise (or so I thought) Seb Rolvenden and the terrified little boy whose voice had been captured on the tape. Because, inescapably, the voice had been mine.

Some forgotten hypnosis session among friends or in a nightclub? That had been Morris's suggestion, but for the life of me I couldn't recall any such occasion, and it wasn't the sort of thing you'd forget . . . Hypnosis hadn't been one of Pat's party tricks, either. Had some mischievous bedfellow recorded it while I'd been talking in my sleep? But how would they have known I was going to have that particular nightmare? You couldn't pre-programme other people's dreams for them.

The only possible alternative was that I'd unwittingly cooked it all up myself, in which case I might as well relax and wait for the men in white coats. No, there'd been an outside agency at work here. Someone had actually got inside my head . . . The detectives, then, seemed to have accepted my mystification at face value for the time being, but one thing I was sure of: they'd be back.

And the words on the tape: someone had hold of my arms, and was presumably dragging me somewhere 'down there' I didn't want to go to. The diction 'Don't want down there' suggested a kid just getting the hang of speech, one of say three years old. But if it had been some sort of Primal Scream situation – an early trauma working its way out donkey's years later – kids were always horsing around with one another, dragging each other here and there, sometimes to bruising effect, too. But not, surely, so that one such incident would etch itself like acid into the subconscious. But again, that would depend on the intensity of the experience.

And Pat? I looked at my watch: five-thirty. Frank would still be at the shop – the police must've interviewed him first. No, I wasn't thinking straight: he must've called them in in the first place to report Pat's absence. Shaken to the core, I went to the bathroom and sloshed my face with cold water, then flung on my jacket and went out to the car.

I found Frank ten minutes later in the sanctum behind his shop, sitting in a massive teakwood chair behind a fretted mandarin's desk, the grimness of his expression matched by that on the Noh mask on the wall above him.

'I honestly don't know what the hell's up this time, Seb,' he began in answer to my urgent enquiry. 'You know how it is between Pat and me these days.'

I avoided his glance as he went on.

'We go our separate ways and so on – but the fact is, she left her car in the garage and didn't take her purse or anything else with her. The only thing I could do was call in the police.'

'Had there been anything, er . . . brewing in particular?' I asked as I paced up and down on the faded kilim.

'Mmm . . . no, there wasn't any particular issue between us – that was the first thing the police asked me – she was just her usual bright, cutting self. Not a cloud in the sky that I could see.'

'What's her usual Thursday routine?'

'Well, during term-time she can be back from the university any time after about four, depending on what she's

221

got on there – students, seminars, meetings, etc. Well, that morning, she told me that it would be one of her early days at the university, and that she was going to work on her book in peace at the boathouse, and that if some stuff came from the States – she'd been banging on about it for ages – would I ring and tell her straight away, since the lack of it was holding up her work.'

'Didn't she have official mail delivered to her office at the university?'

'She said they held it for ages in the post-room – she'd had run-ins with them before about it – and as often as not it went into the wrong pigeonholes, so some items she had delivered here. Well, a packet with an American stamp arrived for her just before lunchtime on the Thursday, and I rang her at the university, and she asked if I could drive round to the boathouse with it later on. I did, at about quarter to five, and found the shutters up at the boathouse and no reply to my ring, which I thought was odd. I thought she must've gone off suddenly, so I went across to the garage and opened it up, to find her car inside, which was odder still. Finally, I went back to the boathouse, let myself in with my key, and found the raincoat she'd been wearing when she'd gone out that morning, with her purse and car keys and so on. I asked around the other houses and moored boats if anyone had seen or talked to her – zilch – so I decided then to call in the law.'

'And there's been no news since of Pat? It's been four days now.'

'Not a thing – no one's reported seeing or hearing from her, and she's not been seen in any of her usual haunts. Seb, you said you'd been round to the boathouse to see her after four last Thursday, about half an hour before I turned up?'

'Yes.'

'Did you see or talk to anyone there?'

'No, there wasn't a soul around.'

In any case, I recollected, I'd been too angry at the time

222

at Pat's having led me up the garden path to have noticed anyone else, let alone talked to them rationally.

'Well,' Frank went on, 'that means you were the last person to see Pat; or rather, not see her, if you see what I mean.'

'You mean, the police only have my word for it that I didn't actually meet up with her in the boathouse?'

'Right, so watch your step with them in future, old son.'

'I suppose they'll have asked you about your movements, too.'

'Not that there was much to tell: I'd spent the afternoon valuing the contents of a house near the wood at Rowhedge – the late owner's son was with me nearly all the time – and I left there around twenty past four. I came back here to the shop, picked up Pat's American packet and set off for the boathouse, arriving there about fifteen minutes later, as I've told you.'

'Have the police been asking you questions about me?'

Frank shook his head. 'They keep things in compartments – never let the left hand know what the right hand's doing – then it's gently backwards and forwards, ever so relaxed, checking your story again each time they come round . . .'

He seemed to know a lot about the police and their methods, I thought, but then my old school chum looked up at me with real anxiety in his eyes.

'It's her having left her things behind, Seb – ID, money, car keys, the lot – I don't like it at all.'

A delicate matter came to mind.

'Frank, I, er . . . don't like to ask – none of my business, and all that, but could Pat have had . . .'

My friend gave one of his snuffly little laughs.

'Was she whisked away by one of her toy-boys, eh? Some hairy young deckhand? That what you mean? I don't think so: for one thing, she'd have needed her purse more than ever . . . On the other hand, you know how she likes to play with people: well, not everybody'll take it.'

I felt a little pang when I remembered that I'd told Detective Sergeant Morris the same thing about Pat: maybe the Detective Sergeant was thinking she'd tried to play with me on the Thursday, and on that occasion, I hadn't taken it.

'Mmm . . .' I murmured thoughtfully. 'I see what you mean.'

'And what have you been up to?'

'I flew to Jersey first thing on Friday morning, and I was over there and in France till Monday morning – doing research.'

'You've told the police that?'

'Yes, of course.'

'I'll bet they'll be faxing Pat's details to all the police stations in France now.'

'This is a real facer, Frank.'

With that, we agreed to keep in close touch till things had been cleared up, and I left the shop and, as if by a homing instinct, drove to Leah's flat in the university grounds. She met me at the door of her flat in paint-stained overalls, and with a bright red bandanna round her head. She explained that she was in the throes of decorating the kitchen, which, when she led me in there, I saw involved a sort of eau-de-nil paint, and it was all I could do to prevent her from shoving a brush into my hand.

'The buggers are supposed to redecorate it themselves,' Leah ruled with a snort, as she climbed back to the top of the stepladder she'd set up against one wall. 'It's clearly stated in the conditions, but I thought: enough of dinge and sleaze.'

My anxiety must have shown, and she paused, brush in hand, and looked down at me from the stepladder.

'What's up? You don't look too chuffed.'

I gave her a shorthand version of everything that had happened to me since we'd last talked, and her eyes sombred over.

'Can you make some coffee?' she said when I'd finished. 'The paint . . .'

I did so, and by and by she joined me at the kitchen table with a steaming mug.

'It looks serious,' Leah said. 'Very serious – even Pat wouldn't just have goofed off with no money or keys. You go out to come back again . . .'

'You haven't bumped into her around the university, have you?'

Leah shook her bandannaed head.

'Parallel lines, and we're hardly on the same wavelength. Occasional brittle smiles across the floor of the Level Six coffee area's about the limit of our communication. And what was that email again you said she sent you on Thursday?'

'Would I care to come over for "Pidgeon" pie – words to that effect.'

'Right, she must've meant this guy who's been stalking you and yours: maybe Pat had a visit from him – after all, you said he'd tried to contact her at the boathouse once before.'

'That's right, after I'd followed him down from Southwold, where he'd had the meeting with Reet.'

'Pat may have included him in her latest mind-game – how else would she have found out his name unless she'd first met him? After all, it's meant your working more or less full-time to suss out that he's descended from the Vickybird.'

I recalled Frank's remark that not everyone might take Pat's winding-up in good part, and feared for the worst.

'Are you thinking what I'm thinking?' I said to Leah.

'That Pat's had some sort of tussle with this Pidgeon guy? Yes . . .'

'It would depend on exactly what trick she's tried on him. For instance,' I conjectured, 'if she'd hinted to him that she knew where there were more Rawbeck treasures,

225

then left him dangling, Lord knows what might have happened.'

Leah frowned as her full upper lip embraced the rim of her coffee mug.

'Go through your visit to the boathouse again.'

I did, with all the detail I could remember, but all I got was another grim shake of the paint-flecked bandanna.

'And you didn't come across anything during your cross-Channel jaunt that might have tied in with Pat?'

'Absolutely nothing, and anyway, she simply wasn't in my mind at any stage of the trip. It was all about Grandfather, the Pidgeons and the Barres – my lot.'

'The Sons of Carrie Bugle ...' Leah remarked with a chuckle.

'And now this bloody tape of my voice the detectives have pulled out of their hat – they said it was found in Pat's office at the university. It's got me fairly spooked.'

'Hypnosis is my bet on that score.'

'I've never been under hypnosis in my life. I can't even imagine how I might hand over my mind to anyone else. No, it's just not on.'

'But that's what makes it look so hilarious on the stage – the po-faced types they get to strip down to their under-pants, stand on their heads, sing like Elvis – the very ones who "can't imagine how", as you've just put it. And you have had these odd fugues from time to time, haven't you?'

I was reminded of my odd lapse on Easter Monday – where did the day go? – but I'd taken Dr Cousins' view at my check-up, and put it down to overdoing things; that and the after-effects of the medication I'd been recently weaning myself off. But then my mind went back to the odd walkabouts I'd gone on in the past – sort of blue plaques in my memory – always after a big emotional upset like my run-in with my son Paul at the cottage in Dunstanburgh when Reet and I had been in the process of breaking up. And always ending in white cliffs ...

226

Could someone, somehow, somewhere along the line have been using hypnosis on me? And didn't you have to plant a trigger in the mind of whoever you were hypnotizing? What would the trigger have been in my case? No, it was too fantastic . . .

'Sorry,' I said, dismissing the issue, 'but I don't buy hypnosis. The fact is that Pat had the tape, and the answer as to how it was made must lie with her.'

'Last Thursday,' Leah went on, 'when Pat was supposed to have disappeared, I'd have left the university around the same time she did. I'd a dental check-up in Wivenhoe at four-fifteen, but no one could've missed her big black Bristol 400 on the road out from the university. And I wonder who this Mr Francis is – the name Pidgeon asked after when he visited your aunt in Malmesbury?'

'I tell you, the name rings absolutely no bells for me – yet another aspect of this mix-up I've got to get to the bottom of.'

'And this address the detectives asked you about before they left you – Cwm-whatsit?'

'Cwmdonkin Drive – they must've found some reference to it among Pat's stuff at her office. I daresay they'll be following it up. Funny . . .'

'What?'

'I seem to have heard it somewhere before, but I can't quite remember in what context. And there's another possible pointer to Pat's movements: d'you recall when she buttonholed us at the petrol station the other week? When she made that remark about your letter to the *Guardian*?'

'Yes, it was a Saturday morning.'

'She was in a tracksuit –'

'Shellsuit.'

'Whatever – anyway, maybe it was her health club morning. There's one in Colchester – I see its van buzzing around from time to time. A white van with the name on it in blue.'

'I think I know the club you mean.'

227

'There's a branch in London, too – same colour scheme – I've noticed it there. It's got a name like a Greek holiday resort – Troiana, Triana, Triada – that's it! The Triada Health Club . . .'

But Leah made no response, and I was damned if I could place the London branch of the health club. I supposed I'd have to leave that one for the time being.

Chapter Twenty-Two

I'd stayed for supper at Leah's, and we'd parted on a serious note. She'd promised to keep her ear to the ground at the university regarding Pat's disappearance, with particular reference to the comings and goings of the police.

Back at home, unaided sleep was out of the question that night, and after nearly three hours of tossing and turning, with the shrill, terrified, taped voice – my voice, for God's sake! – ringing in my head, I'd finally had to pop a tablet. Feeling defeated – I'd been making such progress recently in weaning myself off the medication – as I phased into the light sleep the tablet allowed, my last clear thought was of whether, unknown to me, the childish voice would cry out again unheard that night.

Next morning, Wednesday, I awoke unrefreshed and went through the motions: tub, shave, breakfast, post – all junk – then, like some doggedly dutiful lighthouse-keeper, I went up to my workroom to check my Inbox. Spam was all that I found there, so having machine-gunned these unwanted messengers at the gate with the Delete, I turned to the bit of bio-rewrite I'd been working on. But it was no use: my eyes refused to engage with the text. I tried again with the first sentence: *Tod Slaughter's association with the film producer George King would mark the turning point of . . .* But my mind was rearranging the words into: *Pat Hague's association with Cwmdonkin Drive would mark the turning point of . . .*

I jumped out of my chair and began to pace the room. Damn it to buggery! I had to get to the bottom of whatever was going on before I could settle down to serious work again . . . What the hell had happened to Pat Hague?

I whipped out my mobile, and rang Frank for a progress report – nothing new – then Leah. I hadn't asked for this new stress, she advised, so no disgrace in my popping a tranquillizer. Damned if I would, though . . . No, I'd be no one's crock – get down to work again, set my course, and sail straight through it all. I went back to the computer, and, gritting my teeth, worked through the chapter, and I think made a decent job of it. Then I started on the passage in Chapter Eight of my Tod Slaughter biography my agent had advised me to tweak up, the one about the actor's role in the film *The Crimes of Stephen Hawke*. All about this guy in 1880s London who was an evangelical moneylender by day and a garrotter by night: *Meet me on the terrace this evening, my lord, and we'll come to grips with the business* . . . If only life could be that simple.

I soldiered on till one, then broke off to eat some scraps or other, after which sleepiness overtook me, and I just stretched out on a rug in the sitting room and crashed out for almost two hours. Coming round, I rang Frank again, but there was no reply. I decided to give Leah a rest – what a gift to her I was proving to be! – then, just before five, I had another visit from Detective Sergeant Morris and DC Conlon.

The saggy-faced Morris was as urbanely matter-of-fact as he'd been on the previous afternoon, and Conlon was there with his document case, like a Central European office worker clutching his lunch.

'No word yet about Mrs Hague, I'm afraid,' the Detective Sergeant kicked off from the sofa. 'In the meantime, we're filling out and firming up her most recent movements. Astonishing what a little, newly dropped detail can do. Will you please describe in as much detail as you can the last time you actually saw Mrs Hague?'

'At a filling station – not last Saturday, but the one before.'

'26th April,' Conlon muttered, to a nod from his boss.

'Can you remember which filling station and at approximately what time?' Morris pressed on.

'The big one at Old Heath – I never take any notice of their names – and it would've been round nine-thirty, or maybe nearer quarter to ten in the morning.'

'Were you alone at the time?'

I noticed that Conlon had stopped taking notes, and was staring fixedly at me from deep behind his high, sweaty cheekbones, and his boss's eyes were wary and attentive. This was clearly some sort of cue-moment.

'I was with a friend who lectures at the university – Dr Leah Rooney – and was giving her a lift there.'

Conlon was flicking back the pages of his notebook, clearly for reference.

'This Dr Rooney,' the Detective Sergeant went on. 'Does she lecture in the same department as Mrs Hague?'

'No, she's a psychologist.'

'What would we do without them?' Morris murmured pleasantly. 'And does she know Mrs Hague?'

'Oh, yes – we're all friends.'

'And at the filling station – did you both pass the time of day with Mrs Hague?'

'Yes, actually Pat – Mrs Hague – did most of her talking to Dr Rooney, congratulating her on a letter she'd written to the *Guardian* on the Thursday. I just sort of greeted her – friendly chit-chat . . .'

'"Friendly chit-chat",' Morris echoed as Conlon took notes. 'Did Mrs Hague give any indication of where she was going on that occasion?'

'No, but she was dressed in a tracksuit and trainers, so I guessed she might be off to a health club or something of the sort.'

'Ah! Are you in the health club habit, Mr Rolvenden? Wife's always telling me to sign up . . .'

'I don't think I've ever set foot in one, Sergeant.'

A silence fell, a silence more marked than an exchange of glances: had I put my foot in it somehow?

'Let creaking joints lie, is what I say,' Morris quipped, breaking the tension. 'I understand that, as well as being married to an antique dealer, Mrs Hague enjoys a bit of a punt on antiques herself? Auctions and so on.'

'Yes, for one thing, they tie in with her line as an English lecturer – letters, signed books, writers' realia sort of thing.'

'And prints, Mr Rolvenden?'

'Ah, that – yes.'

'You're friends with Mr Frank Hague?'

'I've known him since I was eight – we went to the same boarding schools.'

'Do you dabble in antiques, too, Mr Rolvenden?'

'No, I can't say they interest me all that much.'

'Never go up to London to the big sales? With Mr Hague, perhaps?'

'No, never – I know he has interests in London.'

Morris remained stone-faced as to my last remark, and turned to something else.

'You mentioned before that Mrs Hague liked to have a joke with you from time to time – a bit of a tease, in fact.'

This change of tack rather put me off my stroke.

'Ah, yes – the Pidgeon pie email. She has a rather zany sense of humour – plays with words to see how you'll react. She's been that way for as long as I've known her.'

'And, knowing Mrs Hague's little ways, you always take this, er . . . winding up in good heart, do you, Mr Rolvenden?'

By now there were beads of sweat on my upper lip – I thought I knew what this was leading up to.

'Well,' I said, with a feeble chuckle, 'as I say, it's part of her personality.'

'Did you meet Mrs Hague at an auction sale in Walberswick, Suffolk, on . . .'

'Friday, 25th April,' DC Conlon murmured in his capacity as remembrancer.

Christ! I thought, here it comes . . .

'Yes, as a matter of fact I did meet her there, Sergeant. There was an interesting print on sale, and I thought it might be relevant to something I was –'

'And did you have an argument with her there?'

'Well, I'd been interested in the sketch,' I improvised, 'and I thought she'd bid it away from under my nose to keep me in suspense – she could give it to her husband to sell on at a profit, anyway, and –'

'And was the print so important to you as to make you shout that you hated her, that you, er . . .'

'"Loathed her with all his being",' Conlon read aloud from his notes.

Another, quite crushing silence descended as both Morris and Conlon stared me out as if I'd been a specimen in a butterfly case.

'I, er . . . lost my rag that time,' was all I could think to say.

Rising from his side of the sofa, Morris smiled a smile of infinite tolerance, while his assistant got up and fumbled with his inseparable document case.

'We all lose our rag at times, Mr Rolvenden,' Morris remarked. 'All of us. Well, thanks again for now – needless to say, we'll be keeping you informed about developments.'

My hands were actually shaking as I showed the pair out, with an irritating and mildly embarrassing little pause in the lobby while Conlon made a quick visit to the bathroom. Once the front door had closed after them, I went back into the sitting room and, hurrying over to the bureau, poured myself three fingers of whisky from the bottle on the tray on top of it. I could already hear the door of the prison cell clanging in my face . . .

Just then the phone rang. I gulped down the whisky, put the glass back on the tray, and ran over to the line phone

233

on the little side table. I picked up the receiver, to hear Frank Hague's voice, incisive and concerned.

'Just to warn you – the law have been round here an hour ago. As far as I could work out from what they told me, it seems they've found a couple of sight-witnesses to Pat's arrival at the boathouse from the university last Thursday.'

'But didn't you say you'd asked around the marina after you went there to deliver the American package to her, but no one there had seen her?'

'Must've been someone I didn't talk to – the paper-boy, or maybe some driver on the same route back as she was on – but the main thing is that it's beginning to look as if you were the last person to turn up at the boathouse before she disappeared. If the coppers come round, be very careful what you say to them.'

'Thanks for the warning, Frank, but you've been pipped at the post.'

'They've already been round there? Of course, you never know how much they're telling you is bluff, but I'd watch out for Morris.'

Frank talked as if he and the Detective Sergeant were already acquainted.

'What were they after at your end, then?' Frank asked.

'They were just more or less confirming what you've just said: my phone call to the boathouse after Pat's email on the Thursday, my drive round there soon afterwards, and, er . . .'

'Yes?'

'Oh, about a stupid spat I had with Pat at the auction rooms in Walberswick a couple of weeks ago – you weren't there on that occasion. I was interested in a print they were offering, and she outbid the whole house just to wind me up – or that's how I saw it at the time.'

'A print?' Frank queried. 'She didn't tell me she'd bought any prints . . . Dammit, though, that was a week before Pat disappeared – surely the police can't be thinking

234

that you'd brooded over the spat for a week, then gone round to the boathouse and, well . . .'

We were already taking it for granted that she was dead, and I knew that neither of us was surprised, in view of the role of tormenter Pat had revelled in. But even now I couldn't talk to Frank about Pat without embarrassment over the fact that I'd jumped into bed with his wife in Jersey a couple of summers before, and again later in England. All the same, grateful as I was for Frank's current warning and information, I couldn't help raising a mental eyebrow in the face of his coolness towards his wife's disappearance. But of course that was sentimentality on my part, as all the wells of communication between them must long since have been poisoned. No, the real wonder was still the fact that he'd put up with her for so long.

'Well,' Frank was concluding, 'just thought I'd better ring up and put you in the picture.'

'Thanks a lot, Frank – I appreciate it. Cheers!'

So, he didn't know that Pat had bought the print at the auction: this tended to confirm that her buying it had been connected with Pidgeon and the Rawbeck Mystery. In turn, it was very much on the cards that her disappearance must somehow tie in with Pidgeon's quest for the lost Rawbeck masterpiece. What if he'd kidnapped her in order to get something that would help him in this? But that was fantastic in view of how much he'd come into the open lately – far too dangerous from his point of view.

I hadn't broached with Frank the matter of the bizarre and disturbing tape of my voice found in Pat's office, for the simple reason that it was supremely unlikely that she would have shared her wheeze with him, especially in view of his tendency to report everything to me. No, it had all the hallmarks of one of her tricks, and I felt cold fury rising within me when I pictured her gloating – perhaps with an unknown accomplice – over an aspect of my life

I'd clearly been carrying around with me for so long while at the same time being completely unaware of it.

It wasn't looking good. I now seemed to have been the last person in the vicinity of where she was before she'd disappeared, I'd admitted to the police that she was in the habit of taking a rise out of me, and, moreover, had confirmed to them that I'd had a flaming public row with her not so long before.

I wondered how DS Morris and DC Conlon had assessed my character on our first meeting? The neurotic, flaky type? Up for anything? And would they have the right at this stage to question my doctor about me? About my breakdown, and my fugues, when, apparently, there'd been whole days in my life when I hadn't really been aware of – or responsible for? – my actions.

No, it wasn't looking good at all . . .

But, after all, I hadn't actually been accused of anything yet, and it was still possible that Pat would turn up again, or send us a teasing postcard from some sunlit, faraway place. What if even now she was sussing out Swansea, prior to her sabbatical, for her Dylan Thomas book project? But at this moment I needed something to take me out of myself: could I drive over and help Leah with her decorating? No, give her a rest from my troubles. What, then? I had to *do* something . . . Something heavy and unthinking – yes, I'd go out and bushwhack the brambly patch at the bottom of the kitchen garden, where I hid the New Zealand compost bins.

A vigorous hour's sweat in the May sunshine did much to restore me – physically, at any rate – so that, by seven-thirty, I was ready to go inside again for a meal. Then, around eight, Aunt Hertha rang me from Malmesbury.

'Hello, Seb? Pidgeon's scooted – to Wales!'

'When was this?'

'Last Wednesday – the day after I told you he'd turned up in the back lane here.'

'Mmm . . . you were gathering rhubarb for a policeman friend of yours . . .'

'That's right – Steve Hunter – well, Steve memorized Ramier's – or rather, as you say, Pidgeon's – car number in the lane, and that evening he spotted the car in the car park of the Four Feathers, and noticed that it was gone the next morning.'

'And Wales?'

'Steve keeps in with the people at the local garage – essential contacts in his line of work – and he found out from one of them that a tall foreigner with his hair in a quiff – unmistakably our Pidgeon – had popped into the shop there and bought an OS map of Wales, then had got into his car and joined the B4040.'

'That would have taken him down to the link with the M4 and the Severn Bridge. Mmm . . . really does look like Wales he was headed for, then.'

'If Pidgeon's still in search of our family,' Aunt Hertha speculated, 'I didn't know we had Welsh connections?'

'Me neither. Did Pidgeon say anything about Wales when you showed him round the house?'

'No, just about your grandfather and his life, and paintings – what I told you.'

'While we're on to things Welsh – or Welsh-sounding – does the address Cwmdonkin Drive mean anything to you, Aunt Hertha?'

'Can't say it does – why? D'you think that's where Pidgeon's headed?'

'Just an address the police mentioned to me recently – anything's possible – but at least you've now given me a lead on Pidgeon's whereabouts. I can't thank you enough, Aunt Hertha!'

'Our enquiries are proceeding!' she said enthusiastically. 'Bye for now . . .'

I put down the receiver and sank back deeply in my armchair. Cwmdonkin, Cwmdonkin – where had I heard the name before? I closed my eyes, and presently an image of an old Bush cabinet wireless took shape against the void. Then the dial of the wireless began to glow, and with memory's eye I could see the matchstick Dad had stuck in the gap of one of the ivorine pegs beneath, to steady it, one of the pegs you pushed to get the various regional transmitters they had in the Fifties.

Next, the wireless of my reverie started to warm up, and a voice started to intone – a beautiful, crackling masculine voice, with the ghost of a Welsh lilt. It was unmistakably the young Richard Burton.

As the voice rolled out the brilliant wordsmithery, I fancied I could smell Dad's pipe tobacco, taste the Tizer I'd been meditatively sipping as the magic of the half-understood words had begun to take hold of me. The voice of my reverie had gone on for quite an hour, then had come the prim, prissy voice of the Third Programme announcer: 'You have been listening to *Under Milk Wood*, by Dylan Thomas, first broadcast in 1953 . . .'

The vision vanished as I opened my eyes wide and sat upright in the armchair. Of course, hadn't Dylan Thomas, the roaring boy of Swansea, the Toast and Tipple of New York, whose biography Pat Hague had been working on just before she'd apparently disappeared, once dubbed himself the 'Rimbaud of Cwmdonkin Drive'?

Chapter Twenty-Three

And Rimbaud rang a bell, too – yes! – I recalled now where I'd last come across the name! On the plaque on the wall of the house in Royal College Street in London, when I'd gone there to check out Rawbeck's Victorian haunts and the crosses on Grandfather's old street map. Rimbaud and fellow poet Verlaine had lived there for a short while in the 1870s. And if Dylan Thomas had modelled himself on the French *enfant terrible*, surely Pat Hague would at least have gone to look at the place in the course of her researches into the Welsh poet's life and influences? The ways seemed to be meeting . . .

By now dusk was gathering, and I got up out of my chair and went over to switch the light on. Already nine o'clock by the clock on the mantelpiece. I knew I wouldn't sleep that night without dope. But there was one thing I could do immediately: ring up Aunt Hertha to act on her invitation to go down and stay with her in Malmesbury. I might be able to take up the trail of the elusive Pidgeon again, and I was desperate to get away for a while to clear my brain.

I rang my aunt, and it was arranged that I'd go up there next morning, Thursday, so, after a wretched night, I got up at six and drove without stopping till I reached the approaches to Malmesbury around lunchtime.

Last time I'd gone up to the limestone town on the hill, in its loop of the Avon, had been on foot, through the stream-cut watermeadows. Then I'd made my way uphill, threading through the great trees on the lower slopes, brushing through the cow parsley and finally entering the town through one of the deep arches that penetrated the curtain wall of narrow, high-gabled cottages, and so, upwards on limestone steps to the ruler-straight High Street, at the end of which, beyond the intact Market Cross, lay the great eleventh-century bulk of the truncated Abbey Church.

This time, though, I was in the aftermath of the arrival of the Jiffy bag from Jersey, and I'd other things on my mind, so I simply drove straight off the M4 and up the A429, going through the little town centre and on to the Foxley road, where the vicarage stood.

Aunt Hertha proved to be in excellent form, in her Fifties outfit of blouse and slacks, with tints of blond worked into her brushed-up grey curls. I left the car on the gravel of the front drive, and followed her into the high-ceilinged lobby of the big old red-brick house. I couldn't help pausing on the black-and-white chequerboard tiles and thinking of Nanny Rolvenden.

'I daresay this house'll be full of memories for you, dear.'

'They're like a sort of pack on your back – it gets heavier with each passing year.'

'Don't I know it! Don't forget I've a good head start on you! If it's any consolation to you, though, when you get to the home straight, the pack gets lighter. The memories are more real than they were first time round, because you've learnt to see them in perspective. At times, they're so clear, it's as if they're waiting for you . . .'

I looked beyond Aunt Hertha's tanned, brave smile, and I could hardly suppress a shudder when I thought of myself at seventy-five, waiting for the arrival of the Ruffian on the Stairs. Perhaps he'd take the form of Julian Rawbeck . . .

'Lunch now!' my aunt commanded briskly. 'Then we've a lot to talk about!'

And so we had – about Aunt Hertha's rackety, useful life as an organizer of medical relief in most of the dodgier parts of the world, family gossip, and my own, less admirable attempts at being fulfilled, solvent and happy. Finally, I gave her a run-through of what I'd unearthed about Grandfather's secret history, and the mess I found myself in now. She stared attentively the while through her library-frame glasses, slightly open-mouthed, until I'd finished my account.

'Of course we all vaguely knew about your grand-father's life as an alleged bohemian in Paris, when he was young, but nothing like this! And now we've a music hall girl in the family – wonderful! D'you really think that when I showed this Pidgeon man round the pictures here, he was looking for the lost painting?'

'*The Ruffian on the Stair*, Aunt Hertha, and if he wasn't looking for that, then he must've been looking for some clue or indication as to where it might be.'

'What, then? And how do you know my showing him the pictures had anything to do with his seeming trip to Wales, if he has gone there?'

'Only one way to find out – thanks for a delicious lunch, by the way! – please lead on . . .'

My aunt led me out of the kitchen to the reception rooms, then to the ones upstairs, where we surveyed the pictures on the walls. Most of these were pencil sketches and watercolours – Nanny's sister Maud had been a keen watercolourist – with a few heavy Victorian oils of the Every-Picture-Tells-A-Story school donated by various dim family members between 1900 and 1920. Nothing of very great interest or real value, just the usual sort of stuff you'd expect to find in an educated, middle-class setting of the period. And all remarkably preserved.

'Haven't really had time yet to get rid of all this junk,' my aunt said cheerfully, as we retraced our steps along the upstairs corridor. 'Except, perhaps, Aunt Maud's water-colours – one or two are not at all bad . . .'

'Such as this one,' I remarked, pausing under one of the said pictures on the corridor wall. 'I know the house well . . .'

It was a carefully done study of Dad's weekend cottage at Capel-le-Ferne in Kent, where, until 1966, I'd spent my school holidays. The watercolour showed a blue-and-white bungalow, in a clump of trees set back from a chalk road, with a solid Norman church in the background to the left. The church was still there, but the chalk surface of the road had long since been tarmacked over; nor had the cottage been painted blue-and-white when I'd known it forty years before. And of course nowadays there was a slight matter of a thousand-and-one other bungalows competing for the space on all sides. Nor did the proximity of the roaring M20 dual carriageway make for an atmosphere of rural seclusion.

'You recognize it?' Aunt Hertha asked with a smile. 'I believe your father sold it just before he died.'

'I know – he got about three thousand quid for it – add a couple of noughts to that for its present-day value. Lord knows who lives there now, but one thing's sure: it won't be much good as a holiday retreat. In the old guidebooks, Capel's always described as quaint and remote . . .'

And then the penny dropped: I could have burst out laughing.

'Did Pidgeon ask you about this picture?'

'Oh, yes – he asked about almost all of them.'

'And did you tell him it had once been a family holiday home?'

'I suppose I might – yes.'

'Excuse me a second, Aunt Hertha – I'm just going to dash down to the car for something.'

I came back with my OS Road Atlas of Britain, and opened it at the place-names index at the back.

'I don't think you told Pidgeon Capel was in Kent,' I said with a chuckle, running my finger down the column of 'Capel' names. 'The first one's in Surrey, but nearly all

242

the rest are in Wales – I think I know which I'd pitch for if I were a foreigner in Britain, especially if my starting-off point was here in the west of England.'

Aunt Hertha chuckled as she followed my indicating finger.

'Yes, I see – well, I hope they'll have a welcome in the valleys for Mr Pidgeon!'

'There's still the other question mark he left here with you.'

'Ah,' my aunt replied. 'Mr Francis . . .'

'Yes, and that was all Pidgeon asked you on that score: whether Mr Francis had been here?'

'Mmm . . . he just said he'd been a fellow countryman of his who might have passed this way years ago in search of your grandfather. I explained that I'd never heard of him, and that in any case I'd only been in this house a few years.'

'Pidgeon didn't press the subject?'

'No – is it very important?'

'It's just that in all my ferretings around, it's the first time the name's popped up, and then only from Pidgeon. I have to get it in frame . . .'

'What'll be your next move, then?'

'The real Capel – my Capel – in Kent, I think, to see if it sparks off any memories.'

'But not today, surely – you're looking hollow-eyed. Let me drive you into town – see the abbey – and then we can have tea somewhere. And you must stay the night – have a clear head for tomorrow . . .'

Of course, Aunt Hertha was right, and the next morning, Friday, I set off refreshed, after the sort of sleep that zonks you out after you've gone without for a night or two. I lunched at Reading, then slipped on to the M25 and round the loop till I could join the M20, which I left at Stanford, and so made my way to the outskirts of Lympne in Kent.

I pulled up outside the castle, and had a look round. It

was the first time I was there since I'd been a boy, when a weekend with Dad's flying chum, Bill Wallace, always rounded off the summer fortnight we used to spend in Kent. Bill had written himself off in a car accident in the Seventies, and, so far as I knew, there hadn't been a Mrs Bill, so God knew who'd be living in his house now. Still, it wasn't far away, and there'd be no harm in looking.

Getting back into the car, I drove slowly along the lane that led to Hythe station, past the caravan site, and there it was . . . I parked the car in a space on the tarmac of the site, got out and started to walk down the hundred yards or so to the house. It was a lot smaller than it had seemed to me as a kid, of course, but a substantial sort of pre-war bungalow nonetheless – still standing on its own in the bland turf landscape, with the conical slate roof, and the chimney straight in the middle. The pebbledash of the outside walls was stained and the green paint of the front door and twin bay window frames was blotchy and cracked. There were faded blinds at the windows, and an old Ford Granada on the concrete apron to one side of the front drive.

All in all, Bill Wallace's former bungalow was a picture of desolation and neglect: clearly nothing had been done to the building since he'd gone. I was about to turn away and go back to the car, when I glimpsed an elderly, white-moustached face peering at me from a crack in one of the blinds. I nodded and smiled in what I hoped was a reas-suring way, and would have left at that point, but then the intent expression on the old man's face focused into unmistakable recognition, and, yes – fear.

I stood and stared back, taking in the features. The mot-tled bald pate of the very old, with a white fringe, big, putty-coloured ears, a long, crease-jowled face, of the same putty hue, the reddened eyes of a bulldog, and the heavy, white moustache which covered the long upper lip. I was absolutely sure I'd never laid eyes on him in my life. In this day and age, to show fear on seeing a prowling

244

stranger outside one's isolated house was a natural enough reaction, but the recognition in the old man's eyes . . .

Refixing my amiable grin, I stepped up the drive to the front door, with its billowing-sailed galleon in the stained-glass window, and pressed the doorbell button briefly, but with confidence. I waited thirty seconds, then glanced up: the gap in the blind had closed. Another half-minute passed, so I rang again, my effort being greeted this time by the rattling of bolts being run home inside. I stooped, and poked the flap of the letter-box open.

'Excuse me,' I said through the gap, 'but I'm looking for –'

'You again . . .' came the elderly quaver. 'I've told you before, he doesn't live here any more – he's dead – brown bread – understand? And if you don't hop it now, I'll ring the police.'

Baffled, I stood back – the old boy was clearly upset.

'I'm terribly sorry if I've bothered you,' I said, loudly enough for my words to be heard through the door. 'I'll be going now – I shan't trouble you again.'

'And see you don't!' came the muffled response from behind the closed door.

I retraced my steps along the lane, with the scared old eyes boring into my back from the gap in the blind all the way down to the caravan site, where I got into my car again. I started the engine, then reversed carefully – I didn't think the old guy in Bill Wallace's former bungalow would have been able to read the number plate at that distance – back on to the road to Lympne and so up back to the M20 and eastwards in the direction of the A20 and Capel-le-Ferne.

What had all that been about? I thought as I bowled along in the tinstream. What had the old man meant by 'he'd told me before'? I hadn't been down there for donkey's years – no, he must have been confusing me with someone else. Bill Wallace had been one of nature's extroverts, and there must still have been droves of people who remembered him from way back, so what more natural than that, finding themselves driving past, at least some of them should stop off from time to time at his old house and ask after him? But I couldn't dismiss so easily the recognition in the old man's eyes when he'd seen me on his drive – you can't blag that, any more than you can hide it.

And I felt a sort of sinking feeling when I remembered the marker nature had put on me – the eyes. To have one green and one brown must be the perquisite of very few, and what were the odds that someone else similarly marked had called before at the bungalow in search of Bill Wallace? To add to my unease, I remembered the white cliffs that had formed the termini of my past unconscious walkabouts – there were white cliffs not a million miles from where I was driving now ...

Just then my attention was claimed by the first scatter of bungalows that formed the outriders to Capel, and I drove down the coast road that skirted East Wear Bay. Soon the familiar, squat Norman tower of the church hove into view above the ribbon of asymmetrical houses, and, yes – there it was – the house in Maud Woodruff's old watercolour.

I slowed down to a crawl till I was almost level with the bungalow. Apart from the depressing sprawl all around, it was fairly unchanged, only the window frames were PVC now, and the door a glossy, shrieking white in what looked like plastic. The garden, too, had been tarted up with pebbles, decking and the rest.

I was just about to pull up, when the *Sold – Subject To* ... sign in the garden and the curtainless windows told their own story. Whether Pidgeon or the mysterious Mr Francis had passed that way, or whether I'd somehow zombied my way down there in some amnesic state in the past – as I'd apparently done at Bill Wallace's old place at Lympne – there'd be nobody in to tell me. I contented

246

myself with taking a mental note of the Folkestone agency on the signboard and drove straight on.

When I finally did get home to Essex and my lighthouse, my heart sank as I spotted, parked on the headland, the car which had previously brought DS Morris and DC Conlon into my life three days before. Morris got out of their car as I got out of mine, and ambled up to me with a relaxed smile on his careworn face.

'Ah, Mr Rolvenden!' he exclaimed jovially, 'we thought we'd lost you . . .'

Chapter Twenty-Four

Once inside the lighthouse, the two officers took up their now customary places at either side of the cane sofa in the sitting room.

'Been on a business trip?' Morris kicked off civilly.

'No, I've been on a visit to an aunt in Wiltshire, on family business. Have there been any, er ... developments?'

'Mrs Hague hasn't turned up yet, if that's what you mean, Mr Rolvenden: it's just that there are a couple of loose ends you can help us tie up.'

'If I can ...'

'Have you ever been to the Sir Colin Campbell pub or the Hatim Tai café in London?'

'Can't say I have, Sergeant – not by name.'

There was a short pause.

'"Not by name ..."' Morris did his irritating echoing act, while his shadow took notes, in between bouts of staring intently at me.

'What I mean,' I began to elaborate, 'is that I may have gone past such places – I'm in London pretty often – or even into one of them on some occasion or other, without really registering their names.'

'That's fair, Mr Rolvenden,' Morris said evenly, 'very fair, so let's try it with some times ...'

'You weren't in the vicinity of the Sir Colin Campbell on Farringdon Road,' DC Conlon piped up, as he read from his notes, 'at 12.26 on Monday, 14th April, sir? Or the

248

Hatim Tai café, also on Farringdon Road, at 12.31 on the same day?'

'Ah,' I said. 'With you now . . . On that day I'd been in town to see my agent, Eve Solander, and afterwards I went to look up some places marked on an old street map I'd been following up, in connection with research I'm doing for a book. I was in the Farringdon Road around the times you mention, and I may have passed by those two places, which were among a number I was checking out. I didn't remember the names particularly, because they didn't turn out to be of any significance to my research.'

'Are you working on the book now?' Morris asked.

'Er, no . . . it's just at the mental planning stage.'

The ghost of a smile played on the Detective Sergeant's lips, but he let that pass.

'And on your 14th April trip to London,' he went on, 'd'you recall stopping off at the Triada Health Club, also on Farringdon Road?'

So that was where I'd come across the London branch of the Colchester health club! The one whose blue-and-white van had triggered off my speculation as to where Pat Hague might have been going after Leah and I had met her in sports gear at the filling station at Old Heath on 26th April. What, though, if Pat had been making for the London one? I was beginning to see the method behind Morris's questioning . . .

'It was marked,' I started to explain, 'or rather the site was marked, on the old London street map I was following up. Again, the health club didn't signify in my researches, and I didn't actually go into it.'

'You don't happen to have this old map by you at the moment, do you, Mr Rolvenden?'

I got up, went over to the bureau, and came back with the 1871 London street plan that had come with my grandfather's things from Jersey. I unfolded it carefully, and handed it to Morris, who took the edges gingerly in his hands.

'Certainly looks old enough,' he said indifferently, 'but the pencil marks could've been put there yesterday . . .'

With this casually uttered, implicit slur on my veracity, the Detective Sergeant refolded the map and handed it back to me. But what he'd said was true enough: the pencilled crosses *could* have been put there far more recently than 1899. Perhaps I'd been too taken up by the thrill of the chase sufficiently to rate that possibility. All sorts of speculations began to open up in my mind, then Morris brought me back to the matter in hand with an abrupt change of tack.

'You've not been well, I understand, Mr Rolvenden?'

My first thought ran to my doctor, but then I recalled DC Conlon's visit to the bathroom on the detectives' last visit here: he'd have seen my tablet bottles on the window sill there . . .

'Bit of a breakdown,' I explained briefly. 'Months ago – I'm well over it now.'

'Good to know that! I suppose it must be a funny sort of life, being a writer – I believe you're the first one I've ever met – doing your head in all the time, trying to come up with new ideas, and living all on your own here – you do live on your own, Mr Rolvenden?'

'I'm divorced.'

'Quite so, quite so – I'm sure it all gets a bit much for you, at times.'

'I cope, Sergeant.'

Morris clasped his hands together in front of him, then looked briefly down at his shoes, while Conlon's little eyes bored steadfastly into me from his corner of the sofa, his notebook and pen at the ready.

'We've quite a bit of data,' Morris said. 'I wonder if you'd like to help us by getting your account of things on paper, Mr Rolvenden.'

'A statement, you mean?'

It was all familiar from films and the telly, but this was real . . .

'Of course, you can have a solicitor present, if you like.'

'There's the one I had in Suffolk,' I thought aloud, 'for the divorce, but apart from him, I don't think I know any solicitors.'

'Up to you, of course, Mr Rolvenden,' Morris said with a relaxed shrug.

I was tired, and just wanted to get it all over.

'All right, then,' I said, 'but I can't tell you any more than I've told you already.'

The statement was taken in the big station in Colchester – 'E' Division HQ – instead of the local nick in Wivenhoe, as I'd expected, which I took as an indication of how seriously they were taking Pat Hague's disappearance. I had to give a detailed – and I mean detailed – account of my movements since I'd first followed up the crosses on the old London street plan on 14th April. They went over and over it all before I signed the thing and was able – on condition that I kept them informed of my whereabouts till further notice – to go out into South Street again and flop into my car.

I sat in the car for a few minutes, thinking about the figure I must have cut in the police station: that of a cracked-up, menopausal male, with a broken marriage behind him, latching on to Pat Hague as a sort of last chance. They'd no doubt have imagined it as a stormy relationship – maybe they thought that, in my obsessive jealousy, I'd been stalking her to the health club in London? As well as to the nearby ethnic café, where maybe she went after workouts? My row with Pat at the saleroom in Walberswick, too, would have tended to confirm the detectives' suspicions about this.

As for my story about my sussing out pencilled crosses on the old street map, well, Morris's obvious indifference on my showing him the street plan was an indication of what he'd thought about that excuse. And DC Conlon would no doubt have got his exact timings of my moochings round the Farringdon Road area on 14th April from CCTV cameras in the neighbourhood. They'd have been especially interested, too, I was sure, in my angry response to Pat's absence when I'd gone round to the boat-house on the day – the hour – of her disappearance, in response to her teasing 'Pidgeon pie' email. I'd rattled the door handle and banged on the shutters in my im-potent rage – maybe, in the minds of the police, that was when I'd snapped and gone off and found Pat, with dire results . . .

They'd doubtless be seeing my flight to Jersey, then over to France, in the light of the above scenario; after all, it was behaviour entirely in keeping with a man who's just done something whose consequences are too awful to face. Perhaps the detectives had pictured me, cornered and out of resources, making my way to the white cliffs of Normandy to end it all, then thinking better of it. Why shouldn't I have then dreamt up a tale about unhappy coincidences, while researching an imaginary book – a book for which Morris now knew there weren't even any preliminary notes – and so come back to England, wily and prepared, to face the music . . . Or something along those lines.

Perhaps it was only because they still had to find Pat, dead or alive, that I was on the loose now: wind me up, let me go, and see where I went. The outlook was far from rosy, but now, with all the day's impressions crowding in on me, I was too confused to think straight, let alone lay sensible plans. I really must talk to Leah. In spite of my weariness, I went out to the car and drove straight over to her flat in the university grounds.

Her little kitchen smelt of fresh paint as, half an hour later, I sat there devouring a pizza and describing what had happened to me since we'd last spoken.

'Keep away from London,' Leah said, 'until this is all settled. The main thing is, the police still haven't found Pat, and it's all circumstantial so far. Did you tell them about the old man in Lympne, and how he reacted when you came to his door?'

'No, I didn't – I see what you're getting at: it'd give them a handle to suggest I was a sort of sleepwalker, not responsible for my actions. I just told them I'd visited some scenes of my boyhood – Malmesbury and Lympne.'

'Did you tell them about the bungalow in Capel-le-Ferne?'

'No, besides I didn't even stop there. I can't get over the reaction of the man in Bill Wallace's old place in Lympne, though. He definitely recognized me, you know ... Is it really possible to visit a place – drive along motorways, ask directions, pay for petrol and so on – without actually being aware that you're doing it? What d'you call it – a fugue?'

'It's never very reassuring to realize how little sentience – consciousness – counts for in nature; after all, the greatest order of living things – the plants – have none at all. And think of all the things – driving included – we do automatically, once we've learned how. The fugue state is now a humdrum fact of psychology.'

'But how do I relate all that to my, er ... walkabouts?'

'In your case, I'd have said dissociative amnesia's the most likely condition.'

'Explain, please.'

'During episodes of it, you forget everything to do with your personal experience, while still being perfectly on the ball as to how many twelves there are in eighty-four or what the capital of Thailand is.'

'Or how to drive safely, to ask garage attendants how much you owe them, and so on?'

'Yes, that goes on unimpaired, just as you don't have to consciously think about it before taking each breath, but your personal stuff isn't at home while the fugue lasts. Most dissociative fugues are to do with shutting out traumatic memories, things your system decides it's better you don't remember or even have to cope with.'

253

'What triggers them off, then?'

'Something that jogs you into involuntarily recalling the damaging thing that happened to you in the past. For instance, if you underwent some horrific experience in an air raid as a child, a backfiring car exhaust could trigger off the memory, and with it, perhaps, the fugue. Or if you'd once been mauled by a wild animal, a cat suddenly jumping up and nuzzling your neck could be the trigger. When the trigger's set off, you may goof off from work, or go away somewhere. Later, you'll just turn up at work again, or come back, and not know what they're talking about when they ask you where you've been.'

'I can imagine how the old guy in Bill Wallace's former home would've felt if he'd found me on his doorstep asking for Bill, who's been dead for thirty years . . .'

'Let's keep our fingers crossed that he hasn't rung the police, after all.'

'Yes,' I said, 'but there are still loose ends to be tied up down Folkestone way.'

'You mean, find out about the last tenants of your father's old bungalow in Capel-le-Ferne, and see if Pidgeon's called on them?'

'No need to go down there, of course, now that I've the house agent's details: I can just ring them up. In the meantime . . .'

'In the meantime, you should get some rest – go straight home to bed.'

I fell in readily with Leah's advice, and, after breakfast next morning, rang up the agency in Folkestone about the Capel bungalow. It turned out that the last owners had moved out to New Zealand to live with their grown-up children. The new owners were moving in on Monday – they'd actually known the former occupants, so they might be able to tell me something I wanted to know on that score.

It was now Saturday morning, so that allowed for another weekend of suspense . . . I went upstairs to work,

254

but couldn't settle to anything, my mind being constantly gatecrashed by images of Pat Hague – what on earth had happened to the bloody woman? – by the scared face of the Old Man of Lympne peeping through his faded blinds, and by the jovial, dead face of Bill Wallace, with his brilliantined hair, shaved straight and level above the tips of his ears.

Now there was a new actor in the shadowy drama, a player introduced by Pidgeon when he'd asked Aunt Hertha in Malmesbury if a Mr Francis had ever passed that way, and enquired after my grandfather, more than half a century before. And had Philippe Barre, on his enigmatic – and, it seemed, final – visit to England in 1955, also made a beeline for the home of his old benefactor of Jersey days? Could this Francis have been yet another wartime comrade of Philippe Barre's? But old Marti in Dieppe hadn't mentioned a fourth musketeer.

And what on earth had become of Philippe Barre, after he'd disappeared in England all those years ago? Blood of my blood, son of my real grandmother, Carrie Bugle – God! – that was going to take some getting used to! I was still assuming that Philippe would have travelled here using his ex-comrade-in-arms Duzko's ID as a means of his preventing his wife's dunning the shipping agents for her maintenance allowance. But what came afterwards? Did Philippe Barre, still in vigorous middle age in 1955, settle down here as 'Duzko'? Could he have found a wife, and even started a new family? In which case there might be people in England now who went up to the National Gallery in London and looked with special understanding at Rawbeck's depiction of Carrie ... But then I woke up – it was so bloody obvious ...

Chapter Twenty-Five

I quickly closed and saved what I'd been working on, then surfed the Internet for back numbers of the local Malmesbury newspaper. Unfortunately these weren't available online, so I shut down the computer and rang a directory enquiries line on my phone. They gave me the number of the Malmesbury paper, which I got through to, and they asked me if I'd write in with details of what I wanted to know. No good – time was of the essence – so I thanked them, and rang up Aunt Hertha, to ask her if she'd help me out.

'Yes, dear,' she replied. 'I can go straight down to the local library, and see if they've copies of the paper for the days on either side of VE Day in 1945, and for August 1955. Failing that, I could always pop over to the newspaper offices, and ask there. What was the name you were interested in again?'

'Duzko Francis or Francis Duzko: D-U-Z-K-O.'

'Right, I'll ring back if I can find anything.'

'Thanks, Aunt Hertha – you're a star!'

Working, then, on the theory that 'Duzko' and 'Mr Francis' were simply the constituent parts of the same name, why shouldn't Philippe Barre, travelling with the ID of his dead ex-comrade Duzko Francis, not have visited the Rolvenden family retreat in Capel-le-Ferne? Just as, fifty-odd years later, Pidgeon seemed to be retracing his steps?

I rang directory enquiries for the number of the

Folkestone local paper, but, when I rang it, I got the same results as with the Malmesbury paper: if I wanted to check their archives, I'd either have to email or write, and wait, probably till next week, for a reply, or come down and look them up in person. Anything was better than skulking, clueless, at home, and, since it was already half-past ten, I'd have to get a move on . . .

When at nearly three in the afternoon I arrived in Folkestone, I went straight to the newspaper offices there, and found what I'd been looking for, tucked away down at the bottom of page four of the issue of 9th August 1955. The body of a man, aged forty-seven, identifiable only by his seaman's discharge book, had been found at the foot of the cliffs south of West Hougham. He'd apparently left his ship in Victoria Dock, London, on the previous day, and it hadn't been established what he'd been doing in the Folkestone area, nor had anyone come forward to identify him or own to having had any contact with him.

The name on the dead man's discharge book had been Dusko Francic, and in the brief mention of the coroner's findings in the issue of the paper of a fortnight later, the verdict had been one of death by misadventure. It seemed that Francic had signed on his last ship – a French-owned vessel – at Rotterdam, and that none of his pay had been deducted by the shipping agents for any dependant's allowance. This, combined with the fact that his last address had been given as a seamen's boarding house in the Netherlands seaport, meant that it hadn't been possible to trace any next-of-kin. The French consul had been duly informed, and that, it seemed, had been that.

So that solved the mystery of my kinsman, Philippe Barre's, disappearance all those years ago. I took photocopies of the old articles, and left the newspaper offices and made for my car again. There I rang up Germain Barre's number in Berneval, so that I might break the news to him of the fate of his grandfather. The hotelier's daughter Liliane took my call at the other end, and promised she'd relay the news to her father, who was at a wedding somewhere. I said I'd keep them in the picture as to further family developments, and rang off. I'd post off two of the photocopies of the respective newspaper articles to Germain in France.

Sitting back in the seat of my parked car, I remembered the VE Day postcard Philippe Barre had sent Marti from England, with its message: *Do you remember?* Well, we'd never know what Philippe had been thinking about now, his memory-traces having been splattered over the rocks at the bottom of the nearby cliffs. I knew the spot where his body had been found – West Hougham – from boyhood holidays. It was just inland, up the coast from Capel. The cliffs went down just south from West Hougham into East Wear Bay.

I drove off up there, and, twenty minutes later, pulled up at the Martello tower that dominates the slopes above East Cliff Sands. I got out of the car, and went and stood on the slope, taking in the busy harbour, with its Channel ferries, and the steep hill of Old Folkestone, with its castle-like parish church on top. It felt good as I did a little walk-about in the fresh sea air, getting as far as the soft *maquis* tangle of the chalk-shelves of the Warren towards Dover, then, accompanied by the song of birds, down the springy turf to the actual cliff edge, with the chalk of the out-jutting curve of the cliff on my left dazzling white in the late afternoon sunlight.

With the smell of the short grass in the mellow sunshine, I shut my eyes and remembered my kinsman, Philippe Barre alias Dusko Francic, who had fallen out of time in the grey-blue vastness beneath me. I remembered again the expression my grandfather had used for a similar remembrance: *pax cineribus* – peace to his ashes. As if in answer, a nightingale began its thin song somewhere, and I opened my eyes and started to walk along the chalk path again, musing as I went.

At one point I craned slightly over the cliff edge, and, all of a sudden, the May sunshine was eclipsed as a dark horror overtook me, its unbidden outrider being the terrified voice of a small boy – my voice – in my head: 'Let go my arms – don't want down there!' I'd have been three when Philippe Barre had last passed this way, and at the time – August – I'd have been with my parents at the bungalow at Capel, just down the coast. Why, our paths might have crossed . . .

I stopped and began to block out a mental scenario of what might have happened if such an encounter had taken place. In my imagination, Philippe, probably hard up, had got wind of where our bungalow was, and was making his way along the path towards Capel, agog to know what the son of his old benefactor in Jersey would make of him. I'd have been playing in the turf, while, out of sight in some sheltered hollow, Dad would've been snoozing among the picnic debris. As usual, Mother would have contrived to be somewhere else . . .

In my reconstruction, then, I'm playing near the cliff path – probably beyond it – in spite of Dad's stern warning never to go near the cliff edge. By and by, a burly, dark, rough-looking man comes into view along the cliff path – I imagined Philippe as looking like his grandson Germain in Berneval – and spots me. In a well-meant gesture, he steps off the path and attempts to take my hand, in order to lead me away from the cliff edge and find who's supposed to be looking after me.

Naturally, I'm frightened by this swarthy giant with the rough hand and funny accent, and I try to wriggle free, in the process possibly getting nearer the cliff edge . . . Alarmed, Philippe grabs both my arms to keep me from getting any nearer the edge, and my terrified, three-year-old self gets the idea he's actually trying to drag me over the cliff . . . I scream in terror: 'Let go my arms – don't want down there!'

My screams wake up Dad, and he scrambles to his feet and dashes to the cliff edge, where he sees a scruffy type manhandling his little boy. He sees red, and, grabbing me away before Philippe has time to explain, sloshes the half-brother he's never met. As I watch, my three-year-old self screaming in horror, Philippe totters back under the blow, loses his footing on the turf, and goes over the edge . . .

Poor Dad! I could just picture him, horrified at what had happened, and wondering how to cope with my distress. In my mental reconstruction I imagined him as he tried to comfort and reassure me: 'Now you're to forget all about the horrid man, old chap – just a nasty dream, really – d'you see what can happen when you go too near the cliff edge? There, there, it's all right now – horrid man's never, never coming back – and no need to tell Mummy, eh? We don't want to upset her, do we? No need to tell anyone, really – why don't we make it our secret, eh? Always . . . Now let's forget all about it, and go and see if Mummy's back yet . . .'

Back in the twenty-first century, I stood staring unseeingly over the indifferent waters of the English Channel. I felt quite out of myself, like a shaman in a revelatory trance. It all fitted perfectly: a complete unity of time, place and motive. After the cliffside horror in 1955, Dad would have taken me straight back to my normal three-year-old's life, and, little by little, I'd have blanked the episode out of my conscious mind. Except whenever, in later life, someone would inadvertently grab my arms, as poor Philippe Barre had done when he'd tried to keep me away from the cliff edge, and then my unconscious would step in and draw the healing blanket of forgetfulness over me. Then I'd go walkabout for a while, until everything was all right again, and I'd come back to myself near white cliffs . . .

Eager to test my theory, I dug in my pocket and whipped out my mobile, then frantically pegged in the number of the Holt. My son's voice came over from the other end.

'Paul,' I began, 'you're just the one I want to talk to – can you remember the time we had that row at the cottage

260

in Dunstanburgh? The one just before your mother and I finally split up?'

'What's this all about, Dad? Where are you now?'

'On the cliffs, near Capel-le-Ferne.'

'I can get someone down there, if you'll just hang on . . .'

I laughed out loud.

'Oh, I'm not thinking of jumping, if that's what you're thinking! Perish the thought on a lovely day like this. No, on the contrary, I feel as if a weight's been lifted off my mind. It's about Dunstanburgh – it's important . . .'

'Yeah, I remember the row – you threw a real wobbly. What d'you want to know about it?'

'Did you grab my arms at any point?'

'Mmm . . . come to think of it, I did – to calm you down. You just pushed my hands away and stormed out to your car and zoomed off . . .'

So that had been the pattern of my fugue incidents: a sudden physical or emotional start, combined with the trigger of seized arms, then forgetfulness and flight to some place of peace near white cliffs, just as, way back in 1955, my father must have comforted me and taken me away from the yawning, nightmarish jeopardy towards which I'd thought the hapless Philippe Barre was dragging me. All a horrible joke, really, like so many bad incidents in life, since my kinsman Philippe had only been trying to prevent my three-year-old self from falling over the cliff. It occurred to me how much the cruel ironist Julian Rawbeck would have relished such a situation . . . Perhaps he'd have wanted to paint my father under the title of *Cain* . . .

'Dad, are you still there?' Paul's voice on the mobile tore me out of my reverie. 'Dad?'

'Yes, Paul, I was woolgathering for a moment.'

'Look, Dad, what's this all about? Why are you wandering around in Kent? I've had just about enough of this –'

'Pat Hague's disappeared, and I'm trying to get to the bottom of it.'

'Disappeared? Have the police been told?'

261

'They're on the case now; in fact, they suspect ... but look, I can't explain now. I'll catch up with you when things have cleared up a bit.'

I rang off, and, realizing how far I'd wandered away from my car, turned on my chalky heels and walked back along the cliff. I hadn't gone far, when a thought stopped me again in my tracks. Cliffs, white cliffs ... I remembered when I'd told Leah about the row I'd had with Reet and Paul in Dunstanburgh in Northumberland, when my son had grabbed my arms, and my fugue state had set in, ending with my coming to beside the usual chalk precipice. Leah had said she knew the area well, having spent seaside holidays there as a child. But the cliffs there were hard basalt – there were no white cliffs in Northumberland ...

Just then my speculations were interrupted again, this time by the bleating of my mobile. I took the call – Reet's voice this time.

'I've just got in,' she said quickly. 'Paul's told me you're in Kent – is it true that Pat Hague's disappeared?'

'Yes, she hasn't been seen or heard from since last Thursday – she left her car behind in the garage at their boathouse in Wivenhoe, and Frank found her coat inside, with her money and keys – everything. She hasn't made contact with anyone since. The police seem to think –'

'Have you been to the bungalow in Capel?'

'I drove past it.'

'You didn't go into the house, or into the garden? It's important ...'

'Neither: I was going to stop – I slowed down to a crawl – but when I saw a Sold sign up and no curtains at the windows I didn't bother, just accelerated and drove away.'

'Right – where are you now?'

'I'm walking along the cliffside path above East Wear Bay, making for my car.'

'Get in it, then, and drive back to Essex – don't stop on the way – and before you go back to the lighthouse, drop in at the police station in Colchester and ask if there's been any news of Pat – anything, so long as you show your face at the station.'

'But what's it all about? In any case, I'm not sure the coppers who're dealing with the case will be on duty on a Saturday –'

'It doesn't matter a toss who's on duty there!' Reet snapped. 'As long as you show your face in the police station – d'you understand?'

'Yes, yes, but –'

'Then after you've reported at the police station, go straight home and wait there till I ring you again. Will you do that? As I say, it may be very important.'

'All right, all right – I was going to go home, anyway, but –'

'And – this is vital – if anyone rings you or talks to you in the meantime – and I mean *anyone* – you're not to give them the slightest hint that you've been near, or especially in, the bungalow at Capel.'

'Right, then – again, I wasn't planning on telling anyone, anyway, but all right – I'll do as you say. But can't you tell me anything more?'

Reet paused, as if she was making up her mind whether to speak.

'Look at today's *Guardian* – the front page. In the meantime, Essex, police station, home and mouth shut about the Capel bungalow. I'll be in touch . . .'

My ex-wife rang off as mysteriously as she'd rung up, and, slipping my mobile in my pocket, I strode along back to my car. I got in, and started off on the long haul home to Essex. As I drove on, I pondered on Reet's latest intervention: what did she know about the Capel bungalow that I didn't? She'd been there in the past, of course, but Lord knew how many years back. She'd still have been at university with me then – hardly out of her teens – and I smiled as I remembered how shy Dad had been around her. She'd been a real cracker then, and that dash of hers tended to intimidate people who weren't used to her.

At this moment, I felt a jag of guilt as I acknowledged to myself how good of her it was to bother about me, but still, I'd have given quite a bit to know where she was coming from in all this. Her agitated tone on the phone clearly showed that she hadn't known about Pat Hague's disappearance till Paul had told her about it after he'd talked to me, but how much did Reet know? Perhaps she'd been in contact with Pat herself, or even was still in touch with her? And why this bloody extra mystery? All I needed . . .

When I arrived in Essex, I reported to the Colchester police station, as per Reet's so-urgent request, and my query about progress in the search for Pat was logged by the bod at the desk – he'd see that my message got to Detective Sergeant Morris as soon as possible – then I left the place and drove for home. As soon as I'd crunched on to the drive there, Aunt Hertha rang up to say that there was no record in the back issues of her local paper of any Dusko Francic having made any impression on the town, either in 1945 or ten years later. We'd likely never know, then, whether Philippe Barre had, using Dusko Francic's ID, come to Wiltshire in search of my fabled grandfather at that time.

Then there was the business of the *Guardian* . . . What *had* Reet's penultimate remark meant? I remembered Pat's collaring Leah and me at the filling station a fortnight before, and congratulating Leah on her letter to that paper, but was there a tie-in between that incident and my ex-wife's remark on the phone this afternoon? I got out of the car and let myself into the lighthouse, and there on the welcome mat, with the unopened mail, was my morning's copy of the *Guardian*.

Tired as I was, I took the paper straight into the sitting room, sat down and read every single word on the front page, but not a jot or tittle of connection could I find with

Pat Hague's disappearance or with any of the matters I was dealing with. Now whatever her faults, Reet didn't go in for silly mind-games, so I read it all again, with the same result. Nothing relevant to me or my activities, except my name, scribbled by the newsagent, across the top margin of the paper. I recalled Leah's embarrassment at the filling station, when Pat had waved the paper under her nose, and a grim suspicion flitted across my mind, only to be dismissed in the same instant. Out of the question – too fantastic . . .

But I had to settle this *Guardian* business straight away, so I rang Reet about it.

'Trust me,' she replied. 'I'll be in a position to explain about that next week – probably Monday, but in the meantime, you should stay where you are.'

I thought about my cherished Sunday fish lunch with Leah.

'Does the exclusion zone extend to West Mersea?'

'This is serious, Seb – deadly serious. As long as you keep away from Kent. One more thing . . .'

'Yes, go on.'

'You've been living in a dream world for longer than is good for you, and I advise you to start getting ready for a rude awakening.'

And that was all I could get out of her. At least I could ring Leah, and confirm our Sunday date at the fish restaurant. I had so much to talk to her about . . . I rang her flat number at the university, but there was no reply, then, with a snort of irritation with myself, I realized it would be one of her Leeds weekends. She'd be in constant attendance on her mother, and a heart-to-heart talk just wouldn't be on. Damn it – it would have to be Monday, then. And what was supposed to happen on the Monday?

But first things first – this business of the *Guardian* had set off all the alarm bells in my mind, and there'd be no rest for me over the remainder of the weekend if I couldn't get to the bottom of it. What was Frank's take on all this? I next rang his flat in Wivenhoe, to find him in, and evidently alone.

'Have you heard anything new about Pat, Seb?' were his first words on hearing my greeting.

'I was going to ask you that . . . I went up to Colchester nick this afternoon to ask for news of her, but neither Morris nor his henchman was around.'

'They've been giving the boathouse a regular turning-over, as well as searching the moored boats and unoccupied houses and huts nearby. There's even been an underwater unit dragging the creek – it's looking worse and worse.'

'Has Morris been asking you questions about me?'

There was a moment's silence, during which Frank's embarrassment could have been cut with the proverbial knife.

'Er, yes, as a matter of fact – quite a bit about your illness and stuff.'

'Mmm . . . I was expecting something of the kind.'

'There's something I was going to ask you specifically, Seb – to help cover your back, you understand – but just shut me up if it's none of my business.'

'What's that?'

'I wondered if you knew if the coppers had been leaning on Reet? I think she should be alerted, in case they get her to make some sort of hostile statement towards you – you know, unreasonable behaviour, and all that crap.'

This was a facer – did I breach Reet's secrecy zone?

'If they have been round to the Holt,' I began, diplomatically, 'I should think I'd be the last person she'd let on to about it.'

'Mmm . . . well, you know best about that.'

Just then I remembered something about my last interrogation by the detectives.

'Oh, yes, Frank – something I'd like to ask you. Detective Sergeant Morris told me Pat used to go to a health club in London – the Triada Health Club. Do you know anything about that?'

'News to me – like so much she gets up to. Why, are they trying to connect you with that?'

'Looks like they're trying to ring all the circumstantial changes they can round my movements.'

Now for the business of the *Guardian*, I thought, and Pat Hague's odd little bit of business with that paper at the filling station the fortnight before, when she'd walked up in tracksuit and trainers, and brandished that Thursday's issue of the paper under Leah's nose.

'Frank,' I began, 'do you remember where Pat was a couple of Thursdays ago? Just a loose end I'm trying to tie up.'

'Mmm ... that'd have been 24th April – let's see ... Hang on a sec – I'll look in my diary. It's here on the desk somewhere ...'

Frank scrabbled about at the other end for about half a minute, then spoke.

'Ah, here it is: she was at some seminar in Cambridge on that day – stayed overnight, in fact – and as there were other functions there on the Friday morning, I didn't in fact see her again till that afternoon, when I drove over to the boathouse to hand her that morning's mail. In fact, I'd been doing a house contents inspection near Clacton since early on that morning, and I didn't get home till after lunchtime.'

'So Pat hadn't been to the flat on first arriving back from Cambridge, in order to pick up her mail?'

'Mmm ... no, I distinctly remember driving over to the boathouse with it. Is it very important?'

'As I've said, just a loose end – can't afford to have too many of them, when you don't know what the coppers are going to spring on you next.'

'Too right. Anything else I can help you with, Seb?'

'Thanks, not at the moment. Where can I get in touch with you tomorrow, Frank, in case anything turns up?'

'I'll be doing a house contents recce up Woodbridge way.'

'On a Sunday?'

'We live in 'ard times, sir – 'ard times . . . Mobile'll find me – you know my number.'

'Cheers, Frank.'

I rang off. So if Frank had been away in Clacton on the Friday lunchtime two weeks previously, he wouldn't in fact have known whether Pat had already looked in at their flat on arriving back from her Cambridge seminar. Come Monday – it was beginning to take on the air of Judgement Day – I'd really have to pull out all the stops to get to the bottom of this.

But just then the accumulated weariness of the crowded day I'd had overcame me, and I let out the mother and father of all yawns. I hauled myself out of the armchair and went into the kitchen to gobble up a pork pie, then went upstairs for a Neronian bath, to be followed by an early night.

Next morning I got up physically refreshed, but with the instant return of my puzzlement and concern over the previous day's events and discoveries. I was being kept away by Reet from my father's old holiday retreat at Capel-le-Ferne, and I'd no idea why. All my ex-wife had told me was that it was for my own good, and that it had something to do with the front page of the *Guardian*, any old *Guardian*, if an examination of yesterday's front page of that paper was anything to go by. And that had given me the chilling suspicion which, if true, would turn my world completely upside down . . .

And all – according to Reet – would be revealed on the morrow – Monday. I further suspected that, if I could make the link between the *Guardian* enigma and the importance of Monday, I'd have it all cracked. But did I want to know? Wouldn't I be happier if I just let it all take its course? Hadn't Reet also said that I was in for some unpleasant revelations? With this dilemma hanging over me, I tried to get on with the day.

I didn't pop out to buy the Sunday paper that morning – I'd other things on my mind – just took a leisurely breakfast, then went upstairs to my computer and worked on several minor outstanding pieces of work. When I came down, I was under the sullen cloud of not having my fish lunch with Leah to look forward to.

After a scratch meal I took a turn in the garden, then came back in, brewed up a mugful of coffee in the kitchen and switched on the radio: *Gardeners' Question Time* on Radio Four. There was a question from a listener who wanted to know how to prevent stored potatoes from sprouting in the sacks. Maybe she was storing them in too warm an environment, suggested the expert, and might he recommend she clamped them outdoors throughout the winter? In a manner of speaking, he observed, she'd be keeping them on ice . . .

For several seconds the hand with which I was holding my coffee mug remained suspended halfway up my chest, as the remark of the garden expert on the radio did its work of suggestion. 'Keeping them on ice . . .' That was it! The last piece of the jigsaw puzzle, the Meaning of Monday Morning . . . I put down the mug smartly on the kitchen table, and hurried into the lobby in search of my Barbour jacket, with the car keys. Reet's warning notwithstanding, and however unsettling my suspicions as to the outcome of the affair, I had to get to Capel well before the new owners moved into the bungalow next morning: a life might be at stake.

Chapter Twenty-Six

I had to get to Capel by nightfall, but afterwards it would be a waiting game, perhaps all night. I took the A12 to the entry to the M25, and so round till I could get on to the M20. I didn't want to get to the coast too early, so stopped for tea in Ashford; by the time I'd started off and got to the opening with the A20, dusk was already setting in. Here, instead of driving straight ahead for the approach road into Capel, I took the road that led through Hawkinge, as I knew there was a little loop of minor roads and lanes south of that township where I could park my car. From there I could make my way discreetly, and, I hoped, unobserved, southward to the back of my father's former holiday home.

All went well as to the general logistics of my plan, but I found it heavier and more confusing going than I'd thought through woods and fenced-off fields in the still evening. It wasn't till after eleven that, sweating and bleeding from snags and brambles, I crashed through a gap in the sharply scented may hedge that all but stood between me and the back garden of the darkened bungalow.

All but, for there remained a rutted lane between the hedge and the scraggy privet barrier which somewhat symbolically divided the back garden of the bungalow from the lane. My normal reaction would have been to crouch under the may hedge till I'd taken a breather and worked out in greater detail exactly what I was going to do, but, if my theory was right, I'd no time to lose in getting as close to the house as possible, so that any intervention on my part could be made in time.

I looked briefly up and down the lane, then darted across it and through a gap in the privet hedge of the garden where I'd spent so many summer weeks of my childhood. I lay doggo on the other side of the privet shield, and looked around: no evidence of the tarting up that had been done on the front garden, nary a square metre of decking or a tin feature. Ah, and there in the moonlight was the old octangular summerhouse I remembered, with its half-railing across the open side. Well, I reflected, this was no time for nostalgia, and, taking a deep breath, I got up and took a step towards the little hut.

I hadn't taken my second step, when a sturdy, spider-suited male figure in a baseball cap appeared soundlessly in front of me and barred my way. I recoiled instinctively, but not before I'd recognized the familiar, scrutinizing stare of Detective Constable Conlon.

'Not in the plan, Mr Rolvenden!' he hissed. 'You'd better come in with us, and don't make a sound . . .'

Conlon's gloved hand closed round my elbow, and, crouching, he led me across the rough sward to the pre-war, revolving summerhouse. Inside we took our places at the rail with another crouching figure, also in a baseball cap. I turned wonderingly to Conlon, but he just laid his finger across his lips, and nodded towards the back door of the house. I squatted down there in silence with my two dark-clad companions for close on an hour, till I began to shiver gently in my oiled jacket. Then there came the faint squeak of car suspension from somewhere down the enclosed lane behind us.

'They must be coming down the back,' Conlon whispered to his oppo. 'You'd better go down to the other end of the hedge and cover the car – I'll send a message now for someone to go and reinforce you.'

The man got up and slunk away into the night, as

Conlon gave terse instructions into a hand radio, then turned to me.

'Let's get out of here, Mr Rolvenden – this'll be the first place they'll check.'

I followed the DC nippily out of the summerhouse and over the grass till we hit a clump of shrubs just outside the back door of the bungalow. The astringent scent of philadelphus soon reached my nostrils.

'Haven't got hay fever, have you?' Conlon muttered, and, after I'd shaken my head: 'Thank Gawd for that – down! – they're coming!'

It was like the rear end of a pantomime horse emerging from the gap in the hedge, then I could make out that the figure was carrying something – like the end of a sagging, rolled-up carpet . . . My heart sank: had I come too late, after all? Then the front end of the panto horse came into view, bearing its end of the carpet. It was an even slighter figure than the first, but, like the first, was clad in what looked like motor-bike leathers. Both their heads were obscured by tight-fitting coverings. Suddenly, the garden was flooded in white light.

'Right!' Conlon's South London voice rang out. 'Both of you stand still exactly where you are!'

The dark figures stood like still-life for an instant, then dropped their burden in the grass and dashed for the side path which led to the front of the house and the coast road. There then came a flash of light over the roof of the bungalow, as if something was being lit up at the front, and was throwing a bright arc into the night sky. The two figures were caught – literally – in the headlights from the road as they stood at the mouth of the path, to be engulfed instantly by scampering figures in tight clothing.

Conlon whipped out what looked like a hunting-knife, and I followed him to the rolled-up bundle on the lawn. He deftly slit through the gaffer tape that secured the bundle, then, with the same speedy deftness, unrolled the carpet.

'Pat!' I gasped, recognizing the putty-coloured face which was pressed, open-mouthed, against the dirty underside of the carpet. Then, to Conlon: 'Is she . . .'

He'd slipped off a glove, and was applying two fingers gently to Pat's neck.

'Pulse is still going – better get the medics over.'

'They're on their way now from the road.' I heard Detective Sergeant Morris's voice above us. 'You definitely recognize this lady as Mrs Patricia Hague, Mr Rolvenden?'

'That's her, Sergeant – no mistake about that.'

Morris smiled his weary smile. 'I daresay you had it sussed out right from the beginning, eh, Mr Rolvenden?'

'It may look like that, Sergeant, but it wasn't till I . . .'

The paramedics arrived with the stretcher, and took Pat away.

'We'll have a nice, long talk about it later, Mr Rolvenden,' Morris said as he turned towards the path and gave an order: 'Bring the woman over here for a minute.'

The small, compact person in leathers, who'd formed the front end of the pantomime horse – now handcuffed to an athletic young man in a baseball cap – was led up to us, and I dropped my head in grief and dismay as I recognized the firm contours of the body in which I'd so recently been losing myself so joyously. All my dark suspicions of the last couple of days were confirmed. I'd been steeling myself against the possibility, but nothing could've prepared me for the bitterness of the fallen blow.

'I know this'll be hard for you,' Morris was saying, 'but I've only met her once, and I'd like to get her identity confirmed.'

'This is Dr Leah Rooney,' I muttered, my voice almost breaking.

I looked up, and the almond eyes were as inscrutable as they were unwavering.

'Well, that's over with,' Morris said as, with a jerk of his head, he dismissed my hope for a happy future and her escort. 'I already know Mr Hague over there quite well – he needs no introduction.'

Frank, the rear end of the horse, his head now uncovered in the glaring light, looked over and gave his nervous little laugh as he was led away.

'Women, Seb!' he called over. 'Bloody women . . .'

Morris turned to me as my shoulders shook.

'We live and learn, Mr Rolvenden – we live and learn . . .' Then, after I'd got my act together again: 'I suppose your car's somewhere near?'

I cleared my throat and sniffed.

'It's parked in a clump of bushes off a side road near Hawkinge.'

'I'll send someone up there to pick it up. I shouldn't think you'll be in a mood for driving: how about my driving you all up to Colchester?'

Just then I noticed Reet and Paul approaching over the lawn – so Reet *had* been in charge down here . . .

'One of our men can follow up in your Land Rover, Mrs Rolvenden, and Conlon can take care of the, er . . . other parties.'

The stuffing had been knocked out of me – I'd lost Leah – and I just fell in automatically with the Detective Sergeant's plan, and presently, with Paul up beside him and me in the back seat with Reet, Morris was driving us in pregnant silence along the M20. The Sergeant finally broke the silence with a question directed back at me.

'When did you finally twig you were being set up, Mr Rolvenden?'

'The white cliffs of Northumberland . . .' I muttered.

'Say again?'

'I told Dr Rooney how I was given to occasional memory lapses when a sort of emotional trigger was set off.'

'Yes, your son here told us about that – when you'd had some sort of upset, and then someone grabbed your arms. Where do the cliffs come in, then?'

274

'I had a row a year or so ago with my wife and son in a cottage at Dunstanburgh, on the coast of Northumberland, and Paul grabbed my arms, so that I went off on one of my amnesiac walkabouts. Well, I told Leah – Dr Rooney – about this, and about the white cliffs where my fugue had ended, and she remarked that she knew that stretch of the coast well, as she'd spent holidays there as a child. Her remark struck me as odd later, because there aren't any white cliffs in Northumberland.'

'Not a patch I'm familiar with,' the Detective Sergeant said. 'Farthest up the east coast I've been's Skegness.'

'Well,' I went on, 'it occurred to me recently that Dr Rooney might have wanted to divert my attention from the white cliffs near Capel, where I now suspect was where I drove to after the row at Dunstanburgh.'

'What made you think that?'

'Well, I started to become generally suspicious of Leah's motives when I noticed her reaction to some play Pat Hague had made with a copy of the *Guardian* in front of me and Dr Rooney at a filling station near my home – Leah was plainly rattled – and this tied in with what my wife told me about the incident the other day.'

'Pat told me all about it,' Reet said tersely.

'And then,' I went on, 'I found out recently from Frank Hague that the day before Pat had waved the paper at Leah and me at the filling station, she'd returned from a seminar in Cambridge, and, according to Frank, she'd gone straight on to their boathouse, where he'd gone that afternoon to give her her mail delivered that morning at their flat above Frank's shop. Now Frank had been out of town all that morning, and my guess was that Pat had returned early from Cambridge, let herself into the flat and found Leah's Thursday *Guardian* lying around somewhere, with her name written on it by her newsagent.'

Morris chuckled.

'Mrs Hague would've guessed that Dr Rooney had left the paper at the flat after she'd spent the night there with

Mr Hague while she'd been at this do in Cambridge. When the cat's away, the mice'll play, eh?'

'Pat thought it enormously funny,' Reet remarked. 'She told me she'd just left everything as it was in the flat – left the mail on the doormat – and gone straight on to the boathouse, not letting on when Frank turned up there after lunch with her letters. She said what a delicious tease she was going to have with you.'

'But nothing to the "tease" Frank and Leah were planning for her.'

'Frank had the guile,' Reet said.

'And Leah the guts,' I capped her.

'And had you other reasons for suspecting Dr Rooney was up to something?' Morris asked me.

'The matter of the crosses on my grandfather's old map, Sergeant: you were the one who reminded me that anyone could've put them there, and at any time.'

'Right – I remember now. Well, why should it have been Dr Rooney in particular who put them there?'

'Because unless the pencilled crosses had been on the map before they'd arrived through the post at the lighthouse, she was the only one who could've put them there before I'd examined the map myself. Leah was there with me when the Jiffy bag containing the map arrived in the post. I opened the bag, and we both looked at some of the other things in it, but before I could examine the map, the window cleaner arrived for his money, as he usually does of a Saturday morning. I went to the door to deal with him, leaving Leah with the map and the other contents of the Jiffy bag.'

'But,' Morris objected, 'that wouldn't have left her much time to pencil the crosses on the map, especially if they had to be marked in specific spots. It would only have taken you a minute or so to pay the window cleaner and come back . . .'

'The window cleaner also doubles as a jobbing builder, Sergeant, and for ages now he's been trying a hard-sell technique on me to persuade me to let him repoint the walls of the lighthouse – it was a standing joke between me and Leah. In fact, I stood at the door argy-bargying with him for a full five minutes or more before he gave up and went away.'

'Mmm ...' Morris murmured. 'Ample time for Dr Rooney to do her thing with the old map – and she'd no idea the map was on its way to you from Jersey?'

'It came to me as a bolt from the blue, Sergeant – there's no way she could've had a plan already prepared for when it came.'

'A clever, cool lady, then, who knows how to make the very best of an opportunity. She marks two or three crosses at strategic points on the map – places she knows Mrs Hague frequents – and leaves you to go and sniff around them, so it'll look later as if you'd been stalking the lady in London.'

'Then,' I took up from the Sergeant, 'after Frank and Leah dope Pat and bundle her away from the boathouse, I'm sent the email – ostensibly from Pat – summoning me there to "eat Pidgeon pie", when Pat couldn't have known anything about the Frenchman called Pidgeon I'm after. Leah knew all about him, though ...'

'And you obliged,' Morris went on, 'even to the extent of losing your rag at the boathouse when you realized you'd been invited on a wild goose chase, and rattled the door handle and banged on the closed shutters. Just like some barmy, disappointed stalker. A stalker, moreover, who was the last person to have any apparent contact with Mrs Hague before her disappearance. On top of that was the row you had with Mrs Hague at the auction sale in Suffolk – talk about grist to their mill! – not to mention the fact that you're still a bit fragile in the wake of your break-down. All in all, as neat a little stitch-up as I've ever come across. But how did you know Mrs Hague would've been taken to the Capel bungalow, and that tonight had to be the night for their finally disposing of her?'

'When I told Leah that I'd been down to take a look at the area round Capel, in search of clues to the disappearance there of my French blood relation, Philippe Barre, in 1955, she made a point of asking me whether I'd actually been *in* the bungalow. And here's where we came in regarding Leah's incongruous remark about white cliffs in Northumberland: I immediately suspected it had been a flimflam at the time to divert my interest from the real white cliffs near the Capel bungalow.'

'Right,' Morris said, 'their plan wouldn't have been ready then.'

'As for the timing of Pat's planned disappearance,' I went on, 'I recalled that Leah had been thoroughly rattled by the *Guardian* incident at the filling station a fortnight ago – how much did Pat suspect about what Frank and Leah were up to? – so if they were going to move against her, it'd have to be soon. Then, when I drove down to Capel and found that the bungalow had actually been sold very recently, and was to be occupied by the new owners tomorrow, I knew Frank and Leah would have to act immediately. From their point of view, Lord knew when the new owners might turn up – they might even drive over this evening to have a preliminary look at their new home, bring friends to see it – anything might happen . . . In fact, when I did drive down here, I was more than half expecting to find I'd cut it too fine, and that they'd already done Pat in.'

'When I told Mum about your phone call from the cliffs in Kent,' Paul said from the front of the car, 'and that you'd told me that Mrs Hague had disappeared, she smelt a rat straight away . . .'

'Yes,' Reet said to me. 'In view of what Pat had told me about Frank and Leah's affair, and the fact that your dad had once had a weekend place on the Kent coast, I put two and two together, and rang to warn you to lay off Capel at all costs. I wanted whatever was going on just to be between Frank and Leah and the police.'

'Though I could've wrung Pat's neck,' I explained to my ex-wife, 'in the end I wasn't really prepared just to sit by and let someone else do it in cold blood, so I thought it was time to come down here, just in case my suspicions turned out to be right. In the event, I'm glad you called in the Law, though, Reet.'

'And right through Leah's involvement with Frank Hague,' Reet went on, 'you suspected nothing, Seb. Pat told me that Frank had gone out of his way to introduce Leah to you at a party in their flat, yet you saw nothing, but just went on thinking you were God's gift, and she'd been bowled over by you . . .'

The passionate scorn in my ex-wife's voice belied the forensic indifference of her actual words up to now, and I understood how Pat, with her sadist's eye for vulnerability, must have played on this while reporting to Reet – or inventing – the details of my now-punctured romance with Leah. However cheap and foolish I felt, though, I couldn't resist an even cheaper and more foolish snap at Reet.

'And it never occurred to you to put me out of my misery?'

I then noticed that my former wife's eyes were full of angry tears, and I think that, if someone had slipped me a loaded revolver at that moment, I would without hesitation have clapped it against my head and pulled the trigger.

'That's rich, Dad!' Paul exploded from up front. 'For a kick-off, it was you who made your own bloody misery in the first place, and for seconds you've a nerve to expect Mum to act as a, a . . . gooseberry to you and this Leah! Mum's got her self-respect.'

'I'm sorry, I'm sorry . . .' was all I could reply to my son's strictures.

'God's gift . . .' Reet murmured, shaking her head.

Detective Sergeant Morris coughed diplomatically, clearing the air.

'The other factor that must've prompted Hague and Dr Rooney to act a.s.a.p.,' he added, 'would've been the tape of your voice they made – or rather Dr Rooney must've made when she'd been, er . . . with you at night. When they found out it had gone missing, they'd have thought immediately of Mrs Hague, and sure enough we found it in her office at the university.'

'Yes,' I said, 'once she'd got hold of the tape, she could've sprung the plot at any moment. Frank and Leah must've been on absolute tenterhooks, with the prospect in front of them of their plan unravelling before their eyes.'

'But,' Reet said, 'Pat with her sick vanity would never have credited Frank with the nerve to do anything drastic against her.'

'Dr Rooney had nerve enough for both of them,' Paul put in. 'D'you know what I think kept Frank with his wife all this time?'

'What?' the Detective Sergeant asked.

'Blackmail. I reckon he was as bent as a clockwork orange, with his boathouse and villa on the Riviera, and just a potty little shop in Wivenhoe to account for it all. Mrs Hague treated him like dirt, and milked him for all he was worth, but he daren't give her the boot. Because she knew too much, and that's why he had to do her in; he and Dr Rooney, who wanted his money, too. Why, the Sergeant here greeted him like an old friend when he nicked him tonight.'

'How does that grab you, Sergeant?' I asked.

'No comment,' Morris said from behind the driving wheel, but his knowing chuckle was all the confirmation we needed for my son's theory that Pat had held on to Frank by sheer blackmail.

'There's just one thing,' Morris addressed the company a moment or two later. 'What if Mr Rolvenden hadn't obliged by arriving in Capel tonight? And what if Mrs Rolvenden hadn't rumbled Hague and Rooney, and we hadn't been called out? There wouldn't have been any incentive for Hague and Rooney to keep Mrs Hague alive, since Mr Rolvenden – the intended patsy – wasn't going to turn up and be incriminated next to Mrs Hague's still-warm corpse. What would have been the point of dumping the body in the Capel bungalow if they hadn't been absolutely sure Mr Rolvenden would turn up?'

'Simple,' I said. 'The police would've received an anonymous tip-off about my visit to my father's late friend Bill Wallace's old bungalow up the road in Lympne, and the old guy who now lives there would've testified he'd seen me in the vicinity on the eve of the discovery of Pat's dead body.'

'Neat,' Morris said. 'That would've done nicely. I can just picture what the investigating officer would've asked the old guy as far as identifying marks went: "And can you tell me if this man had anything particular to identify him?"'

'"One of his eyes was green and the other brown, officer,"' Paul put in in a senile croak.

'If it had come to trial,' the Detective Sergeant said, 'see if any defending barrister could've picked any holes in that one ...'

'So,' I said, 'if I'd told Leah I'd been inside the Capel bungalow when she'd asked me yesterday, Pat Hague would probably have been dead by now.'

'Talk about bloody Lady Macbeth ...' Paul said.

'For all her psychological expertise,' Reet observed, 'Leah Rooney had the typical academic's bitterness: to be cleverer than practically anyone else in pretty well any company, but to be skint. Money's the one gift the gods almost always keep from academics, and the same went for Pat, only she'd hooked Frank, and she was damned sure she was going to hang on to him. That's my opinion, anyway.'

'Pat and Leah were fighting over who should own the goose that laid the golden eggs,' I mused aloud. 'It was a campus struggle, really ...'

'There's another little point that hasn't been cleared up yet,' Morris said. 'The memo we found among Mrs Hague's things in her office at the university: "Visit Cwmdonkin Drive." You may remember I asked you about that, Mr Rolvenden.'

'It ties in with one of the crosses Leah Rooney put on my grandfather's map, Sergeant: at the bottom of what's now Royal College Street in Camden Town.'

'Mmm . . . go on.'

'The French poets Rimbaud and Verlaine once stayed there in the 1870s – I saw a plaque to that effect up on the wall of the house.'

'Where does Mrs Hague come in, then?'

'She's writing a book about the Welsh poet, Dylan Thomas.'

'The *Under Milk Wood* man?'

'The same, Sergeant: Dylan once called himself the Rimbaud of Cwmdonkin Drive, his boyhood address in Swansea.'

'Right, I'm with you . . . Mrs Hague would've been meaning to visit there for background for her book, and her husband would've known that, as well as that she'd have been to Royal College Street, too, to look up the Rimbaud connection.'

'And,' I went on, 'Frank tells Leah about it, so when my grandfather's map falls into her lap, she decides to mark the spot – with the other Pat Hague sites – with a cross.'

'And you follow it up, as you followed up the other crosses – in the footsteps of Mrs Hague.'

'The legend of the Camden Town Stalker is born . . .' Paul said.

'They meant to do for you, Mr Rolvenden,' Morris summed up.

'Frank's always resented you, you know,' Reet said, implacable as Nemesis. 'Starting at school, where he has to run to you for protection, then, later on, he envies you for what he sees as your easy successes – so neat, then, to

282

combine your comeuppance with the convenience of your going down for Pat's murder.'

'Frank'll fix it . . .' my son quoted me.

'You know,' I couldn't help saying, 'it looks as if I've been getting up a lot of people's backs without my knowing it!'

At that, Reet and Paul gave spontaneous hoots of laughter, and, to my astonishment, I felt Reet's hand briefly squeeze the back of mine. Outside the car window, dawn was beginning to grey up the skies, and a silence fell for a few minutes, each of us alone with his or her thoughts. Presently Detective Sergeant Morris yawned, then spoke, as if to himself.

'Well, it's Monday now. In a few hours, if everything had gone to plan with the plot against Mrs Hague, some copper in Folkestone would've been getting a horrified phone call from the new owners of the Capel bungalow – something dreadful found rolled up in a carpet in the summerhouse or the attic – then they'd be ringing us in Essex to nick you, Mr Rolvenden. We'd have thought you'd finally snapped: if you couldn't have Mrs Hague, no one else would.'

'A narrow squeak,' I said, 'but all the same, I'm glad I went down to Capel.'

We arrived in the main police station in Colchester just as it was turning full daylight, and Reet made a statement, then was driven off home by Paul to be in time for milking at the Holt. I was invited to make a few additions to the statement I'd already made so laboriously, after which I was allowed to collect my car from the precincts and drive the short distance home. Once there, and utterly done in by the physical effort and mental turmoil of the last few days, I simply locked the door behind me, staggered upstairs to bed, and crashed out till nearly noon.

On awakening, I blinked round the sunlit spartanness of the tall-ceilinged room, and my first thought was to ring up Leah and tell her all about what had happened, then it all rushed back to me, and I turned my face to the wall again and lamented. What had Reet said about 'rude awakenings'? I finally managed to drag myself up, and so into the bathroom for a cold shower, then I went down to the kitchen to brew up coffee and put some mushrooms on to fry.

I took the coffee into the sitting room and slumped into the armchair in front of the dead ashes of the last fire. I felt stunned, fibrous with dismay. I remembered Reet's little hand-squeeze in the car up from Capel, and compared her part in all this with Leah's – Leah ... Then my eyes wandered over to the mantelpiece and the photograph of Sebastian Rolvenden the First. I got up and walked over to it, examining the anxious stare in the large, long-dead eyes, as I'd done so often in the past.

I suppose we read our own feelings into the expressions on faces in photographs and portraits, for with a little frisson I fancied I saw a new sternness on the austere, trimly bearded face. The Bible in the Jiffy bag from Jersey came into my mind, the Bible with the string marker in it, with the words at the top of the first marked page about the 'woman thou gavest me' tempting Adam. Well, Grandfather, she'd tempted me ...

Just then I smelt the greasy, meaty reek of burning mushrooms, and dashed back to the kitchen to eat brunch and ponder the immediate future. I wasn't looking forward to the trial of Frank and Leah for kidnapping, criminal conspiracy and, no doubt, in Frank's case for the fiddles Pat had been blackmailing him over. I would be a key witness, and dreaded the figure I'd cut in court: that of a shifty, menopausal Lothario. And how was I to face Leah across the court room? I'd a time, indeed, of rude awakenings ahead of me ...

And Pat: when she was well enough to appear in court, would she have recovered her customary cockiness? And would she still be directing her scorn against me from the witness box? But however shabby my philanderings with her had been, however egotistical the way I'd dropped her, at least I'd played some part in saving her life. That went some way, surely, towards redeeming my conduct. Or so I rationalized . . .

I dropped the wholemeal crust on the plate, got up and took it to the range, then went upstairs to try to do some work. At around five that afternoon, I heard the tooting of a car horn on the headland. I went over to the window of my workroom, and, peering out, saw Reet's Land Rover, with my ex-wife, alone, locking the door. Propped against the car was a large plastic bag, such as you retrieve garments from dry-cleaners in, with something flat and square in it. Reet looked up and waved, and, after I'd waved back, I closed and saved what I'd been working on, and hurried downstairs to let her in with her angular package, and usher both on to the sitting-room sofa.

'I'll bet you've had no rest since you left Colchester,' I began, after she'd refused coffee, 'what with the farm . . .'

'I'll get over it – anyway, I've left it to Paul and the students for the rest of the day. You're, er . . . OK?'

'Yes, slept like a top – I'm not looking forward to the trial, though.'

'Your agent'll be over the moon – think of the free publicity!'

There was expectancy in the air, and I found myself trying to appear unconcerned in the face of the challenging presence of the large, square package in the plastic bag. I felt I'd had enough revelations to be going on with for the time being.

'Reet, there was something I wanted to ask you. I didn't mention it in the car up last night, because I wasn't sure you wanted it aired in front of Sergeant Morris.'

'Go on.'

'Why did you bid so much for that print of the Rawbeck sketch at the auction in Walberswick – the *Morte Moriantur* thing, with Grandfather and the Vickybird looking guilty on it? I mean, nearly two thousand quid . . .'

'I may have been wrong, but I thought your peace of mind – your mental balance, even – was worth that.'

'But if it was that important, why didn't you tell me about it?'

Reet's eyes flashed for an instant.

'For the same reason why I didn't come tattling to you about what Pat told me about Frank and Leah – I've got my bloody pride! Nor by the same token do I intend to make this picture lark into a big scene of the Jealous Wife's Revenge.'

'All right, then: what was on the print that you thought might have had that effect on me? I had a good look at it at the viewing, but I didn't spot anything that devastating in it.'

'It was a prelude to something, Seb . . .'

'A prelude to what, for heaven's sake?'

My ex-wife tapped the package at her side.

'To this.'

'But, what . . .'

'Cast your mind back to the last holiday we all had together – you and me, and Frank and Pat – in the Jersey farmhouse.'

'Yes, go on.'

'The solemn little boy who pointed you out to his father in the lane – Le Brocq the school caretaker's son – remember?'

'Yes, he asked his dad if I was the man in the shed, and we all laughed.'

'Well,' Reet went on, 'it stuck in my mind, somehow – the little boy had been so serious about it – so sure . . . Later on, when I was on my own, I went over to Mr Le Brocq's cottage, and mentioned the incident. He laughed, and said it was his grandfather's shed his son had referred to – the kid was always hanging around it. The old boy had accumulated so much junk over the years, it was like an Aladdin's cave in there.

'Le Brocq said he was afraid the old man was getting

past looking after himself unaided, but he knew it would kill him if he had to go into care, so he was delaying it for as long as he could: his wife cooked for the old chap, kept his house tidy, and so on. He told me where old Le Brocq lived, and I went along there. As a matter of fact, I found him in his shed, surrounded by junk. He was very old – gaga and cagey at the same time – but he seemed to come to his senses all of a sudden when I told him I was Mrs Rolvenden.

'Then he asked me bluntly what I was doing on the island, and I told him I was on holiday there with a party, but when I mentioned the incident with his little grandson, his eyes narrowed, and he looked sort of angry. "It's mine," he said, and "It belongs to me." I just smiled and tried to humour him – I hadn't the faintest idea what he was talking about.

'Just then he shooed me out of the shed and shut the door behind us, then stood and stared into my eyes for a while. Then he grinned slyly, and said, "I want two hundred for it – not a penny less. It's mine to do as I like with – two hundred."

'By then I was really curious, so I asked if I might see "it", whatever it was, since I still hadn't a clue what he was talking about.'

Reet then paused in her narrative to reach over to the plastic bag and take out the package, which was wrapped round with stout, dirty brown paper and bound with yellowed twine.

'I've kept it in the bank ever since,' my ex-wife said, as she undid the twine. 'Neither Brogan nor the Frenchman knows anything about it.'

With hesitation in her eyes, Reet handed me the painting, and I smiled, as I fancy someone might smile who's just had a limb blown off, but doesn't immediately take it in. I then gave a sort of croak before reading out the inscription on the little bone plaque at the bottom of the frame.

'*The Ruffian on the Stair*,' I read out, 'and Julian Rawbeck's monogram down in the right-hand corner. So he did finish it, after all . . .'

In the painting I saw the staircase, leading up to the door – ajar – of the tenant, Madam Life, who wasn't in the picture. Above the landing was the stairhead window, edged with narrow, rectangular panes of alternate crimson and blue, the window modelled on that over the pub in Hackney, where in 1893 the Ruffian, Laurence Victor Pidgeon – the Vickybird – had in real life murdered his employer, Mrs Bella Nye. Rawbeck had held this knowledge, like a sword of Damocles, over the Vickybird's head, until he'd freed himself by cutting the artist's throat in the very same room suggested in the painting I was looking at.

But above all, I now knew what had lain behind my grandfather's eagerness to recover the painting, after the Vickybird had stolen it from him and sold it to the Paris dealer, Carbonero, in 1899. As I beheld the hatchet face of the Ruffian – the Vickybird – as he stared out, grinning malevolently from the sombre canvas, halfway up the stairs, I understood that the picture cast doubt on my grandfather's paternity of his son – my father – A.H. And I knew why the little boy in the Jersey lane had identified me immediately from the painting, which had lain so long in his grandad's shed. In the painting, one of the Vickybird's eyes was brown and the other green. My search for my grandfather was over.